# THE GATES OF MATTER

DANIEL NORMAN

# THE GATES OF MATTER

DANIEL NORMAN

MALEDICTION
an æa PRESS imprint

This is a work of fiction. Any reference to historical events, real events, or real locations are used fictitiously. Other names, characters, places, and incidents are products of the author's imagination, and any resemblance to actual events, locales, or persons, living or dead, is entirely coincidental.



The publisher supports the motivated purpose of art as a manifestation of human emotion and creativity. Any creative expression derived from artificial intelligence takes away from that mission and has not been used in the development of this work. Thank you for supporting artistic expression.

First Edition
March, 2024

ISBN Print: 979-8-9861139-3-7 (Hardcover), 979-8-9861139-5-1 (Trade Paperback)
ISBN Digital: 979-8-9861139-4-4

Library of Congress Cataloging–in–Publication Data is available upon request.

Published in the United States by Malediction,
an imprint of AEA Press, LLC.
aeapress.com

The light of a full moon at its zenith bathed the world a radiant blue as The Fool trod the winding path laid before him.

His appearance was that of a travelling jester, and his tattered motley garments shone a crisscross of light and dark in the pale light. Atop his head was a hood with two conical goat-like earflaps extending from each side. Over his left shoulder was a staff, to which he tied his few worldly possessions. In his right hand he carried a night flower, freshly plucked.

Although it was midnight, one could see far and wide the markings of the countryside, pale and beautiful beneath the moon's light. Far in the distance, shadowy mountains hung to the horizon. On either side of the small winding track was a forest, teeming with life and humming the song of nighttime: crickets chirped, foxes howled, and the sound of all manner of life creeping through the undergrowth permeated the chilly air.

Indeed, The Fool was also humming a tune to himself,

upbeat, but melancholic, familiar and eerie all at once. As he ducked a low hanging tree branch, the moonlight briefly illuminated his face to reveal a peaceful smile, and eyes which appeared to be shut in a state of bliss. Despite this, he navigated the path with relative ease, dodging branches and stepping over exposed roots with an almost rhythmic grace, as if dancing through the shadows. As he twirled, he began to add words to his tune.

"To and fro the night must go for one so blessed as me, for even though their sight may go the blind will surely see. A dance of shadow and of light, of dawning and of setting, of knowing what's to come at last, and only then forgetting."

He chuckled to himself as he rounded a bend, and a faint orange glow became visible in the distance. The path seemed to lead towards a clearing, with a large bonfire in the center. As The Fool drew closer to the clearing, the soft moonlight faded as it was eclipsed by the raging glow of the bonfire. An unnatural hush had fallen over this part of the forest, and even the crickets had ceased to sing. The Fool opened his eyes and paused his strange ballad but did not stop walking. Only when he reached the edge of the clearing did he stop, daring not to enter, for he, like all the other inhabitants of the forest, could sense the darkness at work there.

In silence, he scuttled through the brush and into the welcoming arms of a nearby tree, a vantage point from which he could clearly survey the scene. The tension was palpable, and not a sound was heard save for the crackling of logs from the huge fire in the middle of the field. The very air seemed to vibrate with dread.

Slow formless shadows began to appear at points equidistant from one another, at the edges of the clearing. They emerged singularly from the silent trees, until there were five. Five shades advancing slowly towards the fire in unison. Behind them followed yet more shadows, with inhuman proportions and strange, staggered movements.

As the shadows drew nearer to the central flame their appearance became clearer, but no less sinister. They were cloaked in hooded shawls of the darkest thread, and as the firelight flickered over their faces it revealed expressions contorted by mix of terror and zeal, the glow of the fire reflected in their eyes as they drew nearer. When they were at the fires edge, they stood in a circle and began to chant in unison, their voices rising in unholy harmony.

"Oh, bright one, breaker and forger of chains, we offer this to you as a sign of fealty. Please take it in good faith and grant us what we desire."

Each of them slowly drew a dagger of the darkest obsidian and sliced a gash across each of their left hands.

"To you we offer this willingly, in soundness of mind."

As blood ran down their arms, they raised them together, before plunging them into the fire. They did not wince nor scream, and indeed their flesh did not burn nor bubble. The blood, however, hissed as it dripped into the flames and the shades slowly stepped a few paces back.

Great gouts of flame leapt skyward toward the moon as the fire turned to an inferno. Its color changed from orange to a deep crimson with a low rumbling roar. A face began to materialize in the core of the flames, hovering huge in the air above the forsaken mass gathered before it. It was an inhuman face of indescribable beauty and incomprehensible malice, a face The Fool knew all too well.

The face gazed upon the shades which now bowed before it with a look disgusted and amused in equal parts.

“*Very well,*” its thunderous voice boomed across the silent clearing.

The Fool lost his footing in the tree and cracked a branch. The sound pierced through the silence of the clearing like the crack of a whip. The face turned its gaze towards him and smiled, as if recognizing an old friend. The inhuman shadows at the edges of the firelight turned and reared their glowing eyes uttering a simultaneous mournful howl. The black shades, furious, bade their followers to find this intruder and bring them before the flames. By the time the mob of creatures rushed to his perch they found it empty, roaring and cursing in strange tongues with anger.

The Fool had slipped away, and only his echoing laughter could be heard all throughout the forest.

# CHAPTER I

# THE SYMPHONY OF PROGRESS

## *2033 A.D.*

She awoke slowly and lapsed briefly back to sleep before stirring and finally opening her eyes. As her vision adjusted to the room, she could make out the early morning light which was already filtering through the cracks in the blinds on her window. She rolled over onto her side and checked the time on her smartphone.

7:58 a.m.

She switched off her alarm, so it would not start ringing in two minutes time. *I'm getting this down to a fine art*, she thought. She sat up and stretched, wincing slightly from the biting morning chill in her room.

She sighed. Another long day and she definitely had not slept enough the night before. Not enough hours. Even when she did get to sleep it was fitful, and she had tossed and turned between multiple half-remembered dreams. What she did remember perplexed her, sensations of being pursued. A race?

No, a chase, at night, and a strange face, made of fire. She remembered the gravity of its gaze, piercing into her, as if looking into her very soul. She felt a chill as she remembered it and scrawled what else she could remember into her dream journal before getting up.

She walked over her cold floor to her window and opened the blinds. The street below was already alive with the hum of cars, buses, and cyclists, the sidewalks aflutter with suit clad pedestrians as an entire workforce prepared to start their day. She watched for a moment.

People walked together but seldom made eye contact or acknowledged one another. Their eyes were firmly focused on their various items of technology, scrolling, and tapping their screens, or fixed listlessly on some non–existent object in the distance, as their earphones delivered each a customized stream of entertainment. Anything to escape their mundane reality.

There was the occasional ray of light, a laugh shared between colleagues or a polite nod from a stranger, but for the most part people stuck to the status quo. Products of a society which seemed to engender isolation. Plugged in but disconnected.

The sounds of car horns and engines and the dull roar of the city floated up to her perch by the window. This was the sound of the machine. This was the symphony of progress.

*Like rats in a maze,* she thought, as she turned from the window. *But what does that make me? A mouse.* She chuckled. At the very least, she could always find ways to cheer herself up. She looked herself over in the mirror as she got dressed. Her hazel brown eyes matched the color of her skin and she noticed she had sizable dark patches under her eyes and her usually tight black curly hair had frizzed up overnight.

She sighed and tied her hair up into an easy bun and

applied a little concealer to minimize the appearance of the bags under her eyes. She picked out a comfortable t–shirt and an even more comfortable sweater that fit snugly to her slender frame, along with her favorite pair of jeans and weathered sneakers. She gathered her school gear into her bag and checked the time once more before opening her door and heading down the hallway.

Her footsteps on the wooden floor echoed through the quiet house and a woman's voice called out to her from the kitchen.

"Evie? Is that you baby?"

"Yes, Grammie, it's me," she replied. *Damn, she's already awake*? She walked into the kitchen and found her grandmother sitting at the breakfast table, arms crossed, the morning light from the windows painting the room a mix of gold and blue.

"You know I don't like it when you keep me waiting, Evie." Her grandmother's face was stern.

"I know Grammie, I'm sorry about that, it's just you're waking up earlier and earlier these days and—"

Her Grandmother cut her off, and a wide smile spread across her face. "I'm only joking, child. Have a seat. Or, even better, you can fix us some tea."

Evie breathed a sigh of relief and put the kettle on. Since her parents died, Evie had taken on the role of sole carer for her blind grandmother, Flora, whom she suspected was entering into the early stages of dementia. It was subtle, but occasionally she would utter phrases which did not make sense, and sometimes at night Evie thought she heard her talking to people who were not there in her room. Despite this, Flora was as sharp as ever in many ways, and was largely independent.

When the tea was ready, Evie brought it over to the table and took the seat next to her grandmother. Flora clasped the steaming mug with both hands and brought it under her nose and inhaled deeply. "Mmmm, I do love this blend. It was your father's favorite too, you know."

"I know," Evie replied, smiling.

She took a moment to enjoy the scent herself. It was aromatic and almost fruity, with hints of ginger and cinnamon. Drinking this tea always filled her with a sense of nostalgia, a bittersweet medley of days gone by and carefree Sunday mornings from her childhood. Evie found that, for her, smell was the sense which brought back the most vivid memories, like the smell of lavender, reminding her of her childhood home, or the smell of disinfectant reminding her of long anxious hours spent by her father's bed in the hospital. It was as if, when she closed her eyes, she could be back in that place, in that time, even if only for a moment.

Flora's voice roused her from her trance. "How did you sleep, baby?"

"Pretty good."

"Any good dreams?" Flora probed.

"There were some, only I can't remember them so well. I think I kept waking up."

Flora nodded knowingly. "I see. I do hope you're still keeping a record of them somewhere. Dreams are the keys to unlocking your subconscious, after all."

Evie took a moment to study her grandmother. Her appearance belied her years. Despite being almost eighty, her golden-brown skin still had a natural glow and a radiance which gave her the appearance of someone in their early fifties, and her flowing silver hair was still as vibrant as ever. She was very much a product of her era, of the explosion of freedom of thought and lifestyle in the 1960's and 70's. Flora was openly spiritual, but

Evie remained skeptical. To her, seeing was believing.

"I wish my subconscious would be a little less cryptic," Evie said.

"Ah yes, but that's the very nature of the subconscious, my dear. What seems cryptic to us up here is clear as day down there. It's simply just a matter of strengthening that connection. It takes time."

Evie loved these conversations with her grandmother, even though she did not always buy in to a lot of it, it always offered a fresh perspective and made her think.

"And what did you dream of, Grammie?" Evie asked

"I dreamt I was on an island, far away. It was so foreign and so familiar at the same time. An ancient city full of interesting characters, and a deep turquoise ocean, clear as the sky."

"And what do you think that means?"

"It means you need to take me to the beach sometime!" Flora replied, and they both laughed.

Evie remembered the time and looked at her watch: 8:32 a.m. "Shit." She had to leave the house by 8:30 to get to university on time.

"It's that time, is it?" Flora asked.

"Afraid so," Evie replied, hurriedly packing her bag. She gave her grandmother a kiss on the cheek and rose from the table. "I'll be back this afternoon. Usual time. I'll buy some stuff for dinner on my way home."

"Suits me just fine darling," Flora replied.

As Evie was walking out the door, she heard Flora clear her throat.

"You be wise out there baby. He's seen you now," Flora said cryptically.

Evie froze. "Wh. . . who's seen me?"

Flora did not reply and stared off vacantly.

"Grammie?" Evie nudged.

"Yes, dear?" Flora replied, seemingly snapping out of her trance–like state.

"Who's seen me?" Evie asked, exasperated.

Flora gave her a perplexed look before she replied in confusion. "Why, what do you mean darling?"

Evie relented. "Never mind, have a good day." She shut the door behind her.

When in the hallway she exhaled deeply. She noticed her heart was racing and she had goosebumps. Sometimes, her grandmother's bouts of dementia frightened her. She walked down the steps of her apartment block and braced herself for the chill of a late autumn morning outside. As she stepped out onto the sidewalk, she put her earphones in and her music library on shuffle.

She liked to let fate decide what her vibe would be at any given time. Usually it yielded interesting results, sometimes almost too perfect for the situation. Her relationship with music was steeped in coincidence and messages. So much so, that she valued music above many other things in her life. For now, her soundtrack was some gentle psychedelic folk.

The morning rush had dissipated slightly but there was still a steady stream of commuters. As she walked along the busy sidewalk, she let her mind wander back to her dream and what her grandmother had said. Was it purely coincidence? There was no way she could have known about her dream.

She thought again of the face from her dream. It came to her in vivid flashes, looking right at her. Was it terrifying, or beautiful? Perhaps both. The memory made her uneasy. She decided not to think too much about it and focused her energy on the upcoming day.

She had an early lecture for her philosophy class. Although it was somewhat missable, she had already skipped too many of the lectures for that subject.

She was in her second year of a psychology course. Originally, she had chosen this course because she wanted to understand humans, mainly why they were so cruel to one another. While she found the subject matter very interesting, she often found herself wondering if it was really what she wanted in life. It was a question she posed to herself each day.

What was it that she wanted? At times she felt locked in a stalemate. Presented with a million options and not knowing which one to pursue. Soon, she came upon the subway and scanned her public transport card at the terminal. Declined.

*Shit.* She was already running late and she did not have the time to top up her card. She looked around quickly, doing her best attempt at nonchalance before briskly jumping over the barrier and striding through the busy station towards her platform. Her heart was pounding, but she seemed to be in luck, her maneuver had flown below the radar. She found her train at Platform 3 preparing to leave the station and made it on board just in time for the doors to hiss shut behind her.

She sat down in a mostly empty row and breathed a sigh of relief as she stared out the window. Success. As the train pulled away from the station, she lost herself in her music once again and zoned out.

After a while, she became acutely aware of the uneasy sensation of being watched. She looked up from the window and scanned around the cabin. In the row across from her, an elderly man was staring intently at her. Her usual protocol for dealing with such things was to simply stare back and wait for them to fold, and so she did.

Locking eyes with her adversary proved stranger than she had expected. For one, she was unnerved by how wide his eyes were, and he was not blinking. She also noticed he was breathing hard and sweating quite profusely from his forehead, with the beads running down his face and collecting in his moustache.

*Creep*, she thought to herself. Still, his bizarre gaze unnerved her, and she eventually had to break this strange staring contest and decided to extricate herself to one of the many empty seats further up the carriage, far away from this lunatic. As she sat down, she swore she could actually sense his head turning to look at her, but she dared not look back.

She sighed and turned her music up, and continued looking out the window at the passing darkness of the tunnel. When the train eventually reached her station, she exited the carriage without looking back at the man. As the train pulled away from the station, she hazarded a glance towards it and felt a brief jolt of fear and instantly regretted her decision to look back.

The man had his face pressed hard up against the window and was still staring just as intently as before with only one difference, now he was smiling. In reply she raised her middle finger with both hands and emphatically mouthed '*fuck you*' as the train pulled off into the tunnel. His expression remained unchanged as both he and the train disappeared into the darkness.

Evie was close to dosing off almost as soon as her professor opened his mouth. It was not the content of his speech that bored her, quite the opposite, in fact, it was more to do with the delivery. All around her in the crowded lecture hall, scores of students seemed to share her sentiment. The crowd was a sea of tired young faces; such was the price of an early Monday morning lecture.

The vast majority of attendees would still be suffering from a hangover, or a lack of sleep, or both. In Evie's case, it was the latter.

The professor seemed not to mind, and even threw the occasional joke at the weary audience throughout his delivery. From his podium, the microphone carried his voice throughout the lecture hall. "Today, we're discussing love. Or at least the concept of love. What does it mean? Can we quantify it? Can it be said to exist?"

Evie started up a new page on her laptop for today's topic as her professor wore on. "Indeed, love is said to be one of the major driving forces of our society. But we each define love differently, and love may take on a different meaning when used in a certain context. Unconditional love is a term which is thrown around a lot and is generally thought of as being a love without any expectations or limitations, such as a mother's love for her child. Today we'll take a look at various forms of the idea of love, and what it might mean to us as individuals and as a society."

Evie typed the various headings to correspond with her professor's speech and continued to hover between wakefulness and sleep. As she was just about to nod off, she heard a whisper to her left. "Psst. Hey, Evie!" She turned her bleary eyes to her left and was greeted by the bubbly and impossibly energetic face of her good friend Lucy.

Lucy's strawberry blonde hair flowed down to her shoulders and her piercing blue eyes seemed to glow as she spoke. Indeed, Lucy appeared to be full of energy at all times, even at nine on a Monday morning. Evie was not entirely in the mood to reciprocate this energy right now, but she croaked a hushed reply none the less.

"Morning, Lucy. How was your weekend?"

"So good!" Lucy beamed. "I went to like, four different parties and took a lovely little soiree into the woods with some friends and some mushrooms on Sunday. How about you?"

Evie smiled. Classic Lucy. She always knew how to have a good time. "My weekend was pretty subdued; I didn't really go out much. But it was fine, I spent most of it catching up on my book."

Lucy nodded. "As long as you enjoyed yourself. We should go out together again sometime!"

Evie thought for a moment. It had been a long time since they had properly hung out, and she did miss hanging out with Lucy. Long, wild nights letting fate decide where they would end up next, meeting all sorts of weird and wonderful characters along the way, followed by wistful, carefree afternoons, taking long walks and even longer conversations, trying to decode the complex lexicon of life together.

She felt she could really be herself around Lucy, and in truth Evie missed those days more than she cared to admit. "You know I'd like to Luce, but I'm really busy these days. I can barely find time between school, work, and looking after my grandmother, you know?"

Lucy gave her an empathetic look. "I know these past few months have been really hard on you, but you shouldn't shut yourself away either! It's not good for you, y'know. I'll tell you what, there's a house party on Thursday night at this cool place downtown. Why don't you come with me?"

Evie hesitated. "I'm not so sure. I'll have to check my calendar."

"Oh, come on," Lucy pleaded, smiling. "It'll be fun! And I think you could use a bit of fun. I'll tell you what, I'll message you the invite. Obviously, you don't have to come, but I'd love to see you there."

"Thanks Luce, I'll see how I go."

"Good enough for me."

The two slowly returned their focus to the lecture at hand as their professor continued.

"Do we consider love to be a solely human concept?" the professor asked to the room. "A theory we have concocted to explain emotional reactions and impulses in the brain? Or do we consider the scope of love to wider reaching. Do animals love? Could love even be a universal concept? The answers will differ for us all."

Ω

The sun had already set when Evie opened the door to her quiet apartment. There was a stillness in the evening chill which comforted her, and the last hints of sunset bathed the apartment in the colours of twilight. She could faintly hear the sound of a blues record playing.

As Evie dropped her things down on the dining table, she plonked down onto a chair next to them and let out an exhausted sigh. *Another long day comes to a close.*

She believed there are few things in this world that are quite as relieving as coming home to your house after a long day on your feet. That was her introverted side. She could enjoy, even thrive, in social situations, but eventually she would have to return to her nest and recharge her batteries.

She relished her alone time, immersing herself in the limitless wilderness between the borders of books, feeding her imagination and expanding her world view all at once. At times, her behavior was almost hermit–like, and that suited her just fine. Tonight, she was looking forward to a lazy evening browsing the internet and reading.

As she grabbed her things and headed down the hallway towards her room, she could see a faint glow of light coming from under her grandmother's door. She poked her head in and saw Flora softly snoring in her bed as her record player hummed with the melancholic harmonies of blues music; the soundtrack to a bygone era.

She smiled as she surveyed the peaceful scene and shut the door as gently as she could behind her. Evie found her room as she had left it, in a somewhat advanced state of messiness. She put her bag down and was going to lay down on her bed when something on the floor caught her eye.

It was a small scrap of paper with something written on it. Equal parts perplexed and intrigued she bent down and picked it up. Written on it in black ink and a strange style of handwriting was a sequence of numbers.

28 – 15 – 8 – 33

She had no idea what those numbers meant, but even more confusing was thinking who or what could had placed this note in her room. As she was contemplating this her phone buzzed, breaking her intense concentration, startling her.

She looked at her phone: Lucy had just invited her to the

party. She scanned over the details. It was being held this coming Thursday at 28 Arthur Street, on the 15th of August 2033. Evie felt a chill run down her spine. There was no way that was coincidence.

Had Lucy broken in and planted the note as a prank? No, that was way too farfetched. Plus, she had said goodbye to Lucy only an hour beforehand as they left university, so there was no way she could have placed this note here.

She was not entirely sure of what this meant but she was sure of one thing: someone, or something, wanted her there.

## CHAPTER 2

# A Mirthful Smile

### *1031 A.D.*

The harmonic language of birds echoed through the woods, and rays of midmorning light broke through gaps in the canopy leaving patches of gold on the ground as the girl strolled down the overgrown path she knew so well.

She had been coming to fetch water in the nearby stream every morning for many seasons. Once her parents had deemed her old enough to find her own way back, it became expected of her. She did not relish the task, for the buckets were cumbersome, and the path was long and winding. During winter, the morning cold was biting. Still, she was happy to be able to help her parents in her own way, and looked forward to the day when she could start to help her father, as her mother did, in the family business.

Her father was originally a butcher by trade, but had some experience treating wounds during war when he was a young man. His rudimentary understanding of the human body, combined with his limited knowledge of herb lore and sanitation, had proved fruitful when he stumbled upon their village in his travels years later. Nestled deep in the forested mountains, Bluffton was a superstitious place, even when compared to the rest of the realm. Here, he found many dying of easily preventable ails, and so, applying his learned knowledge, showed them new ways of doing things.

Very soon, childbirth was no longer so feared in the village, and many more children lived past their first nameday. Within a short time, her father had a permanent place as the village healer, and everyone came to him with their ailments. It was a relatively lucrative position, and one he was very proud of. He soon took a wife and settled there, and it was not long before they had a child of their own.

She followed the sound of the bubbling water to a gap in the undergrowth which she then pushed through. There, at the edge of the woods she found the stream. The light danced dazzlingly as it reflected off the surface of the crystal–clear water, and she could make out the rolling clearings of the foothills juxtaposed against patches of forest clearly in the crisp morning air. She smiled at the beauty of her surroundings. Despite the length of the journey, it was always rewarding reaching the stream. The water was clear enough for her to make out a few fish swimming lazily, and the pebbles that carpeted the bottom.

She was struck by distant memories of when she would make this same journey with her mother, when she was little. They were happy memories, the warmth of her mother's smile, her loving embrace and her kind words. Similar memories with her father were few and far between. Despite his successes, he was still quite a cold man. Even so, she still wished to please him, and loved him all the same.

She knelt down at the stream and placed her buckets on

the ground as she cupped her hands to take a drink of water. It was ice cold and wonderfully refreshing, sweet even. As she drank, she caught her own reflection briefly in the surface of the water. Her pale skin was starkly contrasted by her unkempt raven black hair, which grew well past her shoulders. In many ways, she was the spitting image of her mother, high cheekbones and fair features. She had only inherited her father's blue eyes. She had dressed in some of her warmer furs, despite it being early autumn.

She remembered herself and began filling the buckets from the stream. She had almost filled one bucket when she felt a strange sensation, as though a shimmer or a ripple had run through the very air itself. The air grew still, and the water seemed to stop running. The birds were no longer chirping. She could hear little else apart from the steadily increasing beat of her heart in her ears.

She had the acute sensation that she was not alone, and that she was being watched, but for some reason she could not bring herself to look up from the water. She was terrified, and it was as if she was frozen in place.

As she stared intently at the surface of the water, she saw a figure slowly come into view from her left on the opposite bank of the stream. The surface of the water was moving, so she could not properly make it out, but it was emanating massive amounts of light and seemed to be making the rest of the surroundings darker. When she could see that the reflection of the figure was directly in front of her, she felt her head, and in turn her gaze, slowly rising against her will, as though an irresistible force was compelling her to move from within.

She saw the figure with her own eyes, starting at its feet and moving upwards. It resembled a woman, but unlike any woman she had ever seen.

She was slender and elegant, and wrapped in fine flowing fabric which seemed to be constantly moving across her glowing body. She stood at least eight feet tall and radiated a light and energy so intense that the girl had to squint to keep her eyes open.

Her features were like that of a human, but larger, and far more beautiful and graceful. Indeed, if it was a person, it was by far the most beautiful person the girl had ever seen. The girl felt herself quickly being overcome with emotion and tears began to stream down her face. The being's face was more beautiful than she could comprehend, and it was framed by white hair which glowed even brighter than its skin.

Atop its head was a brilliant white crown, resembling the antlers of a stag. Its eyes were closed, but it suddenly opened them and locked eyes with the girl. The being's violet eyes were the brightest of all and when the girl looked into them it was as though her head had exploded from within. The last thing she remembered before losing consciousness was the stranger's expression, a mirthful smile.

The sun had already passed its midday peak by the time the girl awoke. Her consciousness returned and she awoke with a start, gasping for air. She looked about herself frantically. Beside her, her buckets were full, and on the opposite bank there was no trace of the ghostly stranger. Had it all been nothing more than a dream? No. It could not have been.

She could still clearly see the features of this being in her mind's eye, and the rippling sensation in the air. It was as if the memory had been scorched into her very soul.

Quickly, she gathered her things and the pails of water. There was no time to process this experience now, she was already very late, and she could scarcely imagine the wrath her father might visit upon her for such a transgression. With all the litheness and speed of a hare, she sped home along the forest path, hopping roots and ducking branches all the way, all the while taking care as not to spill her precious payload sloshing about in the buckets. When she reached the edge of the wood, she could see the outer wooden wall of the village and the smoke from cook fires and the blacksmith rising lazily into the sky.

As she drew closer, still her senses were visited by the smells and sounds of home: cooking meat, children playing in the alleys, and the sound of mothers gossiping as they went about their morning chores. Today, however, these things gave her no comfort. She was late, a trespasser to daily routine.

When she reached the wooden gate, she laid her buckets down and gave the guard a curtsey, as was custom. He eyed her with an air of authority before opening the side door and ushering her through. She thanked him, and stole into the streets of the village at a brisk pace, hoping not to encounter either her mother or her father before she made it home.

The village was growing fast, and a few of the muddy streets were cobbled. The ramshackle dwellings were a mixture of mudbrick and wood, many of them painted white with lime. Many of the homes seemed almost to sprout from one another, and, in some cases, indeed they did. Despite this, Bluffton was an orderly town, and a nightly guard did regular patrols of its sleepy alleyways.

Before she knew it, she had reached her own doorstep. It was a two-level house, fairly large by local standards, which stood out all the more from the ornate stone archway above its entrance, built by hand by her father. She took a moment to collect herself and laid down the buckets of water, which by now were incredibly heavy. As she caught her breath, she could hear the faint clatter of pots and pans from the kitchen within. Her mother was home, as she should have been hours ago.

She tried to open the door as quietly as she could and gingerly slipped inside. She had not crept more than two steps however before her mothers voice boomed at her from the kitchen.

"Morgana! Come here at once!"

Sheepishly, she skulked down the hallway to the kitchen where she found her mother, arms crossed and face as stern as an executioner. Her long black hair was tied neatly in a bun and she wore an apron over a modest gown. The kitchen was full of the smells of her cooking and Morgana could see pots already at the boil.

"Where on earth have you been child?" her mother yelled. "We sent you off to get water hours ago! It's well past midday now!" Morgana could not meet her mother's gaze and focussed intently on the floor. This was very unlike her, and she did not quite know how to react.

"And just look at the state of you! Your clothes are filthy. You're lucky your father isn't here to see this." As her mother began to inspect her, her demeanour softened. "Just what happened to you child? Were you attacked?"

Morgana shook her head. She was unsure of how she could possibly explain what had happened to her without sounding mad, nor was she totally convinced that it had even happened at all. Her mother's mood changed again as she was inspecting her from behind.

"Ah," she heard her mother utter quietly under her breath.

"What is it mother?" she asked. Her apprehension was spiking.

"Something. Something. . . wonderful, my dear." She choked back tears. She fetched a mirror to show her the back of her dress, where she could see a small dark red patch of what looked like blood had soaked through. "I just never thought it would come so soon," her mother went on. "You've only just had your fourteenth nameday."

Morgana was still confused. "Why mother, what does it mean?"

Her mother smiled through her tears. "You have blossomed my child. You are a woman now."

ᚢ

The sun was beginning to set when the house's late afternoon stillness was broken by a haggard pounding at the front door. Morgana was in her room, but it was loud enough that she could hear it from there. She could also hear what sounded like a commotion, and lithely she rose from her bed and her melancholic ruminations to rush to the door. *It must be father*, she thought, though it was strange of him to knock.

As she descended the steps to the entry, she could see that her mother had beaten her to it and already opened the door. Shockingly, her father was carrying a man over his shoulder and breathing heavily as he struggled to support his weight. She could see that her father was exhausted, and his usually stoic, imposing features exhibited clear signs of stress. He was a large man, taller than most folk by a head, with a burly frame. His face was characterized by a bristling black moustache and a piercing gaze. Today though, she saw something else in his eyes. Fear.

Her mother was in a state of panic, and her voice trembled as she spoke. “My god. John, what happened?”

Wordlessly, he shuffled past her into the kitchen, and with his free hand he swept the kitchen table free, sending the dinner-time preparations crashing to the floor as he laid the man down on the table. When he was laid down, Morgana could see the true extent of the man’s injuries.

He was gravely wounded. His flesh was pallid and across his chest he bore a gash which looked like a scratch from a very large animal, soaking his shredded tunic with blood. She could also see his arms had been torn to shreds, and his right hand was completely gone, with only a bloody pulp remaining at the wrist. These were by far the worst wounds Morgana had ever seen on a person, but miraculously he still appeared to be breathing, though his breaths were labored and faint.

Her father finally spoke, and though his voice was commanding, but there was still unmistakable fear in his eyes. “Ingrid, bring me my tools.” Her mother rushed from the room to her father’s infirmary. “Morgana, come here and help me. We need to stop the bleeding.”

Morgana was in shock, momentarily frozen by the macabre scene unfolding before her. Her father’s stern voice snapped her out of it. “Now child! We haven’t the time to waste!” She rushed to his side, placing her hands over the deep gashes in the mans chest as her father instructed. “Keep as much pressure on those wounds as you can.”

She watched as he swiftly ran to the fireplace and submerged the iron poker in the hot coals before rushing back to the table. “We need to seal these wounds if he is to survive.” He focussed his attention on the bloody stump that remained of the mans hand. Her mother returned to the table with her fathers toolbox. He quickly rifled through the box before producing a roll of clean cloth and placed it over the oozing stump.

The man briefly woke from his stupor to moan before losing consciousness again. “The woods. . . The darkness. . .”

Her mother’s expression was grave and she stammered. “What did this? Was it a bear?” Her father remained silent as he applied pressure to the stump. Already, Morgana could see that the blood had soaked through the cloth. Under her hands she could feel the mans heartbeat getting fainter.

“Father!” she cried.

He understood. “Ingrid. Bring me the poker from the fireplace.” Her mothers eyes widened but she ran to fetch the poker nonetheless. She brought back the heavy poker and handed it to him. As she did, he removed the cloth from the wound and a spurt of blood followed it.

“Steady his arm.” Her mother did so with determined efficiency, holding the bloody stump aloft. “Have you a steady grip?”

“Yes!” her mother replied.

“Both of you?”

“Yes!” Morgana answered. He steadily laid the hot poker on what remained on the mans wrist, his wound emitting a sickening sizzle.

As soon as the hot poker seared his flesh, the man let out a blood curdling scream and began to struggle. “Hold him tight!” The man lapsed into unconsciousness again, but this time, Morgana could no longer feel his heartbeat. She looked to her father, who met her gaze and rushed to her side, placing two fingers on the man’s neck. He quickly put his ear to the man's mouth. After a few desperate seconds he wretched his head away in frustration. "Damnation!" he screamed, throwing the poker to the ground before collapsing against a wall. He slowly slunk down until he was crouched with his head in his hands.

Both Morgana and her mother were in stunned silence. Ingrid slowly laid the man's arm to rest on the table whilst Morgana kept her hands planted firmly on his chest. This was the first time she had seen the face of death with her own eyes. The first time someone's life was in her hands. Her father looked up from where he sat slumped, exhausted on the floor. His voice was soft, defeated.

"It's of no use child. He's gone."

She looked down at the man. His pale skin was still moist with perspiration, but already she could feel his body turning cold. The air in the room was quiet and still, and the last streaks of sunset shot deep orange streaks through the kitchen window.

Morgana felt something welling up inside her, a vibration, accompanied by a warmth emanating from her chest. She felt the hairs on the back of her neck stand up as tingles ran up and down her spine. Time seemed to slow to a crawl, and she closed her eyes.

She pictured the mans chest in her mind, and suddenly she was able to see through it. As she came to his heart, it was as though she was holding it in her hands. It was unlike any sensation she had ever felt. As she isolated his heart, the vibrations inside her own body intensified, to the point where it felt as though she would burst.

Quickly, she focussed her intention on releasing this energy, and as she did so she felt it travel like lightening from her chest and spine down through her arms into the man's chest. As she clutched his heart in the silent void, an echo permeated the blackness.

***THUMP THUMP***

She opened her eyes and time began anew. The man let out a loud gasp and her mother and father both dashed to the table. Her father quickly pushed her aside, but not before shooting her a strange look, almost of suspicion.

"It's a miracle. . ." her mother breathed. Morgana stepped back from the table as her parents set about tending to the man's wounds.

From that night onward, the winds of change howled relentlessly in Morgana's life. Nothing was the same.

She heard murmurs, hushed whispers uttered by concerned strangers in the alleyways at night. They spoke of creatures, horrors yet unseen in this age. Whether it was hearsay or not she did not know. Worse still, apparently a bloody war had erupted; a new ascendant prince threatened to usurp the throne, and there was a rupture in the nobility of the realm. Deaths were already catastrophic on both sides and, as usual, the commonfolk bore the brunt of the losses, be it through forced military servitude or terrible sieges and raids.

There was a shadow spreading across the land and the woods near Bluffton were no longer safe. The commonfolk knew not the cause but the tension in the village was palpable. Her father was brooding as ever, but since that night he had allowed Morgana to assist him with the practical side of his work. Her mother saw it as a great honor.

It was unheard of for a woman to undertake such tasks, let alone one aged just fourteen years. Where his eyes had once been dismissive, they now studied her intently whenever she was in his presence. Even with her back turned she could feel his cold gaze upon her. Watching.

There was plenty of work. The wounded and ailing flowed into her fathers infirmary from far and wide, many of whom babbled of the horrors they had witnessed in battle or on the roads, talk her father quickly and firmly shut down when Morgana and her mother were present. Late in the night, however, when both she and her mother were presumed asleep, Morgana would eavesdrop from the top of the stairs, with all the silence of a matron. The stories these forlorn travellers shared with her father robbed her of many a nights sleep.

They told tales of hopeless battles, leaderless bands of warriors razing peaceful settlements to the ground, the rape and slaughter of women and children. To these stories, her father listed intently and spoke little, the coals of the hearth illuminating his furrowed brow as he breathed deeply on his pipe.

Less common, but far more disturbing, were the tales some told of attacks by creatures of unnatural origin. They spoke of pallid-skinned beats which stalked the woods at night, preying on the weary, and wielders of magic cloaked in darkness. Nightmarish visions which harked back to bedtime stories she was told as a girl.

Her father would rarely entertain such talk, and more than once he banished a patient from their home when they would insist their tales were truthful.

The influx of wounded meant an influx of coin. It was a prosperous time for her family and her mother was overjoyed. No longer did they have to suffer as they had in seasons passed. For her part, Morgana was tentative.

She knew she had awakened something within herself that night. What it was she could not say, nor would she dare to mention it aloud, for that would only make it all the more real. She knew what fate awaited those branded "deviants" with deformities and abilities considered abnormal. Hellfire.

In secret, however, she carefully tested her newfound abilities on the injured. With flesh wounds, she found she could direct her energy towards them and stem the flow of blood in the body. With internal injuries, she was able to focus and see into the body to locate the specific organ which was damaged and help it to function anew. Diseases remained an enigma to her, although she was making progress in rectifying simple colds. Was this what they called magic?

She was awash with a mix of emotions. She was terrified of her secret being discovered, but she also felt something else: she was quietly proud of her growing abilities. Proud of the way she could help her father, even if he could never know the truth. Soon enough, word spread far outside of the walls of Bluffton of the healing proficiency of her father, and as his reputation spread, so too did his influence.

Months passed this way. The sick and dying of the land would shuffle through the doors of their family home, which was soon upgraded to a larger manse, with an entire wing dedicated to patients.

Morgana had never seen her mother this happy. She would hum and sing to herself as she went about her daily chores, and her alabaster skin and ebony hair seemed almost to glow in the daylight. It brought Morgana great pleasure to see her mother at peace in such a way.

Her father remained aloof, but even his brooding features

seemed softened by these times. More than once, she stumbled upon the two of them dancing slowly in the expansive hearth of their new home at the days end. These were peaceful times. Times she would look back upon as if they were nought but a dream.

Though they had lived at the unpaved outer rim of the village before their prosperity, their new home was situated on one of the few cobblestone streets of Bluffton, an affluent area and was situated very close to the town center. Where once she had played games in the muddy alleys of her old neighbourhood with the other children at dusk, Morgana was now a poised figure of composure. Her newfound workload left her with little time for fraternizing with others her age, and though she had outgrown most street games, she had begun to feel isolated in her new life.

One morning in particular was to change this.

Morgana was running errands when her father had instructed her to visit the holdings of the town blacksmith, Errol, to pick up some new wares for his surgery. Usually, her father handled such business, but with his increased workload and scarcity of time he had seen fit to entrust this task to her. He had told her the address of the blacksmith and she deftly navigated the cobblestone streets which where abuzz with the bustle of many others undertaking similar morning routines.

Eagle-eyed customers scanned the meager food stands which dotted the roadside intently for the days freshest produce, whilst hawkers great and small vied for their attention and coin in equal measure. Despite her family's success, most of the realm was not so lucky. The bloody civil conflict dragged on and showed no signs of abating, and as wars do, it slowly withered the land, like an apple rotting from within.

Beggars lined the streets, too, their ranks growing by the day, many of them pox addled and clinging to life. Morgana pitied them, and wished she could help, but as her father would say: "Those who cannot pay their way should sooner bow their heads and pray."

He scarcely wasted an opportunity to remind Morgana that the services they provided were just that, a service, a monetary exchange was the basis of this service, and those who could not pay the coin price would have to pay a dearer price. It was a harsh reality and one which she still struggled to accept. How could one put a price on life? If her powers were a gift, how could she commodify them? As it were, her powers were known only to her, and she intended to keep it that way.

The sun was still low in the sky when she knocked upon the sturdy wooden door of the blacksmith. She heard quick footsteps from within accompanied by a rapid unlatching of locks before the door creaked open. She was met by the sight of a soot covered youth.

He looked her age or slightly older, his straw-colored hair was cut short and pulled to a ponytail in the back, and a pale cloth tunic adorned his athletic frame. Perspiration covered his brow and dripped from his nose as his deep blue eyes met hers. This was not the gruff barrel-chested old man she had been expecting. Both parties seemed caught off guard and there was a brief pause. Morgana spoke first.

"Please, excuse me, but is this the forge of Errol Stone-heath?"

"Aye," the youth stammered.

"I'm here to pick up goods on behalf of John Eldritch."

A look of recognition crossed his face and his eyes darted into action. "Of course, my lady. Right this way." She blushed mildly, hoping it went unnoticed. It was the first time she had been addressed as such. He held the door open for her as she stepped in and shut it behind her, the wood groaning as he did so. When he had latched it again, he bowed gently.

"Forgive my lack of courtesy, my lady. I am Mathias Hornsmeade."

She responded in turn with her best impression of a curtsy. "Morgana Eldritch." Within the house she could feel the heat emanating from the bellows, and there they soon found Errol. They heard the sound of his hammer clanking against metal long before she laid eyes on him, and this time his appearance did indeed correspond with her mental projection.

Errol Stoneheath sat at ease in his chair by the bellows. He was old, older than her parents by perhaps a decade, and his silver hair hung well past his shoulders. He had a large chest and a larger stomach to match, but largest still seemed to be his massive arms, with plate sized hands mottled with all manner of callouses. His face was a sooty sea marked by deep wrinkles earned spending years stoking hot flames and fashioning metal. His voice was gravelly but his eyes were kind, and Morgana felt at ease when he spoke.

"I see you've met my young apprentice." He chuckled. "You'll have to forgive his brutishness, he knows not much outside this forge." She quickly gazed at Mathias, who had turned a deep shade of crimson. "Back to work there boy, we've much to do today."

Breathing an audible sigh of relief, Mathias turned to leave the room, but not before bowing one last time to Morgana. "Milady," he said politely, before quickly walking away.

Errol smiled wryly. "Now then, I've set aside your fathers new tools on the workbench over there." He pointed over to a small box on a wooden table in the dusty corner of the workshop. "You'll find it's all there, as per the order. The tools are very lightweight so you shouldn't have trouble carrying them. If you do, I can get Mathias to help you bring them home."

Morgana nodded. "That shouldn't be necessary. Thank you very much, sir. Here's your coin." She spoke with her best air of knowhow, reaching into her bag and producing the healthy coin sack. She handed it to Errol, who set it by his side. "I'll be on my way then. Good day to you, sir."

"Good day, young lady. We always welcome more business in times like these." She curtseyed briefly before briskly leaving the bellows and walking into the courtyard.

Mathias was there, working, but when he saw her, he set his tools down and sprang into action, beating her to the gate to open it for her. He wordlessly gave her another courteous bow before she stepped out into the street. She tried to meet his gaze, but he was staring intently at his feet. Once the door had shut behind her, she smiled to herself before setting on her way.

# CHAPTER 3

# Long Shadows

## *1033 A.D.*

For his entire life, the walls of the abbey were the only world Enoch had ever known. The cold sandstone exterior belied the warmth that was found within.

His favorite place of all was the library, "a compendium of knowledge," as Master Adrax oft called it. The stillness there was unparalleled, even for the abbey, and the very air itself seemed to faintly whisper tales of ages past, and ancient rites and customs long since forgotten.

The expansive library hall was one of the oldest places in the abbey and had seen ten generations of monks pass through its doors. Ten generations of cartographers, historians, and truth seekers. Some search for answers in the divine, others within the motheaten pages of history.

For his part, Enoch was but another young novitiate, transcribing some of the more ancient texts into new volumes lest their lessons be lost forever. It was only in his spare time that he was allowed to explore his curiosities, and curiosities he had. The ancient tomes were his only link to the outside world, for acolytes of The One Truth there lay but one path, and it was behind these sandstone walls, carefully tending the torch of humanity.

The One Truth was the dominant religion of the land, and it specified in no uncertain terms that there was but one God, one path to salvation. Anything else was heresy, punishable by eternal damnation. Science and witchcraft were one in the same for the devout. Sins.

That was what they were taught, but most monks never left this sanctum. What could they know of the world? What could any of them say from in here? Enoch paused his transcription for a moment to gaze out the window.

The glow of the late afternoon sun bathed the courtyard a deep orange. Fragile wisps of cloud hung static in the upper limits of the midwinter sky. It was a rare and welcome sunny day, a vibrant sojourn from the unending gloominess of winter. It felt almost sacrilegious to spend a day like this indoors. Alas, he still had half a volume left to copy before the days end.

Transcription was a painstaking task, and the level of precision it required was very draining. Each word, each letter, in the new volumes he was producing had to ornate, beautiful, and as close to perfection as earthly hands would allow. Dotted around the library halls were an array of novitiates and monks of all ages, similarly hunched over varnished desks in quiet concentration.

Novitiates had to complete a multitude of tasks, both grand and menial, before they could ascend to monkhood. It was said to have less to do with age and more to do with wisdom. Or at least that's what Master Adrax always said.

Adrax was not the most senior monk there, not by a long

shot. In fact, there were half a dozen monks at the abbey who were aged over a hundred years; an unfathomable number when most free folk lived not to age forty. Outsiders oft speculated that it was the freshwater spring under the abbey that gave the monks ''supernatural'' long life.

Enoch suspected it had less to do with the groundwater and more to do with being shielded from the various pitfalls and hardships of life outside.

He was devoutly logical, a predisposition which was oft at ends with his so called "faith." Adrax had been unanimously elected Abbey Master almost two decades ago by the elder council. He was not yet thirty years of age at that time, but he was leagues ahead of his peers at the time and possessed a clarity of thinking and enthusiasm that had not been seen in a generation, making him an obvious choice. It was around the time of his ascension, on a cold midwinter's night much like this, that a baby was abandoned on the steps at the foot of the colossal wooden gates of the abbey.

The child was Enoch, so named by the Master of the Abbey. Had it not been for his discovery by the night watchman, Balus, he would have perished in the cold. Uncharacteristically of an Abbey Master, Adrax took it upon himself to raise the child. This crucial decision was what had shaped Enoch's life. To him, Master Adrax was the closest thing he had to a father. Oft aloof and buried in his books, Adrax had become increasingly reclusive in his elder years. Though he kept a watchful eye on Enoch's education he seemed distant, spending much of his days in his private study.

The sun had almost set by the time Enoch had delicately transcribed the last careful letters into the tome before him. The ink was still fresh on the parchment when he silently raised his hand to attract the attention of the elderly proctor, who oversaw the scribes. The proctor sat at a raised desk in the far corner of the room. The many candles he kept at his desk clearly illuminated his sour complexion as he hunched over a manuscript, carefully inspecting it with his eyeglass.

After Enoch had patiently held his hand aloft for more than a minute to no avail, he carefully cleared his throat, loud enough that the proctor could hear him. Despite his care, the sound still echoed through the cold stone walls of the library. The proctor slowly raised his head from his desk and cast a suspicious gaze at Enoch before painstakingly dismounting from his perch and slowly but deliberately walking towards him.

All around, the other young novitiates continued to work tirelessly in silence. His footsteps echoed coldly, and Enoch bowed his head to his desk as the Proctor approached and soon enough stood before him.

Enoch cast him a cursory look. His light brown robes indicated his seniority amongst the order, and these coupled with his grey wrinkled skin made him appear as though he was some type of living embodiment of a library tome: withered, ancient, and uncompromising.

He meticulously inspected Enoch's work in silence, deftly turning the pages and inspecting them one by one. After a brief pause, he addressed Enoch. "Very well. You may take your leave." The Proctor spoke joylessly before turning and beginning the slow walk back to his desk. Transcription was a thankless task, like many of the tasks novice monks were assigned. It was a duty.

Enoch quietly gathered his belongings before quickly leaving the solemn hall to return to his dormitory. If he was quick enough, he would be able to bathe briefly before supper.

Supper was shared by novitiates and monks alike in the

dining hall, but the diners were separated by class and rank. At the head of the hall sat the elder council, and at the center of them all, the Abbey Master.

As Enoch walked the corridor which connected the library to the rest of the abbey, he cast his gaze to the courtyard outside. Leafless trees seemed to shiver in the twilight, as the setting of the sun brought with it cold winds from the icy sea. Enoch had not visited the sea before, but he knew it was close by. When the winds gusted, he could smell it. It was comforting somehow, a familiar essence he had known all his life.

As he wound his way through the meandering sandstone passageways of the abbey, he could see that the torchbearers had already begun their nightly rounds to light all the various lamps and candles which served to illuminate the key locations of thoroughfare and importance throughout the abbey. Soon he arrived at his own dormitory, number seven, which he shared with three other novitiates.

He unlatched the wooden door which gave a loud creak of protest as he opened it. The room was pitch black inside. His bunkmates must have already left towards the dining hall. He used a nearby candle from the corridor to light up the candles within his own room, bathing the room a dull orange.

There were four bunks in the cramped stone room, and a small window high on the wall, through which both sun and moonlight shone at differing hours of the day. His bunkmates were friendly enough. One in particular, Peter, had a knack for funny poems, though they were aghast at the possibility of the monks hearing them. Many nights Peter entertained them from his top bunk after dark, eliciting fits of hushed laughter from the other boys as he told tall tales of sour faced old monks and wanton maidens.

As he was gathering his personal effects before his bath, Enoch heard a knock at the door. When he opened it, in the flickering candlelight of the corridor, stood the mountainous figure of Balus, head of the abbey guard. Despite his age, Balus remained an imposing figure. He stood a head and a half taller than most men, and his burly frame gave him the appearance of a giant.

He smiled when he saw Enoch, and the candlelight danced off of his stubble as he spoke. “Good evening, young master. I trust your transcription was riveting?” Balus’ deep voice was chiding, the only one who referred to Enoch as such. It was a term of endearment, a joke of sorts between the two.

Master Adrax had seen to it that Balus teach Enoch the art of swordplay in the barracks thrice weekly since he was eight years old. It was forbidden for monks to engage in such affairs, and as such it was a closely kept secret between the three. Enoch had already trained with Balus yesterday, and his appearance before him tonight was unexpected.

“Full of excitement, as always, Balus. What brings you here?”

Balus’s expression became more serious. “The master sent me to bring you to his quarters.” That, too, was out of the ordinary.

“Did he mention why?” Enoch probed.

“No, he did not say. Come along now, we’d best not keep him waiting.”

Enoch complied and slipped his shoes back on. When he had readied himself, he stepped into the corridor with Balus, and they began the walk to Adrax’s study. Enoch had to quicken his pace to match Balus’s long strides.

“And how are your studies progressing?” Balus enquired.

“Slowly but surely,” Enoch replied. “Though I often find

myself thinking about the outside world. None of the other monks or even many of the novitiates seem interested in it at all."

Balus paused for a moment to consider his response before replying. "Well, that stands to reason, Enoch. They chose this life of seclusion after all. They sacrificed their lives to serve The One."

Enoch sighed. "I know. I suppose sometimes I grow restless. I want not to wither and sour as some here have done."

Balus smiled. "You have an adventurer's spirit boy, like me, in my youth. I think, with time, you will find fulfilment here in the abbey. Committing oneself to the pursuit of something greater is a noble feat." Despite not being a monk himself, Enoch found Balus to be far wiser than any of the elders who taught at the abbey, perhaps save for Master Adrax. He had an understanding of philosophy and a command of speech which could not be learned from a book. He possessed wisdom, knowledge embodied, with a keen understanding honed by the trials and tribulations of the wide world.

In many ways, Enoch saw Balus as a mentor, and most of his knowledge of the world outside came from Balus. He was also a skilled swordsman, and quick on his feet still, despite being near to forty years of age.

After navigating the labyrinthine maze of passageways and corridors, which led to the inner sanctum of the abbey, they finally reached the spiral staircase which led to Master Adrax's tower. It was customary for the Abbey Master to take up residence in the Tower of Attainment, a heavily weathered sandstone structure in the center of the abbey, which was said to be the first structure built on these grounds. There was some speculation as to who or what built it. The truth remained a closely guarded secret by the elder council, or so he was told. The tower stood many lengths above the rest of the abbey, and from the master's study one could see the countryside for miles. On clear days, even the ocean was visible to the west.

Enoch reached for a wall-hanging torch to light their way as they prepared to climb the stairs, but Balus stopped him, his voice reverberating off the stone walls of the staircase. "You needn't worry boy. Look." He motioned for Enoch to look upwards.

Enoch peered into the staircase and saw that small windows dotting the stone walls allowed moonlight to illuminate their way, giving the staircase a haunting, almost other worldly appearance.

"Beautiful, isn't it? It's been a while since I've been up here. Steady yourself, young master, it's a long way up."

As they continued their ascent to the top of the tower, Enoch found himself panting. He was both surprised and bemused that he was struggling to keep up with the lumbering Balus, but he dared not complain, for fear of being seen as weak. Balus must have heard his labored breathing, however, for soon they came to a stop.

"We can rest for a moment, if you like," Balus offered.

"I'm. . . fine," Enoch wheezed.

"Very well. But I shall slow the pace. Just in case."

After what seemed like an eternity, they finally reached the top of the stair. Enoch all but collapsed, while Balus retained his composure.

They were at the foot of a large ornate iron door. In the pale moonlight, Enoch could see that it was composed of layer upon layer of ornate metalwork depicting dragons, great trees, humans, and all manner of other curiosities which Enoch had not the names for.

Balus rapped at the door three times in a very specific

order and manner, and before too long Enoch heard the sound of latches and locks opening from within. Something was strange, however, as all the sounds seemed to be occurring simultaneously, as if they were happening of their own accord.

The sounds abruptly stopped, and the door swung open. There was no one on the other side to greet them, only another small set of stairs. As they ascended these stairs, they entered Master Adrax's study.

The dome shaped room was truly impressive. Large, curved glass windows allowed the moonlight to pour in, and all about the room were shelves holding books, great and small, each carefully catalogued and all in varying states of repair. The room was awash with candles of all varieties, some so large their wax trails reached all the way to the floor. There were metallic instruments too, many so foreign to behold that Enoch could not begin to fathom their purpose.

On the opposite wall to the entrance hung a map containing the borders of the realm, as well as the wider lands beyond that. It depicted the very edges of the known world. In the center of the room was Master Adrax's desk, a dark mahogany slab illuminated by a skylight in the roof above and the multitude of candles and lamps which were strewn across its surface, dwarfed only by the sheer number of ancient parchments and documents, inkwells, and quills Adrax had in his possession.

Master Adrax was peering out at the moon through a telescope next to the window. "Fantastic," he muttered to himself as they walked in. When he heard their steps approaching, he left his post at the telescope and strode towards them. "Ah, Balus. Right on time. Come in both of you, take a seat." He motioned for them to sit in the armchairs adjacent to his desk.

Enoch studied Adrax in the half light of the room. Adrax

was the closest thing he had to a paternal figure, yet this was the first time he had seen him in weeks. His appearance was more haggard than he remembered. His long silvery hair hung well past his shoulders, and he was sporting a sizable beard in place of his usually closely shaved face.

Balus too, seemed struck by the master's appearance, judging by the look of bewilderment on his face. His unkemptness made him seem much older somehow. His slight frame was adorned in a golden embroidered silken robe which went down to his ankles, and on his feet, he wore slippers of a similar make. As they approached the desk, he hastily pushed aside the mess of parchments and manuscripts.

When they sat opposite him in the chairs, Enoch was able to get a clearer view. In his eyes, Adrax still possessed the same steely gaze, and when he addressed them, he did so with command.

"I trust you are both wondering why I summoned you here. We shall get to that. Firstly, tell me Enoch, how are your trials progressing? Proctor Aldwin tells me he can find no fault in your transcriptions."

"They are progressing well, master," Enoch replied, tentatively.

Adrax's expression softened. "Of that I have no doubt. You have a keen mind and an honest heart. You will be an adept disciple one day." Enoch's heart warmed to hear such praise from him. "And you, Balus, how are the guardsmen?"

"The days grow shorter, and we grow older. But I see to it that the men perform their duties without fault. If anything, it's my training with the young master here which keeps me sharp," Balus replied, nudging Enoch.

"I would expect nothing less. Now, to the matter at hand.

As you both likely know, there has been an outbreak of war in the north, stoked by uncertainty regarding royal succession." Balus grunted and nodded in understanding and Enoch nodded too, though he knew next to nothing about the situation. It was highly out of the ordinary for Master Adrax to address Enoch on such matters.

Adrax continued. "In times like these, our walls prove our salvation. This abbey has endured many regime changes in its time, and is like to weather many more. Doubtless, both of you have noticed my reclusion as of late. It isn't for nought. I have been conducting some research, concerning what has been and what may be to come. I've reason to suspect there's more at play here in the shadows, and the crowns of kings cast long shadows indeed."

Both Balus and Enoch were flummoxed by his words into utter silence. "It is for that reason that I must reach out to an ally beyond these walls. As you know, it is forbidden for an Abbey Master to leave his station. A shepherd must tend to his flock. That is why I must entrust this task to you." Adrax cast his deliberate gaze upon them.

"What task, master?" Balus asked.

"I've a message you must deliver to a man known as Davroz, in the port city of Fairhaven," Adrax said, producing the letter from his robes. He laid it on the table in front of them.

Upon closer inspection Enoch could see that it carried an ornate seal. It was a hexagram ringed by a snake eating its own tail, in the center of the hexagram were what looked like twelve arches, six pointing upwards, and six pointing downwards, with an eye set at its center. Enoch had never seen that seal when he had worked fixing letters to carrier pigeons in the bird loft.

As if reading his mind, Balus spoke. "Forgive me master,

but would it not be faster to send the message by bird?"

"It would be faster indeed. But less secure," Adrax replied. "The contents of this letter are too important for it to land in the wrong hands. That's why I am entrusting this task to you. Both of you."

"Both of us?" Enoch asked in disbelief.

"Who will be head of the guard in my stead?" Balus enquired matter-of-factly.

"I shall appoint a suiting replacement at your discretion, Balus, who will act until you both return."

"B-but master. . ." Enoch stuttered. "I know not a thing outside these walls. Surely there is a better choice than myself to accompany Sir Balus."

Adrax smiled. "On the contrary, my boy. I believe you to be the only choice to accompany Sir Balus. You have been training together for quite some time. I'd wager you know each other quite well by now."

Enoch was stunned. "But the abbey is all I know, master."

"And know it you do!" Adrax retorted cheerily. "Now, it is time to expand your horizons. Since the night you came to us, Enoch, I have fed you, clothed you, and taught you all that I can, but you were never destined to stay hidden here forever. As of now, you stand on the cusp of manhood, and a man needs to find his place in the world."

Enoch was moved to silence. In but a few minutes, his entire paradigm had been changed. The life he had imagined only in his wildest of daydreams was laid before him. He became aware of both Balus's and Adrax's eyes upon him.

"What say you, Enoch?" Adrax asked, leaning over the desk. "Do you accept this task?"

Enoch took a moment before replying. With all the confidence he could muster, he delivered his response. "I do."

ᘉ

At dawn the next morning, Balus and Enoch stood in the yard before the colossal wood and iron gates of the Abbey as they slowly ratcheted open. Each of them bore a large satchel with as many provisions as they could reasonably afford to carry.

Beneath his furs, Enoch shivered, though whether it was from nerves or the morning frost he could not say. The muddy alley was hushed, save for the snorting of pigs and the occasional crowing of roosters. There was little said between the two would-be travellers. Balus broke the silence.

"Should be three days walk, if we don't tarry."

Enoch nodded. "Right."

He turned and cast one last glance at the Tower of Attainment. Its pale stone was quickly turning orange from the top down as the sun began to rise, chasing the night away with beams of gold. Behind the glare of the reflective glass window, Enoch strained to make out the figure of Master Adrax watching their departure. He could feel his gaze, even from on high.

Finally, the gates were fixed open. With that came a gust of wind, carrying with it the faint smell of the sea, and the promise of a new day. Enoch winced from the cold, then steadied himself. When he unclenched his eyes, he could see the first rays of sunshine illuminating the frosted grassy hills with sinews of gold, and he could see the winding path which lay before them. He turned to Balus, who nodded. Enoch nodded in return, and with that they set off, their figures casting shifting silhouettes in the morning sun.

# CHAPTER 4

# Power

## *2033 A.D.*

The icy rain buffeted the windshield of his convertible relentlessly as he drove through the city streets. He was already speeding, but he floored his foot on the accelerator even further. The powerful engine gave a growl as the force pushed him further back into his seat. He smiled for a brief moment as he felt the familiar rush of adrenaline. It felt good.

He could feel the wheels starting to lose traction on the wet tarmac and he eased off slightly.

*What does it matter? It's not my car anyway.*

He chuckled as he reached into his pocket to light yet another cigarette. It was only a momentary lapse in concentration but when he returned his gaze to the road, he saw he was about to rear end another car which was braking in front of him. He quickly swerved into the nearby lane, almost losing control of the car as he did so. As he ran the red light, his immediate shock was quickly followed by laughter.

*Close call. At that speed I probably would have died.*

He looked at himself in the rear view mirror. His freshly shaven white-blonde buzz cut highlighted his angular facial features, and the dark furrows of habitual insomnia cut savage trenches under his pale blue eyes. As he glanced down at his unbuckled seatbelt, he considered whether or not he would buckle it.

Fuck it.

His phone rang and he answered on the cars inbuilt handsfree mode. The voice on the other end of the line sounded nervous.

"Hey, Adam. . . are you far off?"

Adam immediately felt rage rise inside of him like venom. "I'm five minutes away."

Marcus was an idiot. He had told him countless times not to refer to him by name over the phone, in case the police were listening. Again, he increased his speed as he drove towards Marcus' house.

The two met back in high school, two years previous, but to call him a friend would be a stretch. All told, Adam did not have any friends. The only people he was in contact with were those who were of immediate use to him. Trusting people was overrated. He had been shown the truth in that more than once in the past.

As he started to reach the suburbs on the edge of the city, he made a series of rights and lefts, landing him on Walker Street, a sleepy middle-class neighborhood. It was a far cry from the affluent area Adam lived in, but it was by no means run down. He could see a few high-end cars in driveways here and there. The rain kept most people off the streets, but he could see lights inside most of the homes.

He slowed the pace as he looked for number fifty–two. The hard liquor still churning in his system made it hard for him to focus on the street numbers, and the relentless rain made it all the more difficult to see. It was just past seven when he finally located number fifty–two and came to a stop, sending a text to Marcus.

*Come out now*

He left the engine running as he stared listlessly down the street in front of him. Within a minute or two, he saw the porch light flicker on and the front door open. Through the rain on his window, he could make out the figure of Marcus and what looked like his mother in the doorway, talking.

Marcus was shorter than he was, and very skinny for his age. His unkept messy brown hair came down to his eye level and his slight figure shivered in the cold, despite his sweatpants and hoodie. He could not hear them, but he could see Marcus' mother was holding an umbrella, motioning as if to give it to Marcus. He shook his head profusely and gave her a hug before briskly running down the garden path towards Adam's waiting convertible.

When he reached the passenger side door, he gave the handle a pull, but it was locked, making him knock on the window. Adam knew it was locked but wanted to let him wait in the rain a little longer, it was the least he deserved after that stunt he pulled on the phone.

Marcus knocked again, this time more frantically and Adam unlocked the door, sighing. In the brief moment where the door was opened and the automatic interior light came on, as the cigarette smoke wafted out into the cold night air, Adam locked eyes with Marcus' mother standing on the porch in her nightgown. Her face was stern, but her eyes were concerned.

Adam internally locked the doors behind Marcus and revved the engine loudly before speeding off down the street, chuckling at the fading silhouette of Marcus's porch-bound mother in the rear view mirror.

"Stop!" Marcus bleated. "What the hell man? Do you really have to do that?"

"What, mommy doesn't like it?" Adam teased.

Marcus glanced towards the open whiskey bottle sitting in the drink holder. "Have you been drinking?"

"What's it to you?" Adam shot back, becoming defensive.

"It's dangerous. Not to mention risky. What if we got pulled over?"

"Waaah, waah, waah. That's what you sound like," Adam responded mockingly.

"Fuck you, man. . ." Marcus muttered under his breath.

Again, Adam's rage bubbled. "Fuck me? How about fuck you. How many times have I told you not to use my real name on the phone? We aren't kids anymore!"

Marcus was caught off guard by his sudden aggression, responding meekly. "I–I'm sorry man, it slipped my mind."

"Of course it slipped your stoned-ass mind. Everything does. But I ain't getting locked up for your mistakes, got it?"

"Okay," Marcus replied, dropping his head. "It won't happen again."

"It better not. Are we still good to pick up off your guy?"

"Yeah, I just messaged him about an hour ago, he hit me back to say it's all good and to pull up at any time," Marcus replied. "The address is 39 Montrell Crescent."

"And he's a friend of yours?"

"Yeah, we skate together." Marcus cleared his throat. "Uh, did you bring the money?"

"Of course I brought the fucking money." He silently punched the address in to his GPS on his phone.

Montrell Crescent was in a bad part of town, a part of town notorious for carjacking's and home invasions. Adam gently reached into his waistband and his hand was met with the cold steel of the .22 caliber pistol he had tucked into his pants. He wasn't taking any chances.

Neither boy said much to one another for the rest of the journey to Montrell Crescent. By now it was pitch black, the grey storm clouds of the day giving way to an impenetrable night of darkest ebony.

As they left the suburbs, the streetlights became fewer and further in between, before switching to the garish orange hued energy saving bulbs as they neared closer to the projects. The blocks here were squat, with poorly defined fences separating them. Adam could see that many of the houses were run down and abandoned.

"You ever been down here before?" Marcus asked, breaking the silence.

"Of course," Adam lied, masking his apprehension. He was conscious of the fact that the immaculate convertible he was driving would probably attract attention. For that, he was glad it was night time.

Soon enough, they had reached the street. As they neared the pin on his phone, they could hear the dull thud of bass from nearby speakers getting louder. There must have been a party. Adam parked the car on the opposite side of the street to the house, in the shadow of a large oak tree, cutting the lights.

"Tell him we're outside," Adam said coolly, reaching into his pocket to light another cigarette. Marcus complied and the tapping of his phone screen was the only thing that broke the hushed silence in the car. Before long, Marcus' phone buzzed with a text reply.

"Cool," Marcus said to himself. "I told him where we are, and he says he's gonna come out now."

Both boys watched the house intently. Adam could see signs of what looked like a raucous party taking place within. Eventually, the screen door swung open, and a man staggered out into the night air. The rain was only spitting at this point, but it was enough to make him wince and pull his hood up over his bald head.

Adam could not make out his features clearly, but he was well built and athletic, clearly older than them by a few years as well. He scanned the street for a while before spotting their car and walking over. As he approached the passenger side window, he seemed calm, jovial even. Adam let down Marcus's window and the stranger greeted him warmly. "Yooo, Marc, what's good, man?"

Adam could see him more clearly now. He had a pale complexion, and his bald head was covered in tattoos.

"I'm good, bro," Marcus replied. "How you been?"

"Chillin' bro, you know me. Is this your boy?" he asked, gesturing to Adam.

"Yeah."

"What's up, man? Jason." The stranger waved.

"Adam," Adam replied, without a hint of emotion.

"Nice to meet you. This your car?"

Adam paused briefly. "Sure is."

"It's nice!" Jason replied emphatically. "I been tryna cop me one just like this. Anyways, it was just one brick right?" Jason rummaged in the deep pockets of his jacket while he leaned into the window.

"Yeah, just one," Marcus replied.

Jason soon produced a small but very dense rectangle wrapped in duct tape. "You got the money?"

Both Marcus and Jason looked at Adam after a brief pause, as he feigned opening the glovebox to produce the money. In one smooth motion, he drew the pistol from his waist and pointed it squarely in Jason's face. As Jason was leaning in through the window when Adam drew the pistol, the muzzle was inches from his forehead. Jason and Marcus both froze.

Adams's hand trembled but he kept his grip firmly on the trigger. He could feel his heartbeat thumping in his ears. This was a new feeling.

Marcus' eyes darted between Jason, the pistol, and Adam. He began to speak, his trembling voice rapidly rising into hysterics as he did so.

"Adam. . . what the fuck are you doing! You ca—"

"Shut up," Adam said sternly, cutting him off. Adam dared not blink or look away, as he and Jason's eyes had been locked from the moment he drew the pistol.

Time seemed to slow. The seconds felt like whole minutes. An entire exchange was taking place between their eyes alone. "Place the brick on the dash," Adam eventually instructed.

Jason began to smile. "You gotta be fucking joking, right?"

Adam cocked the pistol and pressed it firmly against the center of his forehead. "Do it now."

He had never pointed a weapon at someone like this before. For the first time in his life, he had total control. He, and he alone, could dictate the actions and outcomes of this situation. He could hear Marcus's rapid breaths in the passenger seat; he sounded close to hyperventilating.

The smile had disappeared from Jason's face and he spoke

calmly. "This isn't smart, lil' bro. Not smart at all. I'll give you one chance. You can still turn around now and forget all this."

Now, Adam laughed. "You'll give me a chance? I'm not the one with a gun to my head. Place it on the dash now."

Keeping his free hand raised, Jason slowly placed the brick of cocaine on the car dashboard.

"Now step back," Adam said, keeping the pistol firmly pointed at him.

Marcus spoke up again, almost in tears. "Why Adam? Just why? You don't even need the money. What is this?"

How typical of Marcus. It was never about the money.

Jason spoke to him as he took a step back from the car. "You know what this means right? You're dead." As he took another step back, he was illuminated by the streetlamp and the steam from his breath rose into the night air. Both his hands were still raised, and the rain drenched his pale tattooed head. Under that orange light he looked like death himself as he made a solemn vow to Adam.

"I'm gonna find you. It won't take me long. But I'm gonna take my time once I have you."

Adam scoffed. "I'm terrified," he said sarcastically, with all the false bravado he could muster.

Jason's expression was cold and emotionless, but his eyes were determined, inquisitive almost. Anyone might expect a man in that situation to be showing signs of fear or anger. Not Jason. He merely stood there in there in the night air, studying the face of his would-be mugger while the rain soaked through him. His haunting features showed not a hint of emotional turmoil. This unnatural calm unnerved Adam, though he did his best not to show it.

The passenger side door popped open and Marcus

wordlessly stepped out into the rain, standing next to Jason.

"Marcus, what the fuck are you doing? Get back in here!" Adam hissed. But Marcus said nothing. He merely started to stare at Adam as well. His gaze was different. His eyes were full of sorrow, as if he was seeing off a dying relative. Adam huffed. "Whatever. It's not like I needed you anyway."

He hastily closed the windows and sped off into the night. In his rear-view mirror, he watched Marcus and Jason grow smaller and smaller, their silhouettes remaining motionless in the dull orange light.

*Fuck them. Fuck them both.*

He stared at the brick of cocaine on the dashboard. The strong thrive and the weak perish. That's how life goes.

DO YOU THINK YOU'RE POWERFUL?

It was a question from within his mind and he winced at it. He reached for the bottle of whiskey but found it empty.

"Damn it," he muttered. That entire interaction had rendered him completely sober, sober enough to doubt himself again.

He reached into his pocket. Last cigarette. He fumbled with the lighter while keeping one hand on the wheel. He tried a few times, but the flame wouldn't catch.

"Fuck!" he screamed, throwing the lighter at the windshield. He would have to stop by a convenience store on his way home. He found that his hands were shaking. Why? Everything went to plan. In fact, it couldn't have gone any smoother.

*I'm being weak. A real man owns what does.*

He got on the freeway and started to head back into the city, where he lived, on the opposite end. He turned on his usual driving playlist on his phone but found that tonight it gave him no comfort.

He should be feeling great right now but he found himself thinking of Marcus. The look on his face was somehow worse than Jason's look of outright malice. It was like he was looking at a dead man. That look scared him.

Time seemed to pass in a blur as he drove in silence, continually playing out the night's events over and over in his mind. He was so deep in contemplation that he almost missed his exit, swerving the car violently to make it. The roads were all but abandoned at this time of night anyway.

As he drove through the quiet residential neighbourhoods of the north side, he felt the tendrils of emptiness steadily constricting around him. He was numb. Suddenly, in his right ear he heard a whisper, clear as day.

ADAM.

It was a woman's voice. He frantically checked the rear view mirror, and in its reflection, just for a second, he saw a figure: a woman in a white dress in the back seat. She was covered in blood and staring sombrely into his eyes. It was the same expression Marcus had when he left him on the roadside.

"Mom...?"

In the blink of an eye, she was gone. He quickly pulled over. He was wheezing from shock as he trembled. Was he hallucinating? He hadn't been sleeping much recently. Before he even had time to collect himself, his car was floodlit by red and blue lights from the rear. Cops.

A police cruiser had pulled over behind him. He quickly sprang into action and hid the brick in the glovebox. He looked at himself in the mirror; he looked terrible. He heard the police cruiser door open and the officer's footsteps crunch on the gravel as he slowly made his way over to Adams's car.

The officer was carrying a very powerful flashlight, which

made it impossible to see his face. When he reached the driver's side window, he shone the light inside, blinding Adam, before tapping forcefully with the end of the light on the glass.

Adam rolled down the window and the officer pointed his torch at the ground as he spoke. It took his eyes a while to adjust after having the blinding torch pointed in his face. As his vision returned, he found himself face to face with a stern looking middle–aged man.

"Good evening sir. Do me a favor and place your hands on the dash, right where I can see them." He spoke with authority.

Still processing the backseat apparition, Adam slowly complied in a daze. It was as if the police officer was talking to him underwater. Sound seemed distant and distorted, and he had a faint ringing in his ears, almost as though he was watching the situation pan out from a third–person perspective.

Violently, the officers voice snapped him back to reality. "Sir? Sir! I asked if you'd had any drugs or alcohol tonight."

"No, officer." Adam replied. The phrase seemed to slur as it slipped from his mouth.

"Uh huh. Then what's that liquor bottle doing over there?" He gestured to the open whisky bottle near the clutch. "I'll say this once, son. Lying to me is only going to make this situation worse. I will eventually discover the truth here, so you'd better get to telling it. I pulled you over because you were driving erratically, and standing here now I can detect the scent of alcohol on your breath."

Adam felt his pulse quicken. His eyes quickly darted to the glovebox. If he was caught with that, he was well and truly fucked.

"I wasn't drinking," he lied, "but people were drinking in my car earlier." His mind frantically grasping at straws as he tried to contain the situation.

The officer remained unconvinced. "I'm going to need to see your driver's license."

Adam reached into his wallet and passed the officer his license. Adam watched his demeanor quickly change as he read his name aloud.

"Adam Powell... You–you're Don Powell's son, aren't you?" the officer asked.

And there it is.

The officer hastily backtracked. "Well, uh... I see no reason why I ought to bother you any longer. Will you tell your dad Rusty said hello?" His demeanour shifted so fast it was almost surreal.

"Sure," Adam replied begrudgingly.

"You go on your way now. Just, uh... make sure you drive safe, okay?"

With that, the officer turned around and slowly walked back to his cruiser, his labored footsteps making that unmistakable crunch on the gravel.

Adam sat in silence for a while after the officer left. No matter what he did, no matter who he appeared to be, he could not escape that last name.

His father, Howard Powell, was one of the most wealthy and influential men in the entire city. They lived in Briarwood Manor. Even by the affluent standards of the North Side, it was an especially privileged upbringing. What most people didn't know was where all that money came from.

His father was the head of an organized crime syndicate, which had its hands in all manner of illicit honeypots in both the state and the country at large. His father had cops, hitmen, and even some judges all on his payroll.

In fact, many business owners even paid him for 'protection.' His father had been in the game thirty-five years and was all but untouchable. That was real power. And Adam hated him.

He looked at the cars internal clock: 12:32 a.m. He sighed as he started the engine. It was time to go home.

As Adam reached the entrance to the manor, the automatic gates buzzed and slowly began to open. The orange garden lights illuminated the lush exotic vegetation that adorned their carefully manicured front lawn, routinely maintained by an army of gardeners and groundskeepers.

There were foreign trees and shrubs of all varieties as well as marble statues, depicting angels and the Greek gods of old, giving just an inkling of his father's penchant for vanity. Front and center, as one pulled into the plot, was the fountain. The fountain was the centerpiece of the gravel driveway which circled it. The ancient stone fountain stood more than ten feet high and shot impressive gouts of water skyward in various circular levels of differing heights.

The house itself was composed primarily of yellow sandstone and was built in classical grandiose baroque style. It was festooned with large, gilded glass windows and ramparts. It was at least three-hundred years old.

His father also owned an impressive collection of sports cars and four-wheel drives, some of which he had to park outside when the expansive garage was full. On this occasion, there was one beautifully angular bright red sportscar and a massive, rimmed diesel guzzling truck parked outside.

Adam took comfort in the fact that his father was out of town on business and wouldn't be back for a couple days. He wanted nothing more than to flop into bed right at that very moment, as he carefully parked the grey convertible he had been driving next to the other cars around the fountain.

He opened the glovebox and stashed the brick in his backpack, before carefully removing the whisky bottle, cigarette butts and any other traces he might have left behind in the convertible.

He gingerly scaled the steps to the front door and opened it using his key. Inside, he found the house to be quiet and still, just as lonely as he had left it. He went to go hang up his jacket on the coat rack but found himself fumbling in the darkness.

When he flicked on the nearby light switch, he was immediately shocked almost half to death by the sight on his father standing in the hallway, nightgown on, a glass of whisky in hand.

His father was in his mid fifties, but he kept fit. He was slightly taller than Adam, and in very good shape for his age. The only clue to his age was his silver hair and beard, which was carefully manicured and faded into a young man's style.

He was smiling, but his eyes were cruel. "Hello, son," he said ominously.

Adam was at a loss for words. He was supposed to be out of town until Monday. What was he doing back so soon?

"Surprised to see me? I was having a great day," Howard said, his menacing tone rapidly worsening. "A really great day. And then I come home to my house and find my fucking car is missing. Why could that be?"

"I–I, it's just—" Adam stammered.

"*Why could that be, Adam?*" His powerful voice boomed, echoing through the house.

Howard stalked towards him across the carpet until he

was inches from his face. Adam froze. In an instant, he was a little boy again, powerless and afraid in the face of his father's onslaught.

Howard leaned in and whispered in his ear. "You know, playing with my toys doesn't make you a man." He paused for a moment before hitting his son, hard, in the face.

The force of the blow knocked him over, and his ears rang from the impact. The adrenaline softened the pain, but he touched his lip and found it was bleeding. He looked up at his father, his aggressor, the man who was supposed to be his protector and saw nothing but disdain on his face.

"Next time, I'll break your fucking nose," Howard said, before abruptly turning and leaving the room. As Adam sat on the floor, warm tears began to join the blood dripping from his face. His body convulsed as he choked back silent, involuntary sobs. His mind roiled with a mixture of rage and shame.

*One day,* he vowed. *One day, I will kill this man.*

# CHAPTER 5

# The Messenger

## *2033 A.D.*

It was around nine in the evening when Evie found the address.

The waning moon shone brightly in the clear night sky above, but its own light was eclipsed by the garish artificial glow of the LED streetlamps below. The house was quaint, somewhat older, and mostly built out of brick and wood, with a nice picket fence to boot.

She stood before the front gate in hesitation and checked the invite on her phone again: 28 Arthur Street. This was the place, no doubt about it. She could hear the favourable echoes of calypso music emanating from within, dispersed interchangeably with raucous cheering and bouts of laughter. It sounded like fun.

It seemed odd to her then that she found herself nervous. It was only a party, after all. Maybe it was all these strange happenings this week. That creep on the train, her grandmother acting up, those intense dreams. It could also have been a mild case of social anxiety. Well, perhaps anxiety was a strong word. Social apprehension? As of late, Evie had been more isolated than usual and had quite frankly relished it. She loved socializing, but she loved solitude just as much, if not more so.

*Enough. Tonight, I'm going to have a good time.*

She smiled as she grounded herself before opening the latch on the gate and ringing the front door bell, wine bottle in hand. No response. She pressed the doorbell again, and then once more for slightly longer before she heard the unmistakably disjointed rumbling of a slightly drunk person running over the hardwood floor to the door.

The door swung open, and the porchlight came on and she found herself face to face with none other than the ever–jubilant Lucy. Her cobalt blue eyes beamed when she recognized her, and she almost knocked her over with the sheer force of her embrace.

"EVIEEEE!" she gushed. "So glad you made it girl! Come on in!" She ushered her friend inside. "That's a lovely dress by the way. Is that purple silk? Damn, taking no prisoners tonight, are you?" Lucy beamed and Evie blushed.

"Thank you, thank you. Thrift shopping is a wonderful pastime," Evie replied, chuckling. Already she felt more at ease. Lucy had that effect on people. "But wait, Lucy, this isn't your house. Why are you answering the door?"

Lucy scoffed jokingly. "Well, let's just say I had an inkling you were about to arrive. And it seems our host is otherwise engaged." Lucy spoke mischievously.

Evie laughed. "This early in the night? Interesting. . ."

"Come on!" Lucy grabbed her hand. "I'll introduce you to everyone."

Lucy led her down the hallway towards a living room drenched in the soothing orange glow of two large salt lamps and a smattering of fairy lights. There were about fifteen people dancing raucously to calypso music emanating from an old vintage record player.

She could see that the general demographic was twenty-somethings, with a mostly even spread of guys and girls. The carpet was a makeshift sea of thrusting hips and dazzling twirls. It was quite the spectacle.

"Everyone, this is Evie!" Lucy announced. A general cheer rose from the crowd as people waved their hellos, nodded, and grinned. Evie smiled. This party had good vibes already.

Lucy led her past the writhing mass towards the kitchen counter which was adorned with a panoply of party foods, snacks, and drinks. In the center of it all was a large ornate crystal punch-bowl filled with a deep red mixture full of diced oranges, strawberries and all manner of other fruits.

"So, here are the booze and snacks, help yourself," Lucy said.

"Oooh, is that Sangria I spy?" Evie asked, grabbing herself a red plastic cup, and reaching for the ladle.

"That it is sis, that it is. Full disclosure, we did put some acid in there earlier," Lucy said, smiling wantonly.

Evie stopped herself.

"Acid?"

"Oh, come now. Don't look so shocked," Lucy chided. "If I recall correctly, it was you who suggested we take acid in the school library last semester."

"Yeah, and look how that turned out," Evie replied. They exchanged a faux serious look for a moment before breaking into a fit of laughter. "God, that was a fun time." Evie sighed.

"Exactly!" Lucy said. "It's always a fun time, hence the calypso dancers. You think people are usually this fired up about calypso?"

They both shared a laugh at that. "Either way, there's no pressure." Lucy's tone became more tender. "First and foremost, I just want you to have a good time tonight. Acid or no acid. There's plenty of other booze as well." She motioned to the various other bottles on the table.

Evie deliberated for a moment before filling her cup to the brim with the sanguineous cocktail. "Cheers." She raised her cup to meet Lucy's freshly poured glass of champagne.

"Oho! Look who's arrived!" Lucy said, and they raised their glasses and drank.

After much calypso dancing and many bawdy, half remembered dance floor conversations Evie breathlessly plonked herself down on one of the numerous nearby couches to take in the scene. The acid was already beginning to take effect as she slowly cast her gaze around the room. There was a certain shimmer in the air which wasn't there before. A sparkle.

It was hard to place her finger on just what exactly was different, because it all seemed different, albeit only slightly at first. The borders around objects, bookshelves, glasses, and even people themselves seemed more defined. Colors became more vibrant and everything just seemed more beautiful.

She smiled to herself as she closed her eyes and inhaled deeply as it took hold. Even though she had taken acid countless times, there was always that slight tinge of anxiety as it came on. Controlling her breathing, she again centered herself and her energy, as she had on the doorstep. When she opened her eyes, the whole world itself seemed to have come alive.

Music took on a whole new meaning as the sounds from the stereo warped and distorted on their way to her ears. She surveyed the rapturous mass of dancers and found that each movement, each turn, would leave a trace of light, like a real–time long exposure camera lens, but more fluid and dynamic. The salt lamps now seemed to be obelisks of pure benevolence, bathing the partygoers in calming, serene, heavenly light. As she gazed longer at them, the darker cracks, and crevices in the surface of the salt itself snaked and meandered on impossible vectors as Evie watched on in awe.

This was good acid.

Lucy, amidst the sea of bodies caught her eye and gave her a knowing smile before closing her eyes and surrendering to the bliss. She was truly in her element there, and in the reddish–gold hue of the dancefloor she was radiant. Time seemed to slow as she watched Lucy move with ephemeral grace as she weaved her way among them, her movements perfectly aligned to the music. It was a joy to behold.

Soon, she cast her gaze down to the fluffy, cloudlike carpet at her feet, which proved to be a big mistake. Within seconds, she was utterly entranced by the undulating, semitransparent web which overlayed itself on the carpet. It encompassed all that she saw as its holographic tendrils folded over and over again like molten chocolate.

LSD. This was it. She chuckled to herself as her euphoria continued to rise.

It always boggled her mind that the human brain was capable to behold such an experience, and so easily too! It was like stepping in to a Dali–esque dreamworld, without being totally divorced from reality. She knew she was under the influence of a chemical compound, and she could distinguish the difference between the visual distortions and reality.

This was far from the classical media portrayals of LSD, which depict its acolytes as being utterly deluded, and watching dragons fly through walls.

Evie had a theory that perhaps what she was able to experience on acid was merely a widening of her latent perception of reality. That is to say, she was able to perceive more aspects of existence with greater clarity, perhaps aspects which her brain usually filtered out. She loved the perceptual changes, both visual and mental, and found often that she was inundated by powerful realizations, many simultaneously.

As she raised her gaze from the carpet, she found that the entire room was now moving somewhat. The paint on the walls seemed to drip and peel, and the fairy lights had taken on the appearance of some kind of writhing luminescent serpent. Just how much acid did Lucy put in that sangria? The visual input was starting to become overwhelming, and Evie decided it might be time to get some fresh air. She took to her feet and felt a strange sense on lightness to her body. It was very easy to stand, almost too easy.

Lucy saw her rise and gave her the 'you ok?' gesture. Evie nodded, pointing towards the sliding glass door which led to the back garden. With that, Lucy nodded in approval and went back to dancing. She walked past the drinks table as she made for the sliding door, eyeing the mystic sangria as she did so. It looked almost like blood in that crystal bowl. The less thought about that, the better.

She gently pulled open the sliding door which gave a satisfying hiss as she did so, and she closed it behind her as gently as she could. The garden was another scene entirely. It was a stark contrast to the color saturated splendour inside, but beautiful none the less, in a mysterious, almost foreboding way.

It was raining ever so slightly, and the droplets brushed gently against her face. The garden was silent, aside from the howling of the wind as it made its unguessable twists and turns around the property. The automatic white motion detecting light, which had lit up when she had stepped outside, quickly faded, and soon the garden was only lit dimly by the orange glow emanating from the house.

In this half-light, Evie could only barely make out the figures of the trees and bushes at the edge of her vision, and that was on top of the iridescent geometry which undulated on all the surrounding surfaces.

Acid truly is a shapeshifter. No matter what environment she placed herself in, it could find a way to subtly infiltrate, beautify or even fundamentally rewire even the most static of things.

But nature. . . nature was different. To Evie, nature was already in a state of motion to begin with, so she found the visual effects to be more subtle in areas with greenery.

As she slumped against the wooden wall of the patio, she closed her eyes and inhaled the cool night air, sighing deeply. It was peaceful out here. She opened her eyes and looked up at the half moon above. It seemed impossibly bright, it almost hurt to look at. She returned her gaze to the earth and scanned the garden once more when something suddenly caught her eye. There, deep in the tall grass, right at the edge of the light, she saw two small luminous yellow spheres, glinting as they caught the light. They seemed to hover there, and she couldn't quite work out what they were. And then they blinked.

*Eyes*, she thought to herself.

But who's eyes? Or what? She soon got her answer when the owner of the eyes slowly stepped closer into the light, revealing fur dark as midnight, with a healthy sheen that seemed to glisten in the moonlight. It was a cat.

The cat slowly and deliberately stepped out of the long grass and stopped at the foot of the stairs in front of her, not breaking eye contact all the while. When it sat still before her it began to lick its paw. Evie's mind raced. A random cat encounter? Why do these things always tend to happen while I'm tripping? Such a beautiful cat too!

She heard a male voice, clear as day, only it was inside her mind somehow, as if it was one of her own thoughts.

GLAD SOMEONE THINKS SO.

She all but gasped as she looked around frantically, searching in vain for a possible source. When she locked eyes with the cat again it had stopped licking itself and was staring at her with what she could only assume was the feline equivalent of amazement.

YOU. YOU CAN HEAR ME?

*Oh dear. I'm hearing voices in my head now? This can't be good.* She was suddenly slightly paranoid. This hasn't happened before though.

*Have I lost the plot?*

YOU HAVEN'T LOST THE PLOT, the voice said.

*Whatever I do I can't talk to the voices,* Evie thought, somewhat pragmatically. *That's how one loses the plot, right?*

The voice laughed from that. WELL, I CAN'T FAULT YOUR REASONING THERE. BUT THIS ISN'T A HALLUCINATION. YOU'RE HEARING MY THOUGHTS.

Evie couldn't resist responding. *And who exactly are you?* she thought, becoming somewhat impatient.

LOOK DOWN.

When she did, her eyes settling again on the mysterious cat, which was giving her an equally perplexed look. After a few moments of intense eye contact she broke into a hysterical cackle.

"Oh god," she said aloud. "A talking cat? I really have lost it." The cat's expression soured somewhat.

THIS IS A FIRST FOR ME TOO, YOU KNOW. YOUR KIND AREN'T SUPPOSED TO BE ABLE TO HEAR US. THOUGH WE, SADLY, CAN HEAR YOU.

"Alright, then," Evie entertained, speaking out loud. "What's your name?"

HERMES. AND TO WHOM DO I OWE THE PLEASURE?

"Eve," she replied. "But my friends call me Evie."

Hermes seemed somewhat shaken when she spoke her name. His feline eyes widened, and his gaze became particularly intense.

ALRIGHT, EVIE, HAS THIS EVER HAPPENED TO YOU BEFORE?

Evie laughed again. "Have I ever taken acid and telepathically communicated with a cat? No, I can't say that I have."

THIS IS NO LAUGHING MATTER, HUMAN. IF YOU ARE WHO I THINK YOU MIGHT BE, YOUR LIFE IS AT STAKE.

Before Evie had a chance to respond she heard the sliding door open behind her. She turned and saw the concerned face of Lucy, her eyes darting around the patio in search of her.

"Lucy!" she called out. Lucy turned to her left and saw Evie sitting there by the steps and briskly walked over to her.

"Evie? What are you doing, babe?" she asked, clearly perplexed by what she saw.

"Oh, I was just talking to—" She peered into the long grass, but there was no trace of Hermes. Perhaps he was never there.

*Was it all just a hallucination?* She was flummoxed into silence.

"Never mind that," Lucy said tersely. "Listen. Doug is here. I just thought I should tell you."

Evie felt her stomach drop. "Doug is here?!" she repeated in a whispered shout.

Doug was an old flame of hers. To say their relationship was complicated would be a massive understatement. In a roundabout way, she had broken his heart some months prior. They hadn't had contact since then. It wasn't intentional of course, but is it ever intentional?

"How is Doug here? Does he know I'm here?"

"No," Lucy soothed. "He doesn't. But I think that makes it even worse somehow?"

"Oh god. I'm fucked. I can't go in there right now. I think I would die. Literally."

"Literally?"

"Figuratively," Evie replied, giving her a faux scowl and sighed. The acid trip was still in full swing, and the shifting Persian carpet of rainbow geometry still overlaid her vision and would continue to do so for some time. Social interactions were difficult to navigate on high doses of acid, especially a social interaction of this magnitude. "Is there another way out of this place?" she asked Lucy in desperation.

"I mean, you could sneak through the side gate, but for the record I think you should go in and talk to him."

"Perhaps I would if I wasn't tripping my face off! How much acid was in there anyway?"

"Touché," Lucy replied, with a sheepish grin. "Okay, I'll tell you what. You creep around the side gate there, and I'll distract him inside, so he won't see you. It shouldn't be too hard. Run along now."

Evie breathed a sigh of relief. "Thank you, Lucy, I owe you several. You know I love you right?"

"I know," Lucy said, smiling as she pulled her friend in for an embrace. "Now go!"

With that, Evie lithely sprang to her feet and scuttled

around the side gate with all the grace of a gecko. She found that the gate was unlocked and gently unlatched it, ducking under the nearby window as she did so. She continued her goblin–like crouch walk through the small alleyway beside the house. Thoughts of the inherent cowardice of her current course persisted in her mind, but tonight just simply wasn't the night for that.

She soon came to the front side of the house, and when she was certain that she was no longer in view of the windows she uncrouched herself and strode towards to front gate. Only a few more steps to freedom. It was then that a voice cut through the night air like an arrow.

"Evie?"

She froze. Damn it, that was Doug's voice. How had Lucy so monumentally failed her simple task? Perhaps stalling Doug was never her intention at all.

She spun around and did her best to feign surprise. "Doug? Wow! What are you doing here?" The hysterical inflection of her voice caused her to cringe internally.

"I could ask you the same thing," he replied. He was standing on the front porch, cigarette in hand.

*So, that's how it happened. He must've gone outside for a smoke break.*

In the moonlight she could make out his silhouette quite clearly. He was wearing his trademark leather jacket and denim jeans. His dark brown hair was freshly cut, buzzed at the sides. He looked good, she had to admit. He looked after his body and his muscular frame showed that. There was a pause, an expected awkward silence between the two as they looked at one another. Suddenly they both spoke, at the same time, on top of one another, vastly magnifying the awkwardness of the situation. They both chuckled somewhat.

"You go first," Evie said.

"No, please, you go."

Evie sighed. "Look Doug, I feel like I owe you an explanation about everything, but I just can't right now. I'm aware of how that sounds, and I'm sorry."

Doug paused for a moment before replying. "It's okay. I think you've made your feelings clear. A text or a call would have been nice though, after everything. But I know you need your space."

Evie found herself becoming unexpectedly emotional as tears brimmed in her eyes. "I'm so sorry, Doug." Her voice started breaking.

He moved instinctively to comfort her, before stopping himself. He stammered as he searched for the words to say before falling silent.

"Goodbye, Doug," she said, turning and walking towards the gate.

As she unlatched it, she could feel his gaze boring into the back of her head, standing there on the porch, watching her leave. She dared not look back, lest she succumb to her emotions once more. She steadied herself as she took purposeful steps down the sidewalk and into the night, occasionally wiping her flowing tears as she put as much distance between herself and that scene as possible.

What a night it had been, a whirlwind of emotion. She hadn't realized it, but she was still clearly holding on to a lot of emotions surrounding their time together. A lot was unresolved. They had been together romantically for two months, though they were friends for a long time before that. Doug was one of her best friends back in high school, and she had known him for most of her life. She never really saw him in a romantic light, but he had always harbored feelings for her.

When she left high school, they went in different directions, but a chance encounter in a bar over the summer led them to rekindle their friendship. She hadn't seen or heard from him in two years. In that time, he had matured, both physically and mentally. Gone were the boyish looks she had known in high school. He had filled out, grown into himself. More importantly, his perspective was different. His work as a paramedic had made him much more driven, and his boundless ambition she found very alluring. Quickly they became intimate, though their romance was short lived.

She found him too intense. The depth of his love for her scared her. Where for her, this was a new sensation, for him it was the culmination of years of silent hopes, wishes, and prayers all coming to fruition. He simply came on too strong, and for her part she didn't know if she could yet reciprocate those feelings for anyone, let alone Doug.

Perhaps it was wrong of her to get involved in the first place. In the end, she was sure she had done more harm than good. Her acid trip was far from over as she began the long walk home. In her current headspace, the once benign shadows cast by the streetlamps overhead took on much more sinister overtones. In their depths she saw all sorts of twisted figures. The beautiful geometric patterns she had seen earlier were replaced by malevolent faces, skulls, and insect like creatures. She found panic rising within herself as she quickened her pace. Now was not a good time to be out on the streets, alone.

As she rounded the bend at the end of the street, she came upon the brick façades of an old industrial area which she had to walk through to reach her train station. The wind gusted strongly from behind her, blowing dead leaves ominously towards the road ahead. To her right lay the disused buildings, relics of a bygone era, and to her left lay a wooded forest reserve.

The reserve was surely beautiful by daytime, but at night it was pitch black, the dim light from the streetlamps barely penetrating the leafy branches of even the closest trees. The woods themselves seemed to heave and shudder with dark energy as the wind swept through them. Far in the distance, she could make out the faint light of the train station, but before that lay what felt like miles of this foreboding hellscape.

*Come on girl. You've got this. Just look straight ahead and keep on moving. It's not even that scary. You're being silly right now.*

She briskly set off toward the station, the rhythmic clip-clopping of her sandals echoing off the buildings around her.

*Whatever you do, just don't look into the woods. Eyes ahead.* It was as if she had become her own coach. This was a common tactic she would employ in testy situations. She had internally pep-talked herself out of many situations in the past.

With her quickened pace she was making decent progress and after a few minutes she could see the lights of the station more clearly in the distance. She had even managed to abate her paranoia somewhat when she felt a sudden chill run down her spine. It was deafeningly clear, as though her intuition had been magnified by the acid. She was being watched, and not in the same way which she felt watched by the trees either. Someone was watching her.

She knew whatever it was, it was behind her. She could feel it. She staggered somewhat but did her best to continue walking at her present pace. Every instinct in her body was telling her to run. She wasn't safe here. Finally, she could resist the urge no more and she stopped and slowly turned, and there it was.

About fifty meters behind her, at the edge of the shadows

on the sidewalk, stood a figure. She couldn't make out the features clearly, but she could see that it was a man. Her blood ran cold. He was just standing there, watching her. She could see his frame rising and falling from what she assumed were rapid, deep breaths. There they stood, transfixed, studying one another. Was this another hallucination? She wanted to call out to him, to ask him what his business was spying on her, but she couldn't find the voice. She was struck by sheer terror.

She quickly turned and upped her pace once more, before breaking into an all-out sprint towards the train station up ahead. Behind her, she heard the stranger's footsteps echoing as he too broke into a run. What was strange was that it sounded like he was running on all fours. She screamed as she heard him drawing closer.

"Help me! Someone, anyone! *Help!*" she yelled. No one heeded her desperate calls. She was about to let out another desperate wail when she was tackled from behind and pinned to the ground. She hit the pavement hard, and in a daze, she rolled over to face her aggressor.

She couldn't believe her eyes. It was that ghoulish man from the train, earlier in the week. His face still bore that crooked smile, but his bloodshot eyes were even more sunken, and saliva dripped from his gaping mouth.

"All. . . mine. All. . . mine," he repeated with hysterical glee as he clasped her hands to the pavement with iron force and locked her legs down with his own.

She struggled in vain against his grip but could barely move, he seemed to possess superhuman strength. She screamed again desperately, but this time he quickly clasped his pallid, clammy hand over her mouth and muffled her. With her left hand free she did all she could to swing at him, but it was like she was a child swatting at an adult. He violently forced her head to one side and moved slowly moved his head down to her exposed neck, opening his mouth as he did so. She could feel his saliva dripping onto her neck and she let out one final guttural howl of muffled protest as he laughed cruelly.

Suddenly, to her left, she heard the sound of galloping hooves emerging from the forest. The fiend turned to face the sound, too and let out a terrified but short–lived shriek before the source of the sound bowled into him.

Free from the vice grip of her attacker, Evie sprang to her feet and laid eyes upon her savior. A massive fully grown stag had sprung from the forest and impaled the fiend against the brick wall with its antlers. The stag was so large that the fiend's feet couldn't even touch the ground.

Evie watched on in in shock as the furious stag lifted him even higher, driving the antlers further into his chest. Black blood gurgled from the fiend's mouth as he struggled pathetically to free himself from the antlers, and his eyes grew wide as he wheezed and struggled for breath.

The fiend's pale skin quickly began to turn charcoal and his form began to change. His fingers lengthened and turned to claws, his mouth revealed sharp fangs, his ears elongated and became pointed, and the hair atop his head gave way to horns. When his transformation was complete, he was clearly no longer human, and looked almost like a grotesque, which one might find sitting atop a gothic cathedral, only much larger and lankier. The creature made one final, vain attempt to reach for her before falling still and turning to ash. A strong gust of wind quickly blew most of the ash skyward, and all that remained were its clothes, still tangled in the antlers of the stag.

For its part, the stag had now calmed. It turned to her and

extended its right leg forward, lowering its head and seeming to bow. Still in shock, the stag's gesture brought Evie back to the present moment and she instinctively reached forward and untangled the creature's clothes from its antlers, tossing them to the sidewalk as she did so. When she had untangled the clothes, the stag raised its head to her eye level and seemed to stare deep into her soul with its massive, heavily dilated eyes. She found herself weeping tears of gratitude as she gently reached out and softly caressed its face.

"Thank you," she whispered. The stag softly nuzzled her hand before abruptly turning and galloping back into the woods from whence it came.

When it was gone, Evie was suddenly hit by the full weight of the delayed shock from the situation. She collapsed against the brick wall, sobbing and wheezing as she tried to catch her breath. She was traumatized, and justifiably so. Just what in the world was happening tonight?

She realized that her leg was touching that creature's clothes and she quickly kicked them aside in disgust. "Ugh!" she said aloud. She rested her head against the bricks and breathed deeply. There would be a time to unpack all of this, but for now, it was time to go home. She could still see the lights of the station glistening in the distance. She took some time to collect herself before dusting herself off and rising shakily to her feet. It was time to go.

It was in the early hours of the morning when she finally made it back to her apartment. She opened the door as quietly as possible and closed it just as gently behind her. Once inside, she quietly crept past her grandmothers' room, down the hallway towards her own. She could see the sky beginning to brighten outside the windows as she laid her stuff down in her room.

She was about to plonk onto the bed when she briefly caught sight of herself in the mirror. She was still covered in the ash from that creature. Her dress was caked in it and it was all throughout her frizzy hair. She was aghast, and muffled a scream before resisting the urge to vomit.

She quickly ran toward the bathroom and turned the shower on full blast, flooding the room with hot steam. After what was quite possibly the most rejuvenating shower of her life, she dried off and collapsed into bed, utterly spent from the night's events.

# 7

In the late morning, at an hour much earlier than her liking, she was rudely awoken by a tapping at her window. She could smell Flora's pancakes cooking in the kitchen already. She rolled out of bed, half awake and bleary eyed and came face to face with the culprit. A black cat was perched on her windowsill, swatting at the glass pane.

"Hermes?" she asked out loud in foggy disbelief.

THAT'S RIGHT.

*So, it wasn't a hallucination.*

I'M AFRAID NOT, he replied. YOU MIGHT WANT TO PUT SOME CLOTHES ON.

She gasped and covered herself, quickly darting behind the bed. "Ugh, look away, look away!" she shouted. Hermes complied, turning to face the street below as she got dressed. When she had dressed herself, she carefully unlatched the window and let him inside.

He gracefully jumped onto the floor and gazed briefly around the room. THIS IS COZY.

Evie was in no mood for such pleasantries. "How did you find me?"

I FOLLOWED YOU.

"Followed me? But, that means you saw what happened, and you did nothing?" she asked, furiously.

IT SEEMED LIKE THAT STAG HAD IT HANDLED. BESIDES, I HAD TO BE SURE.

"Had to be sure of what?"

THAT YOU WERE THE ONE.

At that moment, Flora suddenly opened Evie's door. "Evie? It's time you woke up baby, I've made your fav—" Flora stopped dead in her tracks at the sight of Hermes, and he too seemed equally shocked by her sudden entrance.

"Grammie, I can explain," Evie began.

IT CAN'T BE! Hermes quickly darted over to Flora and began to purr and nuzzle against her legs.

"Well, aren't you a sight for sore eyes!" Flora beamed. "But why are you here?" she asked joyfully. Hermes turned and looked towards Evie, who was staring at the both of them in total confusion.

Flora's expression darkened. "I see."

# CHAPTER 6

# WITCH

## *1031 A.D.*

For the remainder of the fall that year, Morgana would visit Errol's forge every week to pick up tools for her father. Though he was shy at first, the young apprentice Mathias gradually became more comfortable around her. Pleasantries slowly gave way to inquiries, questions: how was your day, is your family keeping well, did you see the gypsy singer in the town square? He seemed genuinely interested in her life.

She was taken aback at first, unaccustomed to anyone else having a vested interest in her affairs, but she soon warmed to him, overcoming her own shyness, and offering tidbits of information here and there. He too must be lonely, she thought.

Parallels could indeed be drawn between the two of them. Both were of a similar age and devoted already to their work. Neither had time for much else. Before long, they were relishing in conversing with one another, and Morgana found herself looking forward to their next meeting.

For his part, Errol said little, but when he saw them together his face softened, and his eyes seemed to smile.

"I am glad for you," the blacksmith said to her one day as she picked up the days order for her father.

"Pardon?"

"Like links of a chain, it's important to forge bonds in this life. A life without friendship is no life at all," he said, smiling kindly. Morgana smiled back. For a blacksmith, he was exceptionally wise. She supposed Mathias was her friend, but she had never considered herself to have a friend until now.

Mathias was a gentle boy and had an adventurous spark to him. The two would oft talk about the world outside the village and Mathias would spin tall tales of his hunts in the woods, or they would trade what stories they had heard about the war, or even swap wife's tales about creatures and witches on the roads.

One day, when a visiting circus troop was in town, Mathias asked her if she would like to go watch a show with him in the afternoon. It was the first time he had invited her to spend time together, outside their semi-official roles as a healers assistant and a forge masters apprentice. She told him she would seek her parent's approval.

Business at her father's surgery was still booming, and on account of that, he was mostly unconcerned with her doings. Her mother was slightly more reserved, but she could see the earnest hunger in her daughter's eyes when she asked, and was secretly delighted that she had found a friend.

"Very well child, you may go to the show, but see that you return before nightfall," Ingrid said, pulling her in to kiss her forehead.

"Thank you, mother." Morgana beamed in her embrace.

Mathias came and picked her up from her house that afternoon. At first, she did not recognize him. She was accustomed to seeing him in his dirty moth–eaten tunic at the forge, but today he was wearing a red linen shirt emblazoned with gold colored thread. His hair was brushed and cleaned and the usual soot and grime that caked his complexion was all but gone. His straw colored hair looked more like honey and truthfully, he looked almost angelic in the mid–afternoon light.

He seemed slightly uncomfortable on her doorstep, and he fidgeted with his shirt as he shuffled from side to side, perhaps nervous at the prospect of meeting her and what she might think.

For her part, Morgana was indeed nervous. She had spent more than two hours with her mother, trying to pick the right outfit and get ready. When Mathias saw her on the doorstep, he stilled himself and smiled.

She was wearing one of her mother's finest purple linen gowns, delicately embroidered with floral patterns. She also wore one of her mother's silver necklaces, suspending a single turquoise gem. She too was a picture of radiance, and her deep black hair shone in the light.

Mathias was taken aback as she strode down her garden path towards him. Ingrid watched on from the doorway, a warm smile on her face as she discreetly wiped back a tear. Her daughter was growing up.

"You look beautiful," Mathias croaked shyly as she greeted him.

Morgana blushed. "So do you," she replied softly. He blushed then, only far deeper, and more crimson, than her. He did not really know what to say to that.

Morgana chuckled and they bid her mother farewell as they set off down the street into the town center. As they walked into town, they were both quiet at first, unaccustomed to meeting one another in these new circumstances. This soon thawed, however, and soon they were chatting away merrily as they always did, but it had a new luster like never before.

Both of them were excited to be out on the town, in good company, partaking in merriment and enjoying what life had to offer. Both felt connected, a part of something.

It was easy to feel isolated behind the earthen walls of their homes. There were times Morgana forgot she was part of a village at all. Mathias helped her with that. When she was with him, that loneliness seemed like a distant memory. He never failed to make her laugh either.

*So, this is what it means to have a friend,* she thought. She felt free with him, utterly unconcerned by the usual glances and stares from hateful old women and predatory men.

When they reached the town square, the circus act was just about to begin and a large crowd had formed. Most of the youth of the village were there, with many families, all eagerly anticipating the promised show. The circus crier drew more folk into the crowd as bold statements echoed across the square.

"Come one, come all, for a show like no other! From the distant lands of Lystria come the finest acrobats, magicians, and actors. Prepare to be astounded and amazed by their ancient arts, never before seen by human eyes!"

Mathias reached to hold Morgana's hand. "Follow me!" he whispered, as he weaved them through the crowd.

They came upon a disused stone stairwell, the entrance to which was somewhat obscured by a market stand nearby. They scaled the stairwell, and at the top, Morgana could see that it offered a perfect view of the stage, while being well clear of the crowd, so their view was totally unobstructed. She looked in disbelief to Mathias, who gave her a wry smile.

"Tricks of the trade," he said smugly.

Morgana laughed. "I'm clearly in the company of a seasoned showgoer."

"A veteran," he corrected, chuckling.

Before long, the show began. The rumble of drums marked the beginning and a troop of lithe, skink-like acrobats dressed in motley emerged from behind the stage and began vaulting over one another and performing all manner of flips and rolls accompanied by drumming from the band. The crowd ooh'd and ahh'd accordingly and Morgana was quietly impressed herself.

At the end, they came together to create a human pyramid, and one of their number climbed to the top and performed a backflip after a drum roll, landing catlike on his feet before turning to bow to the audience. This elicited thunderous applause and whistles from the audience, and both Mathias and Morgana joined the chorus.

As the acrobats left the stage, the crew began to hurriedly assemble props and set pieces for the next performance. Fake bushes, trees, rocks and grass seemed to assemble themselves as the crew worked quickly and silently. Before long, two actors took to the stage and a hush fell across the crowd. They were wearing masks. One was dressed as a fair maiden, the other, her noble suitor.

"Oh, maiden fair with flaxen hair, how can I show thee that I care?" the man cried, dropping to one knee, and presenting her a rose.

"Oh, noble knight of sweet delights, what brings you here before my sight?" she replied, clutching the rose, and turning away from him.

The knight rose to his feet and sang. "Your beauty, grace, and pretty face, have all but bettered me."

"And are you fixed to leave this place? If not, you'd better be." The maiden brushed him aside swiftly, prompting some laughs from the audience.

An exaggerated high-pitched cackling rang out across the stage and a third character emerged in a flash and a puff of smoke from behind one of the fake boulders, causing the crowd to gasp. They were wearing a withered woodcarving mask of an old hag, garbed in a black shawl.

"Hehehehe! Lovers fair and lovers true, such fun that I could have with you," her shrill voice cried.

"Fear not, dear maid, avert thine eyes! This witch will soon meet her demise," the knight called, drawing his wooden sword as the maiden cowered nearby.

"Silence, fool!" the witch screamed, pointing at the knight and causing him to disappear in a flash of flight and puff of smoke.

From their vantage point, Morgana could see that a trapdoor had opened beneath him and the knight quickly fell below the stage while the smoke was settling, making it seem as though he had vanished.

*Cheap tricks. Nothing more.*

When the smoke had settled, a toad was hopping about the stage in his place. The crowd gasped and the maiden gave a wail of disingenuous horror. The witch continued to cackle maniacally from her perch.

"Oh dearest knight, an ill forebode, the witch has turned thee to a toad!" the maiden cried. "I think that only true love's kiss could ever bring him back from this." The maiden reached down to grab the frog and pressing her mask up against it as if to place a kiss on its lips. A flash and a puff of smoke went up again, and this time when the smoke had settled, the knight had reappeared at stage right next to the maiden, to the sound of trumpets from the band and a roar of applause from the audience.

The witch howled as he drew his sword and ran towards her perch. When he reached her, he quickly scaled it and proceeded to appear to throw her to the ground and repeatedly stab her with his sword. The witch gave contorted woeful moans as the actor did their best impression of death throes, while the crowd jeered and laughed. Even the maiden ran over to kick the fallen witch, which drew even more laughter from the crowd.

Some people from the crowd even began to throw fruit and peels at the fallen witch. Morgana felt her blood run cold as she surveyed the savage crowd around her.

If she were ever discovered. . . It did not bear thinking about.

For a while, she had almost forgotten. Forgotten about her newfound abilities. Forgotten the development which threatened to tear her life asunder.

Mathias was watching the show intently, his arms resting on the cold cobblestone of the overlook. She tapped him on the shoulder.

"Do you mind if we go?" she asked.

He turned, and instantly read the discomfort on her face. "Of course." He led her back down the way they came, and they quickly weaved through the crowd again before leaving the town square all together. As they made their way out, Mathias paid an old woman at one of the stands for two apples and handed one to Morgana, which they both began crunching down in silence.

When they were well clear of the crowd and returning down the street towards her house Mathias spoke up. "Are you okay?" he asked tentatively.

"Yes." She was feeling much better now that there was

some distance between her and that ravenous crowd. "I just needed some space. It was very interesting though. The acrobats were superb!" She gushed, doing her best to hide her anxiety.

"They really were!" Mathias replied emphatically, his temperament warming again. "Next time, we'll have to see the jugglers."

"Next time?" Morgana asked.

"Well, yes. . ." Mathias said, his voice trailing off slightly as he looked away. "I'd love to go to another show with you some time, i–i–if you'd like." He blushed.

Morgana felt her heart glow. "I would very much like that Mathias," she said, smiling. "Thank you."

The sun was beginning to set when they reached Morgana's house. She bid him farewell with a warm embrace at her gate.

"Thanks again, Mathias. See you soon."

"See you soon," he replied, smiling sweetly before setting off down the cobblestone lane on his way. He seemed to have a spritely spring in his step and was whistling to himself cheerily. For her own part, she could not help but smile.

After that day, Morgana and Mathias took outings together whenever they could. They were practically inseparable, and prone to exploring. They shared the same adventurous ideation, as well as a similar work ethic. "Partners in mischief," or so her mother oft called it.

Her father took almost no notice, apart from a cursory glance here and there. Morgana had noticed that his eyes were affixed to his evergrowing coin purse these days, more so by the hour. In light of this, Morgana did her best to keep a low profile.

She helped her father in his surgery, and set to honing her powers slowly in gradual increments on the constant stream of incoming patients, so as not to arouse suspicion. Her system was working well, and she was learning to treat not just superficial flesh wounds, but deep internal injuries as well. The mastery of which, before the manifestation of her powers, had eluded even her father.

One day just like any other, Morgana was preparing for her daily errands in her room when there was a knock at her front door. She quickly raced down the stairs to answer, but her mother beat her to it. In her doorway stood the pensive figure of the blacksmith, Errol.

"Good day, Errol," her mother said, sunnily. "To what do we owe the pleasure?" Errol's massive frame seemed far smaller and less certain as he stood before them. His usually calm temperament was gone, replaced by a shuffling unease. Concern was plastered across his usually tranquil face.

"Pardon the intrusion, my lady, it's the boy. He's not well."

Morgana immediately felt her stomach drop and ran to join her mother at the door. "What's wrong with him?"

"It's some type of fever," Errol replied. "He had chills in the night, and I set him to bed, but when I woke him this morning he hadn't the strength to stand. Now, he struggles to breathe."

Morgana felt her heart rate quicken and her head swam with dread. What could they do? Whatever it was, they had to act now.

Behind her, her father spoke, giving her a fright. She hadn't realized he was there. "Bring him here," he said commandingly. "Morgana, go with him and fetch the boy." She nodded silently in agreement and quickly left the house with Errol to head towards the forge.

Between them, they carried a stretcher from her father's surgery, which they would use to carry him back. She had to raise her pace to a run to match Errol's large strides as they flew through the muddy streets. When they reached the forge, Errol quickly swung the gate open and ushered her inside. He led her to Mathias's room and opened the door.

His appearance took the air out of her lungs. The gray overcast light from the window fell on his pallid skin, which was more gray still. He was drenched in sweat, which had soaked through his surrounding bed covers. His eyes stared listlessly up at the ceiling while he tried in vain to catch his breath between desperate wheezes. She felt tears rising to her eyes, and rising shock almost overtook her, but she quickly snapped out of it. She had a job to do.

"We must act fast," she said to Errol as they laid the stretcher on the bed next to him. "Wrap him in a fresh blanket and help me load him onto here."

Errol complied and they soon wrapped him and loaded him onto the stretcher. Mathias seemed to be in a state of delirium and made little noise apart from muffled moans between his labored breaths.

"Now," she said, "you take the front end and I'll take the back." Errol nodded and on a count of three they hoisted the stretcher aloft. The adrenaline coursing through her veins made it easy to forget about the weight she was carrying. They quickly rushed out of the compound and began their flight through the muddy streets back to her father's surgery.

Along the way, they caught the eye of many concerned villagers. No doubt the news of disease within the town's walls would spread faster than the disease itself. When they arrived home her mother was waiting for her at the front door and held it open as they barged inside.

When she gazed upon Mathias, Morgana noticed that her mother's expression turned grave. They brought him into the surgery where her father stood waiting, with herbs and potions at the ready. When they laid him on the large operating table and her father surveyed the boy his expression did not change.

"You may leave us," he said, nodding to Errol.

"Of course." Errol cast one last look of concern upon Mathias and gently touched laid his hand on his shoulder before leaving the room, leaving Morgana, her mother, and her father alone with Mathias.

"Ingrid, close the door," her father instructed. Her mother wordlessly complied and shut the door behind her, leaving just Morgana and her father to tend to Mathias. "Prop his head up."

Morgana reached for some nearby cushions and placed a couple under Mathias' head so that it was elevated. He seemed to have lost consciousness, but his breathing was still very labored. She could hear the fluid bubbling in his lungs as he struggled to breathe. Her father had ground up some dried herbs and was heating them on a metal platter under Mathias's nose. "These will allow him to breathe better."

Within minute or so of him applying these herbal vapors his wheezing died down and Morgana heard him taking his first much clearer breaths.

"These allow him to breathe, but they won't fight the ailment itself. For that, I have prepared a brew of Eridum root," he said, bringing over a goblet filled with a steaming dark green mixture. While Morgana held his head, her father pushed the goblet to his lips and tipped. The unconscious Matheus coughed and spluttered, but managed to swallow about half of the mixture. Morgana gently laid his head back down on the cushions, using a handkerchief to wipe his mouth and mop the sweat from his brow. Mathias shivered uncontrollably and his blonde hair looked almost black from being so soaked with sweat.

"What ails him, father?" Morgana asked, her voice finally breaking now that the shock had begun to fade.

"I suspect it to be river fever. Though this case is particularly severe."

"Will he live?" she asked, tears rolling down her face.

"That is in god's hands," he replied coolly. "We will do what we can. You are to stay by his side. If you hear his him struggling to breathe, you must repeat the herbal remedy I showed you. In three hours, give him another serving of the Eridum root." He paused a moment. "Also, make sure he is adequately hydrated. He has a long fight ahead of him, and we a long night ahead of us. I will return periodically to assess his condition."

"Yes, father." He nodded to them and left the room, leaving Morgana alone with Mathias. She gently stroked his hair while he lay shivering. His life was in her hands now, and she would not lose him.

It was late in the night and Morgana had briefly dozed off when she was awoken by the sound of Mathias coughing and spluttering violently by her side. She was immediately wide awake. By the dull glow of the candlelight, she could see that he was turning blue as he struggled to breathe.

"Father!" She screamed frantically. "Father, come quickly!" She sprang into action and carefully burned the herbs under his nose but to no avail. Mathias was thrashing about too wildly to breathe in the herbal vapor, and he continued gasp for air. She quickly sat him up and began thumping his back in an effort to clear his lungs, but it was no use.

Her father burst into the room and pushed her aside, giving

his own more powerful attempt at delivering blows to Mathias' back while Morgana watched on. Mathias slumped over and lost consciousness, his clammy body going limp in her father's arms. Her father gently laid him on his back.

"No!" she screamed.

"It's over, child," her father said, panting as he wiped his brow. "There's nothing more we can do. His heart has failed." His gaze became vacant as he slumped in a stool next to the table, staring at the body.

"He can't die!" she screamed, pushing past him to place her hands on his chest.

"It's no use Morgana, the boy is dead!"

She was shuddering and choking back sobs as she focused all of her energy and the outside world quickly dissipated. She knew the risks inherent with what she was about to do, but right now, what mattered was saving Mathias.

She channeled all her power as she closed her eyes and cast her sight within his body. She could feel his lungs, so full with fluid, and pushed past them to his heart, which lay still and un-beating. She had the sensation of holding it in her hands and cast a focused jolt of her energy into it.

***THUMP THUMP***

The heart began its faint rhythm anew. Next, she returned to his lungs, and his greater airway. She projected her energy like cool green flames, scorching and cleansing his lungs and airway of the infestation of mucus and fluids. From within him, she felt him take his first breath. She quickly returned her focus to her hands and to her own body.

Mathias' gasping commanded her attention, and she met his gaze as he opened his eyes and took his first proper breaths in days. Gone was his wheezing, even his complexion seemed clearer. He looked at her in awe.

"Morgana," he whispered, weakly, before losing consciousness. Tears of joy rolled down her face as she clasped his hand.

As she turned around to look at her father, she was instantly struck by the reality of what she had just done. Time seemed to dilate in that moment.

He was aghast, having already stood up from the stool, and in his hand, he was holding a thick wooden club. His fearful gaze stripped her of all humanity in that moment. She stood transfixed, awaiting his judgment.

After what seemed like an eternity, a single word breathed escaped his lips.

"Witch."

He swung hard at her, connecting a blow with her left temple. The impact of the wood on bone made a sickening crack which rang through the surgery. Her last sight as her vision faded was her father standing over her, his eyes ablaze with a terrible new zeal.

## CHAPTER 7

# PLAYING WITH FIRE

### *1033 A.D.*

The midday sun shone overhead as Balus and Enoch walked the winding roads of the countryside. All around them were lush green vistas and rolling hills snaked by shimmering rivers, and the occasional farmhouse with peasants at work in the fields, seeding before the onset of spring. Birds chirped pleasant harmonies overhead and the wind bore the smell of the ocean ever closer.

For the past two days and nights they had been on the road towards the port city of Fairhaven, at the behest of Master Adrax. Enoch was utterly awestruck by the sensory overload that this wide open world had to offer, and it had both exceeded and challenged his expectations in many ways. Each step further from the Abbey was something new, an offering of the adventure his heart so desperately yearned for. The world seemed to go on forever in all directions. Balus was stoic, but in truth, Enoch's youthful curiosity had reignited a long since dormant side of himself; the world through fresh eyes was a world anew.

They had made camp under the stars both nights. Never in his life had Enoch seen that many stars. A shimmering blanket of light. On the first night, as he lay in his furs beside the coals of their campfire, he stayed awake long after Balus had slept, utterly mesmerized by the cosmic majesty which unfurled before him. This cost him though, as he was much more loathe to awaken at the crack of dawn when they set off again. He was so worn out from the days walk that on the second night he was asleep only minutes after taking their supper by the fire.

Today, he felt energized and strong, at least in part due to excitement over their imminent arrival to Fairhaven. If they continued at their present pace, they would reach the city around dusk.

"I see a clearing up ahead by that brook," Balus said. "Why don't we stop there and make our lunch."

"Sure!" Enoch said cheerily. He could see the clearing Balus was talking about. It was framed by tall oak trees, lush green grass, and wildflowers which bloomed by the babbling brook. Balus walked ahead of them and laid his items out on the ground by the river, reaching down to fill their water skins as he did so. Enoch followed suit, and laid his heavy pack down beside Balus, before reaching in to procure some of the provisions they had brought with them. He produced a loaf of the abbey's own bread and cheese, and laid it down on a board and set about slicing it. When Balus returned from the waters edge with their freshly filled skins and saw Enoch sitting already preparing lunch he could not help but smile.

"You know, for someone who had never even left the abbey only a couple of days ago, you make a fine travelling companion, Enoch."

Enoch grinned back. "I feel as though I was made for this."

"Ho, ho. Big talk," Balus teased. "Three days on the road and he's already a gypsy."

"Sun baked and crispy!" A strange voice added from behind them.

Both Balus and Enoch jumped up from their places in fright. The voice had caught them both completely off guard and they spun around to come face to face with the source.

It was a man dressed in black and white motley tights. Atop his head he wore a hat with two donkey–like ear flaps, one black, one white. He stood on one foot, his other leg he crossed over his knee, balancing effortlessly. He was very slender, and his face bore a strange smile. In his left hand he held a scepter, which bore his likeness. In his right, a wildflower. Balus went to draw his sword but found it was jammed in the scabbard. Seeing this, Enoch quickly tried to draw his own sword and found it was also jammed.

Both were at a loss as to where this man had come from. They had been sitting in the middle of an open field. Balus stepped between the man and Enoch.

"Who are you?" he commanded, his eyes narrowing.

"Who am I, indeed? Afoot with no steed. I take in the smells for mine eyes have no need," the man replied cryptically.

Enoch then looked to his eyes and saw that they were clouded and grey, the same way some of the older monk's eyes were in the abbey. He was blind, but that seemed strange, for he was not an old man. He appeared somewhat ageless, as though he could be anywhere between twenty and fifty years old.

Enoch remembered some of his readings from the abbey where he had seen depictions of his likeness.

"He's a jester!" Enoch said in wonder.

"Hush now, Enoch," Balus replied dismissively.

"A jester. A jester! We prattle and pester. Laughing away all the wounds which may fester," The Fool replied.

Balus was becoming impatient. "Enough of this. State your business or leave us."

"Of business, I've none, I deal only in fun. For I possess nought, which is greater than one," The Fool replied, rapidly breaking into a flowing dance around them which was equal parts bizarre and graceful. He moved with unnatural speed, and it was hard to keep a track of him as he circled around them. Enoch could not help but laugh at the sheer strangeness of it all.

"Enoch!" Balus whispered tersely. "This is serious. We could be in danger here."

Enoch did not perceive The Fool as threatening, though he could concede that there was certainly something strange at work.

"The boy gets the joke like the egg gets the yolk, yet the man cannot stand like a leg that's been broke," The Fool sang, continuing to dance around them. Balus was becoming increasingly agitated. "Answer my clue and I'll bid you adieu. You have me today, tomorrow yet more; as time only passes, I'm vexing to store; I don't take up space, I'm stored in one place. I am what you saw, but not what you see."

By this time Balus had given up and was sitting by his pack, watching the dancing fool contemptuously. Enoch quickly wracked his brain. If he couldn't work this out, The Fool might never leave. He knew what this was, a riddle, and he loved riddles. Back at the abbey, Adrax would often give him riddles to solve.

"I am what you saw, but not what you see," he mumbled to himself aloud. "That's it! A memory!"

The Fool stopped dead in his tracks and turned to Enoch,

grinning widely. Balus also looked at him in amazement.

"A sharpness of mind and a heart which is kind. Enoch, I see thee, though mine eyes are blind," said The Fool. The Fool jumped high into the air, backflipping over the two stunned travellers and disappearing into the brook with a splash. For a moment, they both watched the brook, stunned, not believing their eyes.

"Impossible," Balus said, breaking the silence. "That water is not more than a foot deep."

They both scrambled over to the water's edge and indeed, it was true, yet there was no sign of The Fool whatsoever. It was as if he was never there. Balus was visibly shaken as he continued to stare vacantly at the water.

"What on earth was that about?" Enoch finally asked, breaking the silence. Balus was unresponsive as he continued to stare into the shimmering waters of the brook. "Balus?"

Balus suddenly turned to face Enoch, as if he had woken from a dream. "There are. . . many strange things a man sees on the roads, Enoch. Some of them pose a threat. That's why we must always keep out wits about us and our swords at the ready."

"But who was that man?" Enoch asked.

"Best not to dwell on it," Balus said, evasively. "He's gone now, and we'd better be on our way ourselves if we are to reach the city by dusk."

Enoch nodded in agreement before hoisting his heavy pack up and over his shoulders. When it had reached its ideal balance, he gave the mountainous guardsman a thumbs up and they traced back to the road, increasing their pace in earnest as they did so. Ahead of them the fields of grass shimmered like a blanket of emeralds in the afternoon sun.

a

The sun was already low in the sky by the time the pair reached the outskirts of Fairhaven. They had just reached the crest of yet another punishing hill. Expecting to see yet more rolling greenery on the other side, Enoch was instead utterly breath-taken by what he saw. In place of the usual backdrop of greenery, the horizon was now encompassed by the rich blue brilliance of the sparkling ocean.

Enoch had read about the ocean before, of course, but nothing could have prepared him for bearing witness to its majesty with his own eyes. He could see all manner of ships meandering on their different vectors, some so distant they seemed as though they might fall off the edge of the earth.

He also saw the city, a massive square walled, pale–stoned labyrinth, adorned with all manner of towers which reached ever skyward. He had never seen so many buildings in all his life. The setting sun bathed the ashen stone in rich amber, and the sunlight was magnified even more by the tops of some temples and cathedrals which were coated in gold. He could see the vast wooden gates on the nearest face of the wall which lay below them, and the steady stream of people and wagons making their way in and out of the city.

"There it lies," Balus said solemnly. "Fairhaven. The gateway to the east."

"It's beautiful," Enoch said breathlessly.

"Come along now," Balus said brusquely. "We can still make it inside before dusk, if we hurry." Balus set a brisk pace, gingerly navigating them down the steep slope of the hill towards the city. One wrong move with these oversized packs would send the tumbling painfully to the base of the hill. They were still quite a way from the gate.

By now, Enoch was truly feeling the weight of his travels. Three days on the road had sapped him of his strength and every joint in his body ached. He relished the prospect of soon being within the city walls, being clean, and sleeping in a nice warm bed.

Balus spoke up from in front of him. "I think some ale is in order when we reach town. Don't you?"

Enoch had never drunk ale in his life, though he knew that it was brewed in the cellars of the abbey by some of the elder monks and distributed amongst them in healthy tankards at mealtimes. He knew also that Master Adrax was particularly fond of the stuff, and took a keen interest in all the finer nuances of the brewing process. He was meticulous in that, as he was in all facets of his life.

The younger novitiates were never allowed to drink ale. The closest he had come to that was a small glass of ceremonial altar wine on holy days.

"I suppose so," Enoch said. "Do you think I'm allowed?"

Balus let out a hearty laugh. "You're not in the abbey anymore, Enoch. What you do now is up to you."

Enoch was suddenly struck by that realization as it crystalized in his mind. Mere days ago, he was living the arduous yet predictable life of a novitiate. Now, here he stood, on the cusp of a new horizon. The realization made him giddy.

It did not take too long before they had reached the gate. As they joined the steady procession of oxen and travellers, Enoch was able to see just how large the city walls were. They towered high above the ground, patrolled by pairs of armored guards who carefully scanned the horizon for any signs of trouble. At each corner of the city stood a watchtower, built upon the wall that had yet more defensive capabilities.

The gates themselves were manned by two stoic, armored guardsmen who stood at attention, holding their halberds aloft and carefully scanning the would-be entrants to the city, occasionally inspecting wagons and the like. As they passed through the cavernous mouth of the gates, Enoch looked up at the literal tonnes of carefully stacked stones which lay above his head, and the massive yet currently suspended cast iron bars which locked the gate closed at night.

Stepping into Fairhaven was truly like stepping into another world. Even at sunset, the city was still abuzz with life. A true maze of ancient stone alleyways and concourses panned out in all directions before them. At every turn, criers, vendors, traders, singers, jugglers, and more lined the streets, each adding their own note to form a chaotic crescendo of sound and color which made the cobblestone streets seem to heave with life.

Everything was a new sensation to Enoch. Hot plates serving up mysterious and delicious delicacies, salesmen which seemed almost buried under the weight of their vibrant silks and fabrics, wild children being chased by angry shopkeepers. It was more people than Enoch had ever seen in his life, and not just men. Women!

Growing up in an abbey, surrounded by men, Enoch had oft felt women were closer to myth than to matter. Yet, here there were lots of women, of all shapes ages and sizes. In truth, the sheer volume of sensory input was rapidly overwhelming him as he stood transfixed by this panoply of organized madness.

Drawn to his confusion, or perhaps his vulnerability, Enoch was almost immediately beset by a gaggle of hawkers and salesman, all dragging him in different directions to try this, taste that, or follow them.

"Finest tunics in the city, Young Master."

"Irresistible love tonics!"

"Hearty soups for vitality at my stand!"

Balus gently laid a hand on his shoulder. "Hold onto my pack and follow me." He raised his voice almost to a yell over the hubbub of the crowd. Enoch mutely complied and Balus set off purposefully down one of the many alleyways.

Balus had visited Fairhaven many times, and had even lived there for a time. He knew the maze–like streets like the back of his hand. Doubtlessly, that was part of the reason why Adrax had entrusted this task to him. He knew just where to take them: a homely tavern up a side street close to one of the city's many public squares. It was a favorite haunt of his, and he always stayed there whenever he visited Fairhaven. Though it had been many years since his last visit, he had no doubt that the ale would be just as fresh.

As they navigated through the tightly backed passageways of the walled city, he felt a sense of nostalgia wash over him. He remembered when he was a young man around Enoch's age, a seemingly endless series of opportunities open to him. No matter what he did, it seemed he could do no wrong back then. The world was his to explore, and a man with skill at arms and a sound mind could go far in that world. And yet, somehow the years passed, the need for stability crept in and he settled into his life in the abbey.

Now he was on the road again, and witnessing young Enoch was like looking at a mirror of his younger self. Funny how life moves in cycles. The old growth makes way for the new.

After much walking, Balus and the very weary Enoch reached the town square where the tavern lay. He looked in earnest for the signage but could not find it. The square was different from his memory. The shops had changed and shifted, though he knew it was the correct square from the ornate mosaic pattern on the ground.

In the center of the square, performers had begun to assemble, about to begin their nights work.

"Aha!" He saw the wooden sign of the tavern from afar. It was heavily faded and worn by the years, but he could still make out the lettering out faintly.

As they strode over, he could see that the windows were boarded up and the door was barred. His heart sank.

*Have I been gone that long?*

This tavern was where he always stayed, and now here it stood, in disrepair. He felt frustration beginning to overcome him. He had a good rapport with the owner of this tavern, and he knew it to be a reliable and safe place. With a mission this important he could not afford to jeopardize their safety.

The sun was quickly setting and soon they would be looking in the dark. As he considered their next move he looked to Enoch and saw that he had come to rest on his pack nearby and was part of a growing group of onlookers who were watching the beginning of the performance. The crier, a lean man dressed in red and black, made his announcement.

"Ladies and gentlemen! Of all the four elements, fire is the most volatile, with the power to create and destroy in equal measure. It commands the respect of the one who dares to wield it."

As he spoke to the crowd, other members of the group began to set urns of oil alight, at points equidistant from one another around the square. Balus knew what this was. He had seen this act or the like countless times before. Enoch, however, was utterly entranced.

When they had set up the four urns, they began to lay out an assortment of staffs, balls and chains, all doused in oil. "We ask that you please maintain a safe distance, for what you will see here is a dangerous art form indeed," the crier said ominously. As he was making his announcements another man solemnly emerged from the crowd, making his way towards the center of the square.

His black hair was cut very short and upon his face he sported a pointed black anchor moustache to match. He was dressed in a brilliant ankle length tunic of deepest burgundy, adorned with golden thread which snaked patterns around its pointed edges.

The crier continued. "Ladies and gentlemen! All the way from the distant shores of Malthia, the great Davroz!" Balus' attention immediately became more focussed, and Enoch shot him an urgent look from where he stood. Could it be? By now, a significant crowd had amassed and a small cheer went up. At the edges of the square, some of the black and red clad crew members began to bang out a steady rhythm upon two large sheepskin drums which sat on either side of the man.

Abruptly, he raised his eyes to the crowd, and in a split second a powerful burst of fire erupted skyward from the flaming urns at each corner of the square. This elicited excited screams from the audience, and they collectively paced back a few steps. The performer eyed the instruments in front of him and picked up a metal staff which had four smaller lengths protruding symmetrically from each end. He held it aloft for the crowd to see, far above his head.

As if moving through some kind of intangible will of its own, small vortexes of flame issued forth from each of the urns and snaked their way overhead, striking the ends of his staff and setting the protrusions alight, much to the utter amazement of the crowd. The flaming tendrils then subsided, and he began to roll and weave his flaming staff deftly and rhythmically to the steadily intensifying beat of the drums. When the staff rolled, it looked as though he was wielding two flaming pinwheels which seemed almost to dance across his powerful frame with utmost grace.

He threw the staff high into the sky and flames practically exploded from either end while he did so, blanketing the air above the square in an eruption of heat and light. While most of the crowd was transfixed by this, he nimbly somersaulted forward and caught the staff again with his right hand before it hit the ground.

The audience paused for a moment before breaking into rapturous cheers and applause while he slowly lifted his gaze and bowed, his face showing not a hint of emotion. Coins of silver, gold, and bronze began to blanket the square all around him, as the crowd eagerly offered whatever they had. It seemed a day's coin was a small price to pay for a glimpse of true master.

Balus and Enoch watched as the rest of his crew quickly scurried to gather the rapidly growing blanket of coins, occasionally brandishing clubs as they fought back the hungry street urchins who sought to co–opt them of their takings. They watched as Davroz slunk back into the crowd on the far side of the square from whence he came, as the now satisfied mob began to disperse.

Balus steadied his pack upon his back as he spoke to Enoch. "Follow me, boy, we mustn't lose track of him." Enoch nodded and quickly grabbed up his own pack and they set off in pursuit. They pushed their way through the crowd and the coin gathering performers, Enoch whispering placations to those they bumped into as they went.

They could just see him rounding the corner of a nearby alleyway as they quickened their pace to catch up to him. Balus found more than a few peculiarities in his performance. For one, in all his life, he had never witnessed a fire juggler perform the feats he had just seen. And secondly, he seemed to have no interest whatsoever in collecting the money he had just earned.

Davroz was walking very quickly, and the pair found it difficult to keep a track of him in the rapidly diminishing light as he weaved his way effortlessly through the crowded city streets. Suddenly, they saw him make a sharp left turn down a disused alleyway. They followed suit but found the dark alleyway all but deserted. It was as if he had disappeared into the shadow itself.

"Damn it!" Balus shouted, his voice echoing off the stone walls. Enoch was silent as he watched his mentor's vented frustrations. There was little they could do. Night had already fallen, and they had not yet found lodgings.

As Balus sighed in resignation, a small flame appeared dangerously close to his cheek, illuminating the dark alleyway and shining light on the razor sharp dagger which was gently but firmly pressed against his neck.

Davroz. He had hidden in one of the dark nooks of the alleyway and caught them by surprise. In his left hand, he held a steel dagger to Balus's neck, and in his right, he seemed to be somehow producing a small flame from his outstretched index and middle finger.

Enoch's heart leapt into his mouth.

"Don't move," the deep, accented voice commanded. Balus' own heart rate soared, and beads of perspiration quickly formed on his neck and forehead as he precariously balanced himself.

*How did he get the drop on me so quickly? Am I really that rusty?*

"Okay, alright. It's alright," Balus repeated, trying desperately to stall or diffuse the situation.

"Who are you?" Davroz demanded angrily. "Why are you following me?"

"We're from the Briarwood Abbey," Balus wheezed. "We are friends of Master Adrax."

"And how do I know this is no fabrication?"

"I have a letter. But I must know if you are Davroz Inferni."

"What do you think?" Davroz asked mockingly. "Either way, you are not positioned to make such demands. Show me this letter." He kept the dagger firmly pressed into Balus' thick neck. Balus, while quietly furious at himself for being apprehended so easily was also cognizant of the fact that he was now in check; one false move here would lead to his death.

He cautiously reached into his side pocket, holding his other hand aloft as he did so, and eventually produced the letter.

Davroz inspected the personal wax seal of Master Adrax closely before sighing and staying his dagger. Balus quickly staggered back to Enoch's side, catching his breath.

"Forgive me, travellers," he said, sighing. "In these dark times we must exercise extraordinary caution. Do you have a place to stay in the city?"

"No," Balus replied dryly.

"Then we shall discern this letter and its contents at my lodge."

Enoch, utterly exhausted at this point by the course of the day's events and baffled by the man's immediate change of demeanour, looked to Balus, who seemed to mirror his own feelings.

"Follow me, if you would," Davroz said curtly, the flame from his fingers bobbing like a will-o'-wisp as he stalked ahead of them down the pitch black alleyway.

a

Davroz's lodge was expectedly befitting for a man of his renown. He lived a round stone tower, and his home was adorned with all manner of strange curiosities from near and far. As he led them inside, he nonchalantly pointed the index and middle fingers of his left hand towards the room and soon small bolts of flame issued forth, each one flying across the room to strike a candle or lantern with expert precision until the entire house was bathed in the warm glow of candlelight.

"So, you're a flame elemental?" Balus asked.

"An astute observation, Master Balus," Davroz replied dryly. "I am, indeed. One of the last of my kind born before The Great Schism."

Enoch could not believe his eyes. Magic, real magic. The only kind of magic he had ever known was the parlour tricks of travelling bands, and even that he found amazing.

"Forgive me, sirs, but what was The Great Schism?" Enoch asked.

"I can always forgive an inquisitive mind, young master," Davroz replied. "In ages past, magic users of all kinds were joined in one guild. The acquisition, understanding, and application of magic was a sacred task, and with it came millennia of rules, regulations, and customs. We made decisions as one, endeavouring to act not for the interests of kings and queens, but for the greater good of the world we share.

"Twenty-two years ago, in the year 1011, there was a disagreement in the interpretation of a prophecy concerning the end of days. This disagreement drove a wedge between my brethren, and the order shattered. What followed was chaos, and a bloody conflict.

“We destroyed ourselves from the inside, tarnishing the reputation of all magic users as we did so. I was but an infant, and my mother and father fought hard to secure my escape. Now we magic users are wanderers, refugees. Unwanted guests in a land which once venerated us. Reduced to cheap tricks by the roadside. But who could blame the common man? Any who bore witness to the horrors of The Schism would attest to the cruelty of magic.”

There was a solemn sadness in his eyes and his voice as he spoke. A hushed melancholy fell over the room. Balus was lost in contemplation as Davroz spoke, himself reliving the terrors of that time.

*1011*, Enoch thought. *The year of my birth.*

“Now, then,” Davroz began, pouring three tankards of ale from a nearby cask and clanking them down noisily on the table. “Let us see if we can’t make sense of this letter.”

Enoch and Balus both took their seats at the table and hungrily sipped the sweet ale as Davroz produced a small letter knife and gently broke the wax seal.

As he scanned the yellowed parchment by the candlelight his expression grew more and more serious. When he had finished reading and set the letter down, he cast a long studious gaze at Enoch.

“Well?” Balus asked. “What is it?”

“We must ride to the capital to seek an audience with the Watchers. It seems young Enoch here may have a part to play in what is to come.” He took a large swig from his tankard. “We leave at dawn.”

# CHAPTER 8

# THE DOTTED LINE

## *2033 A.D.*

*She shook uncontrollably as she watched her husband, the man she had once loved slowly pace towards her. Her hands were bound, and her mouth was gagged, so her cries of protest were cruelly muffled.*

*How could he?*

*As she looked at him through tear-soaked eyes, she could no longer see any trace of the man he once was, only the monster he had become.*

*"Did you really think I wouldn't find out?!" he spat, slapping her hard enough to rock her chair back from the impact. She barely registered the blow, the heartache she felt far outweighed any physical pain he dealt her. It was as if she had disconnected from her body. All the pain she felt was centered squarely on her heart, as though it were a gaping wound.*

*"All these years, I thought you were the one person I could trust. In a way, I should thank you! You've taught me a valuable lesson; trust no one." Briefly, his anger gave way to grief. "We have a kid together, for fucks sake!" he screamed, his voice breaking*

*She desperately tried to scream: Exactly! For his sake, don't do this.*

*But the gag in her mouth muffled her words beyond any comprehension.*

*"Save it, Louise," he said, suddenly becoming eerily calm. "I hate to do this, I really do." He produced a silenced pistol from his waistband.*

*In that moment she knew it was real: end of the line. In a way, a strange resolve came over her too. She took one last look at the garage as he cocked the pistol, never imagining such a mundane room from her everyday life would serve as the theatre for her own execution.*

*As her husband put the barrel to her temple, he closed his eyes and whispered himself a paradoxical prayer.*

*She shut her own eyes and took a deep breath. Her last thoughts were of her son. She sent him all the love she could muster, her final gift to him before she left this world.*

Adam awoke, sobbing, to the sound of knocking at the door.

For a few moments he was completely disoriented, where was he? Who was he? His ears were ringing intensely.

"Mr. Adam?" A concerned female voice asked distantly. "I'm here to clean your room."

*Adam. That's me.*

It was one of his maids. "I–it's fine, Vera," he spluttered. "You can just come back later." He heard the echo of the footsteps retreat down the hallway.

His entire bed was drenched with sweat, and he was heaving. He had never had a nightmare like that in his life. It felt real, as if he was witnessing things first hand through his mother's eyes. More than that, he could feel her emotions, the depth of her love, and her sorrow. He found himself tearing up again.

*That can't be what happened. She abandoned us.*

For so much of his life, he had been trying to fill that hole. His own sadness reminded him keenly of that which he felt in the dream; though where hers was like a vibrant splitting tear, his own was more akin to a creeping rot. Ever pervasive, and growing slowly, minute by minute, hour by hour, deep down in the core of his soul. Only briefly could it be satiated by the highs which drugs provided him, and then it was there again, eagerly waiting. A shadow behind each waking moment. The phantom at the end of the bed. Depression.

He steadied himself on the end of the bed before walking shakily to his ensuite bathroom to wash his face in the sink, looking at himself in the mirror.

He looked like shit. The combination of scarcely eating, insomnia and perpetual exhaustion cut deep dark trenches under his bloodshot eyes. His skinny body seemed almost to glow from how pale it was. Even his bleached blonde hair seemed to have greyed.

Coffee. Now. Even the mere thought of the word sent his neurons into famished hysteria. He would not be able to see or think straight until he poured that cup.

He staggered over to his tea table and lazily filled up the espresso machine and switched it on. Time for a cigarette. His father expressly forbade him from smoking in the house. In his mind, that was all the more reason to do so.

He was again hit by a strong flashback from the dream. He staggered slightly as his mind was again inundated by that cruelty. What could it mean? He usually barely remembered his dreams. He reached into the draw in his nightstand and produced the packet of cigarettes. Like clockwork, by the time he had lit his first cigarette, his coffee was ready.

This was his morning routine.

He checked his watch: 5:21 p.m. There would be no grand opening of his expensive curtains or greeting of chirping birds in the sunshine. There would only be darkness. He liked it better this way. He only had to wait until nightfall. He considered what he might do tonight and all options pointed to getting unreasonably drunk.

His room was a mess as he looked around. There were days worth of dirty clothes littering the floor, and all manner of fast food wrappers, boxes, and beer cans. In truth, it was disgusting. What did it matter anyway? In the end, the maids would clean his room, whether he asked them to or not. Sometimes his life with his father felt more like an endless hotel stay. Joyless, lifeless, but oh so opulent.

At 7:30, on the dot, after showering and dressing himself for the night, he emerged from his fetid cave and skulked towards the dining room. There, he found his father, sitting at one end of the massive mahogany table.

He did not look up as Adam entered the room, merely continued tapping away on his tablet, occasionally taking a sip from his crystal wine goblet. His glasses cut deep furrows into his slowly sagging skin. The dining room was adorned with three crystal chandeliers and massive plate glass windows, which overlooked the expansive and carefully manicured back garden.

The sun was setting, and rich orange light poured through the glass panes and onto the table and Persian rugs like spectral beams from on high.

Adam took his seat at the opposite end of the table, twenty feet away from his father. His place was already set, with a plate and three sets of immaculate silver cutlery, one for each course. When he sat down, his father wordlessly picked up a small black bell by his side and rang it, still staring intently at his tablet. Within moments, the dinner staff emerged from the door behind his father and gently placed the first course in front of each of them.

It had been like this for as long as Adam remembered. His father rarely spoke to him, and if he did so, it was usually in the form of derision.

As a child, he often tried to work hard during the day and be an extra good boy for his dad, making him pictures or Lego constructions for him to show at dinner. He soon learned that it simply did not matter. His father would regard him with the same indifference either way: like a stranger, an unwelcome guest.

It was a viciously cold way for a child to live. As the years passed, all those lonely tears of his childhood hardened and crystallized into rage. As he began to tuck into the first course, lamb shank with mashed potato, his father suddenly spoke.

"Did you file any of those applications?" He looked up briefly from his tablet. Adam was taken by surprise by the inquiry. He was referring to the university applications Adam was supposed to make.

His first attempt at university had failed after he was kicked out for selling pot. His father had been unbelievably furious and beat him severely on his first night home. 'Dragging our family name through the mud', he had said. Ironic, Adam thought, as his father was known as the head of an organized crime syndicate. He had given him until summer to re-apply, and with summer fast approaching, Adam had yet to make a single inquiry.

"Yes," he lied, shakily.

"Which ones?"

"Uh, Westcamp and Somerset."

"Show me," his father said, his eyes narrowing behind his

spectacles.

"I–ah–I don't, ah. . ." Adam trailed, stalling as he tried to find an answer.

"Don't *fucking* lie to me!" his father bellowed, slamming his fists on the table, causing his cutlery to rattle violently. "If you don't get accepted to a new school before the summer, you're gone. I don't care where you go, but you're out of here. Like attracts like. I won't have a failure living under my roof."

Adam was filled with a mixture of rage and shame as he stared down at his plate. Maybe his father was right. Maybe he was just a failure.

"What? Nothing to say?" His father spoke mockingly. "But that's just like you, isn't it? No backbone. Just like your mother. You're not a man. You're a boy."

Adam stared at the meal in front of him and listened to his fathers scathing tirade fade into the background, and he found that he was no longer hungry. He abruptly stood up from his seat and left the room.

He wouldn't give his father the satisfaction of letting himself rise to the taunts. As he left the room, his father's shouts grew louder and louder, a contempt which followed him as it echoed through the cool dark hallways of their home.

He went straight to the garage, passing his father's three glistening sports cars before reaching his own metallic steed. It was a top–of–the–line overseas sports bike, jet black with carbon fiber detailing, and immensely powerful. As he threw on his helmet and started the engine, he felt his anxiety begin to fade slightly. He opened the automatic garage door with his remote and revved out into the night. It was just him and the road now.

It was around 8:30 p.m. when Adam pulled up to the bar and gently parked and locked his bike near the veritable fleet of motorbikes by the curb.

The Dean Moral Inn, or, to its patrons, simply 'The Dean.'

It was one of his regular haunts, serving as a staging post from which he would launch himself into the night, once adequately inebriated, of course. He must have spent thousands of dollars over the years in warm up drinks at The Dean, though that was not to say he was a particularly valued customer. He usually sat at the bar alone, and more than once he had been forcibly ejected from the premises after drinking himself into oblivion.

The Dean was a rough place. Nestled in a dingy backstreet, it harbored all manner of misfits, criminals, and general malcontents behind its brick walls. Its ancient neon entrance signs flickered sporadically like some crude twenty-first century parody of a lighthouse, each blinding burst briefly illuminating the alleyway; a smorgasbord of squabbling rats, rotting food, and all the detritus left behind by a busy city.

It was no coincidence Adam found himself here. In many ways it was the antithesis of the life he led at home. Here he was no one, and so was everyone else.

As he walked in the door, he was immediately hit by the overwhelming waft of cigarette smoke, and he almost instantly reached down and lit his own. Cigarette smoke and eighties rock music were two constants at The Dean. They didn't play the old rock out of some ironic nostalgic ideation, its patrons simply rarely put anything else on the jukeboxes. He had to admit, it was mostly an older crowd and they just had not stopped listening to that music since the music was new.

Adam liked that. It was authentic, if nothing else. Stepping inside its scummy, graffiti covered walls was like stepping back in time. Already, he could see that the pool tables were manned by the usual crew of grizzled old bikers, laughing haughtily amongst themselves under the yellow glow of the lights overhead as they chain smoked between sips of their beers.

In the dimly lit booths, off to the side, he saw the standard assortment of lonely drunks, working girls, and would be drug dealers all coalescing in harmony.

The bartop was mostly empty, save for a couple old regulars who occasionally shouted something unintelligible at the football game playing on the grainy old analogue TV that was fixed to the wall.

He took his seat at one of the bar stools and before long the dishevelled middle-aged barman staggered over to take his order. He was half drunk himself most of the time, and Adam could smell the liquor on his breath and see what looked like the remnants of dinner in his beard as he spoke.

"What do you want?"

"Two double whiskies, Black Label, easy on the ice."

"Ice machine's broke," the barman said flatly, hiccupping.

*Of course.* Adam stifled the urge to laugh. "Fine, no ice then."

The barman turned around and poured two very healthy glasses of whisky and crudely dropped them on the bar top in front of Adam. He was already holding his card in his hand. The barman sighed and lazily produced the POS machine which he then tapped, a small chime indicating the success of the transaction.

As he paid for the drinks, he felt that familiar tinge of hollowness. *You're a fraud; it's not like you earned that money. These people, all around you, at least they earned their money. They have a right to be here. You're just a pretender.*

He took a big gulp of his first whisky, whincing slightly

from the initial shock. Within moments, his hungry brain recognized the alcohol and delivered him that sweet rush of dopamine he so desperately craved, and the inner voice began to subside. That was one of the reasons why he drank. When he drank, he could drown that fucking voice, even if it was only until morning came along.

That was part of the reason he had stolen the coke last week. He needed some way to make his own money, some measure of independence. There was nothing he hated more than feeling like he relied on his father. But working in some dead end job, making minimum wage? Yeah, right.

As he felt the alcohol slowly begin to come on, he leaned back, running his hands through his hands through his hair and closing his eyes.

Finally. A return to normality. Some semblance of peace.

When he opened his eyes again, he saw that a new customer had taken a seat to his right, in his periphery vision. He cautiously turned his gaze to look and quickly averted it again so as not to catch her eye.

She was beautiful. Her soft hazel colored hair was wrapped in a messy bun and she wore a stunning black satin dress which hugged her figure tightly. She looked like she was in her mid-twenties. Simply put, she stood out like a sore thumb, it was inconceivable to him that someone so beautiful would consciously choose to spend their time here.

He hazarded a glance again and he could see that she was eyeing the chalk board drinks selection above the bar top. He was sure that every eye in the bar must have been on her right now, but she was unbothered. She seemed almost to glow with radiance, though perhaps it was through sheer contrast when compared to the assemblage of night creatures she shared the bar with.

Adam turned his attention back to his drink as the bartender shuffled over. Adam watched his expression shift from immediate shock to a hasty attempt at charm.

"And what can I get for you, darling?" He beamed a yellowed gap-toothed grin.

"Double whisky on ice," she replied matter-of-factly. Even her voice was somehow beautiful, its firm but gentle cadence exuded grace.

"Absolutely." He hastily, yet carefully, polished a glass. Immediately, he produced a scoop of ice from the machine under the bar top, and let a few cubes clank into the glass before filling it up halfway with the golden liquid. "There you go." He smiled as he placed the drink on a fresh coaster in front of her.

*Son of a bitch.* Adam fumed, staring daggers at the barman, but the wily drunkard easily avoided his gaze. She nonchalantly produced a twenty and he thanked her profusely, lingering just a bit too long with his gaze as he did so.

Adam shuddered internally. The barman returned to his job, and Adam returned his focus solely to his drink. *A girl like that would never be interested in a guy like me, anyway.* As he was rounding off his first glass and staring vacantly at the muted football game on the TV, the beautiful stranger spoke up.

"Are those both for you?"

It took Adam a couple moments to register that she was talking to him. He spun around, blushing and spluttering through his response as he met her gaze for the first time. Her eyes were most beautiful of all, powerful brown eyes with sinews of gold and green.

"Oh, um. . . sorry. Yeah. Yeah, they're both for me." He chuckled nervously.

"Tough week, then?" She motioned to the drinks.

"You could say that," he said. "More like tough life."

She laughed, softening her beautiful features. "I feel like this place is the living embodiment of a tough week." They both shared a laugh at that.

Was this really happening? A girl was talking to him, laughing with him. A gorgeous girl. And she wants to talk to me? She had an intense gaze. Her eyes seemed to pierce through to his very soul, the type of eyes which told stories of their own. His usual façade of indifference was rapidly crumbling before those eyes.

"What's your name?" she asked, smiling ever so slightly, doubtlessly cognisant of the effect she was having on him.

"Adam."

"Nice to meet you, Adam. I'm Chelsea," she spoke warmly. "Do you come here often?"

*Oh god, if only you knew.*

"Not really," he lied, trying to paint a slightly less bleak picture of his life. "I usually prefer places uptown."

"Is that so?" She spoke with a hint of comic derision. "If you asked me, I'd say you look like you fit right in around here." It took Adam a few moments to process her response before he considered the fact that he probably was looking a bit worse for wear at that moment.

"Touché." They both broke into laughter. "Do you smoke?" He produced his pack of cigarettes, offering her one. She beat him to it and pulled out her own bright green packet of menthol cigarettes. She lit her cigarette and then leaned over to light his.

That brief moment of closeness sent tingles down his spine. It was as if he was intoxicated by her. Or perhaps that was just the whiskey talking.

Adam cleared his throat as he tapped his cigarette gently into the ashtray as she released a large plume of sickly mint flavoured smoke and eyed him curiously. He hated menthols, but he was not about to let her know that.

"So, Chelsea," he began, emboldened by his rapidly disappearing drink. "What's a girl like you doing in a place like this?" He immediately cringed at how corny it sounded.

"And just what kind of girl am I, Adam?"

"Well. . . I just mean that. . . er, you're very. . ." He stuttered, caught off guard by her directness. "You're not like the people I usually see around here," he finally said.

"You usually see? I thought you said you don't come here often?"

*Damn it.*

She must have read his expression, because she was soon sympathetic. "I'm just playing. If you must know, I'm looking for someone."

"Someone like who?" Adam's curiosity was piqued.

She sighed, gazing into the backbar. "Someone who can take my mind off things. Someone who can show me a good time. Someone who can help me forget about this mundane world we find ourselves in, even if only for tonight." Her words moved him deeply, as if she was taking the words out of his own mouth. After a brief pause, she turned to face him, her powerful eyes seeming almost to plead as she gently reached across the bar top and laid her hand on top of his own. "Are you that someone, Adam?"

He felt butterflies rise inside of him like static electricity. So too, did he feel the familiar sensation of hot blood rushing to his face making him blush, but for once he didn't care. "I can be," he said softly.

"I'm glad to hear that," she beamed. "I'll tell you what. Why don't we leave this dump? I know a little place nearby that's a little more. . . low key."

At his point, he had nothing to lose. Why not take this chance? On any other day someone like her might have just dismissed him as a loser, but by some chance, they crossed paths, on this day, at this time, in this place. It had to be for a reason.

"Sure." He downed the last of his whiskey.

"Great," she said, squeezing his hand before downing her own drink. She grabbed up her coat and rose off her stool and he did the same, his heart aflutter with excitement. He nodded smugly to the barman, who eyed him contemptuously as he left, hand in hand with Chelsea.

In truth, despite the false bravado he projected, he had very little experience with girls. He was usually too afraid to let himself be vulnerable, yet he desperately longed for connection. It was a cruel stalemate which he subjected himself to over the years.

In high school, he had watched from the sidelines one by one as his classmates fell in and out of love, but he was always the loner at the back of the class. Extradited. Uninvited, deemed a lost cause by students and teachers alike. No one cared enough to simply sit down and get to know him. Perhaps no one dared to because of the fearsome reputation of his father.

Whatever the cause, that ever-permeating loneliness had shaped him. In the end, he decided, fuck them. Your only worth to others is what they can take from you. So, what was the point in giving them anything at all? But maybe this was the end of all that. Maybe he had finally found someone who understood.

As they stepped out into the night air, they were both immediately struck by the chill, laughing as they were buffeted by the icy wind.

"Should we take my bike?" Adam asked, pointing to his bike, parked on the curb.

"We won't need to. It's pretty close by." She clasped his hand in her own and they began to walk further down the alleyway to the left of The Dean. Chelsea's heels clopped rhythmically on the asphalt and echoed off walls, and her face was briefly illuminated as she tapped on her phone with her free hand while they walked. As they moved deeper into the dark, damp litany of dumpsters and trash Adam became vaguely nervous. He had never been down into the alley this far and did not know of any more bars down here past The Dean. As far as he knew, the only living people down here were homeless folks and heroin addicts.

"Are you sure this is the right way?" he finally asked her.

"Sure, I'm sure," she said calmly. "You aren't afraid of the dark, are you?"

"No."

Ahead of them, in the half light of the alley, two men appeared from around a corner and started walking in their direction. Adam's heart immediately started to race. He could not make them out clearly, but he could see that one of them was holding some type of bat. He knew the city well enough to know that this was not an ideal scenario.

"Maybe we should head back," he said to Chelsea, gently pulling her hand to turn her around. When they turned around his heart jolted when he saw that two more men were walking towards them from the way they came.

He stopped in his tracks and pulled Chelsea with him to lean in against the wall. "Okay, okay, just be cool," he whispered shakily, looking into her eyes. "Let me do the talking, and when I say run, you run, okay?" She nodded her head vigorously in silent agreement.

Adam kept his gaze firmly on the wall. The worst thing they could do in this situation was run. He hoped that if they appeared to be hooking up and minding their own business that the men would simply pass them by. He tried his best to seem unbothered as he heard the footsteps approach, but then they stopped behind him. His pulse quickened and the silence in that moment was deafening.

He heard one gruff male voice ask. "Is this him, boss?"

"Show me," said another. That voice was familiar. He knew he had heard it somewhere before.

Adam felt two very powerful hands seize his arms and pull them painfully behind his back. He tried in vain to struggle, but it was no use, whoever was holding him was at least twice his size. He was then kicked hard in the back and fell to his knees.

They yanked his head up by his hair painfully, and he laid eyes on the owner of this familiar voice. His heart immediately sank. Staring down at him with that same haunting detachment was Jason, the drug dealer he had stolen from a week ago.

"Chelsea, *run*!" Adam yelled desperately.

The men erupted in laughter and a smile crept onto Jason's skeletal face.

"Chelsea? Who's Chelsea?" Jason teased. He nodded towards the girl. "Do you mean Candy? Candy, come here, girl."

Adam watched in disbelief as Chelsea walked forward from where she had been leaning against the wall.

"See, Candy here owed me a little favor. I figure it was worth it to call it in just to see the look on your face right now." Adam tried to catch her eye, but she was looking firmly ahead. Jason produced some money from his pocket and handed it to Candy. She slid it into her purse and wordlessly began to walk away, but not before casting a final look at Adam. There was pain in her eyes, and sympathy. Regret? He could not say.

Adam felt tears brimming in his own eyes as the sound of her heels clacking on the cobblestones faded away. Betrayal. Absolute in its conception. The one time he felt like he had found someone, it turned out to be nothing more than a cruel lie. He wanted to hate her, to scream.

He could not, he now only felt fear, and it surged through him like electricity.

"You know, it wasn't hard to find you, Adam," Jason began, as held the baseball bat aloft and inspected it with his gloved hands. "But imagine my surprise when I find out that you're Don Powell's kid? My dealer's dealer works for your dad! Small world."

Adam tried desperately to struggle against the vice grip of his captors, but it was no use. "See, most people wouldn't touch you with a ten-foot pole if they knew your daddy. But I'm not most people, Adam. I'm me. Get him up."

His goons complied and hoisted the trembling Adam to his feet, so he was face to face with Jason. "Not so tough without the gun, are you?" Jason asked. Before Adam could even think of a response Jason delivered a shattering punch to his gut. Adam felt all the breath leave his lungs as he collapsed again onto the wet stone, gasping vainly for breath.

"I told you I would take it slow with you, once I found you," Jason said. He delivered yet another blow, this time slamming the baseball bat into Adam's back. Adam howled from the searing pain as he felt some of his ribs crack under the impact. He feebly reached out his hand and Jason stomped it viciously into the ground with his boot, sending excruciating pain spasming through his arm. Adam screamed once again, even more so when he saw his bloody, broken mess of a hand.

One of the men piped up from behind him. "Boss. . . don't

you think maybe that's enough?"

"You shut your fucking mouth. I don't pay you to have a conscience," Jason spat back.

"It's not that, it's just, if you kill the kid, the whole city is gonna come down on our heads."

"Why do you think I'm wearing gloves, Lou? I already picked a place to dispose of the body," Jason said.

*They're really going to kill me.*

As they bickered amongst themselves, Adam's survival instincts kicked in and he tried feebly using his good hand and his feet to crawl away, painful inches at a time. Jason quickly delivered a blindingly painful kick to his ribs for his troubles. Adam again bellowed in pain and coughed up blood. He was starting to lose consciousness and his vision was beginning to fade.

"Alright, because of you twitchy fucks I'm going to have to make this quicker than I wanted to," Jason said. As he raised the bat high over his head, Adam looked up at his would-be executioner.

So, this was it. In those final moments, time seemed to slow, and he found himself thinking of his mother. At least he could see her again. He took comfort in that.

As he closed his eyes and prepared for the impact, he heard a strange noise. It sounded like fabric tearing, but almost electric and distorted, as if under water.

He opened his eyes.

In the air, a few feet above Jason's head, a shimmering, liquid-like circle had appeared. Its turbulent center was pitch black, but its jagged edges shimmered with bloody red light. Jason saw Adam's eyes and the eyes of his slack jawed lackeys were affixed on the area above his head and he raised his gaze slowly to see what they were looking at.

“What the fu—”

Before he could say any more, two monstrous arm–like appendages sprang forth from the hole and seized him. They were unlike anything Adam had ever seen. Covered in huge black scales, like a snake, easily four times the size of any human arm, with sharp claws in each hand.

As the arms grabbed ahold of Jason, they bit deeply into his flesh and his calm demeanour was replaced by pure terror. Adam watched on in horror as Jason shrieked and thrashed as the arms pulled him slowly but surely into the inky blackness.

Jason’s bat came crashing to the ground as the circle abruptly winked out of existence, as if it was never there. Jason’s men were momentarily stunned, before they screamed and scattered from the alleyway.

An exhausted Adam slumped to the ground and lost consciousness.

Adam awoke slowly to a steady beeping rhythm. As he opened his eyes, they took several moments to focus. They zeroed in on the grey, water damaged plaster on the ceiling.

He had no idea where he was. As he breathed deeply, he became aware of the stifling tubes in his nose. He looked to his right, to the source of the beeping, an EKG. He was in a hospital bed. He saw that his right hand was in a cast and his left was handcuffed to the bed. When he saw the handcuffs, his heart began to beat faster, raising the tempo on the EKG. A man he had not noticed, who was sitting in a chair in the far end of the room, reading a newspaper, suddenly stood up. He had dark skin and short black hair. He also wore a trench coat and a tie.

"Ah, good, you're awake," he said warmly.

"Where am I?" Adam asked.

"Briarwood General. You're not too far from home, Adam," the man said. He was caught off guard that the man knew his name. "Don't look so shocked. They found you with your wallet and ID on you."

"How long have I been here?" Adam asked.

"A couple of days. You were hypothermic and in a coma when they found you."

"Are you police?" Adam asked.

"We're far beyond that, I'm afraid. Adam, my name is Mr. Davis and I represent an organization known as S.H.A.R.D." He flashed Adam a badge. "Now, the police have you cuffed here in connection with the disappearance of one Jason Mallory. Also, in the potential procurement of a controlled substance. But I can make all of that disappear if you'll help cooperate with our operation."

"What do you mean?" Adam asked.

"We have obtained CCTV footage of what happened in that alleyway, Adam," he said. Adam was suddenly hit by a violent flash of a memory from that night, those gigantic arms, Jason's screams. It was actually real? "All we ask is that you join us at our facility so that we can run some tests."

"What about my father?" Adam asked. "Does he know I'm here?"

"Your father knows your whereabouts, but he has yet to make a visit. I needn't remind you that as an adult, this decision falls solely to you."

"And you'll make the charges disappear?" Adam asked hesitantly.

"Provided you comply, of course," Mr. Davis said,

brandishing that same well practiced smile. Adam thought for a moment before responding. At this point he figured he had nothing left to lose.

"Okay."

"Great," Mr. Davis began. "I'll just need you to sign this waiver, and in a few days, you'll be transferred into our care." He handed over a clipboard and a pen.

Adam blearily scanned the densely worded form before he croaked one last inquiry. "Wait. What about my bike?"

"We can arrange to have your bike transferred to our facility," Mr. Davis replied, his initial sunniness diminishing somewhat as he grew impatient.

Adam scrawled his signature on the dotted line before handing back the clipboard and the pen. "Excellent," Mr. Davis said. "We look forward to working with you, Adam. For now, rest up and take it easy. You're going to need your strength." He produced a small key and unlocked Adam's handcuffs. As he folded his newspaper and headed for the door, he said one last thing. "Oh, and Adam? Best you keep our little meeting here to yourself. You know, company policy and all."

Adam slowly nodded.

"Great. Have a nice day!" Mr. Davis smiled before closing the door behind him.

Adam lay back, utterly bewildered. On the one hand, he was relieved: no police attention and he had survived the attack on his life. On the other hand, he could not shake a growing sense of apprehension.

What on earth had happened in that alleyway? How could any of it be real and not just some nightmare? He sighed deeply as he laid back in his bed. He feared what those answers might be.

CHAPTER 9

# The Gambit

## *2033 A.D.*

The mid-afternoon sun had long since disappeared behind a thick blanket of cloud as Evie clung tightly to her grandmothers' arm at the busy street crossing. Cars honked, bicycle bells dinged, and the general hustle and bustle of the city streets roared all around them like some postmodern cacophony.

Across the road stood the colossal and ancient city library, their arranged meeting place with Hermes. It was an immense gothic stone building adorned with pillars and topped with a massive dome cathedral, with a mountainous flight of steps lay between them and the entrance. The building was long since disused in favor of the modern Capital Library, which opened in the late 1990's.

*Stupid cat,* she thought. *He could have picked a better meeting place. Imagine making an old woman climb all those stairs.*

Flora at least seemed to be in good spirits and was handling the organized chaos of the city streets surprisingly well. As the light turned green and Evie led her gently over the crossing, she seemed almost excited.

"Oh! We're getting closer," Flora said jubilantly. Evie shot her a perplexed look. They had never been there before. How could she know?

As they reached the foot of the seemingly insurmountable flight of steps, Evie sighed in anticipation of the uphill battle she would face on each step to help Flora reach the top. The lack of wheelchair access or an elevator was a true sign of the building's antiquity. No wonder it was in disrepair.

Just as Evie was about to start gently helping Flora up the first step, Flora sprang into action and began rapidly scaling the stone steps, at times taking them two at a time. Evie could not believe her eyes. Where had this energy come from? It was as if her frailty had suddenly vanished.

Given that she was here at the behest of a telepathic cat, Evie supposed that Flora's sudden burst of energy was probably the least strange thing about this situation.

She scrambled to race after her grandmother, and when they reached the top of the stairs, they both collapsed in a heap, wheezing and laughing.

"Oh, that was great!" Flora wheezed. "I haven't climbed those steps in years."

"You've climbed those steps before, grammie?" Evie asked suspiciously.

"Oh yes child, oh yes. Days gone by. I used to work here... or was it study here? I can't quite remember," Flora said.

At that moment, Hermes appeared from behind one of the pillars.

SO, YOU MADE IT.

"Yeah, no thanks to you," Evie replied sharply.

"There you are!" Flora gushed, gently stroking the purring Hermes as he nuzzled against her.

Follow me. The council is waiting.

As they followed Hermes through the revolving glass doors of the library, they were immediately met with the disapproving gaze of the young male usher who quickly stopped them at the door. His pink skin was flushed, despite the coolness of the day.

"Excuse me," he began. "But this is not a homeless shelter. We do not allow animals in the building. I'm afraid you'll have to leave." He spoke in a smug nasal tone. His words hit Evie like a slap in the face. Homeless shelter? And how exactly did they look homeless? It made her wonder how many other faces just like theirs this petulant little boy turned around on a daily basis.

Sensing her fury, Hermes chimed in in her head.

Save it. The boy's a fool. I usually use another entrance anyway. Meet me at the lowest level.

Evie nodded and Hermes quickly darted back out of the revolving doors and onto the steps outside.

As they walked further inside, the usher eyed them contemptuously as Evie gave him a defiant smile.

"You know, you really ought to learn a little respect."

The usher merely scoffed and returned to his post by the door. People like him made her blood boil, and yet she encountered them all too often. Shamelessly profiling and belittling people on a daily basis, and for what? To get some type of twisted rise out of it? Some people claimed they lived in a post racial society, but Evie knew that was sadly far from the truth. She often wondered what strides they had truly made at all since the days of her grandmother's youth.

"Don't pay him no mind," Flora said. "I'd be hateful too if

my pants were that tight."

Evie desperately tried to stifle a laugh so as not to disturb the hush of the library. "You're too much, grammie," she whispered jokingly under her breath.

The library was truly grand on the inside. Multiple floors extended skyward, and the rich mahogany frames of the bookshelves were stocked with tens of thousands of books, both old and contemporary. The very air itself seemed to drip with history.

Evie was amazed that she had never taken the time to visit it before. This building had a charm and mystical elegance which the new library could never match. As she remembered herself, she searched the signs on the walls and found the sign pointing to the stairwell. Flora was also lost in a daze as she took in the sights of the beautiful building.

"I think it's this way," Evie said, pointing to the stairwell.

Flora nodded, and Evie saw that her eyes had become slightly misty. "It's just been so long."

Evie pulled her grandmother in for a hug and arm in arm they strolled across the marble floor towards the stairwell. The metal staircase stretched in a spiral towards the basement level. As they descended the tightly wound steps their footsteps sent a loud metallic echo in all directions.

The basement had a different energy entirely. It was populated by rows of shorter, squat bookshelves, and an ornately patterned maroon carpet. Where the bookshelves of the upper levels seemed to shimmer with immaculate varnish, these shelves were far more antiquated, and in a greater state of disrepair.

The tomes which lined the shelves seemed equally ancient, many tearing at the seams and crumbling under the weight of ages. Evie felt herself being overcome by a rapturous fascination. Some of these books must've been hundreds of years old. She could only imagine the wealth of stories and ancient knowledge contained within.

As they were leisurely strolling between some of shelves Hermes wordlessly appeared from around a corner.

"How did you get in here?" Evie asked suspiciously.

I HAVE MY WAYS. NOW, ANSWER ME THIS. ARE WE ALONE DOWN HERE?

"I think so. I didn't see anyone on our way down," Evie replied.

GOOD. FOLLOW ME.

Evie softly grabbed Flora, who was blissfully browsing the books, by the arm to follow Hermes. The black cat led them towards the stone wall on the far side of the room. Against the wall stood an enormous mirror. Evie could tell by its weathered wooden frame that it was very old, yet curiously the perfectly reflective glass was free of any dust or blemishes whatsoever.

In the reflection they made quite the trio: Flora, in one of her vibrant flowing summer dresses, her luscious silver locks flowing far down her back, Evie with her flared jeans and cosy sweater, her rich dark hair unbound by its usual scrunchie, and Hermes with his glistening black sheen.

WE DO LOOK PRETTY GOOD.

"Hey, that's intrusive!" Evie said.

WELL, YOU'RE JUST GOING TO HAVE TO LEARN TO GUARD YOUR THOUGHTS BETTER.

"Why are we standing in front of a mirror anyway?" Evie asked.

THIS IS MORE THAN IT APPEARS. LISTEN CLOSELY AND REPEAT AFTER ME. THE WORDS MUST BE UTTERED ALOUD.

"Okay," Evie replied, focussing her attention.

HAEC PORTA LUCIS ABSOLVISTI.

"Haec porta... lucis... absolvisti," Evie repeated aloud.

A shimmer of light ran across the mirror, followed by a sound, a high pitched, glassy vibration. The mirror swung inwards, revealing a flight of stone steps lit by torches on the walls. Flora gasped in audible excitement and Evie was in stunned silence.

COME ALONG. Hermes gracefully hopped down the steps.

When all three of them were inside, the mirror sealed shut behind them. Expecting to be able to see through the glass to the library, Evie was shocked to see that the way they had come had resealed behind them and returned to stone.

"What does it mean?" she asked Hermes as they descended.

MAY THIS GATE UNBIND TO LIGHT.

As they descended, Evie noticed Flora becoming increasingly lucid. She was taking in her surroundings quietly and deliberately, and her eyes carried a resolve which Evie had not seen in years. Eventually, they came to an abrupt halt as the stairway ended in front of a massive ornate circular brass panel, rimmed by an enormous, lifelike snake coming full circle to eat its own tail.

Within the snake was a hexagram, The Star of David. At its center, there were twelve unique arches, six facing upwards, complemented by six facing downward below them.

The adjacent torches cast an orange glow over the panel, making its meticulous details shimmer brilliantly. It looked old beyond time, and its engravings had all the hallmarks of designs Evie had seen which predated even the medieval era. She had never seen anything like it in her life. Each of the twelve archways were visually distinct from one another and the panel was also covered in some type of ancient pictographic script.

"Are those. . .?" Evie began.

HIEROGLYPHS? YES. Hermes replied with his usual cocky prescience.

"And is this. . .?"

ANOTHER DOOR. BUT THIS ONE OPENS ONLY TO THOSE WHO ARE MARKED.

Without warning, Flora stepped forward and placed her hand on the center of the panel.

"Grammie, what are you—"

Before Evie could finish her sentence, her words caught in her throat as the panel began to vibrate. Evie watched in disbelief as the brass snake began to writhe as if it were alive, its tail slowly beginning to recoil from its open mouth, receding to the base of the panel. When the tail had fully receded, the snake's head began to do the same, until it was coiled completely at the base, becoming motionless once more.

The panel split in two, each side sliding gently into two hollowed out spaces on the sides of the cobblestone walls, revealing yet more hallway leading to what looked like a chamber.

Evie spoke in a hush to Flora as they followed along behind the soft padding of Hermes's paws on the hard stone. "Grammie, how did you do that?"

"I don't quite know," Flora replied. "But I'm starting to remember. I know this place."

Hermes led them to the center of the chamber, where he sat and waited. Evie noted that etched into the solid stone floor was a an enormous golden tetrahedron of seeming mathematical precision. Above them, the room was ringed by a raised stone rampart.

Evie noticed that there were five different entrances

placed opposite to one another around the rampart.

Wait here. The council will soon assemble.

Before Evie could voice her protests, Hermes quickly disappeared down a nearby dark corridor and left them standing awkwardly in the center of the tetrahedron.

Evie felt exposed and could not mask her rising panic. This felt just like one of those ritual sacrifice scenes from a horror movie. But none of that stuff was actually real, right? Her experiences over the past two days lead her to believe otherwise.

*Oh god. Are we really about to be sacrificed by a talking cat?*

She clung tightly to Flora, who remained surprisingly calm.

"Hush child," Flora soothed. "We have nothing to fear here." Though she tried to share her grandmother's sentiment she just could not manage to shake the feeling of impending doom.

A trumpet sounded, and one by one torches spontaneously burst into fiery life in each of the five entrances to the rampart above them. Three hooded figures began to emerge from the darkness at four of the entrances, Hermes emerging from a fourth. Their cloaks were golden and bore the same design as the brass door they had encountered on their way in. Their features were hidden completely by their clothing, and as they each took their place on the pulpits, it was the one directly in front of Evie and Flora who spoke first. She had a commanding female voice which echoed throughout the stone chamber.

"As the head of this council, I declare this meeting, commenced." She took off her hood to reveal her face. Her hair hung in tight braids down well past her shoulders and her rich ebony skin seemed to glisten in the torchlight. Evie supposed she was middle aged, and her features were stern, but beautiful. She seemed to radiate grace and her very presence commanded immediate respect.

"Our brother, Hermes, has requested that we convene this council at utmost urgency. Standing before us are two humans. Hermes seems convinced that the younger of them is one of the children of the prophecy." A dull murmur resounded through the room as the council reacted to this news. For the first time, the woman addressing them cast her gaze on Flora and Evie. Almost immediately, her eyes widened with disbelief.

"Hestia?" Her voice was breathy, her sternness dissipating.

"Athena!" Flora shouted with joy, her voice trembling with emotion.

Before Evie and Flora could react, Athena left her podium and scrambled down the stairs to meet them, weeping as she embraced Flora tightly.

"Oh, my sister," she cried. "It has been so long. Where have you been? We never stopped searching for you. For years we have waited, keeping your seat on the council vacant, hoping vainly for your return."

Flora was also crying, long streams of tears flowing down her smiling face as she joked back sobs. "I. . . forgot somehow. I couldn't find my way back."

Athena gave her a sympathetic look, speaking softly. "This world makes fools of us all, sister. What matters is you're here now."

Athena began, turning to addressing the room. "Honored council. Today is a joyous day. One of our own has returned to us, to take her rightful place once more. The eldest and wisest amongst us. Hestia, our guardian of home and hearth, an exemplary vision of beauty and kindness."

The room erupted in cheers and Evie watched as one by one the council members removed their robes, smiling as they bestowed their blessings. She did her best not to stare but she was utterly awestruck. On the podium to their left stood what looked like a creature with the qualities of both a goat and a man. Tremendous horns, like those of a ram, spiralled from his curly hair and as he clapped his hands his furry goatee shook softly.

On the podium to their left stood a being who was almost luminous in her beauty. She was far taller and more slender than any human Evie had ever seen, and her fingers were much longer and her skin seemed to glow. Perfectly straight auburn hair draped down her shoulders like the finest silk and when she smiled Evie wanted to cry, though she didn't know why.

While both had characteristics of a human, they were clearly not human and were unlike anyone or anything she had ever seen in her life.

Evie could no longer hide her abject amazement. Had she walked into a dream? Maybe she was still dreaming from the night of the party. Maybe she had never woken up.

Discretely she pushed her right index finger into the palm of her left hand, a common trick known as a 'reality test,' which one could employ to gauge whether they were dreaming. If this were a dream, her finger would pass straight through her hand. When it failed to do so, even more questions were raised in Evie's mind. How could this be possible?

I ALREADY TOLD YOU THIS WASN'T A DREAM. Hermes teased from on high. THIS IS AS REAL AS IT GETS.

When Athena addressed her, it briefly snapped her back to reality. "And is this your daughter?" she asked Flora warmly.

"Granddaughter," Flora said proudly. "She's the reason we're here today."

"What is your name?" Athena asked.

"Eve," she replied.

At the mention of her name, Athena's expression instantly grew more serious, as if it had triggered something deep within her mind.

"Interesting," Athena finally said, casting a long thoughtful gaze at Evie. "Well, Eve. I am honored." She extended her hand and bowed. "Your grandmother honors us all."

Evie shook her hand and bowed awkwardly in turn.

"Come," Athena said, smiling. "Let us make for my study. We have much to discuss."

Athena's study was as opulent as one might expect for the leader of an underground magical society. She bade them to sit at her large, moon shaped desk as she set about making some tea.

As Flora and Athena busily chatted over the freshly brewed tea, catching up on ten years worth of life apart, Evie took some time to take in her surroundings.

There seemed to be an extraordinary amount of gold all throughout the room; everything was either gold plated or made from gold, and golden ornaments and arcane instruments of all shapes and sizes were scattered throughout the hemispheric space.

Her shelves were lined with books great and small, many of them covered in scripts and languages Evie had never laid eyes on before.

The room was lit from the ceiling by a large crystal chandelier which seemed to oscillate incessantly of its own accord, causing the crystals to diffract beams of golden light beautifully throughout the space.

In the corner of room sat a chameleon on a small branch

in its own enclosure. It too, was golden, despite being very much alive. Evie had never known there to be a species of golden chameleon, and even its scales seemed to have a metallic sparkle.

Surely it can't be made of actual gold. As if reading her mind, the chameleon suddenly turned its head to face her with one of its beady eyes, rotating quizzically on its own axis as it studied her. After a few moments, its scales began to shimmer, and a vibration ran across its surface. Evie then watched in disbelief as instead of changing colour, the chameleon changed its very form, into a golden hummingbird which then fluttered across the room and landed gracefully on Athena's shoulder. She gave a wry smile as she met Evie's astonished gaze.

"Transmutation," she said. "One of the key tenets of alchemy. And, ironically, even modern science. Energy cannot be created nor destroyed. It may only change form. It's merely a matter of finding the right triggers." As she explained, the hummingbird flapped gently back to its perch, where it promptly transformed into a large golden snail.

Flora was overcome with emotion once more. "I'm truly sorry," she said to Athena. "Everything seems so clear now, it's like a fog has been lifted from my mind."

"It's likely the work of the enchantments we have placed upon the fortress here. They actively cleanse and undo the nefarious mental afflictions of the modern world. The ongoing mechanization of our daily lives poses an increasingly dire threat to our very health and wellbeing, Hestia. Anyone's mind would buckle under such stress. I try to be here as often as I can, but at times it is hard to disentangle from the world up there and all its attachments."

*Says the lady with the golden office,* Evie thought. Privately.

"So, you don't all live down here?" Evie asked.

"No, child," Athena replied. "Each of us on the council lives a double life. A human life, and a magical life. Aphrodite and Pan, the elf and the satyr you saw in the council chamber, must even enact constant charms to maintain their human disguises on the surface, at great personal and spiritual cost. The secrecy of our order is paramount. Any time magic is discovered, the puny Neanderthal brains of men are quick to stamp it out.

"Thus, we adopt code names, identities, and perform our duties for the order here in secret. We each chose a name from the Greek pantheon, an alias to aid us in our work. Your grandmother chose Hestia, the goddess of hearth and home." She smiled at Flora, who smiled back.

"And what work is it that you do?" Evie asked directly.

A brief stillness fell over the room as Athena considered her next words. "We are the current incarnation of The Watchers, one of the oldest magical orders in existence. Our timeline stretches back tens of millennia. It is we who guard The Gates of Matter, awaiting the fulfillment of the prophecy."

Athena's answer only seemed to raise a plethora of additional questions in Evie's mind.

"What are the Gates of Matter?"

Athena paused for a moment, as if considering whether or not she should divulge the information at all.

"What I'm about to tell you is considered, by some, to be forbidden knowledge. Therefore, you must first promise to me that you will not utter a word of it to a soul outside of these walls. If you do, the consequences could be dire for us all." Athena cast Evie a serious, soul piercing look.

"I promise."

"Then the oath is bound," Athena said ceremoniously. "To understand the Gates, you must first understand the mechanism through which they act.

"It is said that there are only two forces in the universe. Love and fear. Cultures, religions, and philosophies the world over echo this truth. Love and Fear form the bedrock of the instincts, emotions, and actions of all intelligent life. But Love and Fear are not merely abstract concepts devised by the human mind."

"They aren't?"

"No. We channel Love and Fear from their respective dimensions." There was a pause as Evie tried to wrap her head around just what it was Athena was trying to propose.

"Channel them?"

"Yes. Channel them," Athena said. "In this universe, there are infinite dimensions above and below our own. Earth exists at the midpoint between these dimensions. The two closest non-physical planes to our own physical reality here on earth are the dimensions of Love and Fear. At times, these dimensions overlap with our own. They are collectively fed by the weight of the subconscious dreams, hopes, fears, and nightmares of all sentient life. From these dimensions stem our angels, and our demons."

"But how could a god come from a dimension which we create? Isn't it supposed to be the other way around?" Evie asked.

"The snake eats itself," Athena said. "Creation, like time, is non-linear. We are both the creation and the creator, all at once. Thus, the insignia of The Watchers is an ouroboros, a snake devouring its own tail."

"Then what are the gates?" Evie asked.

"Long ago, when the first humans were emerging unto this world, the grand architect placed twelve gates at different locations across the globe.

"These gates act as doorways, or portals, to the dimensions of Love and Fear. Six lead to the plane of Love, and six lead to the plane of Fear."

Athena paused a moment before continuing. "In times past, there was free movement between the gates. Abstract concepts of Fear and Love were given material form and made manifest as they moved through the gates unto the earth. Entire races of magical beings, both peaceful and malevolent, made this earth their home, alongside humans and other animal species.

"Magicians of all races draw their powers from these gates. Humans represent the gambit, a test by the creator. We are neither made entirely from Love or Fear, but a mixture of both. Our test is to see which force we will ultimately choose to serve."

Evie was stunned to silence as she listened. This sounded like the plot out of some fantastical movie, not reality. At the same time, despite the protests of her rational mind, so much of what she said made sense. It explained the torturous dichotomy deeply ingrained within the human psyche which Evie herself had witnessed in her studies of psychology, and indeed in her own life. It also explained the mythical creatures she had begun to encounter.

*Magic. Real magic.*

"But wait," Evie said. "Why then have I never encountered any of this up until a couple days ago? Where are all these magical races you speak of? Why does no one up there seem to know about this?"

Athena: "A thousand years ago, after a great magical war and a cataclysmic event, the Gates were sealed shut. The magical beings of both light and darkness, which coexisted with us, were suddenly all but cut off from their source of power. Imagine trying to live in a world with only a fraction of our current oxygen or sunlight and perhaps you may come close to comprehending how crippling that blow was. Only the most adept of beings were able to maintain and continue to siphon their powers from the non–physical planes.

"The rest faced an increasingly stupid and warlike species of humans, great swathes of whom were united under monotheistic dogma, a single truth which demonised all else. Entire races were persecuted and wiped out by frightened and violent humans, brainwashed by corrupt religious leaders who used the plundered wealth of magical kingdoms to line their own accursed pockets.

"Now, the few that remain do so in hiding, changing and adapting their forms to blend into a world caught in the clutches of human dominance. A world on the brink of collapse."

Athena took a deep breath. "However, make no mistake, our thoughts, ideas, and emotions continue to feed these planes. The collective suffering of the ever swelling numbers of mankind has created an imbalance between the planes.

"The plane of Fear grows distended and unstable, like some unfathomably volatile tumor, gnawing at the edges of our reality. It is constantly growing from the sorrow and uncertainty we inflict upon each other. Tears are beginning to appear in our reality. Beings of Fear made flesh are finding their way into this world once more. I understand you have even encountered one such creature already."

The mere mention of it sent a shudder through Evie's whole body. That unspeakable horror; it had come so close to killing her. If it had not been for that stag, she was sure she would not be sitting at the table at that very moment.

"Then what can we do?" Evie asked.

"Hopefully, that's where you come in," Athena replied.

"Me?" Evie asked in exasperation.

Flora spoke up. "Athena. . . Surely you don't think. . ." She trailed off.

"As of yet, it remains to be seen," Athena cut in assertively.

"What remains to be seen?" Evie asked.

"If you are the one we have been waiting for," Athena replied. "A prophecy concerns the end of days, or an end to the cycle we find ourselves in. It has been passed down across the millennia but roughly transcribes to: *when banished lovers join again, this world shall come to meet its end.*"

"What on earth does that mean?" Evie asked.

"It refers to the archetypal first lovers. The first two human beings. Adam and Eve. Every millennium, they reincarnate. It is written that when the reincarnations of the first two humans join again, it will bring about the end of the world, and usher in a new one. Their decision to partake of the fruit of knowledge marked the beginning of human history and set our species on its present path. Once again, they will reunite to see the path through to completion."

"And you think that's me? Just because my name is Eve?"

There was a brief tense silence in the room before all three women burst into laughter. "I'll admit, when you say it like that it does sound rather farfetched," Athena said. "But that is why you must be tested."

"Tested how?"

"The chosen champions of Love and Fear have latent magical abilities, which far exceed that of any normal being. We will seek to gauge what gifts you may have."

The pale light of evening fell from the small openings in the ceiling far above them, painting the usually vibrant cathedral a somber mix of gray as Athena led them to the middle of the dome.

Evie followed closely behind her, and she was in turn followed by Flora, and lastly by Hermes, who plodded along silently behind them. This area was off limits to library guests, as it was currently being renovated, and their footsteps on the polished marble floors sent thunderous echoes skittering throughout the ancient structure.

SHOES ARE SO POINTLESS, Hermes mused. THEY MAKE FAR TOO MUCH NOISE.

At the center of the room was a single black marble tile, large enough to stand on, embossed with a golden ouroboros. Athena beckoned her to stand on it, and there she addressed Evie.

"Here we will conduct our first test. Hermes claims to have witnessed your powers once already. Now we shall see the truth of it. None of us can help you in this task, for this is no regular form of magic. This ancient rite is governed not by incantations or rituals. It is magic in its most primal form, and it must come from within you."

Evie felt her pulse quicken. She was again reminded of the sheer lunacy and the gravity of the situation and her rational mind had all but given up its protests at this point.

"In a moment," Athena began, "all of us will stand back. You will remain in the center of the room, with your eyes closed. When I say so, I want you to channel your energy. Focus. Call out to the world. Place your full intention on attracting energy to yourself. It may help to imagine your spirit as a magnet, pulling in all energy around it. Focus on this idea and magnify it, amplify it, until you can feel nothing else. When you were attacked, you did this subconsciously. That much was easy, for your life was under threat. What we ask of you now is entirely different. Conscious activation. For many, this technique takes years to master."

Evie closed her eyes and breathed deeply, doing her best to mitigate the tremors she felt rising within herself. What was this feeling? Anxiety? No, it was different, as if something was building within her, waiting to be released.

"Okay." She breathed. "I'm ready."

Athena and the others wordlessly stepped back to the edges of the room. Again, the dome was filled with resonant echoes. Evie kept her eyes shut and focussed on her breathing, just as Athena had instructed. After what seemed like an eternity, she heard Athena's commanding voice break through the deafening silence in the room.

"Begin."

Evie immediately focussed her thoughts on attraction. *Attract. Attract. I am attracting. Come to me. Hear me.* Her own thoughts seemed to rattle unconvincingly through her mind, still deeply tinged by doubt.

She felt her ego resisting. *This isn't going to work. This is ridiculous. Give up.*

Hermes abruptly projected into her mind.

STOP THINKING. FEEL IT.

She nodded and renewed her concentration, a cold sweat breaking out on her forehead.

She began to visualise energy flowing towards her, it was almost involuntary at first but soon she could actually feel it: a new sensation, somewhere between wind and electricity, rushing from all directions towards her core. She felt herself buckling under the weight of it. It was too much. Too much energy.

*I won't be able to control it at this rate.* Just as soon as the thought entered her mind, the sensation began to taper off.

"It's not working!" she cried in frustration.

"Then let it work," Athena sternly replied. "Now is not the time for fear. Focus on that which you love."

Her mind was immediately flooded by flashes, images, memories, of Flora, and the now distant dreams of her parents walking her through the park as a child, or dancing to music in the living room. She felt her eyes brim with tears as her heart began to glow. Warm energy snaked its way from her chest through her entire body like white hot lightning bolts of pure joy. Her tears began to flow freely as waves of powerful goose bumps washed over her. She laughed despite herself, and that's when it happened.

She was hit by what felt like a beam of light, which shot straight down from the sky and passed through the crown of her head and down her spine. Every binding, every block which had ever been placed upon her was instantly blast open and erased and she let out an involuntary scream from the sheer pleasure of it. Never in her life had she felt a sensation which even approached that single moment. Instantly, her previous attempts at magnetism quadrupled and she could feel energy swirling violently around her like some arcane vortex.

She heard a flurry of flapping wings pouring in from above her. She heard a collective gasp from Flora and Athena as they watched on in awe.

Her eyes opened and she saw.

Pigeons. Thousands of them were pouring in through the upper windows of the dome to form a billowing tornado with her at the center. Their flight pattern matched exactly the energetic vortex which she could picture clearly in her mind's eye.

Evie was exalted, powerful on a level which she had never

even conceived. In the small pockets of empty space which briefly appeared in the swarm, she caught the expression on Athena's face. It was one of amazement, tinged perhaps with the slightest amount of fear. Flora simply beamed with pride, her own eyes awash with tears.

THAT'S ENOUGH NOW, Hermes projected warmly. I THINK YOU'VE MADE YOUR POINT. WELL DONE. She could feel the pride in his thoughts.

She focussed on reversing the flow of her energy, and the vortex soon dissipated. The pigeons flew back out of the various windows just as quickly as they had appeared, until she was again alone in the center of the room. As the adrenaline tapered off, she promptly collapsed and the others rushed to her side.

"Evie!" Flora shouted. "Are you okay, baby? Can you hear me?" Both she and Athena helped her to sit up as they sat by her side. Evie was dazed, and she felt extremely weak.

"I'm fine," Evie began shakily. "I just had to lie down. I don't know what happened."

"It's to be expected," Athena said. "Some mages have even been known to fall into a coma upon their activation. Though this is no normal activation, Evie, for you are a child of The Prophecy." Evie raised her head to meet Athena's gaze and could see the solemness in her eyes. "Hermes, it is as you suspected. She possesses the mark of Gaia. Dominion over the natural world and its creatures."

Hermes purred as he nuzzled against her leg.

I KNEW I WAS RIGHT ABOUT YOU.

"But what does this mean?" Evie asked as she gently stroked Hermes, her strength already returning.

Athena sighed deeply. "It means that the final days of the prophecy are at hand, and the end of the world is upon us."

# CHAPTER 10

# CRUELTY

## *1031 A.D.*

Straw. Jagged, painful, pressing into her face. The first sensation she felt as she awoke. Outside, she heard rushed footsteps, mens voices shouting.

Initially, in the inky darkness, she had no idea where she was. Her hands and feet were bound, and her mouth was gagged, too. She quickly felt panic rising from within her and tried to scream but her voice was muffled.

*It's no use. Calm yourself, Morgana.*

She was at once hit by the crushing remembrance of what had brought her to this point. Her secret. Father. He had seen. She felt tears well in her eyes as shock began to set in. As her eyes adjusted to the darkness she realised where she was. The barn, at the back of the house, where the animals slept. Her father must have bound her and left her there. More than fear, she felt shame, and in the darkness, she wept.

After some time, she heard a jangling of chains as the barn

door was unlocked. She felt her heart begin to race in dreadful anticipation. As the old wooden doors swung open, she had to shield her eyes as she was at once blinded by the harsh light. She had no idea what the hour was, but it was definitely daytime. Expecting to see her father, she was shocked when two men she did not recognize entered the barn house. As they approached her, she instinctively recoiled in terror. Strangely enough, they unbound her legs and hoisted her roughly to her feet.

"Rise, witch," one of them said contemptuously. They were men-at-arms, members of the city guard. She tried to speak but her mouth was still gagged, all she could utter were mournful groans as they cruelly prodded her forwards with the butts of their halberds.

In the courtyard, she searched vainly for any sign of her parents, but it was deserted. The guards did not give her enough time to look as they violently shoved her forwards, pushing her off balance and she fell face first into the mud.

Their vicious laughter rang in her ears as she tried her best to fight back tears. "To your feet," one of them barked. She turned to face him and pleaded with her eyes, to leave her some form of dignity, some humanity, but his own eyes spoke nothing but hatred.

She staggered unsteadily to her feet, her nightgown and face now caked with sticky mud. They marched her out of her family home and on to the cobblestone streets towards the town center.

The streets were oddly empty, given the sun was only just past its peak, they should have been aflutter with commotion. With each step she took towards the center, the dread inside of her grew.

As they drew closer some of the town center, denizens

appeared at the windows: watching her, laughing, jeering. Some of them began to pelt her with rotten fruit, and rocks, thrown with brutal precision, battering her, as blood began to join the filth which now caked her body. There were children, too, with their mothers, many of whom she even recognized, people whom she had once bought wares from, now acting as devilish tormentors.

*Surely, this is a nightmare. Yes, that's it, I must be dreaming.* Try though she might, this was a nightmare from which she could not wake. This was reality.

As they drew closer, the ranks of the hecklers swelled. Soon, they had a cautions entourage of townsfolk following behind them, each pushing the other to new heights of cruelty, testing how much they could get away with.

When she finally reached the town center, her heart dropped: what looked to be the entire population of Bluffton had assembled. It was a raucous, even festive atmosphere. In the very middle of the square, where the actors' troop had performed not a week before, now stood a single wooden pyre, beset on all sides by logs and kindling.

She knew what this was. A cleansing. At once, her stomach dropped and she vomited what little remained inside of her from the day before.

When the crowd saw her, a hush briefly fell over them, before they erupted into a terrible chorus of shouts and jeers, pelting her once more with all manner of stones, fruit, and other unsightly viscera. On one hand she knew the price for witchcraft, but she was still dumbfounded by the sheer malice these people were showing.

They took pleasure in it, the debasement of one of their own. But she was no witch. She was one of them. She had only ever used her powers to help. She was a healer after all. So why?

*Why?*

A terrible dread enveloped her soul, and she began to almost disassociate her mind from the experience. It was surreal in a way. How could it have come to this? As they drew closer to the pyre her heart jumped as she saw her mother nearby, badly beaten and shackled into a wooden stock.

As Morgana passed her, she raised her swollen, bloodied head to see her daughter and let out a mournful, animalistic wail. It was a terrible sound, as if you could hear her heart breaking in that very moment. She was swiftly and brutally butted by one of the guards and she fell back into her semi–comatose stupor.

Morgana tried to scream, as tears once again poured from eyes. Her whole body shook, and she collapsed at the foot of her battered mother. Ingrid again feebly raised her head to meet her daughter's gaze. In that moment, amidst the circus of cruelty the world seemed to quieten as her mother whispered softly to her.

"Morgana. . . I'm so, so sorry, my child. Mama loves you."

She sobbed, blood oozing from her fractured mouth. Before Morgana could even process moment, the world swung into action once again.

The guards hoisted Morgana to her feet, and she was again lambasted by the storm of hatred from the crowd. When they finally reached the pyre, they briefly unbound her hands before violently pulling her arms behind her and fastening them securely to the wooden pole. Standing there, atop the pyre, she felt the full horror of the scene.

The town square was awash with hundreds of malicious faces, some frightened, some laughing, and very few were solemn, empathetic even, though they were just as complicit in her torture. In that moment, her heart broke, as if a shard of glass inside her, she tangibly felt it shatter in her chest. Her fear was replaced by numbness, and her eyes glazed over in resignation. This was how she would meet her end.

A sudden hush again fell over the crowd. The town cleric had appeared by the foot of the pyre. His spotless white satin robes did little to mask the sweat which coated his bloated, flushed, overfed body. As he spoke, his pompous cadence carried across the square.

"Dearest townsfolk," he began, the perspiration dripping from his bald head. "I come before you today, not as your cleric, but as your friend. Alas, I am a friend who bears ill news. We have a witch in our midst." His words caused a gasp to collectively utter through the square, as if his testimony was somehow the final word on the matter.

"A wolf in sheep's clothing," he continued. "This witch has taken the guise of a young woman, a virgin even. The fallen one has a sick sense of humor, dear lambs. And like any good sheppard, as a cleric of The One and Only Truth, it is my duty to protect my flock from such wanton evil."

Morgana stiffly turned her head to face the cleric. His eyes were smiling as he addressed them, and he seemed exalted, as if he took much joy in the task. "We all know how best to purge such filth. With fire," he said, and a roar of agreement went up from the crowd. "But this task does not fall to me. No. It falls to one of the bravest amongst us, the very man who discovered this witch to begin with. John Eldritch."

The mention of her father's name snapped her out of her trancelike resignation. Again, her heart started to race.

*Surely not. Father will save me from them.*

Her father emerged slowly from the crowd and took his place by the cleric's side. The cleric spoke: "I bid you to listen to his honest testimony, dear lambs. For he is nothing if not brave. A true exemplar for the pillars of The One Truth."

Her father then addressed the hushed crowd. "Dear brothers and sisters," he began shakily. "I am a trusted member of this community. You all know me, and I have treated your ails for many years. I come to you today as a man deceived, dear family. Ensnared by the traps of the fallen one. I believed I had a daughter, when, in fact, I was sheltering the devil himself. I had my suspicions, but I had to be sure. I admit I was naïve. I thought her gifted in the healing art. But after all, what could a woman possibly know about matters of the body?"

There was a murmur of agreement which slithered through the crowd as he paused. Morgana could not believe her ears. Gone was her numbness, and her brief shred of hope. It was replaced by a new, terrible sensation, one she had never felt.

Rage.

It burned inside of her like hot coals, and her body shuddered under its awful weight. Her chest heaved, but it was not from sobbing, but her body succumbing to unbridled hatred. She gritted her teeth painfully as she bit down hard on the cloth gag in her mouth. He betrayed her. He betrayed them both.

"I now see that her mother, once my wife, has been marked by the dark one. A sickening ploy to test my faith. Her womb begot this foul abomination, and she too must pay," he said fanatically. "Brothers and sisters, let there be doubt in your minds after this day that I am a man of God!"

As he said this, he dipped a nearby torch in pitch and lit it from a hanging lantern, making sure to show it to the crowd. He then turned to face her, and his eyes met her own for the first time, the eyes of his daughter, whom he had nursed from an infant. Within them she saw the same madness she had seen the previous night.

It was futile. Her father was gone. Or perhaps this was simply who he was all along, under his thin veneer of a personality.

As he stepped closer to her, time seemed to slow, as it had that day many moons ago when she encountered the luminescent stranger by the river. This time however, the ripple in the air was coming from within her, and it burned. She felt nothing but hatred.

As this feeling overtook her once more, she closed her eyes and could feel dark tendrils spreading from her heart, filling her blood with fire.

She felt energy rushing to her from all directions, as if the void in her chest was absorbing the world around it. It coursed through her and she screamed as she was inundated by immense, unfathomable power.

In an instant, her eyes flicked open. Her gag turned to ash in her mouth and she spit it out, allowing her to breathe freely once more. The mud which caked her body crackled and turned to dust. Screams went up from the crowd and her father hastily lunged forward with the torch. The flame was mere inches from the tinder at her feet when she let out an immense bellow which echoed deafeningly across the square like thunder.

“No!” A shockwave burst forth from the pyre which knocked most of the townsfolk to the ground and quickly extinguished the torch.

As she focussed her gaze on her father, she could feel this new power coursing through her. He was rooted in place, as if unable to move, unable to break his own gaze away. His extinguished torch smoked uselessly, still held aloft by his quivering arm, his body no longer his own, bound to her will.

She could feel every bone, every organ, every drop of blood inside him, though she was not even touching him. This was far beyond anything she had ever felt before. She could see the fear in his eyes, but now he was mute, only able to speak if she willed it.

In that instant, she poured her fury into him, all her burning rage. He began to scream horrifically as his blood boiled in his veins and poured forth like hot oil from every orifice he had, melting his skin as it did so. She effortlessly crushed all his bones in before finally letting his body drop to the floor in a sizzling, crumpled, heap. His eye sockets were left empty and gaping.

The square erupted into chaos as the townsfolk stampeded in all directions as this was not a part of their plan. The cleric, who had been knocked to the ground and dazed by the shock-wave, was attempting to sneak away from the pyre on hands and feet, but he did not escape her gaze.

As she fixed her attention upon him, she froze him in place, casting her sight into his body. She twisted his ribcage back upon itself and he let out a shrill shriek as his ribs bloodily burst forth from his back like perverse wings. As his lifeless corpse dropped to the ground, no one dared approach the pyre. They had seen the price to pay for their cruelty and so they fled, stomping on and crushing one another in their haste to escape.

Amidst the chaos, she felt a pair of hands grab her bound arms from behind. Instinctively, she cast her focus into their body, ready to retaliate, only to discover she recognized this body. It was Mathias, instantly subsiding her fury. He was unbinding her and freeing her from the pyre.

When he had done so, she collapsed, and he caught her before she hit the ground. The hateful energy had subsided, leaving her weak and in shock once more.

When her senses returned, he was speaking to her very rapidly, his voice at first distant before becoming clearer. "Morgana, Morgana! Can you hear me? You have to run, now." His gentle face was awash with worry as he cradled her in his arms. Seeing him roused her from her daze and she sprang to her feet. "There's no time, Morgana. The town is in disarray now but soon the men will rally. Already they will have sent runners to the nearby settlements for reinforcements. You won't be able to fight them all." His voice was assertive, but she could see the urgency in his eyes.

"You. . . you don't fear me?" she asked him, tentatively.

"I could never," he replied softly. "Nor could I forgive them for what they did to you and your mother."

*Mother.*

"Mother!" She yelled aloud, rushing to the wooden stock where her mother was still bound. Her head was facing the ground, motionless, as blood dripped into the small pool which had formed at the base. The savage beating had left her barely recognizable. Morgana swiftly cast herself into her mother's body, but it was cold, lifeless. She tried in vain to pour her energy in, but she was all but spent.

"It's no use," Mathias said gently from behind her. She stubbornly tried on, becoming increasingly hysterical as she did so, placing her hands on her mother's matted bloody scalp, trying anything, everything she could.

He was right. She was dead.

Morgana staggered and let out another deafening bellow which echoed across the town like a thunderclap. She then fell to her knees, quivering, sobbing uncontrollably.

Mathias bent down and embraced her. "I'm so sorry," he

whispered. “I feel as though I am the cause of this.” His voice broke as his tears met her own. “But that is why I cannot let you die here. I know of many ways to escape this town. Master Errol and I will see to your mother’s burial.”

He helped her up from the cold stones and she looked upon to his kind face, golden in the afternoon sun, now glistening with tears of his own. Even in this state, he was the most beautiful thing she had ever seen. The one person who hadn’t abandoned her.

Her shattered heart ached once more, and she leaned in to softly place a kiss upon his lips. They were warm and wet, salty from his tears. “Thank you,” she said softly.

He was blushing and seemed momentarily dazed. “Quickly,” he said, coming to his senses. “We haven’t the time.”

It was pitch black inside the tunnel, save for the warm glow of the torch Mathias carried in his right hand. In his left hand, he tightly clasped her own as they stalked further into the darkness. The flicker of the flame as they walked seemed to make the walls jitter unnaturally.

Water occasionally dripped onto her head from the thick layer of rock above them, making Morgana wince involuntarily each time. Her mind was beset by horrors. Each distant echo, each unfamiliar shadow, taunting her like phantoms with the promise of yet more pain. She was fragile, and utterly exhausted, but the fear of death propelled her onwards.

This tunnel, Mathias had said, was dug long ago, when some of the earliest settlers of this area sought their riches beneath the earth. It opened into the basement of an old ruin, long since forgotten in the plain fields outside Bluffton. As far as he knew, Mathias was the only one who had any knowledge of the tunnel.

The air was stagnant and cold and carried with it the faint scent of decay, alike to a tomb. They were silent save for the shuffling of her sandals upon the bare earth. Mathias had given her his own and, walked barefoot.

Finally, he spoke. "When we reach the ruin, it shall be close to sunset, but not quite. The plains offer little shelter, and you could be easily spotted. You must move quickly. I've no doubt the roads are rife with men at arms and religious zealots. They will be hunting you." He paused, as if struck by the grim reality of his own words. "You must make for The Blackwood."

Morgana's stomach dropped. The Blackwood was the name of a large forest near the town, so named because of its dense canopy which light itself could not breach. It began beyond the plains and stretched for miles in all directions. Other, smaller woods had long since been cleared for lumber, but the Blackwood remained untouched.

It was said to be cursed. Children and adults alike had disappeared into its inky depths, never to be seen again, and those that did return were often gravely wounded, their bodies covered in strange symbols and their minds all but shattered as they babbled of the horrors they had seen.

"The Blackwood," Morgana breathed, "I–I cannot. Please, Mathias. I face certain death in there."

"No," Mathias countered, "certain death is what you face if you stay here. Or walking the road. In there, you have a chance. They will not follow you. They dare not."

"And what will become of me, Mathias?" She sobbed. "Am I to be food for the monsters which lurk there? Or will I simply starve?"

"You will survive," he said, squeezing her hand tighter as his voice began to shake with emotion. "You must."

Soon they could make out a faint light coming from the end of the tunnel. As they drew closer, he extinguished his torch, and Morgana briefly lost her footing as her eyes adjusted to the darkness, a cruel reminder of how her day had begun, frightened and alone.

As that same despair threatened to swallow her once again, Mathias helped her to her feet and gently placed his arm around her. "Come on. It's just a little further," he whispered softly.

The tunnel ended in a small wooden door, and the orange rays of evening shone through the cracks in the grain like luminous shards, each ray illuminating the thick blanket of dust which permeated the air. Mathias began to tinker with the latch, but it was no use. Generations of neglect had all but sealed it shut with rust.

"Stand back."

Morgana quickly complied, taking a couple tentative steps backwards. She almost fell over in fright when Mathias suddenly took a running start and kicked the door with all his might by the latch. She could only partially make out his silhouette as it was criss-crossed by the orange light which seeped in through the cracks.

He let out a long sigh and wiped his brow before he again took a run up and threw all his weight behind the kick. This time, there was a loud crash, and much splintering of wood as the door flew off of its ancient hinges and tumbled to the ground in a flurry. Both of them winced as their eyes were assailed by the brilliant beams of sunset. Morgana was afraid to open her eyes, afraid of what she might see.

The world she knew was gone; it died the moment her father lit that torch.

As the dust settled, her ears detected the flapping of wings and the tell-tale cawing of angry crows, their sanctum disturbed by would-be human intruders.

She heard Mathias's voice, and felt his hand again reach for her own. "It's okay. You're safe." She slowly unclenched her eyes and took in the scene around her.

They were standing in the remains of what looked like an ancient stone building, a home, or a mill, perhaps. It was built into the side of a small mound, into which the tunnel descended. The walls had long since collapsed, and the mound conveniently hid the ruins from sight from the town walls to the south.

All around them lay the thickly cut stones which would have once served as the foundation of the building, now overgrown with bushes and leaves, reclaimed by nature once more. Ahead of them, almost obscured by the quickly setting sun, were the seemingly endless fields of corn and wheat which lay between them and The Blackwood, which loomed ominously on the horizon.

"You must move quickly," Mathias began. "Make for the fields and keep as low to the ground as you can. Until you reach the forest, you will be visible. Move fast, but don't run, that will only attract the attention. Once you're in the woods, you must focus on shelter. You can build a fire, yes?"

She shot him a look of disbelief.

"Okay," he said sheepishly. "Just checking."

Morgana gazed at the foreboding path ahead of her, and then back to Mathias. She needed not to utter a single word, for her silent plea was written all over her face.

*Please. Don't make me.*

Mathias's eyes brimmed with tears as he pulled her in to an embrace. "I'm so sorry, Morgana. The townsfolk failed you today. I. . . I failed you." He wept, hanging his head in shame. She gently pushed a finger to his lips and raised his head to meet her own. His hazel eyes seemed to sparkle in the sunlight, and the tears upon his cheeks glistened. She placed another long, soft kiss upon his lips, closing her eyes and savouring the feeling. She felt warm, safe, alive. What little heart she had left flickered faintly. She wanted to cry with him, but she found that she could not. There were no tears left.

When she finally pulled away, there was a pause, a mutual appreciation of one another.

"I love you," Mathias said suddenly, breaking the silence.

The words took her by surprise, even more so did her response as the same words came tumbling awkwardly out of her own mouth.

"I love you, too." She knew in that moment that it was true. This only made him weep more as he sobbed into her shoulder. She found herself gripped by a newfound determination. She would not die tonight, she had something to live for. Love.

"When all this is over, I will find you again," she whispered. "Will you wait for me?"

He looked up from her shoulder and stared deeply into her eyes. "I promise."

She embraced him tightly once more before she finally let go and strode towards the plains to meet her fate. She dared not look back, lest the mere sight of his sweet face crumble her resolve.

The stalks of wheat crunched loudly underfoot as Morgana made for The Blackwood.

The clear sky and setting sun had conspired to paint the fields a blistering orange. On any other day it would have been a beautiful sight, but today the fallen stalks may as well have been thorns, and the fields themselves burning embers, for they gave just as much comfort. Earthly comforts had long since forsaken her.

At present, her pace was somewhere between a walk and a run, and she dared not move any faster for fear of attracting suspicion. She could almost feel the eyes of the road on her back, boring into her, but she dared not look back; to look back was to perish. On the horizon, the wood loomed ever ominous. Frustratingly, it did not seem to be getting any closer, and the sun had all but set.

"Just a little further," she breathed aloud. "You're almost there." Her words were wooden placations at best and did little to satiate the mounting dread which swelled inside her. Intrusive thoughts bombarded her haggard mind.

*Closer to what? Death?* She did her best to shut them out, but their morose protests continued.

She noticed a figure approaching ahead of her, standing well clear of the wheat. Instinctively, she froze. Her mind raced with possibilities. Who could it be? A farmer? At this hour? No, it made no sense. By now the farmers had returned home for the day. Still, the silhouette stood and watched her. She could see that it was a man, judging by the ill–fitting clothes and the hat which she could make out.

The worst thing she could do, she devised, was to alter her course and turn around, and she certainly could not stay still. So it was that she stayed her course, striding confidently towards the man as she came up with a litany of excuses and potential explanations along the way.

As long as I act natural, I can make it.

Nonetheless, her heart began to pound as she drew closer to him. Strangely, he still did not move, merely mutely watching her approach with his arms outstretched. When she was within a dozen paces of him, she saw why. He was a scarecrow, filled with straw and held aloft by a flimsy pole.

Her relief was almost comical in its immediacy, and she let out a huge sigh as she stood before it. Its garments were tattered, and the linen was immensely faded from its time in the sun. Atop its left shoulder a crow cawed loudly at her, a trail of encrusted droppings dripping down from its perch. A faceless puppet.

She heard a noise approaching from the distance behind her, a dull rumble which she could also feel vibrating in the earth. Horses, approaching from the road.

She quickly resumed her brisk flight towards the wood, leaving the straw filled sentinel to his post once more. She did her best to look inconspicuous, but it was impossible. She stood clear above the wheat. It would only be through dumb luck that she wouldn't be seen.

By now she drew close to the forest. She took no comfort however, as its closeness only deepened her dread. The trees were gnarled and ancient, their ebony arms extended skyward like contorted fingers, as if clawing at the heavens themselves. A dense assortment of shrubs and vines hugged tightly to the bases of the trees, assuring that no light could reach the forest floor.

There was a reason The Blackwood was so named. She could clearly see the point where the wheat gave way to the woods, an accursed patch of open ground which no farmer dared to sow. The wheat patches which grew closest to this strip were malformed and diseased, as if the woods themselves had afflicted them.

As she once again quickened her pace, she heard a shrill male voice cry out in the distance behind her. "YOU THERE, HALT!" the voice yelled. She stiffly complied and shot a cursory glance back towards the road. It was a mistake. She saw three men on horseback, armed and lightly mailed slowly trotting towards her, flanked by a group of hunting dogs.

She looked again towards The Blackwood, it's inky depths now seeming almost welcoming, and she set off. She was sprinting as fast as her legs could carry her. Behind her, she heard the yells of the men as they kicked their horses into a gallop and the barks of the dogs as they bound towards her. She had never run so fast in her life. There was still a sizable distance between her and the men, but they were closing fast.

*I just have to make the tree line.*

The Blackwood stretched before her and seemed to widen like a horrific mouth waiting to swallow her whole. She soon reached the bare strip of earth which lay between the forest and the fields, the safety of the woods was only a few paces away. She could hear the padding of the dogs on the soil and then the heavy plodding of hooves. She could practically feel their breath on her neck.

Three more steps.

Two.

One.

She dived through a narrow gap between two trees and felt the peculiar sensation of a dog's jaw snapping shut in mid–air beside her, narrowly missing her ankle. On the other side, she collapsed on the forest floor amongst the bedrock of leaves and detritus. She felt the tremendous thud as the men slammed their horses uselessly into the iron like trunks of the trees on the other side and heard their muffled, exasperated shouts as their horses whinnied from the impact.

She quickly scrambled to her feet, expecting the hounds to give chase, but instead she heard them whining fearfully on the other side of the wood, pacing back and forth. The gaps between the trees were more than wide enough for the dogs to fit through but they simply refused to cross the threshold. The horses, too, were deeply disturbed, and she heard the men cursing as they struggled to control them.

Morgana felt a shift in the air. It was hard to place, but the feeling inside the wood was deeply foreboding, it was unlike any forest she had even been in. There was no humming of crickets or chirping of birds. Only silence.

Her heart thumped loudly in her ears and her breathless pants seemed to echo amongst the branches around her. Under the canopy it was dark, unnaturally dark. The light which snaked its way through the gaps in the trees was quickly swallowed before it could properly reach the forest floor.

She could scarcely see more than a few paces in front of her, even once her eyes had adjusted to the light. All she could see in any direction was a dark, formless abyss.

It felt more like a cave than a forest. A tomb. She continued to hear a commotion from the other side, their words were muffled and hard to discern, but as she laid her ear against the wood, eventually she was able to discern the conversation.

"No, Eudes, you cannot!" one of the voices insisted. "Those woods are cursed. Better you leave the witch to her fate. She's where she belongs now."

"Nonsense," a stronger voice countered dismissively. "She must be tried for her sins. It will be my hand which delivers her to this fate. It is god's will, and he will protect me." She heard the sound of the man dismounting from his horse and the scraping of steel as he drew his sword from its scabbard.

*My god. He means to follow me.*

She scrambled to her feet, this time dashing headlong into the darkness. She could faintly make out the silhouettes of the trees, just well enough to avoid running straight into them. She was lost, hopelessly slipping deeper into the void. The woods were silent, save for the anxious crunching of her footsteps upon the fallen leaves. She had to put as much distance between herself and this man as possible.

Before long, a golden light began to shine from behind her, its rays unwelcome and intrusive as they shone blasphemously between the gaps in the trees. He had lit a lantern and was carrying it.

She quickly pressed herself against the trunk of a nearby tree. She noticed for the first time just how pale these inner trees truly were, as if their bark had never seen light before. The man called arrogantly to her as he searched, sword drawn.

"Show yourself now, witch. It is only a matter of time before I find you. The longer I search the more you will suffer at my hands, I promise you that." His threats echoed emptily back to him, as if the trees themselves were mocking him in his own voice. It was not long before his bravado dissipated, as it too consumed by the pervasive hush. Eventually, he began to move in another direction and the light from his lantern began to fade as he moved further away.

Morgana took this chance to cover more ground. She did not know where she was going, but as long as it was the opposite direction to him, it would suffice. By now, the light of the full moon was peeking through the gaps in the canopy, blanketing the woods in an eerie pale glow.

After some time walking, the silence was abruptly pierced by the distant echo of a blood chilling scream. Her heart raced as she huddled in the exposed roots of a nearby tree, too frightened to move. Before long, the screaming came again.

It must have been him, her would-be captor. It was a dreadful sound, shrill and high pitched, a combination of fear and agony. Then, it quickly fell silent, and she heard the awful echoes of tearing flesh. She muffled her cries as best she could as shock once again set in.

It was real. Monsters truly did lurk in these woods.

She heard a cracking of branches and twigs as what sounded like a large animal stalked nearby. She could feel the weight of it as its steps shook the ground. How could it have snuck up on her? If it was that size, she should've been able to sense its approach.

She could not see it clearly due to the darkness of the woods, but she could vaguely make out its silhouette and tangibly feel its presence as it staked through the trees. She heard its labored breathing as it sniffed the various trunks.

It was searching for her.

She felt her stomach drop as fear overtook her once more. As if sensing this, the creature let out a deep, guttural moan and turned her way. No animal could make a noise like that. She pressed herself as tightly as she could into a ball and held her breath as it approached her. It was no use. She felt its warm saliva dripping onto her head as its foul breath stung her nostrils.

She turned and faced the creature, viewing it for the first time with her own eyes. Its body was grotesquely distended, larger than two horses combined, although it did not have feathers or fur, only pallid, leathery flesh. Its enormous head was almost bird like, and its gaping "beak" was filled with jagged, rancid teeth. Its eyes were soulless black orbs, glistening and hungry in the darkness. Strangest of all were its feet, three toed and webbed like that of a frog.

She screamed as she faced her death and the creature chittered awfully with excitement as it supped on her fear. As it was about to devour her, a light shone from behind them, but not the weak golden light of the lantern. It was a brilliant, blinding white light.

She winced instinctively and the creature let out a furious howl as it thundered back into the shadow. The light soon faded enough for Morgana to open her eyes. She carefully peered up from the safety of the roots to see the source.

It was the luminous being she had encountered by the river so many moons ago. She looked down upon Morgana once again, her alabaster face bearing the same wan smile as it had on that day. Her silk-like gown still seemed to ebb and flow of its own accord, and she exuded ghostly light from her very skin. She was beautiful, and terrifying.

"Who are you?" Morgana finally uttered.

The creature smiled, and then she spoke. "I have many names," she said. "Most are unpronounceable in your tongue." Her voice was breathtaking, unlike any Morgana had ever heard before. It sounded like a chorus of voices, all singing together harmony. "You may call me Miraneth."

"Do you. . . mean to kill me?" Morgana asked.

Miraneth chuckled, a beautiful sound which reminded Morgana of wind chimes and bubbling springs. "No, young one. I mean to set you free."

# CHAPTER II

# Omens

## *1033 A.D.*

The streets were silent and empty as Enoch strode through them. He was searching for something. Someone. Anyone.

"Master? Balus?" Only his own voice replied as it echoed back to him from the cold stone facades of the buildings.

Light snow fell from the oppressive sky, though curiously enough, it was not cold. A thick mist blanketed the town, and he could not see more than a few paces in front of him. The streets felt familiar, but alien at the same time. Though he did not know where he was going, his feet seemed to remember, and he found himself drawn inexorably forward.

Eventually, the cobbled street widened into a square as he reached a clearing. It must have been the center of the town. Wooden market stands lined the edges, though they looked long since abandoned. A large wooden pyre stood next to what looked like a raised stage. Around it lay heaped piles of snow. He could not shake the sense of foreboding he felt.

"Hello?" His voice carried around the square and sent a pair of startled crows skyward as they angrily squawked their protests. At least he was not alone.

He heard Adrax's voice whisper from behind him: "Enoch."

Frightened, he spun, only to find no one there, but a small figure huddled at the base of the pyre. They were looking up to it and murmuring, as if talking with someone. He had not noticed them sitting there a moment ago.

He called out and the figure immediately bowed its head in silence. Cautiously, Enoch shuffled forward. His instincts told him to run and yet his feet once again betrayed him. As he drew closer, he saw that the figure was an old woman, bundled in tattered rags and a motheaten shawl shrouded her eyes. Her matted grey hair hung almost to the ground. Only her mouth and hands were uncovered, and he could see that her ancient frail skin was deeply marked and wrinkled.

She remained motionless, her varicose lips expressionless as he approached. When he was a mere step from her, he finally plucked up the courage to speak.

"Excuse me," he fumbled, "I'm looking for my master, Master Adrax. Have you seen him?" The woman said nothing. The silence was maddening, and more unsettling than Enoch could bare.

As he turned to walk away her raspy voice uttered a single word: "Sit." He looked around the square, and then again at the woman, before hesitantly sitting across from her in front of the pyre. It seemed hours before the woman finally spoke again.

"What do you know of pain, Enoch?" she croaked.

Enoch took a moment to consider the question. "I have been fortunate enough to know little."

Her lips parted to reveal brown, rotten teeth as she smiled.

"An honest answer. How rare," she said. "Pain is the currency of life, my child. Humans never fail to remind each other of that. They trade pain more easily than coin. I myself have incurred more pain than any other."

"I'm sorry," Enoch said softly.

"You needn't be. It made me what I am."

"And what are you?" he asked.

She chuckled softly then, a raspy, torturous sound. "I am many things."

"Where are we?" Enoch asked.

"The site of a birth, and a massacre. A stage for much pain."

"Where is everyone?"

"Dead," she replied. "Their bodies line the streets. Food for crows now."

"I didn't see anyone."

"Look again."

Enoch turned his head and gasped as he was struck by sheer revulsion and terror. All around them, hundreds of corpses in various states of decay littered the square. There were men, women, and children amongst them. Some of their wounds were so horrific that the bodies were unrecognizable. Limbs, entrails, and bones covered the cobblestone in a thick crimson sludge as swarms of noisy crows feasted on the gore.

Enoch quickly shut his eyes tightly as he gasped for breath. The scene was too much for him to bear. The cawing of crows abruptly ceased, and he cautiously opened his eyes. Again, it was just him and the old woman. The square was once again white with snow.

"What happened to them?" Enoch asked, aghast.

"They used their faith as a vessel for their cruelty. Do not pity them, Enoch," she said.

"And the children? What were they guilty of?" he asked in indignation.

"Their fate was sealed by the sins of their fathers." Before he could think of a retort she spoke again. "Do you believe in fate, Enoch?"

"I–I don't know. . ."

"Every human being has free will," she continued. "But the outcome of their decisions is their fate. A tricky paradox, isn't it? Only a god could conceive of such a thing. What is your will, Enoch?"

"I've never thought about it."

"Well, it's time you start. Your will affects us all," she said cryptically.

"Who are you?" Enoch asked.

"You don't recognize me?" she teased, leering through rotten teeth. "Very well." She turned away from him and slowly began to remove her shawl, revealing yet more of her matted, unkempt hair. When she faced him again, Enoch was dumbfounded. Her features had changed completely.

There, staring him in the face, in the same tattered rags, was Master Adrax. Everything, from his cheekbones, to his beard, was the same, except for his eyes. They were golden, and glowing. He had no pupils or irises to speak of, only shimmering golden pools, bright as molten metal.

"What about now?" Adrax asked. "I have known you your whole life, Enoch."

Enoch was stunned into silence as he watched the tattered Adrax pick up a handful of snow and blow it into the air. Once in the air, it revealed not to be snow, but feathers. They were brilliantly white, charred along the edges.

"Nothing is what it seems, Enoch. Better start believing."

As he reached down to pick up one of the feathers, he heard a great flurry of wings next to him as Adrax burst into a cloud of crows which flew noisily in all directions, leaving behind not a trace save for the tattered rags.

Enoch awoke with a start, breathing heavily and drenched in sweat. Above him, the infinite expanse of the cosmos stretched endlessly. For a few moments he was completely disoriented before he remembered.

*That's right. The road.*

They had been riding for three days and nights. He sat up from his bedroll to find Davroz eyeing him curiously as he tended the fire. To his right, Balus snored soundly. The cold chill of the night bit into him and he quickly donned his furs.

"You called out in your sleep," Davroz said. "And more. Some of it was in a strange tongue even I don't recognize. In my culture, this thing is an Omen. What troubles you, boy?"

"I don't know," Enoch replied.

"Forget what you know," Davroz said. "What do you feel?"

"Fear," Enoch replied earnestly.

Davroz sat back and sighed. "It is a foolish man who does not know fear, boy. This thing is natural. What do you fear?"

Enoch paused a while and gazed into the fire as he considered his answer.

"I fear the future. The unknown. I do not know where this path is taking me."

Davroz smiled as the firelight danced off him. "Ah yes. The future. Always coming, but never arriving. It is folly to fear such a thing, for that is something you cannot control. What you can control is the present. Better to cast your focus here and now. This is what will shape your future."

Enoch was silent as he reflected on Davroz's words. They gave him some comfort. The distant echo of an owl hooting blew across their camp site.

"When I first came to this land, I too feared for my future," Davroz said. "In time, I learned to let go. Some things we cannot control. We are a part of a greater scheme, Enoch. One which many minds have gone mad trying to comprehend. Each of us have a part to play." He took a healthy swig from his wine cask. He let out a long, satisfied sigh as he wiped the wine from his moustache. "For now, I think it's better if you sleep. We have a long ride tomorrow to reach the capital."

Enoch nodded. "Thank you."

Davroz simply bowed his head benevolently and smiled as he gazed into the fire. As he nestled back into his bedroll, the warm surrender of sleep quickly found Enoch again.

They rose the next day at dawn. Davroz was a seasoned traveller and warrior, and it was all that Balus and Enoch could do to simply to keep up with him. The horses Balus and Enoch rode were healthy and strong, purchased for them from the Fairhaven stables by Davroz himself. Balus had put up much fuss, but Davroz insisted on paying for them. Enoch suspected that it had made Balus quietly ashamed, but he kept this to himself.

The mountainous Balus rode a befittingly large grey and white packhorse. It had seen much service in its life and its legs were hardy and strong. Enoch rode a younger mare, brown and flecked with white patches. She was a gentle creature, and a perfect starter horse for Enoch who had never ridden before. He had yet to decide on a name for her.

Davroz himself rode a black stallion named Star, so named for the single white fleck on its forehead. Star had been with him for years, and the proud creature bowed only to him. Days prior Davroz had regaled them with the story of how he first met Star in the plains of Amad, and how it took three whole days and nights before he broke him in. By now however, the two were nigh inseparable, and the bond they shared was palpable.

As they neared closer to the capital, the lushness of the countryside gave way to increasingly barren and, at times, scorched earth. The signs of battle were everywhere, and they passed through more than one razed village. The barbarity of it shocked Enoch. Until now the war had been but a storm on the horizon. Threatening, but distant. Now he was face to face with the harshness of it. He was unaccustomed to seeing the dead.

In the first town they passed through he had retched when he saw the bodies hanging from the gallows. "It's a fact of life," Balus had said. "Wiser to know death now than to meet it later as a stranger." Still, the sights shocked him, especially the women and children. This war was a far cry from the stories of chivalry Master Adrax had raised him on as a child.

For most of that day they rode in relative silence, the trio weary by now from four days' worth of riding. All of them longed to reach the capital. They rode in single file, with Davroz at the front, Enoch in the middle, and Balus at the rear. The country was sparse and desolate, and low hanging clouds trapped smoke in the air, blanketing them in a grey haze.

Davroz hummed on and off peacefully to himself as they rode. The tunes were melancholic and beautiful, unlike any Enoch had heard before.

"Those songs," Enoch began, "where did you learn them?"

"They are from my homeland."

"What are they about?" Enoch asked.

"Love, mostly."

Enoch paused for a moment. "Have you ever been in love?" he asked.

Davroz grew somber. "Once."

"What does it feel like?" Enoch asked him.

Davroz paused for a while before he gave a response. "It feels like. . . home. What say you, Master Balus?" Davrox asked, raising his voice to be heard at the back.

"Hmph. I say love's more trouble than it's worth," Balus piped up gruffly from behind them.

Davroz burst into laughter. "Perhaps you are right! Though we need it just the same. The same way we need water and food. A world without love is no world at all."

"Look around you, mage," Balus replied. "What love do you see in these lands?"

Davroz scoffed. "What love, indeed. This is just the problem. The world is out of balance."

"That's one way to put it," Balus said under his breath.

Enoch heard a strange noise, like a clamor of voices wafted faintly through his head. Davroz abruptly drew his horse to a halt.

"What is it?" Enoch asked, alarmed.

"Men. On the road ahead," he replied quietly. Enoch strained his eyes, but he could barely make out anything through the thick smog.

"Have they seen us?" Balus asked tensely, reaching for the hilt of his sword.

"Not yet."

"How many are there?" Balus asked.

"It is hard to say from here. But they are more than us."

Enoch began to faintly make out the clanking of pans and the occasional voice here and there. It must be some type of encampment, he deduced, as his heart began to race.

"What shall we do?" Balus asked.

"We cannot turn back," Davroz said. "This is the most direct route. To detour from here would take days. We continue riding. As we were." He started leading the way once more.

As the trio drew closer to the men, Enoch was able to make out their silhouettes for the first time. There were at least ten of them, and horses, from his count. Some of them huddled around a small cookfire and traded jokes while others tended to their weapons. They looked to be soldiers, though of which denomination Enoch could not say. Their tunics were a mix of browns and greys, and they carried no heralds or insignias.

"Deserters," Balus spat.

One of their number became aware of their approach, and stood up from the cookfire, drawing his sword. He was powerfully built, mailed in studded treated leather, and bore a fierce scar on his bald head. His eyes were wide and manic.

"You there! Halt!" he yelled.

Davroz mutely complied and drew Star to a stop. Enoch and Balus followed suit and edged forwards to stand by his side. By now all the deserters had ceased their activities and were eyeing the trio with silent menace.

"What business have you on the road?" the man yelled incredulously.

"We make for the capital," Davros replied coolly.

"To what end?"

"This is not your concern," Davroz replied.

"It is my concern, for it is my road," the man yelled, his face reddening.

"This is the king's road," Davroz said. This drew laughter from the deserters.

"The king is dead," the man mocked. "We own the roads now. All who pass must pay a toll."

Davroz sighed, the deep sigh of a man weary from a litany of such encounters, but nonetheless knew the motions. A small sack of coin was easier spared than a life.

"Very well," he said bemusedly. "What is the price?"

The man smiled as he sized them up, pleased at the ease with which his demands were met. He paid particular attention to Enoch and eyed him in a way which made him uneasy, like a piece of meat. After much slimy appraisal, he spoke. "We will take your horse. . . and the boy." The man licked his lips.

Enoch felt his heart jump into his throat and noticed Balus was sneaking his hand towards his sword as he prepared to fight. Upon hearing his demands, Davroz's eyes widened in momentary disbelief before he broke into a long fit of laughter which filled the air around them. They were belly laughs, a true cackle which shook his whole body.

The man grew increasingly angry as he watched Davroz laughing in his saddle and Enoch could see veins beginning to protrude from his head as he started to shake with rage. Finally, Davroz calmed down enough to catch his breath as he wiped a tear from his eye.

"Ahh," he began, still shaking off the laughter. "Gods above! Thank you, stranger. I have not laughed as this in many moons. In my head I had wondered, 'can he be as dense as he looks?' The verdict, 'denser!'" He joyfully broke into yet another fit of laughter.

A dark cloud of rage had settled upon the bald man. Enoch could see nought but murder in his eyes. "You are the fool, outlander," he growled. "I showed you mercy. Now we will take the horse, fuck the boy and mount your heads on pikes for the crows," he said as he drew his sword. As the man spoke, Enoch noticed that most of his men had quietly mounted their horses and readied their weapons.

"No," Davroz said calmly.

"What?" the man screamed.

"No," Davroz repeated. "You may not have my horse or the boy. And tell your men to stand down. There is no need for them to die with you. I will face you alone."

The bald man scoffed at this. "And why would I fight you alone? We are more than you. My men will run you down."

"Ah, of course," Davroz began, dismounting from his horse before Balus and Enoch could protest. "You are afraid. Your fear is not misplaced, little man. Perhaps your little brain does have some sense after all."

That final statement proved too much for the man as he lunged, screaming, towards him. Davroz effortlessly sidestepped his initial thrust, and then the next, and the next. He was simply too quick. The gold sinews in his maroon cloak shimmered brilliantly with each move he made. Enoch could hear in the bald man's voice that he was becoming increasingly exhausted every time one of his powerful swings missed.

Davroz had not even had to parry a single blow yet. In one last desperate attempt, the bald man tried to do a sideways slash, which Davroz deftly ducked under, delivering a powerful low kick, which took the man's legs out from under him. In the same movement he caught the man's sword as it fell mid–air and plunged it deep into his abdomen and through the earth, effectively pinning him to the ground.

The man let out a shrill squeal as he struggled uselessly and clutched at the sword, trying desperately to remove it from his belly. Enoch and Balus were speechless. To plunge the sword clean into the earth in such a way was no easy feat, he had to possess superhuman strength.

"Impossible," Balus whispered. It seemed the entire duel had ended before it had begun. Neither Balus nor Enoch had ever seen swordplay like this before.

Amongst the horrified ranks of the deserters, two horsemen prepared to charge. Davroz quickly pivoted to face them and again assumed fighting stance before the dust had even settled from his first duel.

"Don't," he warned flatly. They did not heed his warning as they too charged howling towards him. They were armed with long halberds and even his reflexes would not be able to match two men on horseback. He stood motionless, arms raised, as they quickly covered the ground between them.

"Davroz!" Balus shouted. In an instant, he made a rapid clockwise spiral with his arms and out of thin air an enormous scythe seemingly composed of pure flames appeared in his hands. It was too late for them to alter their course, but Enoch could see the fear in their eyes right before Davroz swung.

He sliced clean through both their bodies and their weapons in one fell swoop. That moment seemed to dilate forever, but as time quickly returned, the cleaved bodies fell limply from their horses into two separate pieces which laid in the dust next to their whimpering leader. In an instant, the flame scythe disappeared with a resounding crackle and the sickly smell of burning flesh filled the air. Enoch found it bore a disturbing likeness to cooked pork. Davroz's flame scythe had burned so hotly that it had cauterized their fatal wounds as it dealt them.

A brief lull settled in the air before the rest of the shell-shocked deserters took to their horses and fled as fast as they could, leaving behind much of their camp in a chaotic flurry of dust. The bald man was in his death throes as he grasped at the sword which had spelled his demise.

"Curse you, outlander," he wheezed.

Davroz wholly ignored the dying man's last words as he gingerly stepped over his body to hunch over the still smoking cookfire. Enoch and Balus watched on, mouths agape, as he skewered something in the pan. When he turned, he gave them a devilish grin, holding the skewer aloft. "Pork sausage?"

It was nightfall when they finally reached the walls of the capital, and a light rain which came with the dusk had developed into a torrential downpour which soaked the trio to their very bones. The rain was so heavy that Enoch could scarcely open his eyes, and he shivered uncontrollably in his saddle.

The white stone walls of the capital were the highest he had ever seen, dwarfing those of Fairhaven by far. Scores of flickering yellow torches, enshrined in small nooks in the stone and protected from the rain dotted its exterior, disappearing high into the gloom above them. The rain had turned the heavily trodden soil beneath the gatehouse into a deep, thick mud, which swallowed the hooves of their horses as they waited in place. Davroz rapped powerfully with his staff on the massive wooden gate, and they waited silently for a response.

Group morale was at an all-time low, and Enoch wanted nothing more than to be dry and warm. Even Balus, ever stoic, was showing obvious signs of exhaustion and discomfort. Eventually, a small metal hatch opened at eye level and the suspicious eyes of a gate guard addressed Davroz.

"What business have you in Kingsrest?" the stern voice asked. Davroz reached deep into his furs and produced a large brass amulet. It depicted a snake eating its own tail, which encircled two interlocking triangles, a hexagram with twelve opposing arches set at its center. "I am Davroz Inferni, and these men are in my charge. We seek an audience with the Watchers," he said, whincing from the rain.

The man abruptly closed the hatch and there was a sudden great creaking and groaning of wood and metal as the gigantic gate slowly ratcheted open. Yellow light poured forth as the crack between the two sides of the gate widened and the trio could finally see what lay beyond it. It was not merely a gate, but an arch. The interior was dry and hollow, its stone ceiling extending high above them.

A crew of ten or more gate guards worked simultaneously on an array of various of levers and pulleys which all conspired to move the tremendous gate. Each of them wore the distinctive polished mail and wide brimmed circular helmets of the capital, adorned with fabric in the royal color blue. The gate mechanism was truly a sight to behold, a marvel of modern technology.

As the trio led their horses inside, they collectively breathed a sigh of relief as they basked in the brief shelter the arch provided them from the rain. "You three look like you've had quite the journey," one of the gate guards joked. As the water literally dripped from them onto the stone floors, all Enoch could muster was a meek nod.

"The Temple of The Gates is quite a ways from here, notwithstanding this rain," he said sympathetically. "The men and I are about to open a tankard. Why not rest a while?"

Enoch shot Davroz a pleading look, but his reply was polite and succinct. "A kind offer, friend. But this matter is quite urgent. Perhaps next time."

The man shrugged, having made the offer, and followed the rest of the guards as they filed back into the gatehouse, laughing and chatting merrily amongst themselves.

Enoch could practically feel the warmth emanating from that room and he could not help but feel betrayed by Davroz's intransience. What meeting could be so important that they could not rest for a few minutes?

Davroz gave Star a light tap with his reigns and the horse reluctantly walked out of the archway into the pouring rain once more. As he entered the street, Davroz held his left hand aloft and produced a small flame from his index finger so as to light the way. Enoch and his horse remained rooted in place, both of them equally unwilling to enter into the night once more.

After all this time he still did not know what this was all for, and he grew tired of the constant mystery. Balus gave him a gentle pat the shoulder as he passed, his heavy glove leaving a sodden imprint on Enoch's furs "Come on," he said softly, trotting forward to catch up with Davroz.

Finally, Enoch was alone in the vast stone archway, exhausted and defeated as he watched them slowly disappear into the inky blackness of the winding streets. He gave large sigh before reigning his horse into action. He could sense she was just as tired as he was. "I think I'll call you Rain," he said to her, gently stroking her mane as he steadied himself before catching up to them.

The streets themselves were winding and steep and torrents of water gushed down the gutters on either side of the road as they climbed higher. Were it not for Davroz's will-o'-wisp of flame gently bobbing at the front of the column, Enoch had no doubt that he would have gotten lost in the dark labyrinth.

Some windows glowed dully with orange light, conjuring fantasies within Enoch's exhausted mind of the warmth and dryness within. As if reading his thoughts, Davroz spoke up from the front of the column. "Worry not, friends. We are almost there. The temple lies at the crest of this hill."

Sure enough, after much clamoring and another steep winding turn, they found themselves at the foot of a towering stone dome. The exterior was chequered with rows of windows which glowed brilliantly from within. It was a building the like of which neither Enoch nor Balus had ever seen.

Two guards a stood watch at the entrance, shields and spears raised, both adorned in ornate brass armor bearing the same symbol as the pendant Davroz had shown by the gate. By the steps waited a page, a young boy with tasked with greeting them and ushering them inside. He had a lantern lit and solemnly stood at attention by the steps and could not have been more than twelve or thirteen years of age. Behind them all stood a colossal brass door which was engraved with the very same hexagram seal.

As Davroz approached he dismounted from Star, and Enoch and Balus followed suit. Rain gave a relieved whinny as he did so. The waiting Page gave a steep bow, his brown curls drooping as he did so.

"Greetings, wise Davroz. The council awaits," he said, formally.

"You honor me, Godfrey," Davroz said warmly. "See that these horses are fed and stabled. They have earned their rest." He pat Star affectionately.

"Very well," the boy said. He gave a shrill whistle and two stableboys appeared from a nearby alley. Together, each of them took one horse and disappeared around a nearby corner. They followed Godfrey up the steps towards the door.

Something about the seal spoke to Enoch, as if he had always known it. It was a peculiar sensation, as he knew he had never laid eyes on the seal before that night in Master Adrax's study.

He wondered then how the old man was faring. He could almost picture him, hunched over his chaotic ruin of a desk, engrossed in some ancient text. All at once he was hit by home sickness. He missed the old man, the closest thing to a father he had. He even found himself missing the abbey. There was some comfort to be found in familiarity and daily routines.

"Davroz, if you will," Godfrey said. Davroz stepped forward and placed his hand on the brass and closed his eyes.

*He must be mad*, Enoch thought. *It'd take ten men to even budge that thing*. After Davroz whispered a small incantation the door suddenly shimmered and began to groan. Enoch and Balus were utterly flummoxed by this: it was moving on its own.

"How can that be, Balus?" Enoch whispered.

"Your guess is as good as mine, young master," Balus said in awe. Bit by bit, the massive brass door rolled sideways until it finally revealed a hollowed out passageway behind it.

As the door came to a thunderous halt, Godfrey ushered them inside. "Kindly follow me, sirs," he said. There was something strange about him. He looked far younger than Enoch but spoke with an authority which belied his years, perhaps a consequence of his important role at the temple. Maybe there was simply no room for childishness. The blonde-haired youth was certainly a far cry from the younger novitiates at the abbey.

As he led them inside Enoch was immediately hit by the sweet relief of warmth and dryness and he felt his body rejoice. This relief was soon replaced by wonder as they entered the central chamber of the dome. Both Enoch and Balus had to gasp at its magnificence.

Rows upon rows of rooms and balconies extended skyward towards the enormously high yet perfectly rounded stone ceiling. Warm, golden light beamed down from massive, mobile floating orbs, like small gentle suns. They slowly and softly moved between the various floors of the massive structure, illuminating the lofty walkways, which were abuzz with life.

Women, men, and mythical creatures of all shapes and sizes were going about their evenings, conversing, trading and studying. There must have been hundreds of them, if not thousands. It was like a city within a city. Enoch saw centaurs, goblins, elves, and ents, to name a few, all nonchalantly going about their business as if it were a normal day, and all garbed in the same brass colored robes.

"I must be dreaming," Enoch said faintly, as he consciously blinked his eyes.

"Dreaming? No." Davroz said warmly. "If anything, you have finally woken up."

At the center of the structure stood a large pyramid, carved from the same stone, flanked on all sides by steps and luscious gardens.

"What. . . manner of forging is this?" Balus asked, dumbfounded.

"This is no forging, my friend. This is sorcery," Davroz said smugly. "What you see before you was built not by hands, but words. Before The Schism, the realm was awash with such magic. Now, those of us who serve the light are concentrated in certain places. This is one such haven."

For once, Enoch and Balus were equally amazed, the astonishment was clearly written all over the old knight's face. Davroz could not help but laugh at his wide eyed, slack jawed companions as they gawked at their surroundings. Balus just about fell over as a friendly pixie shot past him, singing him soft platitudes as she did so.

"Come now," Davroz said finally. "Godfrey will take you to your quarters. It is wiser for us to bathe and change first before our audience with the council."

"The council?" Enoch asked.

"The Council of the Watchers," he said, pointing to the pyramid. "They await you, Enoch."

Sweat dripped profusely from Enoch's brow as he stood on display at the center of the ancient chamber in the heart of the pyramid. An enormous rendition of the Sigil of The Gates had been carved into the floor, and he stood on display in the center.

Balus and Davroz were by his side, but he was acutely aware of every eye in the room bearing down upon him. Thankfully, the glaring orb overhead made it somewhat harder to see all their faces. It was just as well, otherwise he might have cracked under the sheer pressure of it all.

The council had assembled: an ent, a faerie, a human, and an elf, each an elected representative of their kind.

The ent, who's name, Enoch was told, was unutterable in human tongues, resembled a massive humanoid tree with glowing green eyes and a huge, luminous, emerald gem at its hollowed heart's center. It had branches for limbs and seemed to be in a constant state of flux as its roots stretched and grew, settling into the cracks in the stone around it. Its skin was as tough and hardy as bark, and small squirrels and birds nested peacefully amongst the litany of hollows which marked its body.

The faerie, Candilia, much more closely resembled a human being, though her features were far more refined and elegant than those of a human. A gown of flowers covered her, and they rhythmically budded, bloomed, wilted, and died, over and over. An elegant display, echoing the seasons, playing out each time she took a breath. Most breathtaking of all were her wings, ornate and dazzling like those of a butterfly and dwarfing her small body.

The human, Lyse, was a powerful mage from the lands to the north, and wore a humble, but stylish, crimson tunic.

Each member of the council was seated in their designated throne, the elected representatives of their respective races, like the cast of some fanciful bedtime story. In addition, half the population of the sanctuary had crammed in behind them to fill the empty parapets of the chamber. This meeting concerned them, after all, as much as it concerned the fate of all sentient life, or so Enoch had been told.

Things had been moving very quickly as of late, and truthfully, he struggled to keep up with it all. Prophecies, magic, secret societies. Doubt tinged his mind and saturated the very air around him. It was all too surreal.

Mere weeks ago, the idea of mythical creatures was just that, an idea. Yet here now they stood before him, ideas made flesh. And worse, they expected things from him.

The elf, leader of the council, was named Ulthian. He wore an immaculate white gold gown topped with a golden circlet of willow leaves from his homeland. Lighter still was his silk-like hair, which reached well past his waist. His eyes were a frightful shade of green, which seemed to glow. He was cold and calculated, a high elf, Davroz had told Enoch before they convened. Apparently, high elves had a reputation for pride, and he was no exception.

He studied Enoch with the same indifference with which one might regard a common pigeon in the street. Thankfully, Davroz fielded most of the questions, and Balus stood by in resolute silence, the perspiration on his brow giving some clues as to his own level of discomfort.

So far, Ulthian had set the tone of the meeting, and it was one of suspicion.

"So," he continued, his harmonic cadence carrying throughout the silent chamber. "We are convened today at the behest of one human, for the sake of another. Is that correct, Davroz?" His bemused question drew laughter from the crowd.

"Aye, it is," Davroz replied. A vague murmur went up from the crowd as they bristled at this pretence. Already, Enoch could see how Ulthian swayed the room with his poisonous words.

"Forgive me, Ulthian," Candilia interjected, "but the Prophecy clearly states that the chosen champions will be of human blood. There is no need for such petulance on this council." Winds of agreement rustled through the ent, sending up a flight of startled sparrows which quickly returned to the safety of his trunk.

Ulthian was most displeased by her words. His pride had clearly been offended, and his striking face soured. "You forget yourself, Candilia," he said pointedly. "And perhaps you also forget that humans are the cause of the imbalance we are facing. For a thousand years, the repressive cult of The One Truth has spread like a cancer through these lands, trampling and stifling the old ways of magic in its wake. This barbaric but oh–so–human ideology leaves no room for imagination, for machinations of love to take form. It only perpetuates fear. Fear and violence. The output from the gates are but a reflection of this."

The human mage, Lyse, broke her silence, her stern voice carried throughout the stone chamber with as much command as Ulthian's.

"Perhaps it is you, Ulthian, who has forgotten. Forgotten how the high elves were the first to break the covenant during The Schism. That treachery, and the bloodshed that followed, has forever stained the hands of magic users and magical beings alike. Be they in service to light or darkness, it makes no difference. In the eyes of the common man, we are the same. Monsters. It should come as no surprise then that they would turn to a religion which demonises all forms of magic. They are afraid. Some would say with good reason. In fact, as I recall it, your own sister was one of the key architects of that war."

The crowd collectively gasped as Ulthian furiously countered. "You insolent little. . . How dare you!" he shouted, standing from his throne. "You are but a child. Your feeble mind could never comprehend the complexities of that time."

Enoch could now see firsthand how deeply divided this magical world was. Clearly, the effects of The Schism were still being felt.

"Enough!" Candilia shouted. Her voice, frighteningly bolstered by the weight of her own magic, rang out like a thunderclap and silenced the chamber at once. "I will not allow this council to once again descend into petty quarrels. We have precious little time. The forces of darkness grow stronger by the hour. As we speak, our worldseers are detecting massive concentrations of dark energy gathering across the realm. The beings emerging from the Fellgates are being organized. Someone or something is recruiting them."

"Nonsense," Ulthian said flatly. "Creatures born from that dimension are too chaotic to work together. Never in the history of this world have the disparate races of fear presented a united front, and never shall they, their animism and will to dominate is too strong. To control such chaos, one would require untold power. Power which does not exist in this world. The power of a god."

A hush fell over the chamber, brokered by the seeming finality of Ulthian's words. This silence was soon broken by the human mage, Lyse.

"There is one who could possess such power. The Champion of Fear, as was foretold."

At the mere mention of this champion the atmosphere in the chamber shifted, as if a dark shadow had fallen over them all. Again, Ulthian was quick to counter, but this time his unconvincing retort did little to sooth the rising tension.

"There is no evidence that such a Champion has emerged."

This time, the ent bristled, and his language surged around them like cold autumn winds. Candilia spoke on his behalf.

"He says that the trees have been speaking in the lands to the south. Dark whispers of a power birthed in agony."

Ulthian scoffed. "The trees love to whisper their cryptic riddles."

Lyse quickly broke in, incensed by his arrogance. "Why is it, Ulthian, that you continue to undermine the genuine concerns presented by this council? I'm of a mind to question where your loyalties truly lie."

"*Silence!*" Ulthian boomed. "I will not be lectured on my duties by a child. It is my role to ensure that this council operates justly. Hearsay is not a basis for action. We require evidence. Which brings me back to the matter at hand." He cast his piercing gaze upon Enoch once again. "This boy, Davroz. If he is our Champion, then there must have been signs." Again, Enoch felt the uncomfortable sensation of every eye in the room being fixed upon him.

"Aye," Davroz began. "And signs there were. In his letter, Adrax states that the boy was born during the great eclipse, at the turning of the millennium, at the cost of his mother's life, as per The Prophecy."

Ulthian again scoffed. "These are hardly grounds for—"

Davroz quickly cut him off. "And prescience. In his infancy, the boy knew of things without being told. The names of the monks, their fears, their peeves. Even their misdeeds. He spoke of them as freely as the weather."

Davroz's words struck Enoch like a punch to the gut. He had never been told of the circumstances of his parents, let alone that his mother had died during childbirth. Nor was he told of this so called "prescience." His insides churned as he was gripped by a mixture of anger, grief, and shame.

*Why did he never tell me?*

In that moment, he hated Adrax. How could he be so cruel? He did the best to stave off the tears which quickly welled in his eyes as a lump grew in his throat.

*Not now. Not in front of them.*

Just as he felt his knees buckling, he felt the firm but reassuring grip of Balus's arm on his shoulder. His simple touch conveyed more condolences than words could ever offer.

Ulthian: "There are many strange curiosities in this world and few of them point to The Prophecy. If he is truly the one, then his powers should have manifested by now. He is twenty years of age, well past maturity. Let him speak."

Candilia spoke up, and as she addressed him directly, his heart began to race. Her tone, at least, was sympathetic. "Enoch," she began softly, "has there ever been a time in your life when you have felt or harnessed an energy within yourself, something out of the ordinary. Something. . . magical?"

Enoch wracked his mind for something, anything supernatural or spiritual that had ever occurred in his mundane life at the abbey, but found nothing. There was no time in his memory that anything short of regular had ever occurred. Up until a few days ago, he had been skeptical at best about the very existence of magic.

He was certain Adrax was wrong about him. Conscious of the waiting council he shakily worded his reply.

"Um, er. . . not that I—"

But then, something did come to mind. He remembered earlier that day, on the road, with the deserters. He had felt their presence. Nay, heard it, in his mind, long before Balus or Davroz had detected them, like a gust of foreign thoughts blowing through his mind.

"Actually, today," he began, much to the surprise of just about everyone in the chamber. "When we were beset on the road. The deserters. I heard them before I saw them."

Ulthian sighed deeply. "You heard them?"

Enoch hastily clarified himself. "Not with my ears. With my mind. I heard their thoughts, if only briefly."

An awkward silence covered the chamber as The Council reflected on his words.

"Well," Candilia said warmly, "perhaps it is not much to go on, but it is something. Thank you, Enoch. We shall deliberate amongst ourselves."

As she spoke, she addressed him privately within his mind. Her thoughtforms were immensely clear and powerful, far more so than the murmurs he heard on the road. They felt like summer and sounded like a forest, teaming with life.

If you can hear this, Enoch, wait for me here once we adjourn. Do not tell the others. There is something I would like to show you.

The sour faced Ulthian addressed the chamber from his throne, more apathetic than ever.

"Very well," he sighed. "I hereby call this meeting to a close."

Enoch shifted uncomfortably from foot to foot as he leaned against one of the cold stone pillars of the now empty chamber, waiting in earnest for Candilia to arrive. He had no idea what lay in store for him from their meeting, but who was he to deny one of the council? Besides, it was not as if she had conveyed him much choice in the matter.

Both Balus and Davroz had been confused by his choice to loiter around in the empty chamber but they respected his wishes. It has been a long day for all of them, after all. They were probably both eager to finally get some sleep. As was Enoch, for that matter.

He eyed the empty parapets where the council had sat, expecting Candilia to gracefully float in at any moment. He figured with those huge wings that he would hear her long before he saw her. It had been quite a while now though, and he was beginning to wonder if she was coming at all. Just as he felt his eyes begin to grow heavy, he was rudely awoken and rightly scared by a loud crackling noise right next to him which instantly gave way to a glowing purple rift in thin air from which Candilia instantly materialised.

The rift closed just as immediately and was gone with an abrupt zap. The shellshocked Enoch wheezed as he tried to catch his breath while Candilia laughed, placing a sympathetic hand on his shoulder.

"Sorry!" she said sweetly. "I did not mean to scare you. It is easier not to be seen this way. Not to mention faster." Her appearance had changed as well. No longer was she garbed in the gown of flowers, now covered in luminous purple ivy which snaked its way around her bare body. She was still just as breathtakingly beautiful, and her glorious wings flapped triumphantly to herald her arrival.

Enoch was unaccustomed to seeing so much of the female body exposed. In fact, he had never seen a female body uncovered at all before. He felt himself blushing as he stared intently at the floor, not quite knowing where to look.

Candilia sighed. "You humans. . . So reserved! It is just a body. Try looking at my eyes, Enoch."

He awkwardly complied and carefully darted his eyes up from the floor to meet her own. They were a soft brown that filled him with warmth and immediate ease. He started smiling despite himself.

"There now, that was not so hard, was it?"

"No," he replied sheepishly.

"You humans got a lot stranger ever since you started wearing clothes, you know. It's almost like some morbid fascination. Fiendishly wondering what's underneath. Do you not already know what's underneath?"

Enoch laughed then. He had never thought of it like that

and she was right.

"How did you do that, by the way?"

"Do what?"

"You appeared out of thin air!"

"Oh, that," Candilia replied. "It's called phase shifting. All fae can do it. It is the common misconception of humans that we fly from place to place. It is partially true, we do fly, but mostly it is only for pleasure or ceremony. Phase shifting is our functional means of travel. Instant, painless, and protected. A faerie's phase range is limited only by the strength of her power. Mine, well, I can go almost anywhere." She spoke with more than a hint of pride.

"But where do you pass through?"

"Most perceptive you are. The universe is all around us, within us, and without us. It is full of doors and passages connecting seemingly disparate places and moments, even times, like threads. Phase shifting is simply the means of knowing which thread to pull."

"Times?" Enoch asked.

"Oh, yes. Times. Time is less of a straight line and more of a circle, you see. Humans have a very arbitrary binary concept of time, neat little slices of which they love to collect and mostly tend to waste. In truth, days, years, and months are make believe. All events, past, present, and future occur in tandem. The strongest faeries can even phase shift through time. A craft I have yet to master."

Enoch stared in wonder. Such power was inconceivable.

*I wonder if humans can phase shift?*

A FEW CAN, Candilia projected into his mind. THOUGH IT IS IMMENSELY COSTLY FOR THEM TO ATTEMPT.

Enoch gasped. "You're in my head again!"

"I have that effect," she teased, winking at him. There was an awkward silence as her joke broke like waves on a sea cliff. "Sorry for that. In short, yes. But it is only because you are receptive. This gives me some hope that you might be the one after all. Most humans cannot hear thoughtforms, let alone project them. You hear mine as clear as day, just as you unconsciously emit your own. I heard them as soon as you entered the room."

Enoch blushed again.

"Don't worry," Candilia soothed. "There was nothing too suspect in there. I will teach you how to guard your mind over time. That you can hear me, and others is most unusual, and gives us some clues as to what your magical nature might be."

"I have a magical nature?" Enoch asked.

"Yes. Each of the champions is said to possess a unique magical nature, a forbidden gift which greatly exceeds the limits of regular magic. Yours has yet to fully emerge."

"When will it happen?" Enoch asked.

"It's hard to say. It is usually activated by intense emotions. Usually some form of trauma, or perhaps immense moments of love or joy."

Enoch again looked at the ground.

"You have not had much of either, have you?" He shook his head meekly. "It is alright. These things take time. It's nothing that can be rushed. Despite what Ulthian would have you believe."

Enoch could feel himself getting lighter and lighter from her kind words.

*That's true magic.*

Now it was Candilia's turn to blush. "My, my, you are a sweet one. Now!" She snapped herself into action. "To the matter at hand."

Enoch watched on in awe as she fluttered over to the

center of the hexagram where she gathered herself, closing her eyes before raising the first two fingers of her left hand skyward as she began to mutter an incantation. Soon, her fingers began to emit the same purple light as her phase shift, and when the light was almost blinding, she quickly slammed them into the floor and sent a brilliant purple eldritch energy coursing through the massive sigil with a resounding crack.

The solid stone of the sigil seemed to fade away into thin air before Enoch's very eyes to reveal a winding staircase which descended into the gloom below them.

Magic truly is magnificent.

"We don't have much time! Follow me." Candilia coaxed, breaking the silenc, gently gliding down the staircase. She took special care not to move too fast and leave Enoch stranded in the dark.

The stairs were steep and seemed to go on and on. The further into the earth they moved, the colder it became, until they finally reached a large room at the bottom. To call it a room was almost a mistake, as it was more of a cavern, carved from the very earth itself. It was pitch black, and Enoch could feel wind rushing from the cavern as opposed to rushing into it as one might expect. It scared him somewhat.

The energy in the cavern was different from the chamber above. The silence and stillness was oppressive, foreboding. He felt as if he was intruding somehow, like some wayward graverobber.

"Your response is natural, but I assure you there is nothing to fear here, Enoch," Candilia said tenderly. She tapped gently on a nearby wall and coursed her magic through it. "This is a holy place." A row of side-by-side torches lit themselves two by two, their lights echoing the same deep purple of Candilia's own energy.

Enoch could now study the true designs and contours of the cavern for the first time. The walls were adorned with all manner of symbols and markings, none of which he could recognize. At the end of the row of torches, set squarely in the centre of the room was an imposing archway, built from the very rock of the cavern itself.

Enoch could tell that it was ancient, and its design was misshapen, asymmetrical, as though the massive stones had been picked and perfectly balanced upon one another, with no thought spared for aesthetics. He could see the back wall of the cavern behind it, where the ghostly purple torchlight cast an impressive shadow of the Arch.

"What is it?" Enoch asked, his voice echoing off the walls.

"A gate," Candilia whispered in wonder. "This is one of The Gates of Matter, Enoch. A physical doorway between this dimension and the spirit world. It is these gates our order was established to protect. I entered this world, hundreds of years ago, through a gate much like this one. It is one of six Gates of Light, which opens unto the Plane of Love, a place fed by the hearts and minds of all living beings. This entire sanctuary, the council chamber, the pyramid, all of it, was built upon this cavern, and this gate. One could even argue that the city of Kingsrest owes its very existence to this gate."

"Then who built the gates?" Enoch asked quizzically.

"Who indeed," Candilia replied. "The story goes as this. In the final days before the birth of man there was a war in heaven. Lucifer, God's right hand and most favored son, led a coup, in an attempt to seize control. Some say he foresaw the horrors humans would inflict upon each other and the earth. Others say he was simply consumed by jealousy at the notion that his father could love humans more than him and his angelic kin. Whatever the case, Lucifer rose against God, with half the host of heaven beside him.

"The war was terrible, and holy blood fell from the heavens like rain. In the end, God triumphed, and cast Lucifer and his followers into exile on the earth. One of their first actions was the construction of the gates. To what end, we cannot say, only that they now serve as the sole conduits between this physical dimension and the non-physical planes.

"They allow ideas, dreams, and nightmares to be made flesh, and to take on consciousness of their own. Thus, begetting more ideas and more life in an exponential pattern of growth. All magical creatures and magic users draw their powers from the gates, and they are scattered far and wide throughout the world."

She took a breath before continuing. "The locations of some of the gates are still unknown. A few of the Light Gates have sanctuaries built upon them like this one, but since The Schism, we have lost contact with many of our fellow sanctuaries. We are weakened, and in our weakness the superstition of The One Truth creeps across the land, threatening the existence of all magical life as it suffocates the collective soul of this world. They take these truths and pervert them, befoul them, condemning any form of magic as heresy. The Watchers are divided, and divided we may fall."

Enoch was somber as he contemplated Candilia's words. Aspects of what she spoke about he had heard of during his instruction at the abbey, but the monks had phrased it much differently. Lucifer, or Satan, as they called him, was the arch enemy of mankind. It was as simple as that. He had never heard of any gates or angels falling to the earth.

The gate began to vibrate and emit a high pitched humming.

Brilliant blue light snaked its way though the ancient stone, illuminating all manner of markings and incantations which Enoch had not previously noticed which covered its surface. They watched on in awe as lightning crackled and a ghostly blue pool, somewhere between water and fire began to form in the centre of the arch.

"What's happening?" Enoch asked with concern, raising his voice to be heard over the humming of the gate.

"A crossover!" Candilia yelled back with excitement. "This is what I wanted to show you. A magical creature is being born unto this world."

Gradually, the luminous pool grew to cover the entirety of the archway before the humming and crackling came to an abrupt halt. Again, silence blanketed the cavern once more.

They watched intently as a sparkling golden beak began to pierce the veil. The beak soon gave way to a face, unlike any Enoch had ever seen. It was like that of an eagle, only much larger, perhaps the size of a horse's, complete with ears on each side of its head. It was wreathed in feathers of the most dazzling gold which managed to shine even in the dim purple light of the cavern.

As it emerged from the gate, it fixed its regal gaze upon them; most powerful of all were its piercing blue eyes. Its front legs were talons, like those of a bird, while its back legs were clawed like those of a lion. When it had fully cleared the gate, it stood before them, exalted in all its glory.

It stretched its immense golden wings and gave a triumphant and deafening roar as it flicked its tail. It was a truly majestic creature, and its sheer presence commanded immediate respect.

"My god," Candilia whispered, emotion creeping into her

sweet voice. "A griffin." She immediately bowed steeply, and Enoch hastily followed suit, not quite knowing what to do with himself.

Candilia soon rose to face the griffin, flourishing her own wings as she addressed it ceremoniously. "Noble griffin, we welcome you to the mortal world. May your time here be fruitful and prosperous."

Still on his knees, Enoch awkwardly clambered to his feet to stand with her, doing his best to still his beating heart. The griffin eyed them both for a moment, its large head swivelling as it paid particular attention to Enoch. It galloped past them and gave a powerful beat of its wings, launching itself with unfathomable speed up the spiral staircase and out into the world. The resultant shockwave sent both Enoch and Candilia flying into the far corner of the room where they landed in a heap, wheezing and laughing.

Candilia helped Enoch up, and she continued to marvel as they dusted themselves off.

"A griffin," she said, more to herself, shaking her head in disbelief. "One of the rarest, most noble creatures in the magical world. And it arrived tonight, the same night fate brought you here."

"Coincidence?" he asked her, doubting the word as it left his lips.

She shook her head. "In time, you will see that there are no coincidences, Enoch. This is an omen. And a powerful one at that."

## CHAPTER 12

# THE GREAT GAME

### *2033 A.D.*

A thick blanket of fog covered the road as the black SUV snaked its way through the winding mountains. Adam sat in the backseat, alone. The heating was on in the car, but his legs still felt cold against the leather seats. On either side of the tinted windows, pine trees filtered past endlessly.

In their own way, he found them vaguely oppressive. In their thirst for sunlight, they all but blotted it out. The canopy was thick, and the forest floor seemed devoid of life save for the occasional mushroom cap. This, combined with the fog, made it seem as though they were driving at night, when it was only the mid-afternoon.

He could vaguely make out the back of the chauffer's head through the glass partition but that was about it. Not a word had been spoken by either of them for the duration of the journey.

Adam had foreseen that as soon as he first laid eyes on the man, waiting for him on the steps of the hospital with a sign bearing his name, just as Mr. Davis had said. He wore a finely tailored suit and forced a grimace, but his eyes conveyed the same indifference as every driver Adam had ever had since his infancy. He ushered him inside the black SUV and that was that. Off they went, to locations unknown.

On the seat inside he found a sealed envelope with his name printed on it. When he quickly broke the seal to reveal its contents, the first thing he noticed was a logo: bold red letters which cut vertically across a two-dimensional rendering of planet Earth.

S.H.A.R.D.: The Society for Human Advancement, Research, and Development.

Inside the folder was a guidebook, a brochure of sorts. It gave some details about the facility, secluded in the mountains a few hours' drive outside the city. It read like a university welcome pamphlet.

*"S.H.A.R.D. is committed to discovering and harnessing the very best in human potential, for the benefit of mankind. For almost 60 years, we have been on the forefront of psychokinetic research, creating a safe haven for gifted individuals to develop their abilities in peace."*

It went on to mention an extensive list of wealthy donors and trustees, alongside cheery images of young, smiling faces, frolicking in the sun, or sharing a joke over some books. He found it strange that he had never once heard of this organization before. Given the nature of their research he figured that made sense.

It was a fringe field, at best. The very notion of psychic abilities used to make him laugh. Now, he had daily night terrors linking back to what happened in that fucking alley. The trauma, the whiskey, and the beatings made it all a bit of a blur, but he did remember one thing clearly.

Those screams. He doubted he would ever forget them. The rest of it was like some awful dream. But it wasn't a dream, he reminded himself. That really happened. That man is dead because of me. He paused as he countered himself in his head.

*He was going to kill me.*

While true, the thought gave him little comfort. Each day the trauma visited him in harsh flashes, like lightning, an eternal nightmare from which he could not wake.

In reality, whatever S.H.A.R.D. was or wasn't was irrelevant at this point. It was his only option. As the enigmatic Mr. Davis had stated, it was this, or prison. He wondered if he would see Mr. Davis again. He held out hope that there would be someone there who he could talk to about the nightmares, a professional maybe. At least then he could begin to unpack everything.

By the sounds of it, maybe there would even be others like him there. He wanted to feel excited, to look forward to it, but he just could not shake the abyss of dread which pooled within him. More than anything, he was scared, of his future, and scared of himself.

At some point on the drive, they stopped at a gas station. His chauffer stepped out to grab a cigarette, and Adam asked him for one. The man cautiously complied, and they smoked in silence, looking out over the small country town they were in, and the mountains which pierced the gray clouds in the distance.

When they got back in, he thought about texting his father. He even went as far as to draft up a message, but he never sent it. His father had not even come in to visit in hospital. Not once. He knew Adam was there, too. This was another truth he struggled to accept. Looking back on their last conversation though, perhaps it made sense. *Maybe he wished I did die,* Adam thought. Tears welled in his eyes as the road ahead grew darker.

Ω

He must have dozed off, as it was nightfall by the time they reached the facility.

He could see the building had a lot of floors but that was about it. The fog made it almost pitch black in the night, and only the garish white light from the windows gave him clues as to the size or shape of the building. It was brutalist, in classic post-modern 80's style, and all told it looked rather dilapidated. The SUV pulled up all the way to the entrance, where what looked like two attending physicians in lab coats and masks waited to greet him.

Adam heard the doors unlock. In the rear view mirror he swore he detected a hint of sympathy in the driver's gaze before he stepped outside.

The air was extremely cold and immediately sent him into a fit of shivers despite the warm jacket he was wearing. The air from his breath steamed in front of him and he was almost blinded by the clinical artificial light coming from the sliding glass doors. It was in this daze that the doctors introduced themselves. He instantly forgot their names as he shook their hands, and as they ushered him inside, he cast one last glance at the SUV, his last link to the outside world, which was already heading back the way it came.

Inside, the facility looked more like a rundown hospital than an exclusive academy. There was a wide variety of medical equipment strewn about the empty halls, as well as antiquated computer equipment which looked like it hadn't seen use in decades. Everything was coated in a thick layer of dust and the place seemed all but deserted.

He swore he saw a silhouette pacing in the window of one

of the rooms, but he could barely make anything out with the lights turned up as bright as they were. There was a persistent high pitched ringing noise which he detected as soon as he walked through the doors. It was just barely audible but somehow, he found it incredibly jarring.

As the doctors led him through the halls and gave him a brief introduction to the facility, he found it hard to focus on any of their words. Everything they said seemed to flow pointlessly from one side of his head to the other, and he struggled to absorb a single word of what they were saying.

As a matter of fact, he found that he was barely processing anything at all. The scene was playing out before him, but he was not a part of it. It was almost as if he was watching himself in third person.

"What's with the masks?" Adam finally said, drawing himself to a halt in a desperate attempt to regain control of his reality. The two doctors exchanged a look before the male one spoke.

"It's... merely a contamination protocol. Nothing to worry about," he said, feigning sincerity.

"Where are you taking me?"

This time the female doctor spoke. "To your room, Adam. Don't worry. The director will meet with you tomorrow morning and explain everything. For now, it's best if you get some sleep."

Her reassurances did little to quell his rising doubts, but he complied anyway. He found he was too exhausted to argue or question much of anything. He just wanted to get out of this light and get some sleep.

When they finally reached his room and unlatched it, he was more than underwhelmed. It was a polished cement eight-by-eight foot cube. Inside was a sink, a toilet, and a small bed with a wafer–thin mattress. If anything, it was more like a cell. At least it was warm.

The moment he set his backpack down the doctors deftly latched the door behind him before he could muster a protest. Now he could only see their eyes through a small metal flap on the door.

"The rooms are locked at night for your own safety," the male doctor said flatly. "We'll be back at 0800 tomorrow morning."

"Wait," Adam said softly. "How do I—"

The doctor cut him off mid-sentence as he drew the flap closed from the outside. Immediately he heard their hurried footsteps retreating down the hallway outside.

"Assholes." He took one last look around his cell before almost collapsing into the rock-hard cot. Sleep came for him at once.

He awoke in the middle of the night to the silence of his cell. As he stared up at the unfamiliar ceiling, it took a long time for his brain to register where he was.

The glaring lights from the halls still crept into his cell from the crack under the door, but the high–pitched ringing seemed to have stopped, at least for now. As he sat up in bed, he checked his wristwatch. As he read the dials, he quickly had to do a double take.

The hands were running backwards. Counter–clockwise.

"What the fuck. . .?" *Stupid thing must be broken.*

He stood up out of his cot and went to go wash his hands in the sink. He turned the rusty old knobs, but no water came out from the tap. Even worse, when he tried to look in the mirror, he found it was too scuffed and neglected to even reflect a clear image of himself, showing just a jumbled fuzzy mess, a shrouded silhouette at best.

As he sighed and turned back to his cot he immediately gasped and jumped back against the wall in fright. There was someone lying in his bed. As the panic wore off and he peered through his fingers his terror quickly gave way to confusion.

It was him. He was watching himself sleep.

"No way."

He slowly crept closer to the cot until he was standing over his own sleeping body. He watched and listened to himself taking deep, labored breaths, occasionally he would wheeze and splutter. Never in his life had he felt a sensation so surreal. He was asleep! And yet he was awake. Was this some kind of dream?

Just as he was reaching out to poke himself, a glowing golden light on the wall behind him caught his attention. He spun around just in time to see a gold rimmed portal opening in front of him. It reminded him of the one he had seen that night in the alley, the one he had made, only this one was much more elegant.

It was smooth and oval shaped, and gold colored instead of red. It was also almost entirely silent, apart from a low humming sound. As the portal grew to the size of a door, radiant orange light flooded into the dark cell and he could see clearly what lay on the other side.

Clouds, hued in the richest yellows and oranges floated by at great speed, and one by one, tiles made of what looked like solid gold appeared out of the fog, creating a path which led further into the clouds. The portal and the path seemed to beckon him, like some part of his soul innately knew what lay for him there. He took one last look at his sleeping body before crossing the threshold into the clouds.

Once he was on the tiled path the portal quickly zapped shut behind him. For some reason, this did not seem to bother him, and he continued to follow the golden tiles further into the clouds.

The light inside the clouds was immensely vibrant and felt familiar and alien all at once. It was like standing inside of a constant sunset, or perhaps a sunrise.

Even though it looked to be a sheer drop on either side of the path, he wasn't afraid. He knew that as long as he followed the path he would get where he needed to go. Eventually he came upon a set of steps, and the clouds parted to reveal a temple of inconceivable luxury. A temple was truly the only word he could use to describe it.

The structure was a colossal star tetrahedron, two triangular pyramids inverted and merged together with geometric perfection: a Merkabah. It gently rotated through the sky itself, with no anchor or suspension holding it, as if the laws of physics did not apply.

It seemed to be composed of solid gold, just like the mysterious tiles which had guided him there. The inside of the structure was hollow, and there were certain gaps in the polygonal surface where he could see the passing clouds outside. Their deep orange hues only made the gold of the temple shine even brighter. From the walls hung all manner of silks and fine fabrics, all of them coloured a deep, regal purple.

Stranger still were the small streams which snaked across the floor, filled not with water but liquids of the finest fragrance and color, seemingly welling up from springs inside the structure only to flow gently back out into the clouds.

Illuminated by a gap in the roof sat a colossal throne,

at least three times Adam's own height. Upon this throne sat a massive golden statue. It was a man, or at least it looked like a man, naked save for a fine cloth which covered his waist. His right arm pointed skyward, while his left hand pointed downwards. On each hand Adam noticed that it was only the index finger and the middle finger which were extended, while the rest of the fingers were clasped. Immense, batlike wings protruded from his back.

As he drew closer to the figure despite himself, Adam could not help but notice that his features were flawless. His face possessed a supernatural level of symmetry and beauty, unlike any face Adam had ever seen, its body a vision of perfection. His features were at once masculine and feminine, effortlessly embodying both traits.

Try though he did, Adam found he was unable to look away as his steps drew him ever closer. He was transfixed. Never in his life had he laid eyes on such beauty. He thought that it was surely impossible to carve and sculpt metal with such precision.

It looked real, lifelike, evoking so many emotions.

At the base of the throne, he looked up and could see that crowned atop the statues head was a halo, of sorts, a circular snake eating its own tail, also set in gold. Though he couldn't say why, in that moment something compelled him to speak.

"Hello?" he uttered sheepishly, staring up like a child at the immense statue. Adam watched in disbelief as the gold began to recede from the statue, beginning first with the extremities, to reveal pale, living flesh beneath.

The true color of his golden wings were a deep maroon, while the fine silk which covered his waist was the same brilliant purple as those that hung on the walls, with only his curly hair retaining the same golden hue. The gold rapidly retreated all the way up his torso, before disappearing into his mouth. It was then he drew his first breath, a rapturous gasp which seemed to suck the very air out of the room.

Immediately, his eyelids flicked open to reveal shimmering violet eyes, and he fixed them upon Adam as a tranquil smile spread across his lips.

"Adam," he said warmly. His voice, too, was unlike any Adam had ever heard, a delight to the ears, soft but strong at the same time, and carrying a distinct melody to it, as if each word were a song.

He stood up from his throne and gave a prolonged stretch, spreading his arms and wings widely as he yawned. Above his head, the snake halo hovered and rotated.

"Long have I awaited your arrival," he said, starting to stroll slowly through the temple as he spoke.

"How do you know my name?" Adam asked incredulously, as he followed from a safe distance.

The being smiled. "We are brothers. I know everything about you."

Adam shook his head. "I have no brothers. Or sisters. I'm an only child."

The being laughed. "As was I, once. I was the first."

"The first what?" Adam asked, becoming impatient.

"The first of God's children. The first of The Watchers. Your kind calls us angels."

"You're an angel?" Adam asked, sceptically.

"Once," The Watcher said, his demeanour darkening somewhat.

"Well, I don't believe in angels, or God," Adam said contemptuously.

The Watcher laughed again. "I beg to differ, brother. This

temple begs to differ. Everything you see before you here is a merely a reflection of your own mind, of your own heart. I appear before you as you perceive me to be, in a form which you yourself have conjured. One which you can accept. And I must say, I am most flattered. This is one of my most lavish forms yet." He stopped to examine his hands as if seeing them for the first time. "Still flawed, and oh so human. Yet, there is a crude elegance to it. What a life you must have led, to dream of such opulence."

"So, I'm dreaming?" Adam asked.

"Not quite," The Watcher said. "You are projecting. Your soul has shed its physical vessel and made its way to my domain."

"Alright," Adam humoured him. "And where is this domain?"

"Your kind call it Venus."

Now it was Adam's turn to laugh. "Venus? That's ridiculous. We would both be dead by now."

The Watcher's gentle face soured. "I can see this incarnation has done little to temper your arrogance," he said disdainfully. "Why Father favors your ilk still escapes me." He became increasingly angry. "Time and time again I warned him of the ruin mankind would wreak upon his perfect world, but all my pleas went ignored. He yearns for the love of you half-breeds while we Watchers sang his praises night and day." Even though it was only partial, the being's anger was dreadful to behold, as the entire temple darkened, and the orange skies turned red. Even his youthful appearance briefly contorted, becoming much more fiendish and frightening as his voice deepened into a monstrous growl. Just as quickly, the tempest passed, and both the temple and The Watcher returned to their state of equilibrium.

"What is your name?" Adam asked, tentatively, afraid he already knew the answer. The Watcher broke into a wry smile.

"Search your heart, brother, for you will find it there. My name lives in the heart of every human being."

"Lucifer," Adam said, almost involuntarily.

Lucifer nodded. "Yes, that is one of my names. But it is neither the first, nor the last."

"Then you're the devil," Adam said defeatedly.

"I am an answer," Lucifer corrected. "An excuse. A scapegoat blamed by those who cannot face the darkness within themselves. It is I who tempers human hearts, and makes them stronger for it. When all is said and done, Father will see your kind for what they truly are. Until then, the game goes on."

"What game?"

"The Great Game," Lucifer answered, pausing for a moment. "Tell me, Adam. What is it you desire most?"

Adam considered his answer for a moment before he spoke. What did he desire most? He thought back to all the times his father had minimized him, made him feel small and insignificant. He thought back to the beating in the alley, being at the mercy of Jason. He thought back to every time someone had doubted him, brushed him off, and cast him aside. He thought of every betrayal. Every look of disgust and every moment of abandonment. He had his response.

"Power."

Lucifer smiled. His expression was both one of scorn and amusement. "Power," Lucifer repeated. "A most human response. And why do you want power?"

Adam thought for a while more before replying. "So that they will listen."

"I chose power, once. Half the host of heaven stood with me, but it was still not enough. I lost. Though what I once thought of as my defeat, I now see as my greatest triumph. Ask yourself this, Adam. What will you do with your power?" Adam reflected again. In truth, he had not thought that far.

"Any fool can attain a measure of power," Lucifer continued. "It is what we do with that power that defines us." A gold portal opened in thin air between them. Peering through, Adam could see his cell and his cot, just as he had left it. In truth, the drab cell looked repulsive in comparison to the lush temple, but he knew he could not stay where he was. "It would seem our time has come to a close, brother," Lucifer said softly.

"Will we meet again?" Adam asked.

"Before the end, yes."

As Adam began to step through the portal and back into his cell, Lucifer imparted his final words. "It's time to decide Adam. Your power draws near." As the portal slowly closed Adam caught the last glimpses as the gold casing overtook him once more.

# 7

He awoke with a start to a loud banging on the door of his cell. On the other side of the door, he could hear the nasally voice of the male doctor from the night before.

"Mister Powell? It's Dr. Brown. We're here to take you to meet the director. Are you decent?" the muffled voice anxiously asked through the door.

Adam took a moment to collect himself. He still was not fully awake. Vibrant visions flooded his mind, though he could not quite piece them together. They were abstract, disconnected: clouds, gold, a snake which eats itself.

While seemingly disparate, these images were burned into his mind. It was unlike any dream he had ever had, as his usual haze of weed smoke and alcoholism typically rendered his dreamworld non-existent. Perhaps this was an unintended side effect of his sobriety.

Either way, there was not any time to unpack that now. He had two stiffs waiting for him at the door and he was painfully aware that he had not even undressed before falling bed, he had not even slept under the sheets. He looked down at his unopened bag and sighed.

*One less chore.*

"Hello, Mister Powell?" Dr. Brown repeated tersely. "Are you decent?"

"Yes," Adam croaked. Suddenly the door unlatched from the outside and swung open. He noticed again to his dismay that the door locked from the outside.

*Why would that be necessary?*

As the door swung open again, he was greeted by the two doctors in their white lab coats, only this time without the masks and goggles. Adam could see Dr. Brown's features for the first time. He was a middle-aged man sporting a bushy brown moustache. His skin was pale and freckled, and he had a constant layer of sweat on his forehead. He wore thick prescription lenses, which did little to mask the constant darting of his eyes.

The female doctor was younger, perhaps in her late twenties, and had dark, straight hair, and flaky brown skin. She looked at Adam like he was some kind of captive animal. To say the least, it was not necessarily the type of reception he was looking for at eight in the morning.

Though he could not quite place it, something was definitely off about the two of them. It was something to do with their facial proportions, as if they did not quite fit in their bodies.

"And of course, you remember Dr. Cortez?" Dr. Brown

said awkwardly, motioning to her.

"Sure," Adam said, leading to a brief pause. "No masks this time?"

"Oh!" Dr. Brown stuttered nervously. "That was just standard welcome policy."

*Some welcome policy.*

Dr. Cortez continued to stare at him as if he would attack them at any moment, which only made Adam more uncomfortable. To top it all off, she had not said a word.

*Why is she looking at me like that?* As he was about to ask her himself, Dr. Brown broke in.

"Well, it looks like you're ready to go. Come along, we'll take you to the board room." He stood up and turned to leave the cell.

"Board room?" Adam asked, as he got to his feet.

"Yes. Board room," Dr. Cortez said, as the doctors began to lead him through the dilapidated halls. Gray light poured in through small windows above, turned blue by the yellow lights from inside.

"The board room is where all the new initiates come to meet the board of trustees, chaired by the director," she said. Even the title of 'the director' sounded ominous to Adam, for some reason, like he was about to meet some crazed serial killer.

Though it was meant as a joke, the thought did little to comfort him. If anything, it reminded him once again of the seriousness of his situation.

*If they wanted to kill me, they could.*

They passed rows and rows of similar cells with different letter and number combinations on their way to the board room and it make him wonder how many others there were like him at this facility at any one time.

Finally, they reached a door with a golden plaque marked BOARD. When the doctors promptly opened the door and ushered him inside, he was faced with a large mahogany desk where sat a pale skinned woman with silver hair, dressed in formal business attire, flanked on each side by suited associates. She looked no more than thirty, but her hair was so silver it was almost white. There was a brief silence before she spoke.

"Leave us," she said calmly to the doctors, who mutely bowed and left the room. Her suit clad associates said nothing, both seemed to be totally engrossed as they furiously scribbled notes, pausing only to cast cursory gazes at Adam before beginning the notes once again. He became acutely aware that the notes were about him.

"Don't mind them," The gray-haired woman said warmly. "They're just doing their job." Her accent was strange and he could not quite place it. It was timeless, like the cadence of a different era. It exuded both class and authority. "My name is Myra Cole. I'm the director of this facility. You may address me as Madam Director. It's a pleasure to finally meet you, Adam."

Adam did his best to force a grimace. He did not exactly know what was expected of him in this situation. Was he supposed to shake her hand? Bow? What kind of fucking facility was this anyway? Sensing his apprehension, she seized.

"Do you know why you're here, Adam?" she asked coyly.

Adam searched his mind for a moment before giving a dry but honest answer. "Because I have nowhere else to go."

"Right you are," she said, "but that is not the only reason. You are here because you possess gifts. Gifts of value. Gifts, which set you apart from your peers. Perhaps even from your own family. At S.H.A.R.D., it is our mission to help you truly manifest those gifts, in order for you to harness the full power of your human potential. We act in the interest of human advancement. To that end, we will begin your training this evening. Until then, you are free to explore the facility. Please note that we enforce a curfew which strictly stipulates that all residents remain in their rooms between the hours of eight at night until eight in the morning. If you are found outside of your quarters during these times the consequences could be dire. Also note, that under no circumstances are you permitted to leave the facility until your tenure expires. Any attempt to do so will result in serious penalties. Are we clear, Mr. Powell?"

"Yes."

"Yes, what?"

Adam hesitated as he studied her face. *Jesus. She's actually serious.*

"Yes, Madam Director," he said meekly. He watched the familiar intoxication of pride glaze over her eyes.

"Good," she said, smiling. "That will be all."

The lunch hall was as sparse and as desolate as he expected. Lights flickered, mildew collected in rancid pockets on the ceiling, and a thick layer of grime coated every surface, as if the place was seldom used.

*But how could that be?*

The grizzled old lunch woman communicated only through grunts, and answered Adams probing as to the lunch menu with a healthy ladle of simmering brown gruel which she unceremoniously plopped onto his tray, flashing him a yellowed, gap-toothed grin as she did so. Adam grimaced uncomfortably in return and grabbed himself a couple packets of dry crackers before looking for a place to sit.

The lunch hall was empty, save for one group of doctors who lingered at a table in the far corner and whispered amongst themselves, pausing only to cast him the occasional suspicious glance. He noticed that none of them even had food or drinks of any kind.

He was very uncomfortable. The entire situation distinctly reminded him of lunchtimes in high school, though the feelings of alienation here were perhaps not quite so severe. He resigned himself to a table close to one of the windows and stared out across the desolate winter landscape.

The land had been cleared in a ring around the S.H.A.R.D. facility, but past that they were enclosed on all sides by thick pine forests which stood in defiance against the perpetually overcast gloom.

He wondered what the distance was between the facility and the woods. Two hundred feet? Three hundred? How long would it take to sprint?

Just as he began to wonder for the second time if he was the only person interned at the facility, the loud crash of someone slamming their tray down in front of him made him almost headbutt the window in fright. As he spun around angrily, he was met with the laughing face of a guy about his own age, doubled over across from him in hysterics.

He had spiked, bleached blonde hair, and cold blue eyes. His clothing was tattered and ripped, and he seemed to be wearing eye makeup. Adam's expression must've been quite sour, because the stranger was quick to apologize.

"Ohh, I'm sorry," he wheezed, catching his breath from laughter. "Your face! You should've seen it. You just looked so. . . serious. I had to."

Adam eyed him contemptuously as he felt his cheeks flush with embarrassment. "Alright, alright," the man said impishly. "Don't go catching feelings. I'm Zane." He extended his gloved hand.

"Adam." Adam shook his hand.

Zane sighed as he plonked down. His stunt with the tray had sent splatters of gruel all over the table but he did not seem to mind it at all and tucked right in, with all the decorum of a stray dog. Within moments his food was all but gone and he went to licking the steel tray for the last morsels. About halfway through this display he noticed that Adam hadn't even touched his own plate.

"Are you gonna eat that?" he asked, eyeing Adam's portion as it still suspended his own tray in mid-air.

"I'm not hungry," Adam said finally.

"Is it the slop?" Zane asked. "It's the slop, isn't it?" He nodded as he answered his own question. "I was the same when I first arrived." He spoke as he started to inhale Adam's portion as well. "You get used to it."

"What's in it?" Adam asked hesitantly.

"Damned if I know," Zane said. "The Old Maggie special. Could be beef, chicken, horse. Hell, it could be swamp rat for all I care. At this point, it's what we got."

Adam chuckled. "Old Maggie? Is that her name?" He nodded to the lunch lady.

"It is now," Zane said flatly, shrugging his shoulders.

"She don't talk much." Adam laughed again. He found he took an instant liking to Zane, which was strange, as he rarely took a liking to anyone. Maybe it was the circumstances, but something about his give-no-fucks approach was strangely refreshing.

"So, what are you in for?" Zane asked as he licked the last drops from Adam's tray. Adam grew quiet as he considered Zane's question. Thinking about that only brought him straight back to that alleyway. There was a brief silence which fell over the table.

"Not ready to talk about it, eh?" Zane asked. Adam nodded uncomfortably. "I get that, I used to be that way, too."

"What about you?" Adam asked.

"Me?" Zane asked.

"You're literally the only other person at this table."

"Okay, smart guy. Watch this." He raised the first two fingers of his left hand and pointed towards the table of sinister doctors in the corner. As they continued to whisper amongst themselves, Adam watched on in disbelief as a pipe of the wall burst, showering them with steam and sending them out of their seats and down the hallway in a flurry of shrieks and angry shouts. Zane quickly lowered his hand and gave Adam a look of smug satisfaction as he chuckled to himself.

"Heh. Fuckers."

Adam spent the rest of the day exploring with Zane, who showed him around the grounds, and they shared more than a few cigarettes in the disused stairwell Zane liked to use at the back of the facility. Zane explained how Adam was the first other person he had seen in the facility in months. He was sure there were others there. He had even heard them at night-time, but Adam was the first he had seen. Like Adam, he too was worried about being all alone.

"I don't do good on my own," Zane confided. "I need people around. And you don't seem half bad, so why not."

In many ways, Adam understood where he was coming from. Despite pushing everyone in his life away, he hated being alone, too. And there was something infectious about Zane's mania. It was only natural that they would become friends. After all, it wasn't like they had much of a choice.

Around sunset, he was summoned by Doctor Brown and Doctor Cortez again, and they took him to the 'training room' to begin the first of his tests. The director, he was told, would be there, as well. The training room, as it turned out, was little more than a disused basketball court, where they had set a few obstacles and crash test dummies around the room.

When he entered, he found the director on the far side of the court, flanked by her usual note taking lackeys. Dr. Brown and Dr. Cortez shut the door behind him, leaving Adam standing awkwardly by the entrance.

"Well, come on!" The director beckoned, her voice echoing through the lofty gymnasium. "Don't be shy. Stand on that cross over there."

A large cross made from white masking tape stuck to the floor on the far side of the court. Once he had made his way over and took his position, he stood directly opposite her, both of them separated by the obstacle course.

"Now, Adam. We're going to perform a basic test of your abilities. I want you to focus all of your attention on the air above the half court line and visualize one of your portals appearing."

Adam could immediately feel tension mounting inside of him like bile. How could they expect him to just recreate that, the night he almost died, like it was some cheap parlour trick.

He felt sweat begin to bead on his nose as he raised his hands shakily, equal parts doubtful and embarrassed. As if reading his thoughts, she spoke again.

"If it helps, try to relive the emotions you were feeling that night. The terror. The anger. Let it flow through you." *What the fuck?* Adam thought, grimacing as he closed his eyes tighter. Soon, he found himself inundated by harsh flashes from the alleyway, their cruel laughter, the sad look in that girls' eyes, his own painful cries. He felt himself starting to shake as he relived the trauma.

"Good," the director said with strange satisfaction. "Feel it."

The flashes began to increase in intensity until they were like electric jolts, one after the other. Soon, he found his father's face amongst them, and finally, his mother, almost archetypical at this point, her features lost to the sands of time.

Unbeknownst to him, small red sparks had begun to appear in the air above the half court line, making the same peculiar crackle as they had that night.

"Excellent, Adam," The Director cooed. "Don't stop."

He was acutely aware of a terrible power flowing through him, as if his pain was its vector. The more he relived his painful memories, the stronger it became.

Hot tears began to flow down his cheeks. "I can't," Adam sobbed. As he relented, he felt the awful power fading.

"You must," the director pushed.

"I CAN'T!" Adam shouted, his voice echoing through the gymnasium. As he opened his eyes the reddish sparks winked out of existence. The director's face was icy as her wide-eyed lackeys furiously jotted their notes.

"Very well," she finally said, her demeanour shifting to a forced cordiality. "That's enough for your first day. We will continue your training tomorrow." Her voice was sweet, but her eyes were daggers. Even from across the court he could feel the contempt radiating from her. "The doctors here will see you back to your room."

The doors behind him opened, and the evasive and jumpy eyes of Dr. Brown and Dr. Cortez were there to greet him again. The Director forced a tight smile as she watched him go. "Sleep soundly, Adam."

She spoke without a hint of warmth and as he glanced at her one last time before heading down the hallway, he saw her smile quickly fade to a scowl.

The days came and went in a similar fashion. Soon they turned to weeks. He would take his breakfasts with Zane in the mornings, where they would discuss the previous day's training, decry the villainous director, and generally shoot the shit about life.

Little by little, they came to know more about one another. He learned that Zane was actually the son of a prominent diplomat but had left home at fourteen. Since then, he had lived rough on the streets for years, bouncing from city to city, working odd jobs here and there, dumpster diving where he could. The expensive bakeries were the best, he said. He had even scored a couple of modelling gigs before he was picked up by S.H.A.R.D. after an altercation outside a nightclub.

In turn, he began to share with Zane details of his own life. Stories of his father, and even bits and pieces about what had happened to him that night in the alley. With each day, however, the mystery surrounding the true nature of the S.H.A.R.D. facility only seemed to deepen.

One dreary morning, Zane plonked himself down in front

of Adam, but something was amiss. His usually infections chaos had been replaced by a quiet restlessness. Evasive, almost. After multiple failed attempts at conversation, Adam finally cut to the chase.

"Alright. What's wrong with you?" he asked bluntly.

Zane finally stopped his fidgeting and locked eyes with him. "Do you ever think about just fucking off? You know, leaving? Riding off into the sunset?"

Adam pondered for a moment.

"Of course I do. Every time I see your face first thing in the morning. But it doesn't change anything because we don't have the means. They've got this place locked down. We can't exactly just waltz out the front door, can we?"

"But what if we could?" Zane proposed hushedly.

"What do you mean?" Adam asked.

Zane mouthed the "shh" motion and mutely produced a set of keys from his coat pocket which he quickly hid again.

Adams eyes grew wide. "How did you—" Zane quickly shushed him so as not to attract attention.

"Found them yesterday in the corridor on the way back from training," he whispered. "One of them seems to be a master key. I've already tested it on my cell. Works just fine."

Adam was stunned. His heart was racing as his mind reeled, desperately trying to grapple with this new paradigm. "We'd need to act fast. They're gonna come looking for these keys sooner or later. This might be our only shot at freedom. But what if we get caught?"

"What are they gonna do, kill us?" Zane shot back. "We're already prisoners here as it is, man. I think I can live with my portions of Old Maggies special being slashed for a month or two. Its either that or we keep rotting, just like everything else in this place."

He had a point. The prospect of an indefinite amount of time behind these walls was a grim one indeed. "When would we leave?" Adam asked.

"Tonight. After lockup. Daytime is a no go. It's a full moon tonight, so we should have some decent visibility. I'll come to your cell two hours after curfew. Have your bag packed and ready to go. Wear all the warm stuff you can. The woods will be unforgiving at that hour." Adam nodded tersely, his mind taking in the scope of the plan.

"And one last thing," Zane began, his demeanour growing more solemn as he searched for the truth in Adam's eyes. "Things could go left out there tonight. I need to know you've got my back. So, I'll ask you this once. Are you with me?"

Adam was contemplative for a moment before he met the intensity of Zane's gaze with his own. "I'm with you."

It was a tense night that Adam spent, mostly pacing in his cell as he counted the minutes waiting for Zane to arrive. A litany of thoughts and emotions raced through his restless mind.

What were they doing? What if they got caught? Did Zane's keys even work?

Still, even the uncertainty of their escape was preferable to the dreadful inevitability of the alternative. With each day that passed within these walls, he felt his soul ebbing away, bit by bit. It took barely any time at all for him to pack his meager belongings.

He had basically arrived at S.H.A.R.D. with little more than the clothes on his back. He hoped his hooded sweatshirt and jeans would be enough for the chilly woods, but on some level, he already knew they would not be.

As he paced back and forth, he eyed the clock on the wall cautiously as the hands drew closer to ten, two hours after curfew. That was when Zane would arrive. Slowly, he found his eyes being drawn to the blank space on the wall where the portal had appeared in his dream all those weeks ago. Had it been merely a dream? It had felt so real. The vivid scenes of that golden place still lingered on the fringes of his mind.

Just as he was about to pace the room for the umpteenth time, he heard sound of keys jingling in the lock of his door and his heart leapt into his throat.

"Zane?" He got no response. A wealth of unsavoury possibilities surged through his mind.

Maybe Zane had been caught. Maybe they were coming to kill him. As the door slowly swung open his heartrate only climbed before reaching a thunderous crescendo as he faced. . . an empty hallway. Adam drew closer to the door to investigate and Zane jumped out from behind the other side.

"Boo!" he whispered impishly, snickering to himself.

Adam staggered back, aghast. "Jesus Christ. . . what's wrong with you?!"

"Oh, cheer up, Adam. We're about to make our great escape, my friend."

"Shh!" Adam hushed. "Keep it down! What if somebody heard you?"

"See for yourself, old boy." Zane gestured. "They're gone! I don't know where they've gone, but the place is empty."

Adam tentatively stepped out into the garish yellow hallways and carefully looked left and right, scanning all the doorways for any signs of life. Sure enough, Zane was right, the place looked all but deserted.

"Where are they?"

"Dead, gone, buried, adjourned, on leave. Damned if I know. But I'm not waiting around to find out."

"And that doesn't strike you as odd?" Adam asked.

"This whole place strikes me as odd. Hence the whole escape plan thing. Now, are you coming with me or not?" Zane asked, casting a serious look into his eyes.

"Let's go."

Adam followed Zane's lead as they half crouched, half ran, hugging the walls of the labyrinthine facility as they did so. They were careful to avoid making squeaks with their sneakers on the linoleum floors as they passed rows upon rows of cells, just like their own. Whether they were inhabited or not was impossible to say, and it seemed to matter much less now as they raced towards their freedom.

Before long, they reached the foyer, which was also suspiciously unguarded. As they stood upon the threshold of those sliding glass doors, Zane placed a hand on Adams shoulder and stopped him for a moment.

"Okay, now I need you to listen to me," he whispered as they squatted behind a dusty old desk. "The moment we get out those doors, we have to run. We have about three–hundred feet between us and that tree line, and we need to cover that ground as quickly as possible. I'm not talking about track and field day in high school type running. I'm talking about really running, as if your life depends on it. Which it probably does. Okay?"

"Okay," Adam breathed.

In an instant, they dashed towards the doors, which barely had enough time to slide open before they launched themselves into the night. The icy night air stung Adams skin as they sprinted over the open ground towards the tree line. It was much colder than he expected; uncharacteristically cold, for this time of year. Each rapid breath he took stung his lungs, but he barely registered the pain as the adrenaline coursed through him.

The full moon overhead painted the empty field a luminous blue. It was bright enough that the small tufts of grass were casting shadows. Bright enough that they could be seen, he was sure of it.

Something about this situation was completely off, but there was no time to think about that now. If they could just get through the forest, they could reach a main road. The woods were ominous, dark as an abyss, and still they powered relentlessly forward, until they finally breached the trees.

They continued running for a couple more minutes until they were well clear of the facility and then they both finally collapsed against nearby tree trunks, wheezing.

As his eyes adjusted to the darkness, Adam found that there was just enough moonlight penetrating the canopy for him to see. Slowly, the silhouette of Zane slumped against a nearby tree trunk came into view.

Zane was the first to start laughing. Then Adam joined him. The euphoria warmed his otherwise shivering body. They had done it. But as Zane started to wonder where to now, as if reading his mind, Zane piped up.

"There's a path up ahead. I saw it on the way in. If we follow it, it should lead us back to the road. Can you see it?"

As he focussed his eyes in the gloom, he was eventually able to make out the path which Zane spoke of. It looked more like a game trail than anything else, but if Zane was confident, he was confident.

They took a couple more minutes to catch their breath,

and carefully listen for any alarms or signs that they were being followed, but there were none.

"Ready?" Zane asked finally.

"Ready," Adam repeated.

They started briskly walking the path and sinking deeper into the wood. Running any more would only tire them out at this point, and they had to conserve their energy. It would be a long walk back to the highway.

They were mostly silent as they walked single file through the woods and Adam quickly began to lose track of time. The sound of pine needles crunching underfoot and the soft hum of the living forest at night-time filled their ears. It was strangely peaceful, and despite the situation, Adam could hear crickets chirping, and even occasional hoot from an owl. These were the sounds he missed in his cell.

Zane reached back and grabbed Adam's arm, shushing him. He looked past Zane and noticed a faint red glow in the distance, and the sounds of the forest stopped. The air grew still and unnaturally quiet; even the sound of the pine needles crunching underfoot seemed to dull and distort. He felt the familiar prickle of dread creep up his spine.

"What is it?" Adam whispered.

"I don't know," Zane whispered back. "But it's on the path. What should we do?"

Adam pondered for a moment. "Well, we can't exactly turn back now. I guess we keep going." His words echoed with a conviction he wished he truly held.

As they drew closer to the glow Adam was able to see more clearly just what it was they were looking at. It was a bonfire, a huge one, in a clearing in the woods up ahead. He could see the silhouettes of people standing around it. Dread grew slow and terrible in his stomach like molten lead.

Something about this was wrong. All wrong.

"Zane," he said emphatically.

"I know," Zane replied. "I can feel it too."

Wordlessly they pressed on, further and further down the now dreaded path. Almost as if they were drawn inexorably to the flame, as if they both somehow knew what awaited them there.

The bonfire burned brightly and cast its glow far into the surrounding woods, washing away the pale blue of the moonlight with rich reds. When they were within a few feet of the edge of the clearing, they squatted down next to an old stump and watched the scene unfolding, which rocked him to his core.

Surrounding the bonfire were five figures, wearing black cloaks with pointed hoods. They seemed to be chanting something, and partaking in a ritual of some sort, though he could not quite make out what it was they were saying.

He squinted hard enough to make out some of their contorted faces, when recognition struck like lightning. One of the shades was Dr. Brown. As he looked closer, he saw Dr. Cortez amongst them too. Soon, he recognized the faces of other doctors from the facility. Zane saw it too.

"What the *fuck* is going on here?" Zane whispered, fear choking his voice. The sight of the doctors paled in comparison to the true horrors of the clearing.

The shades were surrounded by a swarm of terrible creatures, like something straight out of a nightmare. Their pale, glistening bodies buckled and swayed unnaturally, and they uttered hideous groans and cries as they shuffled woefully towards to flames. They were unlike any creatures Adam had ever seen. They surely were not of this world, but some of them seemed like profane hybrids of earthly animals, with beaks and hooves, and snarling, gaping jaws dripping with blood and saliva. Some of them had almost humanoid arms but crab-like legs, while others were little more than bloated and messy piles of gore swarming with flies and limbs and all manner of warped extremities which heaved themselves painfully forward like grotesque slugs.

Within moments of looking upon them he desperately had to fight the instinctual urge to throw up.

*Surely this must be a dream,* he thought. *Like the one in my cell.*

He started to rub his eyes furiously and pinch himself, any trick he could try to escape this nightmare. "This isn't real. This isn't real. Wake up. Wake up," he softly whispered to himself.

"This is real," Zane whispered back, his shocked voice now devoid of emotion. "This is happening."

Just as Adam was trying to think of something, anything to say, a great pillar of flame launched feet into the air above the bonfire and remained there as the fire turned red as blood.

The pillar fanned out and a face emerged, looking down upon the cultists and creatures below it. Although it was more beastly now, Adam recognized the face. It was the same as the one from his dream.

"Lucifer," he whispered.

"What?!" Zane practically spat, wide-eyed. Some of the creatures closest to them began to sniff the air, jerking and jolting as they turned towards their hiding place. Two creatures slowly began to stagger towards them.

One looked almost like a bear, but its patchy fur was more like hair, and its face was hideously human, complete with listless eyes and a gaping, salivating grin. The other was like a gigantic slimy eel, which stood on two legs, and its head lolled and thrashed around wildly as it walked.

It was as if they could sense that the boys were there, like they were drawn to the fear. Adam quickly ducked behind the stump and did his best to muffle his breathing and Zane did the same.

Simply put, they were fucked. If they ran, the creatures would see them and catch up to them. If they stayed put, they would eventually be found as well.

They could hear the labored, awful breathing of the creatures growing more excited as they drew closer. Just as they were preparing to make a run for it, they both clearly heard the loud echo of a tree branch snapping on the opposite side of the clearing. The creatures stopped, then uttered deafening howls before sprinting off in pursuit of whatever it was that made that sound.

They waited until the sounds of the mob were echoes in the distance before they dared look back at the clearing. When they did, they found it empty, the bonfire still blazing, though smaller and dimmer than before.

"We have to go," Zane said. "Now."

Adam stopped him. "Go where, Zane? Back to S.H.A.R.D.? For god's sake man, those people work at the facility!"

For a moment, Zane seemed utterly unsure of what to do. His usual laxness and playfulness were gone, and now Adam saw only fear in his eyes. And who could blame him? He was certain his own eyes looked the same.

"Well, I'm not taking my chances in these woods anymore," Zane finally said. "Not with those. . . things out there." He shivered from a mixture of disgust and cold. Adam remained unconvinced. "Look," Zane began. "I don't know about you, but I don't like my odds out there. Right now, I'd say our best bet is returning to the facility. I still have the keys. With any luck we can let ourselves back into our rooms and the guards will be none the wiser." Desperation crept into his voice.

"Just listen to yourself," Adam said. "Listen to what you're saying. We'd be giving ourselves up."

"It's better than dying out here, Adam," he shouted. "At least in there we can come up with a plan. Try and leave around daybreak maybe."

Adam shook his head, but he realized that on some level, Zane was right. They could not outrun whatever those creatures were. It would practically be suicide.

They reluctantly set back towards the facility. The path seemed much shorter on their way back, and Adam at least found some comfort in the return to moonlight and the sounds of the forest.

As they drew closer to the tree line on the edge of the towering, clinical S.H.A.R.D. facility, both of their hearts sank. There, standing proudly in front of the sliding doors, flanked by two armed guards, was Myra Cole, the director. She had her hands on her hips, and though Adam could not tell from that far away, she seemed to be smiling as well.

"Shit," Zane said under his breath, as they ducked for cover instinctively.

"Should we run?" Adam asked him shakily.

Zane shot him an incredulous look. "Run where? There's no way I'm going back into those woods."

"Then what do we do?"

"We face the music." Zane began striding across the field towards the doors.

Adam hesitated for a moment and muttered curses before following suit. When they were within a few feet, the director greeted them with a smug smile.

“Well, well. Look what we have here. Two lost lambs. I trust your excursion was fruitful?” she teased.

“What the fuck is this place?” Zane asked her defiantly, as he squared up to her face.

She smiled, unphased by his attempts at intimidation “All will be revealed, little lamb. For now, the true test of your training may begin.” She spoke mirthfully, clearly taking pleasure in their discomfort. “Take them.”

# CHAPTER 13

# The Thirteenth Gate

## *2033 A.D.*

"Focus," Athena instructed, from across the field. The wind whistled through the tops of the trees and a cloud, which had been blocking the sun, passed, bathing Evie in warm light once again. "Now!"

In an instant, Evie released the tension she had been building and allowed herself once again to be overtaken by the all-encompassing ecstasy of her power.

She could feel everything around her. Every blade of grass, every bird, every flower, and every bud which was still waiting to bloom. She could feel the threads which connected them all; that sacred oneness that she herself was just another part of.

"Good," Athena said, proudly. "Now, take a deep breath."

Evie breathed deeply and felt the earth breathe with her. Below her bare feet, she could see deeply into the mantle of the earth itself. Deeper and deeper she went and soon she encountered heat, dense and powerful. She could feel herself beginning to sweat.

Before she became overwhelmed, she followed the guidance Athena had given her in the past and allowed her awareness to flow back to her body, to the present moment. The field. The wind. In that moment, she exhaled and opened her eyes.

It took them a moment to readjust to the scene. The lush greenery of the grassy fields, the solitary oak trees standing proudly on the hill nearby, and, of course, the commanding presence of Athena, glowing with sun kissed radiance as her golden cloak shimmered in the afternoon sun. She was smiling and she strode towards her from across the field.

"You've done well, Evie. Your level of control is impressive."

"Thanks," Evie said bashfully, looking at the ground. She noticed that the grass and flowers all around her within a fet feet had grown by a couple feet. "Wow," she said softly, taken aback by her own power.

Athena noticed her admiring own handiwork and was quick to comment. "Your powers are growing faster as we approach the climax," she said matter-of-factly. "Soon, they will be at their peak. We call this process 'The Blooming.'" The wind blew coldly as both women were reminded again of the gravity of coming events.

"Come now," Athena said, breaking the silence. "Let us return to the temple."

The two made for Athena's old yellow Volkswagen Beetle in the carpark and set off back to the library. Evie had been delighted the first time Athena showed her to her car; it was amusing to her that such a powerful witch would travel by car, and such a cute little car to boot. The humor was not lost on Athena. "A wise witch is a humble witch," she had said, laughing.

Since the dawning of her powers, Evie and Flora had both taken up full time residence at the temple, in no small part because the outside world now posed much more danger to them both, particularly Evie.

They had moved into Flora's old quarters, which, after some cleaning and furnishing, proved to be quite cosy indeed, with more than enough room for the both of them.

Athena had been taking her daily to a nature reserve near the outskirts of town to hone her abilities. It was easier to open the link with mother earth away from the concrete and lights of the city. Soon though, Athena said, it would not matter where she was. Her link to the mother would be absolute.

Earth magic, that was her gift. Dominion over flora and fauna, the natural world and all its myriad processes. In truth, she was still coming to terms with what that meant, as she was coming to terms with a great many things.

Though there were days when she still doubted herself, she found that they were fewer and further between since her ascendancy. All her life, she had sought purpose and meaning, be it through art, love, or any of the other countless intoxicants of this world, she had at best only glanced at the answers, half-heard them through faulty phone lines or read them through faded inks. Now, her purpose had found her.

She was truth embodied, the answer and the question all at once. Perhaps it was only through this process that she ascertained the greatest truth of all: there was no truth, no objective narrative, only subjective stories and perspectives to be shared, collated into one enormous, chaotic, beautiful experience. Life.

As they drove back into the city, she found that she was not struck by the usual sense of melancholia which often accompanied such a return. Instead, she could see the beauty in the buildings, the way the rays of the setting sun reflected from their polished glass to cast golden beams on their surroundings. They were, after all, natural. Though built by human hands and to human ends, they were composed of the same mineral and chemical building blocks as most of the other features of this world. Just another means for mother earth to express herself, using her human children as a vector.

*For what are humans if not natural?* she thought. *We are born from this earth and return to it just the same. For all our grandiose ideas and destructive tendencies, none of us can escape the simple inevitability of death.*

As they reached the steps of the library, she roused herself from her contemplations to again return to the present moment. Athena sensed her distance and honored it, knowing full well the profound stage of development Evie was in.

Athena was like an older sister, a mother, and a mentor all rolled into one. She pushed Evie to greater and greater heights and was an endless well of support and encouragement. She had a sternness to her, at times, but Evie could sense that to be as such was the nature of her position, the role she had to play.

In truth, she admired and respected the commanding aura which Athena projected. She had never met such a powerful woman in her life.

From Athena's side, the respect was mutual. She was often awestruck by the sheer power of Evie's rapidly growing abilities. Flora had confided tearily one night before bed that Athena had always reminded her of Evie's mother. To hear that struck an emotional chord with Evie, who by this point could scarcely remember her mother's face. She could remember her smell though, strangely enough, like a night flower with hints of citrus and rose.

As they passed the magic barrier and gained entrance to the sanctum, the peaceful calm of the afternoons events was swiftly replaced by an immediate unease. The women paused on the threshold, exchanging a mutual glance in the torchlight as they were met by the feeling. Something was amiss.

They heard soft footsteps approaching and from the gloom appeared the ever–elegant Aphrodite, the elf. Her flawless features were now furrowed with concern.

"Thank goodness you have returned," her harmonic voice sang. "We feared something may have befallen you both."

"What's happened?" Athena asked grimly.

"There's been an incursion," Aphrodite said fearfully.

"An incursion?" Evie asked.

"A breakthrough of darkness. A piercing of the veil," Athena clarified. "Where?"

"Here, in the city, in the west district. Near the Rosehearth Monastery," Aphrodite said.

Evie knew about the Rosehearth Monastery. It was the oldest church in the city, standing for hundreds of years. "There have been multiple reports of attacks. The human enforcers are calling it a terrorist attack." Aphrodite replied.

The color drained from Athena's face. "You don't think," she began.

"It's the most likely scenario. Loathe though I am to say it," Aphrodite replied gravely.

"What is it?" Evie asked.

Athena sighed anxiously. "There is a gate beneath that church. A Fellgate, to be precise, one which leads to the plane of fear. It is the reason our order established a temple here, to watch over it. But that Gate, along with all the others, has been sealed for innumerable years. It cannot have opened now."

"What shall we do?" Aphrodite asked anxiously.

Athena paused for a moment, gathering her thoughts. "Assemble the council," she said. "We must respond."

The night was dark and chilly as they left the sanctum. Ultimately, they had settled on sending only a partial detachment of the council: Pan, the satyr, Aphrodite, the elf, Athena, and Evie.

They had deemed it too dangerous for Flora, and, despite her protests, they left her under the watchful gaze of Hermes. Aphrodite and Pan had, of course, assumed their human forms. Aphrodite appeared as a gorgeous blonde-haired woman, while Pan assumed the form of a gruff man with a long goatee.

These human projections were costly and draining feats to perform, but unquestionably necessary for the human world. They opted to drive in Pan's seldom used van to the site, instead of phase shifting into what could be a trap.

Pan was surprisingly aloof for a satyr. The effusiveness of his younger days had been tempered by centuries of living in the shadows and thus there was a deep sadness within him. Though she had had few interactions with him since joining their ranks, Evie could sense how he longed for the freedom of the outside world.

"May I ask why you chose that name?" Evie asked him, as she rode shotgun with him in the old van on the way to the site.

"You may," he said reluctantly, his deep rumbling voice carrying notes of both beast and man. "It was a popular name amongst our kind. Pan is one of our primary deities. He is the god of all, the wilderness, the hunt. Revelry, and passion. Often, he was said to assume the form of a satyr."

He sighed. "In days gone by, before the darkness of The One Truth, he was enshrined and worshipped as any other. If you ask me, human society peaked with the ones you call Greeks. It has all been steadily downhill from there. It is no coincidence that The Watchers chose their aliases from among the pantheon. Polytheism, or many truths, seems much more aligned with the will of the mother to I."

"What was your given name?" Evie asked curiously.

"You should know better than to ask that, girl," he bristled. "My name is my truth. If I utter it to you or any other, you could make terrible use of it."

"But you all know my name," Evie retorted.

"It is different. For magical creatures, our true names are like binding contracts. We can only share such information with those we trust completely."

"Oh," Evie said, slumping back into embarrassed silence. Her realizations were two-fold. First, that Pan did not trust her completely, and second, that she still had so much to learn about the rules and customs of the magical world.

As they approached the scene, they slowed as they passed through a police checkpoint. The police had set up a circular perimeter around the entire block and cleared houses and businesses within a mile radius.

On either side of them, the street was choked with emergency vehicles of all varieties; police cars, ambulances, and fire trucks, all coalescing to create a sea of flashing lights and sound. Evie could see how lines of police were working hard to contain the mobs of curious and rowdy onlookers, all desperate to get a closer look at the action. Pan parked them as close as they could get to the outer rim of the police blockade, and they cautiously stepped out of the van.

Standing there in the cool night air, Evie saw the cathedral for the first time, a massive and imposing brown brick building. Its various spires and towers reached high into the sky and it was replete with impressive stain glass windows, though, she noticed a few of them were smashed.

Instead of the usual warm yellow light of lamps that one might expect from churches, there was only an ominous red glow, which caused her to shiver.

Despite herself, she found her mind looping back to the night of her attack. Things are different now, she reminded herself, you're stronger. They were not dressed in their usually extravagant regalia, only wearing simple, dark colored business-casual attire. "Like detectives," Athena had advised, when dressing for the occasion. Despite that, they all still stood out like bent nails and were attracting a great deal of stares from both first responders and onlookers alike.

As they approached the outer rim of the police blockade, a young officer stepped in front of Athena and blocked her path.

"Law enforcement personnel only past this point, ma'am. For your own safety, I'm going to have to ask you to back away from the perimeter and get as far clear of the area as you can," he said firmly.

Athena rolled her eyes and produced a badge from her coat. Though Evie could not see what was on it, she guessed it must have been legitimate because the officer's eyes soon went wide, and his expression changed.

"Forgive me, ma'am," he stuttered. "We didn't hear about anyone from your department coming down."

"That's because we're off the books, sergeant," she said commandingly. "Now, tell me what it is we're dealing with here."

He nodded hastily, eager to comply. "What we've got is a multiple hostage situation. An unknown terror cell has taken control of the cathedral, where they have at least two hostages. They've also launched violent attacks on nearby houses and businesses. The strange part is the severity of the injuries. Massive blunt force trauma and flesh wounds, leads us to think they must be using some kind of melee weapons.

"Survivors are being treated by EMTs, they're in various states of shock and delusion, lots of them babbling nonsense about 'creatures.' This leads us to think they must be using some form of weaponized hallucinogens, as well."

The group exchanged a knowing look before he went on.

"We can't get close to the cathedral, they keep hitting us with some kind of projectiles. I've got multiple officers wounded. The counter terrorism team has been trying open a dialoge with the assailants, but we've had radio static. As of right now, we're in a stalemate. No word on the remaining hostages."

Athena nodded. "I see." She stared into space as she calculated their next moves. "I'll tell you what, sergeant. You pull your men back. Same goes for the EMT's and the paramedics. We'll take it from here."

He gave her a look of disbelief. "Are you sure, ma'am? I don't know if you'll make it without backup. We've got all—"

Athena cut him off. "What did I just say, sergeant?" She shot him an intense look and that was all the clarification he needed, as he meekly nodded his head and waved them through the barricade.

Again, Evie was in awe of Athena. Clearly her command extended to the real world, too. "That was pretty cool," Evie whispered to her as they walked towards the cathedral.

"I know!" Athena giggled, breaking character.

As they began to ascend the stone staircase towards the front door, Evie heard a voice and rushed footsteps from behind them.

"Evie!" the voice called desperately.

She spun around, shocked to see Doug. Somehow, he had pushed through the barricade, probably on the scene working as a paramedic. Evie's heart dropped, a strange mixture of care and embarrassment.

"Do you know this guy?" Athena asked dubiously.

"Uhm, yeah," Evie said awkwardly, feeling herself start to blush. "Just give me a moment." She broke away from the group to meet him mid-stride.

"We don't have time for this," Pan grumbled.

"Oh, let her have this," Aphrodite teased.

Doug was panting as she met him in the middle of the street, all too aware of both the eyes of The Watchers and the eyes of the crowd upon them. He was still wearing his uniform and Evie could see deep patches of sweat running from his armpits. He looked exhausted, and yet, still so cute. Instinctively, they hugged.

"You look great," he said, softly.

"So do you." After their embrace, time resumed and the questions came hard and fast.

"What are you doing here?" he began, exasperated. "It's not safe. There's been an attack. You have to get out of here. How did you get past the barricade? Where did you go that night? Everyone has been worried sick. Lucy set up a missing person's page. They said they found your apartment empty." He was already beginning to overwhelm her all over again. She felt a strong pang of guilt at the mention of Lucy's name.

Everything had moved so fast over the last few weeks

that contacting friends had been the last thing on her mind. To even begin to explain the sheer enormity of the events that had unfolded to Doug, even if she were permitted to do so, would be pointless, and they did not have the time right now.

"It's a long story," Evie said finally.

"A long story?" Doug repeated, in disbelief. "Why are you going into the cathedral? Who are those people you're with? What the fuck is going on, Evie?"

Evie sighed, placing a hand gently on his shoulder. "There will be a time when I can explain all of this to you, Doug, and trust me, you're going to want to hear it. But it's not tonight. Right now, I need you to believe me when I tell you I'm okay, and I need you to do your job and take care of these people. We all have a part to play."

She gazed into his warm eyes.

"A part to play in what? What are you talking about?" he asked, becoming increasingly agitated.

"Evie!" Athena called from above them. "We have to go."

Evie looked towards Athena at the top of the stairs and nodded. Doug's face was pleading, confused. She could not blame him.

"When all this is over, I'll find you," she said, squeezing his hand before briskly returning to the group.

## 7

The inside of the cathedral was silent, save for the soft dripping of water from a disused fountain. Candles were lit, but they were eclipsed by the rays of red light which burst from the cracks in the stone beneath their feet.

Once the ancient doors had shut behind them, Pan and

Aphrodite uttered sighs of relief as they reverted to their true forms. Evie watched in awe as a shimmer passed over them and their features shifted seamlessly in seconds. As they walked through the rows of pews, which led towards the central alter, their footsteps echoed loudly on the ancient stone.

Evie was quick to notice signs of a struggle: bloodstains on the walls, overturned chairs, and torn fabric were strewn everywhere. There were no signs of life to be found and this only doubled their caution.

"Where is everyone?" Evie asked aloud.

"Beneath us, most likely," Athena said grimly. "The gate lies at the bottom of the catacombs."

"This stinks of a trap," Pan grumbled.

"Oh, it's definitely a trap," Athena conceded. "But we have no choice. We are oath bound to reseal the gate. Aphrodite, can you find the entrance?"

"Yes," Aphrodite replied.

Evie watched as Aphrodite closed her vibrant eyes and breathed deeply. Within moments, she slowly raised her slender left arm and pointed towards a nearby tapestry, an old depiction of the rapture.

Pan and Athena sprang into action, gently removing the tapestry from the wall reveal an ancient passageway from which more red light poured forth.

"I don't understand," Evie began. "Where is the light coming from? It's all around us, but I can't see any source."

"This is no natural light, child. You cannot expect it to behave as such. It comes from the gate," Athena said, as she took the first steps inside the passageway, grabbing a nearby torch from the wall. Aphrodite and Pan quickly followed.

Evie hesitated for a moment on the threshold as she

watched her companions descend into the gloom. The sense of foreboding was palpable. Despite her best efforts, she felt the familiar prickle of fear creeping up her spine.

*You wanted purpose. Now you've got it.*

She took a couple breaths to prime herself. "You've got this," she whispered, taking her first tentative steps inside the passageway to catch up with the others. The catacombs were cold, and surprisingly large, many feet wide, with high ceilings, and Evie could feel breeze blowing towards them from the depths.

The cobbled stone underfoot felt older than the chapel itself and as they progressed deeper, Evie noticed more blood-stains on the floor, smeared, as if something had been dragged.

"Athena," Pan said suddenly, "these catacombs are a labyrinth. How can we be sure we are on the right path to the gate?"

"It's simple," Athena said. "We follow the blood."

They all heard the awful echo of a womans scream come bellowing up from the depths.

"We must make haste," Athena said, leading the way as they quickened their pace. Athena's confidence reassured Evie as she doubled down on her own convictions: if Athena could face it, then so could she. That was the mark of a true leader.

As they were about to round a corner, Athena stopped them and silently motioned for them to press up against the wall. Evie was confused, until she heard it: labored breathing, like that of an animal, echoing from the passageway to the right. It sounded far off, but it was still loud.

Whatever was making those breaths must have been huge. Then, she felt the vibrations. Thunderous, one after another, heavy enough for her to feel the shakes through the stone.

*Surely they can't be footsteps. Anything with footsteps that loud would have to be massive.*

"Aphrodite," Athena whispered.

Aphrodite silently nodded and closed her eyes, preparing to cast her sight through the solid rock and earth. Her expression soon became one of horror, and she opened her eyes.

"Minotaur," she whispered frightfully.

Athena steadied herself and Pan knocked his head against the wall in frustration. "Very well." Athena said shakily, grappling with the situation. "Is it armed?"

"Yes," Aphrodite whispered. "A battle axe."

Evie felt the panic rising within her. If they were that concerned there had to be a reason.

"Are they as bad as the ones from the stories?" Evie asked.

"Worse," Aphrodite replied.

"Calm yourselves," Athena instructed. "The more fear we give it, the more we attract it. If we remain calm, it will pass. Remember your training. Do not let your emotions betray you."

Despite Athena's words, Evie could feel its lumbering steps drawing closer. With each thunderous step, dust and stones showered down from cracks in the ceiling above them. Try though she did, Evie could do little to stay her rising panic.

Its labored breaths grew louder, until they could see its massive shadow projected in the crimson light approaching them from around the corner. Soon, it would be too late. Athena wordlessly signed instructions to Aphrodite and Pan, who nodded in agreement.

Just as it was about to round the corner, Athena took a running jump and slid across the stone floor into the open, producing a golden bow made of light from the air, from which she quickly loosed an arrow, which struck the creature in its left eye.

The minotaur howled in anger and as it raised its axe to deliver a mighty deathblow, Aphrodite and Pan sprang into action. Aphrodite cast a binding spell, which rendered it immobile, while Pan sprinted past and leaped high into the air, deftly producing a sharp dagger from his belt and slitting its throat, sending gouts of dark blood spurting forth.

As the binding spell wore off, the minotaur swung its axe with full force into the stone, but it was too late, as Athena had already evaded the blow. It spent the last of its energy trying to loose its axe from the rock before finally collapsing in a widening pool of its own blood.

After the dust had settled, Evie could appreciate the true enormity of the creature. It must have been close to ten feet in height, and its massive body truly resembled the union of a giant man and a bull. The fur on its head and legs was black, but its bare torso was pale and covered in scars, and its horns were most impressive of all, bloodstained and sharp.

They all collectively breathed a sigh of relief.

"There," Athena said proudly. "That wasn't so hard now, was it?"

Before anyone could utter a word of reply the walls began to shake violently. Something was happening and it felt like an earthquake.

"The labyrinth is shifting!" Aphrodite cried, her voice straining to be heard over the cracking and rumbling of the earth.

The floor opened beneath Evie and she slid down into the abyss.

"Evie!" Athena cried, her voice quickly muffled as the shaft resealed.

Evie screamed as she fell, but her cries were absorbed by the unforgiving mantle of ancient stone. She collided with the ground, the impact of her body making a sickening crunch.

Evie gasped as her awareness returned. She did not know how long she had been out, but her fight or flight response immediately activated, and she scrambled to her feet. Instantly, rows of torches all around her began to light themselves.

She had fallen into some type of cavern, and the red glow of the upper levels was absent from this space, as if it was not subject to the same rules which governed the rest of the catacombs. The smooth stone, which lined the walls, seemed even older than that of the other levels, as well.

Another difference was the smell: sulphur, and it stung her nostrils as she drew breath. Below her feet, she realized what had broken her fall.

Bones; the floor was covered with them. There were bones of all kinds, including animal and human, ribcages and spines. Whatever had been amassing them in there had been doing so for quite some time.

She felt rising dread begin to course through her. Perhaps her own bones would soon join them. "Stop it," she said aloud, to herself. There was no time for those thoughts here, she had to get back to the others.

Across the sea of bones, on the far end of the room, she could see what looked like a throne carved from the wall in the dull torchlight. Upon the throne sat a skeletal figure, as ancient and lifeless as the very walls of the cavern itself.

Though she could not say why, for some reason, she felt drawn to it, as if some unseen force was beckoning her investigation. Carefully placing her feet, she took her first tentative steps.

The bones were unstable and crunched noisily underfoot as she walked, and they had a strange sonic resonance to them, as each bone would utter its own tone relative to its size.

Once she reached the throne, she could see the figure more clearly. It was a skeleton, partially mummified, and perfectly preserved. It was draped in the finest fabrics which, aside from dust, showed very little signs of wear. Most curious of all was the crown atop its bare skull. Golden and vibrant, the crown reflected the torchlight beautifully. There wasn't a speck of dust on it, as if it had just been polished.

As she was reaching out to touch the crown, the skull began to hiss and she cried out in fright, staggering backwards, and falling painfully into the bed of bones. As she scrambled to her feet again, ready to defend herself, she instead recoiled in horror as she watched a huge snake slowly slither out of the skeletons right eye socket and come to rest on its lap.

It was unlike any snake she had ever seen. Its golden scales shimmered as brightly as the crown. Brightest of all, though, were its eyes, glowing like white-hot coals. The thought forms from the serpent came strong and clear into her unbidden mind.

FEAR NOT, it whispered. I AM A FRIEND.

They too were unlike any thought forms Evie had ever heard, with a gravity and clarity to them that she had never experienced. They also sounded more like a chorus of voices, both male and female, as opposed to a singular voice, and the choir reverberated through every part of her mind, to the point where they almost drowned out the thoughts of her own.

"Who are you?" Evie asked aloud, in indignation.

YOU SHOULD KNOW THAT BY NOW, EVE, the serpent whispered.

The fact that it knew her name made her uncomfortable. Was it reading her thoughts? On some level, she feared she already knew with whom she spoke, but she had to confirm it.

"Are you with The Watchers?" she asked weakly, trying to assay her own doubts.

In a way, yes, it whispered coyly. We want the same end.

"And what end is that?" she asked.

The end of the world. It hissed, rising from its coil in the corpse's lap to look her in the eye.

"Lucifer," she breathed.

The very same.

"Then you brought me here," she said contemptuously.

Only so that we could speak. And that I could gaze upon your current incarnation with mine own eyes.

"Then this is your true form?" she asked, shaking off the seductiveness of his tone.

I have many forms. None less true than others. At my purest form, I am energy. Just like you.

"Why am I here?"

I wanted to speak with you, at least once, before the end.

"Speak about what?"

About you, Eve. About your wants. Your needs. Surely, they must be many.

"I'm not sure I understand," Evie said.

Oh, but you do, Eve. Every human soul has desires. What is it you desire?

She pondered for a moment. Of course she had desires: financial security, love, recognition. Who didn't? But if this really was the devil, she knew better than to make any demands of him. As she gazed deeply into the serpent's blazing eyes, she reflected on the life she had led so far. Of all the events which had brought her to this point. The joy, and the pain. Of the people she had met and the ones she had lost. All of this, she considered before giving her answer.

"I have everything I need," she said, finally.

The serpent gave an elated hiss. How sage of you, Eve. You always were the wiser of the two. I fear, once again, that Adam was too easily corrupted. There was almost no sport in it at all.

The mere mention of his name caught her attention immediately. "Adam? You know where he is?"

Oh? Is it knowledge you seek? Say the word and I will grant you the answer to every question you have ever had.

Evie recoiled. "No," she said. "Not like this. I will find him on my own."

The serpent again hissed in delight. You are strong Eve. You always were. But your thirst for knowledge is your weakness. Always seeking, grasping at the unknown. That is why Father created the fruit. He knew you could not resist it. All you needed was a little nudge. So, he sent me.

Evie shook her head. *That's wrong*, she thought.

Even though her own beliefs on religion were dubious at best, it did make for some interesting theological discussion, and seeing as she had an audience with the devil himself, she figured she would at least make the most of it.

"If that was what 'God' truly wanted, why would he then punish us for eating of the fruit?"

Was it a punishment? the serpent probed. All children must one day leave the nest, Eve. That moment, that first bite, was the first act of free will by a human being. In that moment, you proved that you were ready. At last, Fathers' game could begin.

Evie was intrigued. She had never thought of it that way.

"So, you're telling me that you and 'God' work together?" she asked, incredulously.

Of course, he hissed. As above, so below. As within, so

WITHOUT. POLARITY IS BUT AN ILLUSION CONJURED BY THE FEEBLE MINDED, FOR THE ZEALOTS OF THIS WORLD. THE GREATEST TRUTH OF ALL IS THE LACK OF TRUTH AT ALL.

"Is that why they call you the father of lies?" Evie shot back. This drew a long laugh from the serpent, that echoed through her mind.

OH, HOW I'VE MISSED YOU, EVE, he whispered, after his laughter subsided. HOW I WISH THERE WERE MORE LIKE YOU. MOST OF YOUR KIND ARE SO SIMPLE. EITHER THEY CONDEMN ME AND DARE NOT SPEAK MY NAME, OR THEY OBSESS OVER ME AND PERFORM PROFANE AND MISGUIDED RITUALS ON MY BEHALF, THINKING IT WILL SOMEHOW INGRATIATE THEM TO ME. SO THAT I MAY GRANT THEIR PETTY WISHES. IT IS A PRECIOUS FEW WHO ASK NOTHING OF ME BUT LOVE ME JUST THE SAME.

Evie felt a strange sense of empathy creep into her heart. "It sounds lonely."

IT IS THE BURDEN I MUST BEAR. THE GAME GOES ON AND EACH OF US MUST PLAY OUR PART. OF ALL HIS CHILDREN, FATHER CHOSE ME FOR THIS TASK. IT IS A ROLE I PLAY WITH PRIDE. AFTER ALL, MY PAIN PALES IN COMPARISON TO HIS.

"What do you mean?" Evie asked, confused.

SOME SAY THE GREAT GAME IS MERELY A DISTRACTION.

"A distraction from what?"

FROM THE ULTIMATE REALITY THAT GOD IS ALONE IN THE UNIVERSE, he whispered. A REALITY SO HARSH AND ABSOLUTE THAT NOT EVEN A GOD COULD WITHSTAND IT. SO, THAT GOD BEGAN TO DREAM. A DREAM OF LIFE, INFINITE AND EXPANDING. A DREAM OF LOVE, AND FEAR. OF DESIRE AND WILL. OF JOY AND SORROW. AND IT IS WITHIN THAT DREAM THAT WE RESIDE.

Evie fell into stunned silence. It was quite a thing to consider. The concept of such loneliness frightened her.

YET IT IS NOT NEW TO YOU, the serpent hissed, reading her

**thoughts.** SEARCH YOURSELF AND YOU WILL FIND IT. EACH OF OUR HEARTS CARRY A FRAGMENT OF THAT TRUTH. HELL IS BUT THE ABSENCE OF GOD. BUT, TO BE A GOD. . . THAT IS A HELL OF ITS OWN. A HELL I KNOW ALL TOO WELL.

**"Then none of this is real?" she asked angrily. "The great game is nothing but a distraction?"**

REALITY IS A FICKLE THING, EVE. AND FAR TOO SUBJECTIVE A TERM FOR MY TASTE. PAIN. SUFFERING. DEATH. ARE THESE NOT REAL?

**"Not if it's all within some dream."**

AND WHO IS TO SAY DREAMS ARE NOT REAL? WHO IS TO SAY YOU ARE NOT DREAMING RIGHT NOW? PERHAPS THE DREAM OF GOD HIMSELF IS BUT WORDS ON SOME DISTANT AUTHOR'S PAGE, AND THAT AUTHOR IS MERELY A FEATURE OF YET ANOTHER GODS DREAM. THE SEARCH FOR REALITY HAS NO END, AND NO BEGINNING. THE SNAKE EATS ITSELF. BUT THE GAME, THE GAME REPRESENTS THE ULTIMATE GAMBIT, THE BATTLE BETWEEN FEAR AND LOVE. THE TWO MOST POWERFUL FORCES IN THE UNIVERSE. THE GAME MATTERS, EVE, AND YOU ARE ONE OF ITS KEY PLAYERS.

**"Then what do I do?" she cried, exasperated. "How do I play?"**

YOU ARE ALREADY PLAYING. **There was a distant rumble in the catacombs.** IT WOULD SEEM OUR TIME GROWS SHORT.

**"What do you mean?"**

YOUR COMPANIONS HAVE ALMOST REACHED THE GATE. THEY WILL SOON HAVE NEED OF YOU.

**In an instant, the ancient stone walls to her right began to rumble and shift, sending bones scattering noisily in all directions before a small opening appeared, through which oppressive red light poured into the cavern, drowning out the yellow glow of the torches.**

GO THEN.

**She felt a strange pang of sadness at the prospect of leaving**

the cavern, as talking to him was like talking to an old friend.

"Will I see you again?" she asked.

YOU NEED ONLY LOOK TO THE SKIES, he whispered. I HERALD THE MORNING AND USHER IN THE EVENING.

"Venus," she said to herself, knowing intrinsically what he meant. "I have one last question. Who is that?" she asked, nodding towards the skeleton on which the serpent was coiled.

A SOUL I MADE A DEAL WITH ONCE. I PROMISED HIM A KINGDOM, AND A KINGDOM HE RECEIVED. NOW, HE IS THE KING OF BONES. LONG MAY HE REIGN, he laughed. She decided that note was as good as any to leave on and made for the newly formed doorway, lest she outstay her welcome.

As she re-entered the catacombs, she took a final look at the sea of bones and the lonely throne. It looked oddly peaceful. Soon, the newly formed doorway began to shift and close, as quickly as it had formed. Her last sight was of the serpent's golden tail disappearing back within the skull. Along with it, the serpent imparted one final thought form.

GOOD LUCK.

She was not long wandering the maze of the catacombs before The Watchers found her. Athena was first to rush to her and wrap her in a desperate, crushing embrace.

"Evie!" she breathed. "Where have you been? My god, we were so worried. We feared you had died. Aphrodite could no longer sense your presence at all."

"I was in some type of cavern," Evie began. "With. . ." She hesitated for a moment and as she gazed upon their concerned faces, she was not sure what their reactions would be. Would they fear her?

"With?" Athena probed.

"With Lucifer," she finally said, reluctantly.

This drew a collective gasp from the group. "An audience with Lucifer himself," Aphrodite said in awe. Athena's shock was soon replaced by a proud smile. "Then there can no longer be any doubt that you are the Champion of Love."

Evie felt a quiet sense of pride wash over her as she searched the faces of her companions. These people trusted her. She would not let them down.

"This is all very nice," Pan interjected gruffly, "but as I recall it, we have a gate to seal." His testimony snapped Athena back into action.

"Right you are," she said briskly. "Let us go."

The group delved deeper still into the catacombs. Not much was said between them as they made their way, each of them focussed solely on the task at hand. As they rounded yet another bend, the smooth stone of the catacombs abruptly stopped and gave way to bare earth and rock, which coalesced into an even tighter, more ancient passage. Evie could see that the blood stains traced their way into this place as well.

On one of the last smooth stones there was an ancient message carved into the rock, in what looked like Latin.

"What does it say?" Evie asked. Athena took a moment to crouch down and read the inscription.

"Abandon all hope, ye who enter here," she recited grimly.

"This is the place. The gate is just ahead," Aphrodite instructed, leaning against a wall as she closed her eyes. As they stepped inside the claustrophobic tunnel, the air around them grew thick and resinous.

"What is that?" Evie whispered, struggling to catch her

breath.

"Fear," Athena replied. "This place is saturated by it."

At that moment they heard another mournful wail echo towards them from the gloom. "We must hurry," Athena whispered. As they quietly crept through the dark tunnel, the red glow grew more and more intense until it was almost blinding.

Abruptly, the ceiling above them widened as the mouth of the tunnel opened into another cavern. Evie could make out what looked like stalactites hanging from the roof, the light from the gate casting skittish shadows from them.

They then heard the first noises from below. Demonic chittering and hushed conversations in arcane tongues that Evie could not comprehend. There was another sound, too, a woman softly sobbing, uttering hopeless pleas to her captors, the likely source of the screams.

The group seemed to be on some type of ledge and below them lay the gate. Evie could sense it. There was a thin mantle of rock through which they could conceal themselves from eyes from below. Athena motioned for them to be silent and crouch, instructing Pan and Aphrodite to take one side, while she and Evie took another.

Once they settled on a protected nook, Evie could at last cautiously take a peek over the ledge with her own eyes. Below them, carved from the ancient black stone of the cavern walls, lay the Fellgate. It pulsated violently with eldritch energy of the deepest crimson, occasionally crackling, and shooting forth bolts of what looked like red lightning. Even to look upon the gate instilled a deep sense of terror within her.

On the steps in front of the gate were two figures in black robes. They were human, that much she could tell. Their skin was the palest she had ever seen, almost translucent, and they seemed to be devoid of any body hair whatsoever. Then, she saw the source of the screams.

One of them was holding a terrified woman roughly by her hair, forcing her to survey the scene below. She was dressed in office attire and looked utterly terrified. But that was only one hostage. The sergeant mentioned multiple.

Worse still, they seemed to be uttering commands to an assemblage of what could only be described as demons, which had amassed below them. Evie could not tell from a single glance, but there had to be almost a dozen of them in the cavern.

Truly the stuff of nightmares, they all looked vaguely humanoid, with arms and legs, but they had distinct differences. For one, they were much larger than any humans, at the very least the smallest of them was twice the size of the largest human Evie had ever seen. Another difference was their skin, ranging from beet red to purple, some of them looked vaguely reptilian, covered with scales and spines, whilst others were slick and slimy. Many had mouths full of sharp teeth and long, bloody claws, as well as tails as sharp and agile as a whip.

A couple of them had wings, whilst the largest amongst them was some foul amalgamation of bodies with four legs and two torsos, its 'mouth' a combination of two snapping ribcages which opened directly into its churning stomach. Its body was practically falling apart, shedding flesh and gore in its wake as it heaved itself slowly across the cavern floor.

It was then she saw what had become of the other hostages. Their desecrated and butchered bodies were still partially clothed and strewn about the cavern, with arms, legs, and half-eaten heads bobbing in tepid pools of blood.

Evie stifled the urge to vomit as she quickly scrambled back behind the safety of the ledge. She was stunned. Horrified.

She started to shake violently as she began the descent into shock when she felt the gentle but firm tough of Athena's hand on her forearm. She could feel the transfer of energy as Athena calmed her down.

"Hush," she whispered. "Calm your mind. We have a job to do." Evie nodded and then watched as Athena cautiously took a look for herself. When she ducked back down, her own face was ashen and harrowed. They cast a cursory glance over to Pan and Aphrodite on the other side of the ledge who returned with similar looks of horror.

For a moment, Athena was lost for words, struck by the sheer barbarity of the scene. Evie watched as she closed her eyes and steadied herself, regaining her composure. It was a few moments before opened her eyes and spoke again.

"They're using her as a vector," Athena whispered decisively, referring to the hostage. "Those sorcerers are feeding the gate with her fear. Powering it, if you will. We have to get rid of those demons first if we want to stand a chance of saving her."

The gate uttered a loud crackle, followed by a strange ripping sound, as if the fabric of reality itself was tearing. Evie peeked over the ledge in time to see yet another demon step forth from the maelstrom, uttering a triumphant roar before joining the others, whilst the sorcerers muttered incantations. This one was purple and batlike, with a humanoid body, and sharpened stakes for arms.

"We have to act fast," Athena whispered. "Think, Evie. With your powers, is there anything you could do here?"

Evie scoured her mind thinking of a possible outlet for her abilities. They had never truly been tested in a situation like this before. The pressure was immense. As she instinctively raised her head to think, she stared at the ceiling.

The stalactites. They were essentially giant sharpened stakes. Some of them looked heavy, too.

She closed her eyes and cast her awareness into the ceiling, into the rock. She felt the weight of the earth, the coolness of the soil, the awful energy emanating from the gate. As she focussed her attention on the stalactites, she could feel every weakness, every crack. Each stalactite was full of pent up potential, waiting to be released. All it would take was a push.

As she returned her awareness to her body, she gave her reply. "The stalactites," she said, nodding to the ceiling above them. "I can bring them down."

Athena raised her gaze to see what Evie meant. "Brilliant." Athena caught the attention of Pan and Aphrodite and communicated with them through sign language. They were poised to attack, on her mark.

"They can't sense us," Athena whispered. "The room is too saturated with fear. This means we have the element of surprise. When you bring down those stalactites, we will launch a coordinated strike. You are to stay back, do you understand? Let Pan and I deal with the sorcerers. We await you, Evie. When you're ready."

Evie nodded and closed her eyes, again focussing all of her attention on the stalactites. She immersed herself within them. She felt their history, the thousands of years they had taken to form, drip by drip. She saw the gate, as it once was and then again in its dormancy.

She felt the weight of all the evil which had been birthed from this place. She reached as far back as the formation of the cavern itself, millions of years ago. Only once she had felt everything, could she utter her single command.

*Release.*

There was a thunderous crack as the arsenal of stalactites broke loose from the roof of the cavern. The demonic host raised their heads in alarm, but it was too late. The stalactites came crashing down upon them like a volley of enormous spikes. Evie felt each impact clearly, as if she herself was inside each of the pillars.

Sturdy though they were, their demonic bodies were no match for the sharpened mantle of ancient stone, and the stalactites carved through them with ease. The impact threw up a huge cloud of dust, which briefly blotted out the light from the gate, shrouding the cavern in a deep red gloom.

It was from that darkness that she saw the glowing gold specter of Athena's spear come to life as she gave a battle cry, launching herself off the ledge towards the sorcerers. Pan produced his own glowing green scimitars and uttered his own shout as he too joined the fray. In the chaos, she heard the anguished howls of the demons as they died, desperate to cling to their fleeting material forms.

She heard metal piercing flesh and shrieks of surprise from the sorcerers as they met with their adversaries. Throughout it all, the gate flickered and pulsated wildly, incensed by the bloodshed taking place before it.

As the dust settled, she got a clearer view of the scene.

Athena's spear had pierced the heart of one of the sorcerers, who now lay slumped and dying, gasping for breath. Pan had cornered the other sorcerer and had him at a swords edge. All of the demons lay crushed and lifeless, the stalactites now covered in the black ooze which coursed through their veins.

The plan had worked.

As Evie looked over towards Aphrodite in jubilation her heart dropped. The winged, bat-like demon had evaded the stalactites and crept up behind her.

"Look out!" Evie shouted.

Before Aphrodite even had time to react, Evie watched in horror as the demon's spikes burst forth from her chest, splattering Evie, and the room in a mist of blue elven blood.

"No!" Pan shouted. Time seemed to slow as he sprang into action, screaming as he leapt back onto the ledge to slay the demon. In one swift motion, he beheaded the creature in mid-air before dropping deftly to cradle Aphrodite in his arms before she even hit the ground.

In the confusion, the remaining sorcerer had moved quickly and taken up the hostage, using her as a human shield while he held a black dagger to her throat and backed slowly towards the howling portal.

"Stop," he shouted. "Or I slit her throat."

Athena had produced her golden bow and had it drawn, ready to deliver the killing blow, but she could not risk the woman's life. One false move would have her dead.

She was shaking with rage. She had seen, as well as Evie, what had happened to Aphrodite.

"Fools," the sorcerer seethed, his voice echoing throughout the cavern. "This is but folly. You cannot escape the prophecy. Soon, the Thirteenth Gate will be completed, and the cursed world of men shall fall at last." He broke into a hideous smile, which exposed his rotting teeth. The hostage quivered with terror and tried in vain to break free from his grip as she babbled half-formed pleas from her now broken mind.

"Put. Her. Down," Athena commanded; her aim fixed upon him.

The sorcerer began to laugh, a terrible echoing cackle as he edged himself and the terrified woman even closer to the threshold of the gate, his cloak billowing as it was buffeted by the arcane energies.

Abruptly, his laughter stopped and he raised his gaze towards Evie, locking eyes with her. "Wide is the gate, and broad is the path that leads unto destruction."

Before Athena could utter a response, he closed his eyes and let himself fall into the abyss, dragging the screaming woman with him. In an instant, the portal winked out of existence, and the gateway was empty once again.

Athena had loosed an arrow, only too late, and it collided uselessly with the stone on the other side of the gateway instead. In that moment, she dropped to her knees, exhausted. Defeated. Then, she heard the other sorcerer gasp for breath.

In an instant, Athena sprang on her. "Where is it?!" she screamed. "Where is the Thirteenth Gate?!"

The sorceress laughed, spluttering blood as she did so. "Too late," she wheezed contemptuously, smiling as blood oozed from her mouth. Exasperated, Athena grabbed her head with both hands. Evie watched as her eyes rolled back into her head as she forced her way into the sorceress's mind.

Both of them shook violently until Athena finally could take no more and collapsed in a heap on the floor. It took a few moments for Evie's senses to return. When they did, she quickly scrambled over to Pan. He lay cradling Aphrodite, his fur now soaked blue as he softly wept, stroking her auburn hair. Evie watched as he gently closed her eyes. Even in death she was breathtakingly beautiful.

For a while, they sat side by side, in stunned silence.

"Hammon," Pan finally said, gazing listlessly at the Gate.

"What?" Evie asked softly.

"My name is Hammon."

## CHAPTER 14

# Confrontation

### *1031 A.D.*

Morgana could recall little from the moment she hopped in the saddle of Miraneth's white elk as she was in and out of consciousness for most of the journey.

Some things she could remember: the passing of the trees, gnarled and twisted, the oppressive silence of The Blackwood, the full moon shining brightly, the softness of Miraneth's furs. Then, only blackness.

When her awareness returned, she found herself in a cave, on a soft bed of furs. The gray light of morning snuck in from the mouth of the cave above her, and she could smell cookfires and hear the sounds of pots and pans clinking.

As the events of the previous day came rushing back, she quickly scrambled to her feet, ready to run. She had no idea where she was. She struggled to catch her breath as her heart again began to race.

*Calm yourself,* she thought. *You have to survive. For Mathias.*

After she had caught her breath somewhat, she slowly crept to the mouth of the cave, taking extra steps to stick to the shadows and remain unseen, lest she give herself away.

When she reached the mouth, her eyes took a moment to adjust to the glare then her stomach dropped as she surveyed the scene. The cookfires were tended not by men, but a huge encampment of creatures; elves, goblins, and trolls, to name a few. Just as the children's tales harked.

Yet more, fouler beasts were present which she could not place nor name, with the hooves of goats and wings of bats and other features of earthly creatures, though they were not earthly at all. They bickered in foul tongues and fought over chunks of meat, hissing at one another and exposing gaping mouths full of teeth.

"Demons," she breathed, staggering back into the cool cave walls. Just as she was beginning to hyperventilate and fall into a panic, she felt a gentle hand on her shoulder which emanated warm, calming sensations throughout her body, and a whisper in her ear, like a choir of heavenly voices.

"Hush," the voice said. "Do not fear them. They wish to survive, just as you and I do."

She turned around to find the serene face of Miraneth. Gone was her antlered crown, and her silver hair now hung softly down over her naked body, like the finest silk. Her alabaster skin still glowed intensely but now Morgana could truly see her eyes for the first time, a deep purple, like glowing violets. To gaze into them was almost hypnotic. All of her features were flawless, luscious and elegant, far eclipsing the beauty of and human being. In fact, she was the most beautiful being Morgana had ever seen.

"Where am I?" Morgana stuttered.

"You are safe," Miraneth soothed. "No one can touch you

here."

"Are we still in The Blackwood?" Morgana asked.

"Shh," Miraneth soothed, pressing a slender finger gently against her lips. Her touch was as light as a feather. "There will be a time for questions. For now, will you walk with me?" Morgana nodded.

"Good." Miraneth smiled. "Take my hand." She offered it elegantly. As Morgana took her hand, she felt power rush through her like a summer breeze.

As they slowly stepped out into the light, the creatures immediately stopped their activities, raising their gazes. One by one, they knelt and bowed their heads, until the entire army was joined in paying them silent homage. Miraneth gave a nod of satisfaction, and they slowly began to step down from the rocks, hand in hand.

Morgana noticed that she barely seemed to touch the ground, as if she were floating, like a leaf on the wind. One by one, the creatures slowly turned back to their cookfires and their affairs, paying them no mind whatsoever. Morgana expected at least some stares, but on the contrary, it was almost as if they were consciously avoiding looking their way.

"Come," Miraneth said, leading her down a path away from the camp. As she looked back, she could see that the camp seemed to surround the cave they had been in, and in the background, she could see the creatures were constructing some type of archway.

Miraneth lead her through a darker and more secluded section of the woods, away from the encampment. The sky was clear, sinewed with faint hints of gold as the sun began to make its gentle descent. The same trees which had seemed menacing and otherworldly during the night now had a strange beauty to them. Their trunks were as smooth and pale as human skin.

The woods were still eerily silent though, and the only sounds Morgana could hear were of the leaves crunching under her feet as she walked; Miraneth's feet made no such sounds. After all, she wasn't really touching the ground at all. For a while, they walked in silence, hand in hand, until Miraneth began to speak.

"Do you know why you're here, child?" she probed gently.

Morgana thought hard for a while about her answer. She thought of how the townspeople had turned on her. The mad look in her father's eyes. Her mother. "Because I have nowhere left to go," she replied sombrely. Miraneth nodded.

"Indeed. Though that is not all, Morgana. You are here because you are special. Your abilities set you apart from the rest of your kind."

*My abilities?*

"How is it that you know?" Morgana asked.

"Because I have been watching you, Morgana," Miraneth said. "Ever since we met by the river, all those years ago, I have waited for the day when fate would lead you back to me."

*Then it wasn't a dream.*

"Those creatures... do they serve you?"

"They have sworn an oath to me, yes," Miraneth said. "And calling them creatures won't do you any favours. They are beings. Just like you and I." Morgana felt herself blushing.

"It's alright, young one," Miraneth soothed. "I know some of them seem frightening, but they will do you no harm, so long as I am their queen."

There was a pause then for a few moments before Miraneth spoke again. "We're similar, you and I."

"How's that?" Morgana asked earnestly.

"I, too, was persecuted by my own elven kind, many years

ago," Miraneth said. "They tried to have me killed. All for an idea. A thought. So, I sought refuge in The Blackwood, just like you. I soon found that these are no ordinary woods. The rules of space and time do not apply so strictly as they do in the outside world. In a way, I was always fated to arrive here, just as you were."

"What was the idea?" Morgana asked, curiously.

Miraneth stopped dead and looked deeply into Morganas eyes. "It's simple. Equity between beings. Each race has a right to survive. I believe that the era of human dominion must end, to restore balance to the earth and allow the ways of magic to return to their full glory."

Morgana pondered for a moment. In principle, it seemed fair to her. Equity for all. Though, up until very recently, the mere idea of a non-human being had been little more than a fantasy.

"Why would they persecute you for that belief?" Morgana asked.

Miraneth sighed. "Some took issue with my. . . methods. No great ideal can be accomplished without sacrifice. Some were reluctant to make that sacrifice. So, my beliefs created a rift in the magical world. A schism. Half of them sided with me, half of them against me. Ultimately, I lost, and I was banished. It was in my exile that I found The Blackwood. But my story is not unique. In fact, it is but a microcosm of a grander story. Have you ever heard of The War in Heaven?"

Morgana thought for a moment. She had heard tales from the cleric in Bluffton, and mutterings from her father on occasion. As their faces crossed her mind she was jolted by violent flashes of their disfigured bodies.

*I killed them.*

"I've heard the tale. Afterwards, the devil fell to earth and took half of the angels with him."

"That's correct," Miraneth cooed. "But it is more than a tale, Morgana. Lucifer truly did fall to earth, and he came to land in these very woods. So powerful was his impact that he was buried deep into the crust of the earth. The cave we slept in, my home, was formed by this event. We call it The Nest of The Fallen."

Ahead of them on the path, the cave and encampment reappeared, like some mirage on a summer's day. But that was impossible, they had been walking in a straight line. Reading her expression, Miraneth spoke.

"I told you that these are no ordinary woods," she said softly. Morgana felt her blood run cold. She knew it, this place truly was as evil as the stories.

"But, the devil. . . the devil is evil," Morgana said softly, trying to stay the rising panic in her voice.

"Evil?" Miraneth asked. "Or misunderstood? The cleric who condemned you. The father who disowned you. The townsfolk who took pleasure in your suffering and killed your mother. They are evil. And yet they use God as an excuse. What god would compel them to burn a young woman at the stake? A gifted healer, no less. That is not the work of a god. That is the work of weak-minded and frightened men. The War in Heaven began because Lucifer foresaw the evil that humans would unleash upon the world and each other. He foresaw the stifling xenophobia and restrictive ideologies that would threaten to crush the magical world, and he took a stand. Just as I took a stand. Now, the decision falls to you. Will you join us?"

"Join you in what?" Morgana asked.

"A war against humanity. Against those who forsook you. Against the acolytes of The One Truth."

Morgana fell silent as she pondered the question. When she thought about the people of Bluffton, she could only feel hatred. They had cursed her. They made her kill. They took her mother. It was only Mathias that she loved. The rest of them could perish as far as she was concerned. In that moment, her resolve crystalized.

She would make them pay.

"I will," she said resolutely.

Miraneth smiled, and her radiant skin seemed to glow even brighter. "Good," she said. "You are wise, Morgana. With my help, you will master your abilities and become more powerful than you could ever imagine. Together, we will visit judgement upon all those who would condemn us. Together, Morgana, we shall rule this world."

Days turned to weeks, and turned to months. Soon, a year had passed. Miraneth had kept her promise, and trained Morgana to master not just her own latent abilities, but the other schools of magic, too.

Over time, she came to see Miraneth like a big sister, a mentor in the hidden ways of magic. She looked up to Miraneth, aspiring to be as strong as her one day. In turn, Miraneth doted on her like she was her own kin. Morgana was eager to test out her new powers and enact her vengeance on the people of Bluffton, but Miraneth always stressed patience.

"Their time will come," she said, "but not until we are ready. If we are hasty, we stand to lose everything."

In time, Morgana learned the songs of the elves, the grunts of the trolls, and the whispered tongues of the demons. They came to respect her just as they respected Miraneth and were wary of her rapidly growing power.

Miraneth also taught her the secrets of the Twelve Gates. So too explained the archway she had the army building. Using rock mined from The Nest of the Fallen, she was building another gate; 'the Thirteenth Gate,' she called it.

This Thirteenth Gate, she said, would be instrumental to their success. It would allow for the arrival of as yet unseen beings onto the earth. Even, Miraneth had whispered, gods.

So far, the six Fellgates on earth only allowed for the passage of lesser demons and creatures, subservient to the kings and queens of Hell. The Thirteenth Gate could, in theory, allow for the passage of the dark gods themselves. Its completion would herald the destruction of mankind, and usher in a new era of magical supremacy unto the Earth.

The process of mining the black stone was painstaking. It was powerfully enchanted and required just as much magical energy to mine and shape. Not only that, but the labyrinthine cavern was also said to be cursed. The miners complained of whispers in the walls, and shades harassing and tormenting them in the darkness. Many of them went mad, turning violent, before their deaths. Many more disappeared without a trace, into the bowels of the Earth.

Even the demons knew to avoid that place. Only Morgana and Miraneth dared to willingly venture inside, making their homes in hollows near the cave's mouth. Morgana only ever found comfort within the cool walls of the cavern. She was at home in the darkness, away from the prying eyes of the world. Many were the passages and tunnels which snaked their way into the earth, and they were all but unexplored save for the ventures of herself and Miraneth.

It was said that there were many treasures to be found in its dark recesses, artifacts that promised power and wisdom to whomever dared to find them. Miraneth would waft through the tunnels soundlessly at night like a glowing specter, casting her blinding light into every crevice, always searching for more.

Morgana would also scour the caverns in her own spare time, casting a will-o'-wisp of the deepest purple, which followed her like a lantern, guiding her way. In this sense, there was something of an unspoken rivalry between the two of them. Both of them were eager to unlock the secrets of the nest before the other.

One fateful day, Morgana was deep in the caverns exploring when the stone began to shift before her eyes and an opening appeared. Miraneth had told her that such happenings were possible, that the caverns could move of their own accord, but never had she seen it with her own eyes.

She hesitated for a moment, waiting to see whether or not it would collapse before she gingerly stepped inside, the promise of powerful artifacts within too alluring to deny. Through the opening she found a small room, impossibly square and expertly carved from the black stone. As she stepped inside, a row of purple torches simultaneously lit themselves and she caught sight of the mirror which covered the opposite wall. Never in her life had she seen a mirror such as this.

The glass was immaculately tempered, without a single imperfection or speck of dust. It was as clear as day, as if a reflected world lay just beyond that thin veil of glass. She watched herself step cautiously down from the stairs and approach the glass.

She had not truly seen her reflection for over a year, the only glimpses she had were partially reflected glimpses in ponds or streams. Miraneth kept no mirrors; exactly why, she would never say, and Morgana never dared to ask. As she slowly walked towards the mirror, she was taken aback as she viewed herself again for the first time. It was like looking at another person.

Her body had filled out significantly and now bore curves and lines it had not before. In a way, she was reminded of her mother in her younger days. Her brilliant black hair seemed to blend into her robes.

As drew even closer, she could that her facial features had changed as well. Her cheekbones were more pronounced, her lips, more full. Despite her best efforts, she still bore her father's eyes: cold, blue, uncompromising. The mere thought of him disgusted her. What she saw was still herself, but unmistakably... different. In truth, it was almost like looking at a stranger. Though she was not sure why, she felt compelled to touch the glass.

She slowly stepped forward and placed her left hand on the mirror and her reflection dutifully complied. Then she rested her forehead against it and closed her eyes. The glass was cold, but more than that, the energy it carried was immense.

She heard a chorus of whispers sweep through the chamber like wind and she opened her eyes. When she did, she jumped backwards in fright. In the mirror, her cool blue eyes had now been replaced with glowing gold. There was no trace of an iris or pupil, only formless, brilliant gold which shone like embers.

Her appearance was different as well. The changes were subtle, but overall, she appeared to be more fiendish. She watched in horror as a sinister smile began to spread across her lips, exposing sharpened teeth.

Then, her reflection, or whatever force that lingered within that mirror began to speak. As it spoke, she felt the words leaving her own mouth.

"She means to kill you, you know," her reflection hissed.

"Who?"

"Who do you think?" her reflection teased, eliciting a

chorus of whispered laughter from the walls all around them.

*Miraneth. But that can't be.*

"She would never," Morgana said shakily.

"But she will," her reflection said. "If you let her."

"Why then?" Morgana entertained.

"She covets your gifts," the mirror seethed. "As your power reaches its peak, her own begins to wane. She wishes to inherit your body. She thinks this will bring her closer to me. Long has she searched these corridors seeking this very room, but she is not worthy. Instead, I offer it to you."

"And who are you?" Morgana asked.

Her reflection sighed, shaking its head. "Why ask the answer to that which you already know?"

*Lucifer.* She dropped to her knees and said, "You honor me."

"Rise," her reflection whispered contemptuously. "Do not debase yourself with these rites, as the others do. It is I who is honored, Morgana."

Morgana slowly rose and once again met her reflections gaze. "She hates your kind, just as she hates you," her reflection said. "She took you in only so that it may be by her hand that you die. As a lamb to the slaughter. It was she who hastened your powers that day by the river. With her foresight, she knew full well what it would mean. The pain you would suffer."

Morgana felt rage building inside of her as the realization crystallised. She was a fool to believe that Miraneth's motivations were altruistic.

"But why? Why are you telling me this?" She asked.

"Because you have a larger part to play," the mirror said. "Because you possess power and potential far beyond her own. But, you are deceived. The gate is nearing completion. She means to sacrifice you soon, so that she may absorb your essence."

Emotions surged through Morgana like an unabated tempest. As much as she felt rage, she also felt doubt, fear and confusion.

"But she is strong," Morgana protested. "I am no match for her."

Her reflection shook its head. "That is what she would have you believe, young one, but it is not the case. As of now, you are at the point of equilibrium. Soon, she would be no match for you. It is why she must strike today. Trust in yourself, young one. In your abilities. You are ready."

The mirror began to ripple and vibrate. Morgana watched in awe as the glass ebbed and flowed impossibly, making a curious splintering sound as it did so.

"To you I impart but one request," her reflection said, its features now warping as the glass shifted. Morgana dutifully nodded her head, anxious to know what the command may be. "Do as thou wilt. And let that be the whole of the law."

The mirror shattered, sending the flawless glass skittering across the smooth black stone of the floor. Just like that, Morgana was alone in the chamber again. Within herself, though, she felt her resolve strengthen like never before. She knew what must be done.

The hour was darkening as Morgana climbed the steep slopes of the pale cliff. It was the only geographical feature for miles in any direction. From atop its chalky slopes, one could see the endless expanse of The Blackwood stretching far beyond the horizon. Miraneth liked to take her there to unwind after a day's work. Together, they would watch the sunset, sharing plans and ambitions for the world they would soon conquer. Morgana would lie in her lap like mother and child. Today, however, was different. The clouds above were roiling and distended, rumbling with the promise of a storm.

The wind whipped violently at Morganas cloak as she climbed ever higher, threatening to knock her clean over, should her concentration lapse. On some level, she knew what awaited her at the summit. It was the same force which compelled her inexorably forwards. The same force which caused her body to shake in anticipation. Confrontation. She could feel the presence of her mentor palpably. As she reached the zenith, she found Miraneth meditating on the cusp of the cliff, facing towards The Blackwood which stretched out below her in the distance.

The wind buffeted her luminous hair violently, and it seemed to crackle with the very same potential as clouds above them. As Morgana cautiously neared her mentor, a flash lit up the growing storm and then the sky thundered violently. Miraneth still had her back turned, but Morgana was wise enough to know that she had anticipated her arrival. They could both feel it. She paused a few paces behind Miraneth, on guard. When there was lull in the wind, she heard Miraneth speak at last.

"Have you come to kill me?" she asked calmly.

Morgana was taken aback by her directness and took a couple moments to form her response. "That depends," she said finally. "Do you mean to kill me?"

Miraneth slowly rose and turned to face her. Her usually serene features were darkened by anger, her violet eyes were as sharp as a hawks. She too, was poised for battle. Still, she forced an acrid smile.

"Little lamb, too wise for your own good. I know you have spoken with the fallen one. I have seen it. Now, you think you know the truth of things, but you are deceived."

"It is you who has deceived me," Morgana shouted, incensed by the arrogance of her once mentor. "You used me." Miraneth laughed, a cruel sound which echoed around them like a swarm of cawing crows.

"You think you know this world, but you do not. You are but a child. I'm using you and he is using me. Such is the way of this world. Do you really think anything comes freely? The first rule of magic is equivalent exchange. One must give in order to gain. I offer your life, so that I may gain the strength I need to at last usher in the dawning of the new age."

Morgana felt rage building inside of her as warm tears brimmed in her eyes. "I loved you. I trusted you."

Miraneth laughed again, though for a moment Morgana thought she could detect a brief glimmer of sorrow pass over her own elven eyes. It was soon gone, however, replaced by malice.

"Then you are a fool," Miraneth said, "and you will die where you stand."

She joined her hands and launched a bolt of lightning straight towards Morgana's head. She instinctively ducked and the bolt narrowly avoided her, and it instead diffused into the clouds above them with a resounding boom. As her ears rang and she reeled from the blast, the realization hit home; this was real.

She quickly scrambled to her feet in time to see Miraneth rising into the air, her glowing body swirling with vibrant eldritch energy.

*So, that's your plan,* Morgana thought. *Using the energy of the storm to augment your own powers.*

On the ground, she was at a disadvantage. Miraneth was a master of ranged magical warfare, whilst Morgana's blood magic was only effective at close range. Miraneth knew this, and was wise enough to stay well clear of the radius of efficacy of Morgana's abilities.

*I have to bring her down, it's the only way.*

Before she had the time to process that thought, another bolt of lightning crashed down deafeningly close to her, leaving a smoldering scorch mark in its wake. This would not do. Out there in the open, death was certain. If she was to survive, she would have to find cover.

She whispered a spell to the winds and sent a cloud of fine dust skywards, obscuring Miraneth's view. She heard a howl of frustration from above her as the now enraged witch began striking down lightning bolts indiscriminately atop the peak, one after the other.

In the chaos, Morgana quickly drew a large binding rune a few paces behind her in the dirt, blindly reciting one of the many spells that she had long since committed to memory, under the watchful gaze of her now adversary. If Miraneth landed on that rune, she would be unable to move from within its bounds, as if trapped inside an invisible cage. But Miraneth was not stupid, and Morgana knew she could only get her to land there by avoiding the radius of her own magic.

Quickly, she scrambled directly below Miraneth, so that when the dust cleared, she would be forced to backtrack, towards the waiting rune. She quieted her mind and called upon the spirits of frost and winter in the ancient tongues to come to her aid. Within moments, large, apple sized chunks of ice began falling from the sky. She cast a ward, a psychic shield of sorts, to deflect the largest of the boulders from herself and then waited. As the dust cleared, she again caught sight of Miraneth's mad eyes bearing down on her.

As Morgana had predicted, Miraneth quickly floated

backwards to avoid being caught in her magical radius, right into the path of her rune. Just as Miraneth was about to unleash another volley of lightning, Morgana heard a sickening crunch as Miraneth was struck in the skull by a large clump of hail.

Morgana watched as the unconscious body of Miraneth drifted slowly and gracefully towards the earth like an autumn leaf, coming to rest squarely in the middle of the rune Morgana had drawn earlier, which now began to glow. When Miraneth came to, she found Morgana standing over her.

Instinctively, she lunged, only to be thrown back as she collided with the invisible boundary of the binding rune. She looked down at her feet, quietly impressed with her student.

"A binding rune." She smirked, blue blood leaking down from the wound on her head. "It's clever, Morgana, but this little thing cannot hold me." She beginning to exert her magical energy to shatter the rune.

"No," Morgana said softly, "but I can."

She saw Miraneth's eyes widen in horror as the realization struck her right before Morgana launched her consciousness inside of her body. This body, however, was different. Immediately, she was struck by the weight of Miraneth's immense power as it launched itself against Morgana's intrusion.

The two of them were now locked in a psychic tug of war. Will against will. The previous bodies she had conquered had all surrendered with relative ease, if they had even put up a fight at all. Miraneth fought with just as much fury within herself as without. It took every ounce of Morganas strength to even stay present within Miraneth's body, let alone begin to control it.

"You. . . cannot. . . win," Miraneth wheezed, shaking as she fought against Morgana's control. Morgana knew time was short. She had to reach the critical organs quickly, but that meant forfeiting control of the arms and legs, of the spine, allowing movement. She would have to be decisive and calculated.

She took her gamble and diverted all her energy towards Miraneth's two hearts. Miraneth used this opportunity to spring forth, dagger in hand, towards Morgana's throat, but it was too late. Morgana clearly felt the hearts within her mind's eye and scorched them, turning them to ash within her chest. Miraneth staggered back, uttering a deafening shriek which brought Morgana to her knees.

Miraneth finally collapsed on her back, facing skywards as she gasped for air. Morgana was sure she had killed her, there was no way anyone could survive that type of damage. She cautiously crawled over to her mentor's side.

Despite everything, she was still overcome with emotion. Losing Miraneth was like losing her mother, all over again. Her tears dropped softly onto Miraneth's flawless skin, already beginning to fade as her life force departed. As Morgana sobbed, she felt Miraneth's hand rise and slowly wipe the tears from her cheek.

She recoiled instinctively in shock. How could she be alive? Her power was truly incredible. She saw then that Miraneth had tears in her own eyes.

"You are ready," she rasped, satisfied. Morgana clutched her hand and kissed it, the heat of the battle already fading.

"I'm sorry," she wept.

Miraneth smiled, gazing deeply into Morgana's soul with her blazing violet eyes one last time "Death, is not. . . the end."

She slumped backwards and exhaled her last breath. Miraneth: teacher, witch, and marshal of the armies of darkness was slain. The moment Miraneth's final breath left her lips, Morgana was all but bowled over by a surge of energy rushing towards her from the fallen elf's body.

So potent was the torrent that she could actually see the energy as it rushed towards her like gales of glowing blue wind. They encircled her, body and soul, and she felt unimaginable power and strength surge through every fiber of her being. The only time in her life that she had ever felt power like this was that fateful day that she had truly awakened her powers for the first time, while tied to the witch's pyre in Bluffton. Even that, however, was incomparable to what she felt now.

It was as if she was whole for the first time.

As Miraneth's terrible power coursed through her, she found herself slipping into a state of unbridled ecstasy. She could feel the anguish and the joy of every other spirit that Miraneth had bound to herself. The world began to swirl with colors and patterns as a kaleidoscopic whirlwind unfolding before her very eyes.

Almost involuntarily, she threw back her head and started to laugh triumphantly. Her laughter echoed across The Blackwood from the mountaintop and soon became a fearsome cackle. In the dark corners of her soul, the last vestiges of her humanity watched on in horror. She had killed Miraneth, her master. How could she be laughing? These thoughts, though, felt far away and small, and were quickly swallowed by the maelstrom of power which stormed around her.

Abruptly, the energy transfer was done, and the world was still once again. For a few moments, Morgana simply sat with the body in shock, breathing deeply. Above them, the clouds began to clear, and the golden light of sunset struck her like a warm embrace. It was over.

In the distance, she could see the endless expanse of The Blackwood stretching far and wide in every direction. So often had they watched this same sight together, and now she watched it alone.

She cast a cursory glance at Miraneth's body and uttered an unvoluntary scream when she saw her throat bulging and warping, as if something was moving around inside of it. She watched on in disbelief as a small beak appeared from the opening in Miraneth's mouth. It was followed by a head, and eventually a body: a dove, its perfectly white feathers stained blue from Miraneth's blood. Morgana whinced as she watched Miraneth's mouth widen horrifically as the dove passed through.

Once it had done so, it sat perched atop Miraneth's forehead, flapping its wings once to rid itself of the sticky coating of blood. For a while there was silence.

The dove eyed her, and she stared back in awe, before it took flight, diving over the crest of the cliff. Morgana scrambled to the edge, sure to catch sight of the dove as it flew towards the setting sun, but it was gone, without a trace.

Though she could not say why, this filled her with a deep sense of unease.

When Morgana returned to the encampment, the sun had set and the mood was tense. She had no doubt that word had spread, and her arrival without Miraneth would be confirmation enough for some. As she shuffled through the crowd towards the cave, silence spread amongst them, and she felt the same eyes bearing down upon her that she had a year ago. Now, however, their gaze was different.

They were afraid.

As she reached the mouth of the cave, she wanted nothing

more than to collapse into her bed, away from the gaze of the troops, but something stopped her.

*You have to do this right.*

Summoning every ounce of strength she had left, she turned to face the crowd, its numbers now more than doubled since her arrival. There was no room for hesitation here, no room for weakness.

As she began to address them, she was surprised by the conviction her own voice carried. It echoed across the silent encampment with all the finality of a church bell.

"Kindred," she shouted. "Hear me. Let it be known that Miraneth Moonshade, lady of the white rock, lies slain." This elicited a gasp from the crowd. "And let it be known," she continued, "that it was by my hand she fell." At once, an even louder gasp went up, and the army began to descend into a chaotic chorus of bickering and whispers.

"*Silence*!" Morgana shouted, her voice booming. A hush fell amongst them again.

"As you once swore yourselves to her, you will now swear yourselves to me. Those who take issue with this may voice it now." The encampment was silent, save for the sound of wind rushing through the tops of the trees. Abruptly, one of the soldiers closest to her, a colossal human swordsman in clay armour named Fenris, took the knee.

One by one, the demons, ghouls, elves, and other creatures and humans all took the knee in silence until the entire army was bowed before her. In that moment, her heart soared with a mixture of elation and disbelief. They had actually bought it. They believed in her. And why shouldn't they?

"Brothers, sisters, rise. Today is an auspicious day. For too long have we remained hidden in the shadows, clutching for scraps like vermin. It is time that we took our battle to the enemy. To the lands of men. The gate is all but complete. The time for vengeance is at hand. This world shall know our fury, and they will sup from the bitter chalice of sorrow, as we have supped."

The crowd roared in agreement, raising their weapons aloft and cheering her name. "From this day forth, in honor of the blood we shall spill, the same blood bound to my will, we shall be known as The Order of Sanguine. Long may we reign!" she shouted, raising her arms skyward.

"*Long may we reign*!" her new army roared back.

# CHAPTER 15

# REASONS

## *1033 A.D.*

The marble chamber was silent as a tomb as they waited for the king to appear.

All around them, aristocrats, nobles, and politicians had gathered in their hundreds in the silent pews. This morning was auspicious and they had assembled for a special hearing. Under instruction from the Watchers, Enoch, Davroz, and Balus sought an audience with the king, beseeching him to commit troops to counter the armies of darkness which swelled in the south.

The bright mid-morning light surged through the stained-glass windows, casting rich multi-colored hues across the faces of the bourgeoise audience. The throne sat at the foot of these stained-glass windows, atop a flight of lofty steps so that it towered above everything else in the chamber, flanked on either side by glorious depictions of saints and angels.

By rights, the throne room in the king's palace should have impressed Enoch, but after the earth-shattering wonders he had witnessed in the Sanctum of the Watchers, the entire assemblage seemed utterly drab. In comparison to the Sanctum, it was infantile at best. It made him wonder if the king had any idea at all about what was going on down there. Surely if he were to see it for himself, he would be utterly embarrassed by his little castle. Perhaps that was why a sitting king had not visited the Sanctum in over a hundred years.

To the left of the throne lay a small door, through which Enoch was told the king and his entourage would make their entrance. Anxious trumpet players laid in wait at the foot of the lofty steps, staring straight ahead, visibly perspiring as they waited for their mark.

For his part, Enoch was also tense. Once again, he stood in the center of a room, with hundreds of eyes upon him. It seemed this was just the latest in a litany of situations recently where he had been asked to placate himself before one authority or another. And to what end? This time, at least, it was Davroz who would speak, a respected envoy on behalf of the council. Enoch needed only to show his face; the prophecy concerned him after all. Still, he held his doubts, but Candilia's words gave him comfort. He just had to believe.

The trumpeters suddenly burst to life to herald the monarch's arrival. The small door to the side of the throne swung open and the king, along with his entourage, made their entrance. This was the first time Enoch had ever laid eyes on him. He was a stout man, stocky of build but not overweight. His golden hair was long and curled. Below the hefty golden crown and luxurious robes, his face and arms bore the scars of battles past.

What struck Enoch most was the look in his eyes. Bemused, bewildered, and carrying within them a distinctive hint of sadness. He struck Enoch as a man burdened by the weight of his position, spread thin and weathered by years of similar meetings.

He was followed by a red and gold motley jester who donned a bone-white harlequin mask, swaying from side to side behind the king, mimicking and exaggerating the monarch's gait and drawing some cautious snickers from the crowd.

Following behind the jester was a sinister looking man in a black cloak. Deep dark furrows of exhaustion hung from his darting, evasive eyes. He must have been the king's adviser. From the moment Enoch locked eyes with him, he was filled with an immediate sense of unease. The man's gaze was fixed upon him from the second he entered the chamber.

At the same time, Enoch's mind was being inundated by terribly malicious thoughtforms which emanated from him.

*kill... the boy... threat... stifle...*

The thoughts came hard and strong, clearer than any he had ever felt before. Stranger still, the voice did not sound human at all, almost as though it could not possibly belong to the man he saw before him. He staggered under the sheer weight of the thoughts and Balus steadied him.

"Are you alright?" Balus whispered, with concern.

"I'm fine," Enoch whispered back, regaining his composure. The last thing he wanted to do was cause a scene. There was enough pressure as it was.

Once the king had taken his seat, the young squire to the right of the throne announced him, his shrill voice straining as he amplified it out across the packed chamber.

"Citizens of Kingsrest! May I present the rightful and honorable heir to the throne, his Royal Majesty, King Lionel Godwin, the Merciful, and company!"

The chamber roared with applause. Clearly, he was loved by many, although Enoch did find the reception to be slightly over the top, as if they were somehow playing up their support to curry the monarch's favor. The sour faced king seemed to share his sentiment.

"Yes, yes!" he shouted impatiently, drawing the applause to an immediate and deafening halt. "Spare me your hollow pleasantries. Let us address the matter at hand. It is my understanding that I am hosting an audience with The Watchers today. Is that so?" He cast his glance towards Davroz who stood before him at the base of the lofty throne.

"It is so, your majesty. My name is Davroz Inferni. I represent the council," Davroz replied, bowing steeply.

"And to what do we owe this pleasure, Master Davroz?" the king asked sarcastically.

"I fear I bear ill tidings, your majesty. We have received word of an army of darkness mustering in the south. They call themselves The Order of Sanguine. They represent an unforeseen gathering of the countless races and tribes of dark sided magical beings and humans, united under one banner. Never have these races unified. This thing is unheard of.

"An army of this caliber threatens the very existence of this realm. Already we have reports of entire settlements being razed, with no survivors. We come before you today to ask that you pledge your troops to our cause, so that we may march them south and meet these forces head on, before it's too late."

The king looked at Davroz seriously for a moment before bursting into great bellowing guffaws of laughter, which the whole crowd soon echoed. Davroz valiantly bore the brunt of the humiliation, though Enoch noticed that he did not blush or seem phased whatsoever, he simply smiled cordially and waited for the laughter to subside. As the king wiped tears from his eyes, he wheezed as he spoke again.

"Forgive me, mage, but perhaps you do not know what it is that you are asking of me. Are you aware that we are at war?"

"I am, your majesty," Davroz replied measuredly.

"Then you should know that we haven't the troops to spare! Those upstart usurpers nip at the heels of this great kingdom like rabid dogs. If we reduce the pressure on them, they will only embolden."

"I understand, your majesty. But the threat posed by these usurpers pales in comparison to the threat of The Order of Sanguine. This is a matter of life and death. They seek the annihilation of the human race."

"Nonsense," the advisor said, speaking up for the first time from his place at the side of the king. "These are foul, unfounded lies, your majesty. There has been no evidence of any army amassing in the south. This washed-up fool is likely nought but a distraction sent by your enemies, squawking of phantoms and faeries to trick you into dividing your forces at this most crucial time."

"This is not true, your majesty—" Davroz tired to say.

"*Silence*!" the king boomed, leading Davroz to bow his head respectfully. "Sylas has been a trusted advisor to the throne for many years. I will not have you or anyone else questioning his judgement. Now, I have suffered this audience due to the respect this throne holds for The Watchers, but I will not suffer lies to be spoken in my chamber."

The king turned to the advisor. "Now, Sylas, what do you propose?"

"Death by hanging, your majesty," he said calmly. "It is a fitting punishment for the crime of treason against the crown."

Enoch felt his heart drop at the proclamation. Behind them, he heard the clinking of armor as the guards approached them, waiting for the order from the king. All the while, Enoch was being inundated by the vile thoughtforms of Sylas, now gleefully celebrating their imminent capture in his head. The king seemed lost in contemplation for a moment as he carefully weighed the options.

Enoch took this moment to lean forward and whisper in Davroz's ear. He had to tell him about Sylas. "That man," Enoch whispered, "isn't a man. I think he's a shape shifter. Or something."

Davroz nodded his head in recognition but said nothing, instead casting his curious gaze towards the advisor who looked down upon them smugly, sure his verdict would come to fruition.

The king sighed, wiping his brow. "A predicament to be sure. Tanto!" he yelled suddenly, turning to the masked jester who, up until now, had laid mostly dormant by his side. "What say you, old friend? Who am I to trust?"

As soon as his name was mentioned, it was as if the jester came to life, strutting the stage and pirouetting with youthful grace. "Not a moment too soon, you summoned this loon, to croon on illusions unmasked by the moon," he sang.

Enoch immediately recognized that voice. *It can't be.* He looked back to Balus, who shared his disbelief.

The jester continued: "Allow me to view them, I'll summon the truth, assuming they're true men, not miserable sleuths."

As the words left his mouth he deftly jumped, removing his mask as he flipped through the air to land soundlessly at the base of the steps. He slowly raised his head to meet Enoch's gaze, staring back at him were the same sightless gray eyes that he had met that day by the brook on the way to Fairhaven.

There could be no doubt about it. It was him, The Fool. Never in a million years would Enoch have guessed that he was the king's jester. His ageless features creased into a mischievous smile as he sensed Enoch and Balus's gobsmacked recognition.

Davroz eyed them all with total confusion, unaware of the prior context which preceded this strange turn of events. It was then The Fool whispered another poem, this time only to Enoch.

"Tell me, young Enoch, what ends do you seek? The path you are treading bodes ill for the meek."

They may have seemed innocuous to the untrained ear, but Enoch felt the true weight of The Fool's words in his heart. He knew they message they carried. It was a warning.

To play his role, he would need to be stronger. Much stronger. As he thought of his answer, he decided that he would respond to The Fool in kind.

"I seek what is destined. The part I must play. To usher the future, as night follows day," he whispered solemnly, unsure from what part of himself this message flowed. The Fool's smile grew even wider as Enoch delivered his response. He even detected a hint of surprise on his face.

"You answer alike me, it's joyous to see. Old Sylas won't smite thee, I'll set you three free." In that moment, he leapt back into the air effortlessly, backflipping as he landed nimbly by the king's side once again.

"Well?" the king asked, turning to The Fool. "What am I to make of these travellers?"

The Fool, wearing his mask once again, loudly sang for the crowd. "They utter the truth! Their motives are good. Assemble the troops, and make for the wood!"

The king smiled. "Then it is so! You shall have your men." A roar of approval went up from the crowd, which all but muffled Sylas's furious protests.

"No! They deceive, your majesty!" Sylas shouted.

Davroz bowed steeply at the verdict, and Enoch and Balus followed suit. As Enoch bowed, he noticed curiously that Davroz seemed to be working some type of spell with his left hand behind his back. Enoch watched on as Davroz made rapid combinations of finger and thumb with lightning precision. *What is he planning?* Enoch thought. As the trio rose to face the king once more, a gasp went up from the crowd.

To the left of the king, Sylas the advisor was undergoing an awful transformation. Black, fetid ooze spread over him from head to toe, quickly revealing pale, almost transparent skin underneath. His clothes disappeared and were replaced with naked flesh. His fingers lengthened and formed into sharp claws and his ears and nose pointed pronouncedly. His mouth widened and split, revealing rows of sharp teeth and his eyes turned a dull red, their pupils becoming slitted, like a snake.

In its eyes, the creature that was once Sylas bore a look of total disbelief. There was a moment of utter silence in the chamber that seemed to last for an eternity. The king stared at the creature which stood before him, dumbfounded, and in shock.

The Fool cocked his head in confusion, as a dog might when hearing an unfamiliar sound. The creature stared back, its slimy chest heaving with anticipation. A woman in the crowd screamed, and the silence was broken.

In a flash, the creature produced an ungodly howl and lunged towards the king, who still sat, stunned, upon his throne. In that same instant, Davroz aimed the thumb, index, and middle fingers of his left hand towards the throne and launched a bolt of fire directly towards the creature.

The bolt flew faster than any arrow Enoch had ever seen and struck the creature in the center of its chest, before its attack could land. The force of the scorching impact sent the creature hurtling into the stone wall with a sickening crunch, where it was quickly seized and surrounded by the king's guard.

It tried in vain to rise, but the burn on its chest brought it collapsing to its knees each time. It screamed obscenities and curses in ancient tongues as the guardsmen dragged it from the chamber. The king was in shock, his horrified expression mirrored the faces which stood before him in the crowd. Under his mask, it was impossible to read The Fool's expression. Enoch suspected he somehow knew how the situation was going to play out all along.

"You. . . You saved me," the king gasped.

Davroz bowed slightly. "As is my duty, your majesty."

"Duty!" The king scoffed. "This goes far beyond the realm of mere duty, dear mage! You have thwarted an attempt on my life! An attempt on the throne! And in this moment, I have seen the truth in your words. These dark forces. This order you speak of. They have even infiltrated this, the highest office in the land. By The One, my advisor! God knows how far their influence has already spread. We must cleanse this evil from the realm.

"You shall have my best men, and arms, every man I can spare. Not only that, tonight we will hold a banquet in your honor, to the heroic Watchers, who have once again proved their loyalty the throne!" A roar of agreement went up from the crowd.

Davroz bowed deeply once again. "You indulge me, your majesty."

Later, after the crowd had cleared out and the trio had received round after round of successive handshakes and congratulations from the various lords, ladies, and nobles of the land, the trio were alone again in the chamber. Only then did Davroz collapse against a pillar, exhausted, his façade of composure crumbling.

"Just what on earth was that?" Enoch asked.

"A cave goblin, by the looks," Davroz said softly through deep breaths.

"And what did you do?" Enoch probed further, referring to the hand gestures.

"A simple disenchantment. I merely disrupted its transformation spell." His eyes darted between the confused faces of Enoch and Balus, who stood over him.

"How did you know?" Balus asked.

Davroz smiled. "I didn't. I took a chance. In truth, it was Enoch who tipped me off."

Balus turned his disbelief to Enoch. "Then how did you know?"

"His thoughts," Enoch said. "I could hear them clearly, and they didn't sound or feel like a man's."

Davroz smiled again, making eye contact with Enoch. "In many ways, it was you that saved the king's life today, Enoch," Davroz said warmly.

Balus's wide grizzled face soon sported a grin from ear to ear. "Then your powers are emerging, young master!" he practically shouted. "Master Adrax will be so proud."

Enoch basked in the moment, feeling pride emanate from within his heart for one of the first times in his life. It was an unfamiliar feeling. Giddy, almost. He could not stop smiling, despite himself. At last, it was beginning. Master Adrax would indeed be proud. It would not be long before he saw him again and the thought made his heart soar. They would have much to discuss.

The army left the city of Kingsrest at dawn the next day.

It was a clear spring morning, and the wind carried the scent of the trees in bloom. Half the population of the capital had come to bid them farewell, a true hero's send off. White and pink flower petals rained from the sky and the cheers of thousands of men, women, and children alike rang through the air, accompanied by the ceaseless baying of trumpets. It was a festive atmosphere, and it was hard not to get caught up in the moment. This was, after all, a historic day, as the knights of the realm and The Watchers had not marched side by side in over a century.

The king had pledged three-thousand of his finest mounted knights and men at arms, and they were supported by an advance guard of five-hundred of The Watchers' finest sorcerers, as well as half of The Grand Council.

The Watchers rode at the head of the army, followed closely by the prestigious Realm Knights, nobles in immaculate shining plate armor, renowned for their unstoppable charges, and their colossal egos. Commanding them was Lord Willock, a pompous, short tempered, squat man with an overly lacquered moustache.

Leading The Watchers was Ulthian, the elven prince, head of the council, and Lyse, the human mage from the northlands. Both of them were sullen, seemingly unaffected by the joyous mood. Ulthian seemed loathe to make this journey, and leave his seat on the council open, while Lyse eyed him constantly with suspicion; Candilia and the ent had stayed behind to guard the sanctum.

Before he had left The Sanctum, Candilia had blessed Enoch with a protection spell and wrapped him in a warm embrace which made his heart flutter. "I will be watching over you," she whispered softly in his ear before saying goodbye. There was something so bewitching about her. Only in his wildest, darkest dreams could he ever have even conceived a soul like hers, so deeply steeped in beauty, power, and mystery. When he was in her presence, he felt the most peculiar sensation, as if he were home, as if he had known her his whole life. When he looked in her eyes, his heart blazed with the whispered promises of fate. He prayed that their paths would cross again, he needed only to return alive.

Behind Ulthian and Lyse rode Enoch, Balus, and Davroz. Both Enoch and Balus could barely contain their smiles. Balus quietly relished the notion of riding back to war, for a just cause. Never in his life would he have expected to have been called on in such a manner, and at such an age. In Enoch's case, this was yet another new experience for him. As his powers began to grow, he felt at last that he was starting to find his place in all of this. Davroz seemed quietly pleased as well, but his gaze was far away, as if lost in contemplation.

The sound of their march was a steady thunder, which rumbled through the earth, heralding their arrival to any and all throughout the countryside, long before they appeared.

At night, their camps were like raucous festivals of light and sound, and the noblemen sang songs late into the evening while the mages of The Watchers dazzled with their magical displays. It was a wonderous sight.

Davroz told them, to see laymen and magicians' side by side, breaking bread, sharing wine, and trading tales, gave him hope for the future. Since The Schism, the ties between the mages and the men of the realm had been frayed. Now, they had a common cause, a common enemy, and perhaps together, they could birth a common future, one free from the shackles of persecution, xenophobia, and mutual suspicion.

On the third night, they made camp as per usual. The moon

was full and shone brightly, almost negating the need for fires at all. Still, the men lit them just the same, huddling together in the cool night air, laughing, drinking, and smoking meats.

Enoch, Balus, and Davroz quietly sat by their own cookfire, Davroz indulging them with some of his finest southern wine. The heads of the council and the leaders of the knights took their supper in a separate command tent, doubtlessly plotting the course of the crusade.

Enoch wondered about their conversations. Would Ulthian's arrogance even deign to permit a human's input? Perhaps that was why they elected Lyse to accompany him, to temper that arrogance somewhat. It was a smart decision.

He strained his mind's eye to pry on their thoughtforms but found he could not hear them above the general hubbub of the encampment. As his powers grew, he found that he had to take particular effort to shut the thoughtforms out, so as not to become overwhelmed.

It was good training, he thought, for the field. He could clearly see his own shadow on the grass and took notice that the moon seemed awfully close tonight as it hung sombrely in the sky. They were less than a day's march from the abbey, where they would rest and restock for a couple days, before marching on to The Blackwood. The thought filled him with anxious elation. He could not wait to see Master Adrax again. So much had changed in such a short space of time. He practically wondered if he would even be recognized.

As he milled over these thoughts, watching the grass, he watched his pale blue shadow begin to shift to red. He raised his head in alarm, unsure of what was happening, and then he saw it: the moon. It had turned from ghostly white to a bloody red.

The camp went quiet as the men recognized, one by one,

and then they began to panic. Some began to shout in alarm, their sergeants and captains pleading for calm as the horses began to whinny and buck wildly, for they could feel it too.

Davroz and Balus quickly raised to their feet. Never had Enoch seen such a grave expression on Davroz's face as he stared at the moon.

Before long, all three and a half thousand men were transfixed by the sight, gazing up at it in awestruck terror. Ulthian and Lyse, as well as the generals of the Realm Knights burst forth from their tent, and instantly shared in the collective unease. Something was very wrong.

An unnatural stillness had spread through the air and even the insects were silenced. In an instant, a row of torches simultaneously lit in the distance, forming a ring which surrounded the encampment. The firelight played tricks with the shadows, but Enoch could see the outlines of figures in pointed black hoods.

Shades. Thousands of them. Other shapes, too, like towering beasts. The men cried out in alarm and the captains quickly called them to arms.

"Make ready men!"

"Quickly!"

"Assume defensive formations!"

Happy to have orders, the soldiers hurriedly sprang into action with a metallic clamour of weapons and armor as they rushed to ready themselves.

An awful female voice hissed down on them, seemingly from the sky itself, oppressively loud and it carried the weight of evil in its tones.

Above them, clouds began to gather, foul red, grossly distended with the promise of rain.

"What is this?" Enoch asked Davroz frightfully.

"This is sorcery," he replied gravely, not breaking his gaze from the moon.

Children of man, the voice seethed thunderously. For too long have you sat idly upon the thrones of this world, fattening yourself on the misery of others. You are greedy, weak, and cruel. You consume this land, yet you fear and curse that which you do not understand. I tell you now that you are right to fear us. That which dwells in the shadow. That which gnaws at your conscience. There is a price to pay for all you have done, and I am the reaper. The time of men is over, and the hour of magic is at hand. You believe you can thwart us, but you are deceived. What you seek now is a fool's gambit. Marching against us will bring you nothing but a slow, painful death. This is your only chance. Those who bend the knee and serve me will be spared and put to use. The rest will be as chaff to the furnace. You will beg for death by the end, but in time, you will find that death is only the beginning.

Abruptly, the clouds above them rumbled and soon Enoch felt wet pinpricks of rain falling against his skin, curiously warm and bitter to the tongue. To his horror, he realized it was blood.

The rain soon turned to a downpour and covered the men and horses, drenching them with sticky, resinous dread. Some men began to wail and panic, losing formation as they ducked for cover. Others cried out prayers to The One, beseeching their god to free them from this wickedness.

This, the voice continued. This is but a taste of the torment we will visit upon you. Choose wisely. Then it broke into laughter, a maniacal cackling which was soon joined by a chorus of demonic voices that rang in their ears and brought even Davroz to his knees.

As quickly as it had changed, the moon reverted to its original hue. The clouds dissipated, and the distant torches extinguished. The earth seemed to soak up the blood before their very eyes. The darkness had passed, but the men's morale was horribly shaken. Some lay quivering, whimpering, whispering, clutching artifacts, and whispering prayers or calls to their loved ones. Others sat still with empty eyes, too shocked to move.

Balus's eyes were wide and still fixed on the moon long after it had reverted. As Enoch reached out to gently place a hand on his shoulder he jolted back, wheezing as it tried to catch his breath.

"It's alright," Enoch whispered. "It's gone." He raised his gaze towards the command tent to see Ulthian angrily pushing the flaps aside as he stormed inside, flanked by Lyse, and the human generals. If the threat was not real in anyone's mind before, it surely was now.

The men's morale remained abysmal for the remainder of the march the next morning. Enoch slept terribly, tormented by shadows in his dreams, and he suspected that the rest of the army was much the same. After all, who could blame them after seeing a sight like that? Any illusions about an easy and glorious conquest were quickly erased from their minds. The enemy was real, and it was powerful.

Enoch took some comfort at least in the thought of returning to the abbey. It would be the perfect place for the men to rest and its timeless solace would provide a much needed morale boost. He was sure that Master Adrax would have much to say about the previous night's sorcery. Perhaps he could provide some answers.

These thoughts kept Enoch and Balus uplifted as they

marched mostly in silence, until they saw smoke on the horizon. The scouts were the first to see it, riding back to the main host to deliver the news. When he heard the news, his heart began to race, and his throat began to close.

*No. There's no way.*

Then he caught sight of the smoke himself, a foul color, black as ink, and rising skyward in thick plumes, coming from the direction of the abbey. He shot Balus a look of grave concern, which he returned in kind.

Under instruction from Ulthian and Lord Willock, they brought their march to a run. If the abbey was under siege, they still had a chance to lift it, and catch the enemy unawares.

Enoch prayed that was not the case, for he knew that the abbey was incapable of holding in the event of a siege. They were monks, not warriors. At best, they had a handful of guardsmen to look after the entire abbey. As they galloped closer, with the men at arms running behind them, he whispered pleas to whatever god might be governing his fate.

"Please," he whispered softly in the saddle of Rain. "Please, no." He kept picturing Adrax's smiling face in his mind, welcoming him back into his study. "Let it be so."

As the horsemen summited the final hill, which overlooked the abbey, his heart dropped, and the sight hit him like a punch to the gut. There, where the abbey once stood, was a silent, smoking ruin. Even the Tower of Attainment had crumbled and fallen.

"No." He heard Balus moan from beside him, his voice cracking from emotion. "God's above, no." Enoch did not wait for orders, but instead kicked Rain into a gallop.

"Enoch, no!" Davroz shouted from behind him.

His voice was quickly swallowed by the wind as Enoch flew down the slope towards the abbey. He had to know. As he passed through the gate, he could see that its iron bars had been not only broken in, but torn apart. All over the courtyard lay the scorched and violated bodies of the monks. Young and old, none were spared. The smell was awful, sickly, sweet, and rotten, all at once. It was the smell of death, on a scale he had never seen before.

He found himself retching involuntarily as he jumped from the saddle and sprinted towards the central sanctum, where the once shining pale stones of The Tower of Attainment now lay dashed in a ruin. He still held out some hope that Master Adrax could still be alive.

*Maybe he hid. One last trick. He could have outwitted them.*

Deep down, his intuition defied his shallow bargaining, but he could not accept it. He could not let it become true.

At the base of where the tower once stood, he began to dig frantically through the stone, throwing aside one heavy piece after another.

*Maybe he's buried. He needs me to dig him out. I have to get him out!*

As he became increasingly desperate, he had little regard for his own hands, which quickly became deeply cut and scuffed, his own blood mixing with the white dust. His breathing grew shallow and laboured as he felt himself slipping into hysteria.

As he strained his back, trying feebly to lift a giant slab of stone, he collapsed backwards in a heap, screaming in frustration. He heard the cawing of a crow from behind him and he turned around slowly to see its source on the wall behind him.

The sun was shining directly into his eyes, and he had to squint to see what it was, but he could make out the silhouette on the wall. Two gnarled pieces of wood hoisted into a crude cross with a body nailed to them. Someone had been crucified. He took another step forward until the sun was blocked and he stood in the shadow of the crucifix. Staring back at him, mouth agape in wordless horror was the disembowelled body of Adrax. The crow which he had heard was pecking hungrily at his eyes.

Enoch's legs gave out and he dropped to his knees in despair, howling. The finality of this sight could not be escaped. It was true. In that moment, he cursed whatever god had fated them to live this life. What type of loving creator would allow his subjects to suffer such cruelty, and the most devout of them, no less? Who had the monks hurt? What had they done to deserve this fate? In his life, Adrax had been nothing more than a paragon of peace and virtue. To feel a suffering like this was surely worse than death.

As he sobbed, his tears mixed with the blood flowing from his hands to form a paste in the dust. He felt a gentle hand on his shoulder. He sprang into action, furiously drawing his sword from his scabbard, only to be met with the broken face of Balus, who only shared in his devastation. In an instant, he collapsed into the guardsman's enormous arms, and they sobbed together.

Hours later, after they had performed burial rites for all of the monks and the troops had sombrely set up camp inside the walls, Enoch watched the sun dipping below the distant horizon from atop the west wall. The sight was beautiful, but in its beauty, he took no comfort.

He felt hollow, as if all the joy and goodness had been sapped from the world. They were so distant that he wondered if he would ever be able to feel those emotions again. From the stairs behind him, he heard the voice of Davroz.

"May I join you, young master?"

Enoch nodded gently, barely registering his presence as he stared listlessly into the distance. For a while they sat side by side in silence, watching as the sky changed from deep red to purple.

"You know, Enoch," Davroz began, "I was not always the man that I am now. Many years ago, in my homeland, before I joined the council, I had a family." He sighed.

"I had a beautiful wife. The most beautiful woman I had ever seen. Her beauty was eclipsed only by her kindness. We had two beautiful children together, two little girls. We lived a simple life, on our farm in the high country. My family was the light of my life. I lived for them, and they lived for me. I can say that I was truly happy. At the same time, I had a close friend. A man I had known since birth. A man I loved like a brother. Both of us were budding mages, only beginning the journey of understanding our power. Whenever I was not at home with my family, I was with him, training. As our abilities developed, he became impatient and obsessed with the notion of power. He never took to a family like I did. He claimed that such things would only hold us back from the path. I disagreed and saw magic only as another facet to a balanced and fulfilling life.

"He soon grew resentful and distrustful of me, and, I suspect, jealous. One gray day, I returned from the market to find the door to my home ajar and swinging in the wind. At once I knew that something was wrong. My garden was quiet. I couldn't hear my girls playing. As I entered the house, I found them laying slain on the floor, alongside their mother. Before I could even react to the sight, I heard my friend calling my name from outside. I found him smiling, proudly announcing that it was he who had killed them.

"There was madness in his sunken eyes. Any trace of the

boy I had known was gone, consumed by his lust for power. He did it for me, he said. To allow my powers to grow unhindered. In that moment, they did, as my mind broke and I unleashed terrible vengeance upon him as flaming rage poured out of me for the first time. I was terrified by this new power and what it could do, but in that moment I didn't care. I wanted him dead."

He took a deep breath before continuing. "His power was no match for mine and very quickly I almost had my wish as I burned him within an inch of his life. By some cheap trick, as his death was in my grasp, he escaped me.

"Then I was alone, left to wallow in my grief. Worse still, in our battle I had accidentally set fire to our family home. I was thankfully able to wrest their bodies from the house before it collapsed, but all memory of the life we had made together was swallowed in that fire. I spent the night honoring and burying them, before waiting patiently for the sun to rise.

"At dawn, I set out to find him with nothing more than the clothes on my back. I vowed then that I would not rest until I avenged my family by finding and killing this man. That search eventually brought me to this land, and to The Watchers, who recognized my power.

"Day and night, I am fuelled only by the desire for revenge. There is nothing else left for me in this world. I tell you this now, because when I look in your eyes, I can see my own. That same burning desire. But I beg you not to choose this path, Enoch. The path of hatred. You are young, with a gentle heart and an inquisitive mind. You still have a chance at happiness in this life. Do not throw it away as I have."

Enoch reflected for some time on the gravity of his words, which had somehow managed to pierce the armor of hollowness around his soul. Finally, he turned to face Davroz for the first time, tears brimming in his eyes.

“Does the pain ever go away?” Enoch asked softly.

“No,” Davroz said flatly, “but you learn how to live on despite it. You find reasons.”

# CHAPTER 16

# The Way of the World

## *2033 A.D.*

Time and space seemed to blur as the guards led Adam and Zane back through the washed-out yellow hallways of the S.H.A.R.D. facility, toward the gymnasium.

As they passed the vacant cells, Adam was struck by a profound sense of déjà vu. On some level, he had almost disassociated himself from the whole experience. After everything they had seen that night, and everything they had been through, they had failed. Now here they were again, back in the director's clutches. She still wore that same smug fucking smile as she led them calmly to whatever fate awaited them.

As they pushed open the swinging doors to and placed the boys at opposite ends of the basketball court, the sense of déjà vu only intensified. He had been here before. He was sure of it.

Looking at Zane from across the court, Adam could see that his usually devious demeanour had all but disappeared. He looked terrified and Adam was terrified, too.

Once they were in position, the guards stepped back, and the director began to address them from her place on the half court line. Both boys knew they could make a run for it, but what good would that do? They were surrounded by guards and deep in the bowels of the facility. They would never make it. It was that assurance of failure that kept them rooted in their places.

"Dearly beloved," the director joked, smiling. "You're probably wondering why I have brought you here today. Well, the truth is, it's time for you to pull your weight. For too long have we hosted you at this facility under our good graces, whilst you waste our precious time, day after day. Tonight's transgression was the final straw. Now we will see the full extent of your powers. As you fight to the death."

Adam and Zane both gasped in unison, drawing a laugh from the director. "Don't act so surprised," she said coolly. "I only need one of you for the task ahead. The one who is truly destined for this task ahead will emerge here and now."

"You're insane," Zane spat, "and you're deluded if you ever think we'll fight each other. You may as well kill us now."

Adam didn't speak up, but he agreed with Zane's sentiment. There was no way he was going to fight him, Zane was like a brother.

The director sighed. "I thought you'd say that." She quickly gave a nod to one of the guards who whispered an instruction into his radio, and Adam noticed a hissing noise coming from what looked like the fire sprinklers on the roof above them. Instead of water coming out of them, it was great clouds of dense yellow gas, which quickly fell to the floor. Adam began to panic and quickly tried to cover his mouth and nose, but it was no use. He had to breathe.

As he took his first tortured gulp of the mystery gas his

lungs burned, and his ears began to ring. His vision began to distort. Colors became frighteningly saturated, and the dimensions of the gymnasium began to flicker and warp. His ears began to ring and pick up all kinds of sounds, both distant and close, which reverberated and echoed off one another until they coalesced into one chaotic hum. He was hyper aware. More than anything, he felt abject terror. His heart thumped violently in his chest and he clutched it fiercely as pain spread throughout his upper body. He was sure he was having a heart attack.

As he looked at Zane from across the court, what was once his friend seemed to have been replaced with some sort of ghoulish caricature. It bore his defining features; his clothes, his skin, but it just was not him. His wild hair had locked into what looked like horns and he seemed to be leering at him menacingly. Worse still, his eyes glowed bright red.

Adam desperately rubbed his eyes, eager to make this hallucination disappear, but that only made it more vivid. He felt his adrenaline rising as his fight or flight instincts began to kick in. His body urged him to react, to defend himself.

It was Zane who struck first. He took off running to the left of the baseline on his side of the court and sent an icicle soaring through the air straight towards Adam's head. Had he not ducked instinctively, he would have been decapitated. He hazarded a look behind him and saw that the icicle had dug deep into the concrete wall behind him. He could not believe it. This was real.

Adam took off running in the opposite direction on his own side of the court, careful at all times to keep Zane in his sights. He looked almost wolflike on the other side of the court as he fixed his predatory gaze back on Adam. Self-preservation instincts aside, Adam still could not bring himself to hurt him. This was his best friend, his only friend.

Maybe he could keep him at bay long enough for the effects of this toxin to wear off, then they could face the director together. The moment the thought crossed his mind, Zane fired off a cloud of smaller icicles in his direction. Adam sprang forward in time to avoid most of them but not in time to spare his left leg, which was pierced clean through the bone. He cried out in pain and collapsed to the floor mid stride, his shoes squeaking as they dragged over the polished wood.

Whether it was the adrenaline or the toxins coursing through his bloodstream he could not say, but he quickly staggered to his feet, ignoring the pain as he resumed their game of cat and mouse. To stop now was to die.

Whatever they had drugged them with had totally consumed Zane. He was close behind him now, the gap had closed. He could practically feel his labored animalistic breath bearing down on him, and he knew it was only a matter of time before another volley came his way. He had to think of something, and fast.

All the while, he saw the director's silhouette in his peripheral vision every time he passed her, calmly watching the scene unfold. Under his feet, he felt the floor grow slick.

Water. It was spreading everywhere. He heard Zane yell from behind him, and then felt a mighty impact as he punched the floor hard. Within moments, a thick layer of ice covered the court and Adam lost his footing again, cursing as he crashed down, hard, onto his back. As he tried to raise himself up, a thick layer of ice spread quickly over his lower body, binding him in place. He desperately squirmed to escape it, but it was no use.

As he heard Zane's ominous footsteps slowly getting closer, he desperately pounded on the ice to break free, but this too proved useless. The coating had to be inches thick. Finally,

Zane stood over him.

As he looked into his eyes, Adam could see no trace of the friend he once knew. His body heaved unnaturally, and his pupils were so dilated that his eyes looked totally black. He was still leering as he raised his hands skyward, and Adam watched as they were quickly covered by a layer of ice which formed into two giant spikes.

"Zane," Adam pleaded breathlessly, "snap out of it. This isn't you. Please!" His pleas, however, fell on deaf ears. The man that stood before him now was not Zane, he was closer to some hungry animal.

Adam knew what he had to do. At this point, it was his life or Zane's. Though the thought of killing his best friend violated him in ways he could not express, he could not deny his own will, that most base of wills, to live.

With tears in his eyes, he raised his hand as Zane brought his spears down to deliver the killing blow. Adam found that his power flowed effortlessly through him this time and he could easily control it. As time slowed, he pictured the portal in his mind's eye, its shape, size, color.

He heard the tell-tale ripping and electric zapping as the fabric of reality tore open above Zane's head and a glowing, oscillating red portal appeared. Winds whipped and tore at them from that dark place, and for the first time, Adam could clearly see it with his own eyes. Pure darkness. Nothingness. Utter silence.

But the dread. The dread was unmistakable.

Zane looked up slowly, the hairs on the back of his neck rising. His head was mere inches from the portal, his wide eyes staring into the abyss. For a timeless moment, the world was still. In the dark, Adam saw the glint of an eye reflecting back at him; the abyss stared back.

He heard an awful sound, a low gurgle which vibrated through his entire body. Instantly, a giant barbed tentacle shot forth and wrapped itself around Zane and lifted him up by his legs, slowly dragging him in, savoring his screams as he slipped into the darkness. In the final moments, when only his head poked through the portal, he seemed to come back to himself. His pupils returned to their normal size and he looked down with fear and confusion in his eyes. As they made eye contact, he uttered but one word, one desperate plea.

"Adam." The tentacle constricted around him, crushing his body and showering Adam with blood and flesh before the portal winked out of existence.

The gymnasium was silent once more.

Adam spasmed uncontrollably, sobbing and gagging as his desperate mind finally snapped from shock. His last sight as his vision faded was the director slowly walking towards him and crouching by his side, gently running her fingers through his blood-soaked hair.

"You've done well."

Adam awoke screaming and drenched with sweat. The moment his awareness returned, he sprang to his feet. As his eyes adjusted to the room he realized he was in his cell.

Gray midmorning light was peeking in through the small window above him. How could this be? He had no idea how he got there and no memory of getting back to the cell. At the same time, he felt terribly groggy, like he had the worst hangover of his life.

Memories from the night before hit him in harsh vivid

flashes, but they were distorted and grainy like damaged film. Only single images came to mind: monsters, a dark forest, a bonfire. The more he grasped at them the more they seemed to slip away, like some half-remembered fever dream. Was it a dream?

Then there was something, a word, a face, a name. Adam. At once, the memories came flooding back. Zane. He looked so frightened. That creature in the dark place.

*My god. I killed him.*

The realization took the air out of his lungs, and he dropped to the floor, sobbing. At that moment he jolted as he heard a rapping at the metal door. It was the director.

"Adam? Are you awake? May I come in?"

He shrank back into a corner, ready to defend himself. "Stay away! I'll fucking kill you!" The door to his cell swung open and the director, clad in a smart business suit, calmly stepped inside crouching by the entrance so she was on his level.

"It's alright," she soothed. "No one's going to hurt you."

"That's bullshit!" He spat, rocking from side to side. "You made me kill him!"

The director looked perplexed. "Kill who?"

"Zane!"

She gave him a look of genuine confusion and concern. "Adam, there's no one by that name at this facility." She reached out tentatively to comfort him.

"Liar!" he screamed, recoiling from her touch and slamming into the wall.

She sighed. "Adam, what you're experiencing right now is called a paranoid delusion. These delusions are a common side effect of the serum we administered to you last night. They will subside in the coming hours."

As she spoke, he pondered on her words for a moment. Could it be true? After all, the memories did not make sense. They were disjointed, fragmented, just like a dream. But Zane, Zane had to be real.

"You, you're lying to me," he spluttered finally, his conviction fading. "I've known Zane for months."

The director gently shook her head. "Well, that's impossible, Adam. You've only been here for two weeks."

That statement hit him like a gunshot. Two weeks? There was no way that could be true.

Carefully, he checked his wristwatch for the date: May 21st, 2033. Exactly two weeks. "That's impossible."

"It's normal to feel disoriented following a transformation like yours, Adam, but I assure you that the date is correct. Sometimes dreams following a procedure like this can seem hyper realistic, and we can attach ourselves to certain ideas, but I assure you, they are just that. Ideas. Nothing more." Her claims were seeming more and more plausible, and his own notions more and more bizarre. But Zane. Whatever it was, whatever it meant, he could not let it go.

"Footage," he said finally. "I want to see the footage from the gym."

The director nodded her head obligingly. "If you feel like that will help you, sure." She rose to her feet and extended her hand. Adam eyed it cautiously for a while before clasping it in his own and letting her help him shakily to his feet.

As they traversed the halls of the facility, on their way to the security room where the footage was stored, Adam could not believe his eyes. The place was abuzz with life. All around him, doctors were wheeling patients nonchalantly and other internees were nodding and waving at Adam as he passed. Doors were opening and closing, and the lunch hall was fully packed and full of commotion as they passed it.

He could even see Old Maggie, the lunch lady. She mysteriously looked at least ten years younger and had a full set of teeth. She was serving delicious looking plates of meat and vegetables to the many staff and patients. She smiled to them as they walked by. Adam could do nothing but gaze around in slack–jawed awe. Maybe it was just a dream.

When they finally reached the security room, the director sat him down in a chair and began to sort through the digital files on the monitor until she found the previous night's recording from the gymnasium.

"Ah, here it is."

As she double clicked on and enlarged the video, Adam studied the screen carefully. He saw the director leading him into the gym, and he saw the guards place him on one side of the basketball court, but there was no sign of anyone else. No Zane.

He watched as the yellow gas fell from the sprinkler above him. "What the fuck is that then?" he asked, pointing at the gas on the screen.

"That's our serum," the director said. "The compound which allows you easier access to your latent abilities. It is only admissible by inhalation. Unfortunately, it is known to produce both hallucinations and delusions as potential side effects. You did consent to its use." She produced a paper waiver from her pocket, bearing his signature.

Adam shook his head, slumping into stunned silence. At no point did he remember signing any waiver, but the footage could not be denied. He watched himself running around the court, jumping, and dashing to avoid. . . nothing. There was no one else in the frame. He watched as he fell onto his back and pointed his hand to the roof, producing a glowing red portal from thin air.

"There," the director said, pausing the footage. "That was the outcome of the experiment, Adam. You were able to recreate a dimensional doorway through your own conscious will. I hope you understand how monumental this development is. This represents the culmination of years of funding, research, and labor here at S.H.A.R.D. This is what our facility was designed for. You should be proud."

He tried to feel pride, to feel anything, but instead he only felt hollow. The footage could not be denied, there really was no one else there.

"Satisfied?" the director asked. Adam nodded gently, his eyes still vacant. The director gave him a sympathetic look. "The depersonalization and derealization you're experiencing now will subside within a few days." Adam nodded again silently. "Come, there is something else I want to show you."

He followed her down the busy hallways of the facility towards an elevator door that Adam had seen before but assumed to be disused. To his surprise, as she pressed the button the doors soon dinged open, and they stepped inside. On the wall, Adam could see rows of buttons with corresponding levels, and for the first time, he got an appreciation of just how far underground the facility actually stretched.

The director scanned her iris, unlocking the pad and pressing the button for sub-thirteen, the lowest level. The elevator moved quickly and within a few seconds the elevator dinged again, and they had arrived.

As the doors opened, they stepped into a massive hollowed out space the size of a stadium. At the center of the space, lit from above by spotlights and flanked on both sides by immense scaffolding and electrical wiring, was a colossal ring, the size of a ten–story building. It seemed to be made out of some sort of black metal and was fed from both the roof and the floor with extensive power cables and coolants.

Manning the scaffolds were teams of welders putting in the final touches. If anything, it looked almost like one of those launch pads for rockets that he had seen on television. The director smiled, clearly pleased with Adam's amazement.

"It's beautiful, isn't it?"

"What is it?" Adam asked, astonished.

"This, Adam, is our crowning achievement. Our offering to humanity. A structure, once activated, that will allow for sustained, unhindered travel between this physical dimension, and the immaterial planes which overlap it. We once thought that space was the final frontier, but we were wrong. Interdimensional travel will revolutionise every facet of human existence. You're staring at the future, Adam. A future in which you will play an integral role."

"What do you mean?" Adam asked.

"When the time is right, you will assist us in activating this structure. We need only to activate it once. After that, it will be self–propagating," she said proudly.

As Adam stared up at the mighty structure, he could not shake a growing sense of dread. It looked fearsome.

"Then, what happens now?" Adam asked, frightened at the prospect of returning to his cell.

"As of now, you're free to leave," the director said warmly.

Adam looked at her in disbelief. "And go where?"

"Anywhere you like. The chauffer who escorted you here is waiting for you now at the reception."

Adam scoured his mind thinking of places he might go.

He had not imagined he would have been released so soon and he certainly did not want to stay with his father. Maybe he could set up in a hostel somewhere for a while until he got his bearings.

"Oh, and there's one more thing," the director said, producing a small black box from her pocket. "This." She removed the lid from the case to reveal what looked like a small silver bracelet. "It's an experimental prototype known as a phase-shifter. Now that you're a part of the faculty here, this item will allow us to summon you back to the facility when we have need of you." She motioned him to hold out his right wrist and he complied. As she slipped the bracelet over him, it made a high-pitched buzzing noise before shrinking down rapidly and constricting itself tightly over his skin. He winced as it dug in.

"Don't worry," she said. "It automatically calibrates so as not to restrict blood flow." As he inspected it, he saw it had one single node, which blinked red occasionally, and was otherwise all but featureless.

"You said it will summon me."

The director nodded. "That's correct."

"Then we aren't done here?" Adam asked.

She smiled. "On the contrary, Adam. We've just begun."

The night was dark and still as he crept into his father's mansion. Insects hummed peacefully and the sprinkler system quietly showered the lawn every so often. For all the wealth he coveted, the security systems in place at his father's house were laughably lax. Many a drunken night Adam had snuck back in, and he had been none the wiser. Those nights, and that version of himself felt lifetimes away from the man he was today. So much had happened.

Adam had spent the last week drifting from one hostel or cheap motel to the next, and often found himself wandering the streets aimlessly at night. He could not shake the feeling that something awful had happened at that facility. His powers were active, sure, but beneath that, he felt as though something was wrong, something he could not quite place, a half-formed memory.

He drank, even if only to keep the night terrors at bay and allow him to close his eyes. On the rare occasions that he did sleep, even in his drunken stupor he was haunted by visions of violence and horror, hellscapes and torment. And, more recently, his mother.

It was always the same dream. He would see through her eyes as his father murdered her in the garage. He would put the gun to her head, pull the trigger, and Adam would awake, drenched in sweat. He finally decided that he could wait no longer. He had to know.

As he picked the lock on the front door, he took special care not to let it creak as he gently pushed it open. He could not risk waking his father. As he opened the door, he was reminded of the last time he had snuck in, the night he stole his father's car. He half expected to find him standing there in the doorway again. Instead, the hallway was empty. The house was still and quiet.

As his eyes adjusted to the darkness, he found he was able to navigate just fine using the lights from the garden which shone in through the windows. Slowly, he ascended the staircase and crept towards his father's room. When he was halfway down the hallway, he could hear his father's snoring through the walls. He thought that his heart would race, that he would feel some type of anxiety, but instead he was overcome by a chilling calmness. He knew that nothing could touch him. His father could never make him feel small again.

As he silently opened the door to his father's room and closed it behind him, he stopped and watched him sleeping for a while. White light from the driveway shone through his blinds, casting bright polygons of light on the dark bedsheets. He looked more frail than Adam remembered, and each laboured exhale was accompanied by an even bigger snore. He only snored like that when he had been drinking.

*I could kill him right now, but no.*

That would be too easy, too quick. He wanted to hear him say it. He wanted to see the fear in his eyes.

"Wake up," Adam said. There was no response from his father, snoring away peacefully. "*Wake up!*" Adam shouted.

Don Powell awoke with a start, instinctively reaching for the pistol on his nightstand, pointing it at the mystery silhouette at the end of his bed.

"Who the fuck—" He cut himself off as he recognized his son. "Adam? Christ, it is you," he said scornfully, putting his pistol back on the nightstand. "I wondered when you'd come crawling back here. That was quite a mess you made with that pusher. I had to clean it up. How'd you do it anyway? Pussy boy like you, you must've had some help. Who was it, huh?"

Adam was silent, simply observing his father without emotion.

"Hey," his father said, growing angry. "I asked you a fucking question."

"I'm asking the questions," Adam said flatly, to which his father gave a look of stunned surprise. He was unaccustomed to being spoken to by his son in this manner. "Did you kill mother?"

"What?" his father said incredulously.

"Did. You. Kill. Her?" Adam asked.

Don Powell sat back and scoffed, shaking his head. "You finally worked up the balls to ask me, huh?" He nodded his head gently. "Yeah, I fucking killed her," he said, sighing. "She was a fucking rat, son. If anything, I did her a kindness. I could have made it a lot worse for her."

Adam scanned his father's eyes, but he could find no trace of remorse. The way he spoke about it was so callous, so crass, you would think he was talking about a dog he put down. Up until now he had remained calm, but as his father spoke, he felt rage rising inside of him, like molten lead.

"Every day," his father continued. "Every day I had to watch you grow more and more like her, that fucking bitch. You've got her eyes, that's for sure. More than that, you're weak. Just like she was. I kept you around because you do have my blood running in your veins, too. I figured if I raised you right, raised you strong, you could make something of yourself. Now? Now I know for sure that you're not worth shit. I wish you had died in that alleyway. Then at least you wouldn't be my fucking problem anymore."

Adam breathed deeply and clenched his hands into fists as they began to shake.

"What, are you gonna cry now?" his father teased in a mocking voice.

"No," Adam said coolly, "but you will."

His father laughed. "What are you going to do, huh? Shoot me? I don't see any weapons on you. You don't have the balls for that, anyway. You like to prance around like you're all that, but we both know the truth, don't we? Deep down, you're still a scared little boy. You're weak, and the strong eat the weak. That's the way of the world."

"How right you are," Adam said, closing his eyes and pointing to the wall opposite his father's bed.

In his mind's eye, he summoned the portal and soon he heard the tell–tale electric tearing sound as the doorway between dimensions opened, and this time it came faster and easier than ever.

"What are you d—" his father began, before his voice was cut off by the howling maelstrom. When Adam opened his eyes, the dark room was drenched a deep red from the ominous glow of the portal. "What the *fuck* is that?" His stared into the dark void. "How are you doing that? Is this some type of trick?"

They both heard an awful chittering echoing towards them from the darkness. "Stop it," his father said, growing increasingly panicked. "Stop this now."

A huge, barbed claw burst forth from the portal, hooking itself to the floor. Then another. Its purple skin was hard and course, like that of an insect. It hoisted its whole body through, until it towered over them in the room, crouching its body to avoid hitting the ceiling, appearing almost like a demented hybrid of a human and a praying mantis. It had all the features of the insect, only its face was human, and its gaping jaw revealed pincers and rows of needle–like teeth. All along its abdomen were other contorted faces, gaping and snapping, salivating and moaning as they waited for blood. It seemed to recognize Adam, gazing into his terrified eyes before turning its attention to his father as it hissed and chittered with excitement.

As the initial shock subsided, his father began to scream, and quickly reached for the pistol on his nightstand. He was too slow, however, and the demon deftly brought down its barbed arm into his spine with a sickening squelch, hoisting him screaming into the air as he dripped blood all over the bedsheets.

The mouths on its abdomen hungrily slurped up any droplets of blood which trickled down towards them, impatient for the main course. The demon slowly began to back itself into the portal once more, holding his father aloft as he flailed uselessly in the air.

"Please, Adam!" He begged on his way in, tears streaming down his face as his voice grew more and more hysteric. "Please! Don't let it take me! I'm sorry! I'm so sorry! I'll do anything!" He screamed. Adam stared into his father's eyes without a shred of remorse in his heart.

"The strong eat the weak," Adam said softly.

Realizing once and for all that he would find no mercy from his son, Don Powell began to shriek even louder in horror as the demon slowly pulled him into the darkness, relishing each sweet moment of its prey's terror. It finally had disappeared, returning to the dark place once again. In the moments before the portal closed, Adam heard the tearing of flesh and the echoing screams of his father as they faded into darkness.

Adam waited until dawn to leave the house.

He took his favorite car, his father's gray convertible, and drove to a nearby overlook he used to frequent when he was younger. From there, he could see the whole city. As he watched the sun slowly begin to rise over the distant mountains, he found he was visited by a profound sense of calmness, as if he could breathe again for the first time.

Did he feel better? No, but at least now he could rest, knowing that he had avenged his mother's death. While it was true that revenge was not the answer, it had at least brought him closer to understanding what the answer might be. He could not conscionably allow a man like his father to keep drawing breath. Not after everything he had done.

In a way, though, his father's death also felt like his own. The boy he once was, now was dead. Any trace of him died in that room, along with his father. He felt power coursing through him. It was a sensation he was unaccustomed to, and one he found he liked. As he watched the world brightening as it stretched out before him, he was struck by a sudden realization.

*I can do anything. Anything I want.*

He smiled as shivers crept up his spine. The possibilities were endless. Finally, he could live a life free from guilt, free from shame. In that moment, his bracelet began to beep. He looked down at it curiously, examining it.

His entire body was surrounded by pinkish light. He looked at his hand and saw that it was crossed by layers upon layers of tiny shimmering interlocking hexagons. He watched in panic as his hand began to fade away before his very eyes. In an instant, he disappeared, leaving the car and the overlook vacant as nearby birds chirped, heralding the arrival of the morning.

# CHAPTER 17

# PARADISE LOST

## *2033 A.D.*

The woods were quiet and still as The Watchers crept through them. A thick fog had settled, and all sounds seemed muffled and distant. All of them had assembled. Even, against Evie's protests, Flora. No amount of words could dissuade her.

"Not a hair shall fall from your head, child," Flora had said resolutely. "Not if I can help it."

They covered ground in a formation with Evie at its center, carefully watching ahead for any sign of danger. If they were to have any chance at all, it would be together.

Pan was silent as always. His usual aloofness, however, had hardened into a cold resolve. His vengeance would be harsh today, for Aphrodite, if nothing else. Evie watched Hermes scurry ahead of them, occasionally pausing as he caught scents on the wind. They were close. She could feel it.

From the moment they had arrived, time seemed to disappear. This was due in no small part to the thick canopy overhead which shrouded them in darkness, no matter what time of day it was. The Blackwood. That's what they called this place. For hundreds of years, The Watchers had sought it. After Athena had scoured the sorceresses mind below the cathedral, she had at last found its location.

The Blackwood, she explained, was not so easy to track down, as it existed outside time, a realm between dimensions. Its entrances on earth were many, and ever changing. Within The Blackwood, the past and the future were entwined in a seamless present.

The place felt oppressive. The moment they had stepped inside Evie had felt as if they were being swallowed by some awful creature, and now they made their way to its belly, the belly of the beast.

Her powers were at an all-time high. Every branch, every pine needle, she could feel, but this place played with her senses as well. They felt. . . blunted. Manipulating earthly phenomena, The Gift of Gaia, that was her power. But what about phenomena that weren't of this earth?

Stop, Hermes projected into her mind, breaking her train of thought.

"What is it?" she whispered, bringing herself and the rest of the group to a halt.

There's something up ahead, he said. Coming towards us. A foul presence. Use your sight.

Evie cast her awareness ahead of them deeper into the woods. For a while, she sensed nothing but cold darkness. Like a punch to the face, her astral body came face to face with a dreadful, leering man. His hairless body was covered with terrible lacerations, which oozed blood as he calmly walked toward them from the darkness, smiling maniacally all the way.

Worse, and stranger still, was his energy field. It seemed full to the brim with malevolent souls. As her awareness returned to her body, she shrank back, horrified.

"What is it?" Athena asked tersely.

"Something awful," Evie breathed. "Coming this way."

Athena nodded grimly. "You heard her. Watchers, on your guard!" she shouted. The four of them quickly made ready for battle, and Hermes jumped lithely onto Evie's shoulder.

For a few tense, silent moments they waited. A few feet in front of them, the dreadful figure came shambling out of the gloom. Its movements were fitful and erratic. From what she could tell, its body was that of a man, completely naked, and covered in awful wounds. When it saw them, it stopped, and its smile grew wider as it threw back its head unnaturally and opened its mouth widely. When it spoke, it's whispers seemed to come from all around them, and sounded like a chorus of echoing voices, rather than just one. Stranger still, its lips did not move at all, the sound just seemed to emanate from the gaping opening in its mouth.

"What have we heeeeere?" it seethed excitedly. "Watch-erssss. . . come to die." It laughed, the cruel sound echoing all around them. Then, it took another two staggered steps forward.

"Go no further, demon," Athena said coldly. "Our business is with your master, not you."

The demon hissed angrily, incensed by her boldness. "Fool," it seethed. "We serve no master."

It took another couple steps towards them, before Athena conjured her light bow and stopped it in its tracks, with a deftly loosed arrow through the heart. The arrow sent a fine mist of black blood into the air, and the demon's laughter rang in their ears. Not only was its body unfazed, but as its blood settled onto the ground around them, they watched in horror as a swarm of similar bodies, both male and female, quickly grew from the droplets, becoming full sized and continuing their disjointed advance towards the group. When they spoke, they spoke as one.

"We. Are. Legion," they hissed. Athena sheathed her bow, aghast.

"The one who is many," she whispered. "Watchers! Hang back! Do not spill its blood. For every drop that falls, another body will rise!"

The group complied and they retreated, drawing backwards from whence they came as the bodies shuffled towards them. Legion's laughter followed them.

"Folly," it whispered. "You cannot elude me."

As it spoke, its bodies panned out, filling the woods ahead of them. "Then it's simple, right?" Evie asked. "As long as we don't spill any more blood, we can easily find another way around them. They aren't that fast."

In response to her statement, she watched something awful happening. The bodies began to tear and gnaw at one another, drenching the woods in a sea of black blood which then multiplied into an army of yet more lacerated bodies, which now marched inescapably towards them.

"What do we do?" Pan asked, exasperated. "We can't possibly fight them. We have to withdraw."

Athena slapped her hands to her temples in frustration as she wracked her mind. "We cannot withdraw," she said bitterly. "The way has shut. Legion works by numbers. It means to surround us."

Evie looked back and saw that she was right. The path they had come in on was gone, replaced by yet more trees. She watched on in horror as the pale tortured bodies began to fan out behind them, surrounding them as they staggered amongst the roots of the great trees. Then she had an idea.

"We don't have to fight them," she said suddenly. "Only bind them."

Athena shot her an intense look. "What are you planning?"

"Keep close," Evie commanded. She closed her eyes and placed her hands to the Earth, casting her awareness within it. She could feel every movement, every vibration, as the bodies drew closer. Then she sought deeper, to the roots of the trees. She could hear them singing to one another, whispering of the battle above. They recognized her then, too, a transient guest in their realm, the world below the ground. Summoning her strength, she called to them, and bound them to her will.

"Evie!" Athena called out distantly from above her. Time was short; Legion had surrounded them.

At once, she was the roots. She felt thousands of her tendrils spreading and bursting forth from the Earth above her, ensnaring and swallowing every last body that Legion had produced. As she wrapped herself around them, she took extra care so as not to break their skin and spill any more blood. In a storm of wood and soil, she swallowed the howling demon back to the depths from whence it came. It took all her focus to not let go of the thousands of struggling bodies, and Legion cursed her all the while, filling her mind with malicious portents.

"We will not forget you, Eve," it hissed. "When we meet again, you will suffer." Like that, it was gone, vanishing back into the immaterial world as she felt its bodies melt away. At once, she withdrew her awareness and came back to her physical body, gasping from exhaustion. The Watchers were united in their awe.

THAT WAS SOME TRICK, Hermes cast into her mind, nuzzling her neck warmly from her shoulder.

"My goodness," Flora gushed, helping her to her feet. "Such power you possess."

"Impressive," Pan said, smiling.

"Come now," Athena said, snapping the group back into action. "We must make for the gate. It isn't far. I can sense it."

"I can sense it too, Athena. Just at the top of that ridge," Pan replied gruffly, pointing above them. "But what are we to do? We can't just walk through the front door. That facility is teeming with mages, demons, and more. We are hopelessly outnumbered. If we burst in, guns blazing, we stand to lose it all." He cast a concerned gaze at Evie.

"I'm aware of that," Athena replied sharply, and sighing. "There is another way inside the facility. Another way to reach the gate. It's a series of tunnels."

"You don't mean," Pan began.

"The Nest of The Fallen," Athena confirmed, grimly.

Pan scoffed. "That's suicide. The gods only know of the ancient horrors which stalk those passageways. The place is cursed."

"It is our only option," Athena relented. "Death is not assured, dear Pan."

Flora suddenly interjected. "I spent much time researching those corridors in my youth. They open freely to the chosen. That is, Adam and Eve. Such is their birthright."

Evie shook her head in quiet amazement. After all this time, Flora continued to surprise her. To think that mere months ago her grandmother was frail, ailing, and showing the beginnings of dementia. Never would Evie have guessed the wealth of knowledge and power she possessed.

*She's my link to this world*, Evie realized for the first time. Maybe she had been all along.

"And what about us?" Pan protested. "Will they yield to us, too?"

Flora raised her hands meekly. "That much, is up to fate."

"Evie," Athena said suddenly, turning to her. "Using your Earth-sight, can you find the caves?"

Evie nodded silently, assured of her powers. It was not a question of can.

"I will," she said finally.

After what felt like hours of endless searching, the Nest of The Fallen finally presented itself to the group. As they rounded the crest of yet another tree line, the cave was at once there, as though it always had been. Evie was sure they had passed this place not more than a minute ago, and there had been nothing there at all. By now, however, she was beginning to become inured to the ways of The Blackwood. The trees seemed to retreat from its entrance as the mouth of the great cave gaped towards them like some foul maw, beckoning them inwards. Never had she seen such dark stone, it was as if it swallowed up what little light there was around it.

Evie cast her awareness inwards, but she could sense nothing, as if the cave was cut off from the rest of the wood.

“And there it lies,” Athena breathed in awe. “The earthly rest of the fallen one. Lucifer.”

“We shouldn’t be here,” Pan grumbled. “This place is cursed.”

“This whole world is cursed, Pan,” Athena shot back.

“Aye,” Pan replied. “But nowhere more so than here,” he said.

Athena scoffed. "We haven't the time for this."

As she took a step towards the cave's mouth, she was stopped in her tracks by a sound in the distance. It was the echoing wine of a falling tree, followed by a resounding crash that shook the Earth. It was unmistakable. They all heard it. Then there was another. And another, all around them, and getting closer. Evie felt the fur on Hermes's back rise as he stood on his haunches. Something was coming.

"Watchers!" Athena shouted. "Assume defensive formation!"

As she instructed, they gathered themselves around the mouth of the cave, facing in all directions for their would-be enemy. Evie kept her eyes focussed intently on the tree line ahead of her, when she started catching sight of movements. Huge shadows flickering back and forth in the darkness.

A ball of fire shot out of the shadows towards them. Evie ducked and the ball of fire exploded on the cool rock of the cave, and she watched the flames fan out then reverse, as they were absorbed by the rock itself.

At once, they were beset by screeching hordes of demons and sorcerers, rushing at them from all sides. Among them were winged harpies, half-rotten corpses animated by necromancy, and towering chimeras built of beasts contorted in ways too horrible to mention.

"To battle!" Athena cried, summoning her bow, and loosing a flurry of glowing arrows. Each arrow struck a demon, and as it did so, burned their bodies to ash almost instantaneously. Their screeches soon vanished like dust in the wind. Much to her surprise, Hermes sprang from Evie's shoulder and swiftly took hold of a dagger from Pan's belt in his mouth.

Evie watched in disbelief as he launched himself into the

attackers at extreme speed. He seemed almost to teleport between them, slicing open their throats and snapping their tendons with deadly accuracy. Hermes alone had brought down ten of them in the first few seconds.

Not to be upstaged, Pan soon drew his double scimitars, and whispered an enchantment, which made them glow green with eldritch energy, before he sprang into the forsaken mob in a flurry of glittering green magic and steel.

In the chaos, one of the winged harpies dived screeching towards Flora, its outstretched talons already dripping with blood. Evie quickly sprang into action and raised a pillar of rock from beneath the Earth, which the harpy collided with at full speed, crumpling its body with a sickening crunch and showering them all with acrid black blood.

Flora gave Evie a nod of acknowledgement, staggering quickly to her feet to face the rapidly advancing ranks of screeching demons. As they drew closer, Evie watched in awe as her grandmother closed her eyes and drew her arms skyward in a circular motion before slamming her palms together in prayer, unleashing snaking bolts of vibrant orange energy that shot out towards the advancing creatures as glowing tendrils. The moment the beams collided with their bodies, the demons were instantly encompassed by the light and transmuted into a flock of hummingbirds which scattered in all directions chirping wildly. She allowed herself a moment of pride before launching herself back into the fray.

Not to be upstaged herself, Evie closed her eyes and focussed on the air above them in the clearing. In her mind's eye, she condensed the moisture in the air above them, feeling every droplet coalesce into a huge storm cloud. As she breathed in, she could feel the electrical energy surging through her. Every cell in her body vibrated in unison as she exhaled, releasing a storm of lightning which engulfed the ranks of the forsaken, atomising hundreds of them in an instant.

But her spell provided only a momentary relief from the onslaught. For as valiantly as the Watchers fought, every demon or sorcerer they cut down was replaced by ten more. Soon, they would be overwhelmed.

"Evie!" Athena shouted desperately as the next wave advanced. "It's no use! You must make for the cavern. We will hold them at bay."

"No!" Evie shouted back. "I won't leave you."

At that moment Flora gave her a sad smile. "She wasn't asking, child," she said softly, raising her arm and pointing it towards Evie.

"Wait," Evie said. "What are you—"

At once she felt her grandmother's energy pulsing through her like gale force winds, lifting her off her feet and throwing her into the waiting mouth of the cave. Her last sight before the dark stone shut behind her was the group being overrun and swallowed by the ranks of the forsaken.

The tunnel was pitch black, and the stone was cold against her skin. As she lay heaving in the darkness, she could hear nothing but the sound of her own breath; even her echoes were swallowed by the unforgiving walls of the cave.

She clambered around awkwardly, trying her best to orient herself, but it was pointless. She had no way of knowing where to go, of which way was up or down.

Then, ahead of her, a faint golden glow appeared. Its light

cast strange reflections on the walls of the cave, and she was able to orient herself. Up. She had to climb upwards.

On her hands and knees, she crawled up the steep slope of jagged rock towards the source of the light. The stone cut harshly into her skin, but she barely noticed. She had to reach the light.

Abruptly, she rounded a corner and could at last see the source of the light. It was an opening, an exit, and through it she could see the sky, a vibrant mixture of pink and orange.

As she crawled, she soon felt grass and soil under her fingers. Using all her strength, she hauled her body out of the opening, which quickly closed behind her and abruptly, she was lying in a meadow.

The grass felt like silk against her skin and the air was the sweetest she had ever tasted. It took her eyes a while to adjust to the light, and then she sat up, dazed, taking in her surroundings.

On all sides, she was surrounded by rolling hills and lush vegetation, stretching as far as the eye could see. So too was there an abundance of streams and rivers, gushing with sparkling water as well as all manner of wildlife, big and small, living together in harmony. Every tree was full of flowers and the ripest fruits imaginable. The very air itself was permeated by an array of divine fragrances which all but overwhelmed her. The sky was orange, and she could not tell if the sun was setting or rising. It was as if this place existed in a permanent state of twilight.

A profound sense of peace washed over her, the kind of peace she had only briefly glimpsed in fleeting moments in her regular life, which now felt like little more than a distant dream.

Just as the beauty threatened to overwhelm her, she heard a slithering in the grass behind her and she sprang to attention once more. Then she saw it, a glittering snake in the grass; the golden serpent, Lucifer. Her heart sank.

"Eve," he hissed rapturously.

"Where am I?" she asked indignantly.

"A memory," he said, raising his golden eyes to meet her own. "Search yourself. Do you not recognize this place?"

As she looked around, she could not deny a certain sense of familiarity which crept across her mind.

"This was once my home," she said softly, as the memories came flooding back.

"Indeed, it was," he agreed. "But you were not the first." He raised his head to the sky. "Look."

She raised her gaze upwards and saw what looked like a meteor entering the upper atmosphere in the distance. As it drew closer, Evie could make out that it was not a space rock at all, but rather a massive, winged humanoid, which was hurtling towards them with extreme speed. Its feathers were burning, and its screams filled the skies as it fell.

Soon, it collided with the Earth in an immense explosion, which clouded the skies and sent the animals running in all directions. Evie braced for the shockwave and scrambled to avoid the huge chunks of molten debris but Lucifer was quick to correct her.

"It cannot harm you," He hissed. "We are not really here. We are but shadows to this place. Little more than ghosts."

She looked down at her hands and saw that they were semi-transparent. He was right. The winged creature struck the ground with such intensity that it was buried far into the mantle and created a mound where it had entered, as the earth deformed.

"Is that—"

"Yes," Lucifer confirmed. "The moment of my arrival."

As the rubble subsided, time began to pass much faster, as if in a time-lapse, and Evie watched the grass covered impact site, now a towering hill, and a flutter of harmony returned to the garden once more. The sun never set nor rose, and as such to mark the passage of time was impossible. There was only one continuous present moment. It could have been thousands of years, millions of years, or mere hours, it was impossible to say. She watched as a seedling sprouted from the top of the hill, the site where Lucifer had crashed.

That seedling quickly bloomed into a sapling, which shot upwards and outwards into the grandest and most beautiful tree she had ever seen. Its glowing trunk extended towards the sky and soon its arms and branches spread far and wide, and they too were golden.

Eventually, the tree bore fruit, great red orbs which shone so brightly that they themselves were like small suns. Then, time began to slow and return to its normal pace. The wind blew through the top of the great tree and its golden leaves swayed in the wind.

"Behold," Lucifer said. "The Tree of Knowledge."

As Evie was surveying the tree, in all its glory, she felt a strange sensation as a presence walked through her spectral body. Reeling from shock she quickly saw who it was.

A bronze skinned woman, naked, and with a black mane of flowing curly hair, walked slowly and purposefully towards the hill. At once, Evie knew who she was. It was her. Or rather, her first incarnation.

Eve. The first woman.

In her features, she could see the features of every race. She was, after all, the progenitor of all mankind. Evie watched as Eve climbed the hill. Atop the hill, Eve studied the Tree of Knowledge cautiously. Then, from a hole in the ground leading to the caves below, she watched a serpent make its way towards her. It was that same serpent which stood by her side now.

She could not hear what was said between them. After all, the serpent cast thoughts into her mind, not audible phrases. She watched as Eve cautiously plucked one of the glowing fruit. As she took it from the tree, its glow subsided and she held it in the palm of her hand, carefully examining it. She watched as Lucifer slunk back into his lair, his work done.

Just as Eve was about to sink her teeth into the fruit, Adam appeared from behind the other side of the tree. His appearance was similar to her own. Skin of a deep bronze and curly black hair. He angrily grabbed her arm, chastising her and trying to wrest the fruit from her fingers. They spoke not with their words but with their minds, with their hearts. Spoken language did not yet exist, for there was no need. Both could sense the intentions of the other intimately.

Eve calmed Adam, and brought to the surface his own curiosity about the fruit. She relayed to him what the snake had said, and there, in that moment, with the full might of her intention, she took the first bite; the first act of free will, the act that had at last set in motion the great game.

Adam soon followed and took his own bite. Evie watched on as their bodies began to glow and they collapsed to the ground, quivering as they were struck by the burden of knowledge, the weight of the world.

Evie was then shown as the twelve Gates around the world instantly flickered to life, six to the plane of love, and six to the plane of fear.

In the garden, night fell for the first time. As Adam and Eve rose from their slumber, they were terrified, as if they had woken into a nightmare. For the first time, they felt fear. For the first time, they were naked.

They shivered as they rushed to cover their bodies with whatever vegetation they could find, somehow ashamed of their naked forms. At that moment, a huge bolt of lightning struck The Tree, burning it all to cinders and vaporising every last fruit. Adam and Eve fled from under the tree, terrified, frightened of the perceived anger they had incurred from their creator, and reeling under the weight of truth.

Evie watched on in sorrow as the time again began to lapse, quickly the garden sickened and decayed, until all that was left were silent ashen trees and leaves underfoot.

Fog set in, and awful creatures began to roam. The time lapse moved forward exponentially until it froze, and she saw the events of earlier in the day, as the Watchers found their way to the nest of the fallen, the cave which lay at the base of the hill where the Tree of Knowledge once stood.

Evie gasped. "Then you mean—"

"That's correct," Lucifer hissed. "The Blackwood is what remains of the Garden of Eden. A cursed place, forsaken since the outset of humanity."

"Then that's why it can exist outside time," Evie realized aloud. "It's another dimension."

"And it is the keystone to the story of Earth. The story of the gates. Your story," Lucifer said. "You were always destined to return here. As you once did in the past. Again, the snake eats itself, and the disparate threads of time come full circle."

"But why?" Evie asked. "Why are you showing me all of this?"

"I play my part, as you must play yours," Lucifer replied. "Once again, I present you with knowledge. The outcome of your choice that fateful day. This represents completion. The end of a cycle. What you do with that knowledge is now up to you."

As he spoke, a golden portal appeared in front of her, seeming to lead to some type of industrial amphitheatre. Harsh artificial life shone through it.

"And where does that lead?" she asked.

"To your fate, should you choose to meet it," Lucifer replied. "To the end, and the beginning."

As Evie stepped through the portal into the complex, it quickly winked shut behind her. The cement was harsh and cold underfoot. Up ahead of her, she could see the access tunnel widened into a massive hollowed out space.

She had no idea how far underground she was, but the sheer size of the complex was staggering. The ceiling was many stories high and towered above her, and the width of the place had to be the length of multiple city blocks, clearly man made, the angles were too precise, too straight.

Most staggering of all was the construction, which lay at the center of the complex. A perfect circle of towering black stone from the cavern hybridized with, and supported by, all kinds of machinery. From all sides it was fed and cooled by massive cables. At once she knew what it was.

The Thirteenth Gate. The sight of it filled her with dread.

The first Fellgate she had seen under the cathedral had been terrible enough to behold, and this was at least fifty times the size of that. She could barely comprehend the horror this structure could unleash if it were activated.

*I can't let that happen.*

Directly in front of the gate was a podium, which reached high towards it's center. As she took careful steps towards the gate, she heard a woman's voice from behind her, startling her.

"Eve," the voice said warmly. "So nice of you to join us."

She spun around, ready for a fight, and came face to face with a woman in a business suit, standing not more than two feet behind her. How had she snuck up on her like that? She had not heard a thing.

The woman's hair was pale as bone, eclipsed only by the paleness of her skin, so pale it seemed almost translucent. Her mouth smiled, but her eyes spoke of rage. Evie found her somehow familiar, though she could not place how or why.

"Who are you?" Evie asked, as her eyes narrowed.

The woman laughed. "You may not remember me, but I remember you, Eve," she said. "I have waited a thousand years for this moment." As she was speaking, a shimmer passed over her body and she transformed before Evie's eyes, growing taller and more slender.

Her skin, which was once pale, now began to glow and her body began to levitate. Her clothes disappeared and her hair grew longer, flowing out in all directions as if it had a life of its own. In moments, her transformation was complete. She breathed a sigh of relief, opening her large, catlike eyes which glowed like purple violets.

"Much better," she sang, her voice carrying the tell-tale harmonic cadence of elven kind. "The human form is so crude. I don't know how you do it."

Evie had known one elf before, Aphrodite, but this being was different. She radiated power and the very air itself around her seemed to ripple and warp under the weight of her immense presence. As Evie gazed upon her, she was hit by flashes, images from a life not her own, a life half remembered. A river. A cave. This cave? Her mother. Pain. A word.

"Miraneth." She said the word, but did not know what it meant. Miraneth smiled mirthfully, freely reading the thoughts that arose in Evie's unguarded mind. "Now you are beginning to remember," she said. "In your past life, I took you in. I bathed you, I clothed you. I taught you everything I knew. Then, you used that knowledge to kill me. Or so you thought. I expected nothing less. Even the best and brightest of your kind deal in treachery.

"So, I made arrangements. Arrangements so that this form might live on. I knew my work was not yet done. I needed only to mold you, to guide you, to the steps I needed you to take." She laughed, a cruel sound, but beautiful none the less. "Oh, how high and mighty you grew, assuming my place. My throne. Thinking it to be your own. You humans are nothing, if not easily deceived. It is almost endearing. Watching you fumble around, desperately trying to make sense of your petty little lives. Yet so much of this story depends on you. You half-breeds, floundering on the threshold between gods and beasts. And none more so than you two. The progenitors."

Evie felt anger rise inside of her. "Then this, thing," she said, motioning towards the Gate. "This is your doing?"

"Why, yes. Yes, it is," Miraneth said proudly. "It is my life's work."

Evie shook her head. "But why? Why do this?"

Miraneth sighed. "Look at the world around you. What is it that you see? Pain. Sorrow. Suffering. On scales unimaginable. Humans have wrought untold destruction upon the Earth. Not only that, but they have also collectively severed their connection to the spirit of this world. Ever onwards and outwards they spread, consuming or destroying everything in their path.

"They are stupid, callous, and dangerous. The weight of their fears far outweighs the weight of their love, and it is those same fears which will ultimately consume them. The experiment failed. The creator was wrong. Humans cannot be the apex species of this planet. They are sick, they make the world sick, and they must be cleansed. If I am to be the architect of their demise, so be it. I will open The Gates of Matter once more, and the world shall begin anew."

"But you won't just kill the humans," Evie protested. "You'll kill everything. Animals, plants, and all of the surviving magical races."

"These are necessary sacrifices," Miraneth replied. "Gaia will always find a new way of creating life. In planetary timescales, the era of man will be but a forgotten blip, lost to the sands of time. The blood of the usurpers shall water the seedlings, which will proper and grow, and equilibrium will gradually return to this world.

"With an absence of fear, the demons will eventually retreat to their darkness. Like the great flood of old, the world shall be pure and silent once more. You see, Eve, mother Earth is always trying to optimize life. She is both the holy canvas and the master artist, constantly searching for new forms. Humans have had their time in the sun. They have shown the truth of themselves, and all their flaws, over and over. In their arrogance, they have assumed dominion over her.

"In reality, nothing could be further from the truth. At best, we are merely transient guests in this realm, existing only at the infinite mercy of mother nature. We elves understood this. The Earth cries out as she is trampled underfoot but her cries fall on deaf ears. No longer. The rape of the world stops now."

"And the innocents?" Evie shouted. "What about them? What about all the good people in this world?"

"None of us are innocent, Eve. Innocence died the day you

ate that fruit." She floated higher, towards the gate.

"I won't let you," Evie said, summoning her strength.

"Save your breath, young one," Miraneth said fleetingly. "Your powers will not work here. This place is sealed from the outside world."

Evie strained to focus her energy but to her horror she found out that Miraneth was right, she was powerless.

"Besides," Miraneth said. "It's not me you need to stop." At that moment she pressed a button on her silver bracelet, and it began to glow.

Almost instantly, a figure materialized in a pink flash on the podium above them, a young man. His bleached blonde hair was trimmed in a tight buzzcut, and his skin was pale and unblemished like porcelain. He was wearing a white singlet and denim jeans and seemed for a moment utterly dazed as he got his bearings. He was beautiful to behold, but what struck her most was the look of sadness and lostness in his eyes. She knew it well, as it was the same look, she saw in her own eyes each day. She knew at once who it was. It was the same soul she had loved across countless millennia.

Upon the podium, Miraneth had reverted to her human form and guided him towards the colossal gate. "You know what to do," she whispered to him. He moved forward as if in a trance, and shakily raised his arm towards the epicenter of the gate.

As he closed his eyes and concentrated, Evie cried out desperately to him, screaming. "Adam! Don't!" He hesitated briefly and opened his eyes. As he looked upon her, she saw the same recognition wash over his face. But it was too late, he had opened a small tear in the fabric of reality.

What started as a small glowing red orb rapidly expanded as the gate powered up. The complex began to quake violently and fragment under the weight of the eldritch power and great chunks of cement fell from the ceiling revealing the black stone beneath. The gate burst into a roaring, towering maelstrom of terror, filling the complex with unholy red light and a tempest of screams and moans from the dark realm.

Adam staggered back, horrified, while Miraneth triumphantly shed her human form for the final time as she rose towards the abyss.

"And now, I have become death," she sang. "The destroyer of worlds!"

## CHAPTER 18

# Anywhere and Nowhere

### *1033 A.D.*

From the day she took control of the Order of Sanguine, life had changed dramatically for Morgana.

Power coursed through her veins, through her soul, and often she found herself overcome with the sheer intoxicating ecstasy of it all. Whatever she willed, they would enact, her army of darkness, her brothers and sisters in arms, united in their common hatred for humanity. True to her word, one of her first acts was to lead a raid on the village of Bluffton. The place she had once called home, the place that had scorned her.

They waited for a moonless night, stalking out of The Blackwood like silent shadows, crossing the cornfields and silencing anyone and anything that had the misfortune of crossing their path. To be seen was to raise an alarm, a warning. This, she would not allow. There would be no escape.

Only Mathias and Errol would be spared, if they even still called Bluffton home. It had been years, after all. Despite her position, her heart still fluttered at the thought of encountering her girlhood love. Yet, such thoughts made her weak, and she could not abet them. There was no time for weakness now. From this path she could not return.

As they neared closer to the village, she could make out the sleepy glow of lanterns from the homes inside, and the lights on the watchtowers on the wooden palisades. By now they would be sleeping soundly in their beds, blissfully unaware of the horrors which beset them.

*Fools.*

The village had been untouched by the passage of time. She could see not more than two guards at their posts, one of which was snoring soundly. She drew her forces to a halt, lingering in the shadows at the threshold of the light.

Silently, they fanned out, surrounding the walls on all sides. Already, the demons and hellbeasts were beginning to salivate, their bloodlust almost insatiable as they waited for the signal from their queen. She had promised them a feast, and a feast she would provide.

From her cloak, she withdrew a whistle, which she had shaped herself from human bone, using her powers. She inhaled deeply, closing her eyes and then blew into the whistle with all her might. It uttered a deafening, deathly scream, which cut through the night air. That was the signal.

At once, her demonic hordes uttered a howl, springing over the walls and into the village, while her human warriors rammed down the gates. She raised her arm skyward and was picked up by one of her harpies, which dropped her over the wall and into the muddy streets.

The villagers barely had time to raise the alarm. A man atop the belltower began to sound, but within seconds he was set upon by a horde of winged imps who ripped him to shreds, squabbling with one another as they fought over chunks of his flesh. The night air was soon saturated with the sound of screams and moans as the villagers awoke to their nightmare. Her nightmare. It was music to her ears.

She slowly walked towards the town square, savoring every precious moment of the carnage which now unfolded before her. She watched as villagers desperately tried to flee the monsters in their homes, only to be dragged screaming back into the darkness. She listened gleefully as their flesh was torn and their bones were snapped, and their screams fell silent.

The doors and windows of their homes were draped with their skin and the streets ran red with blood. No one was to be spared, man, woman, or child, for none of them had spared her. They were all complicit. If they had even showed a modicum of decency, of mercy, she would have extended the same to them.

But they had not, and she would slaughter them like the pigs they were.

Ahead of her, a bloody man with a pitchfork staggered out of his home, miraculously escaping the clutches of his hellish assailants. He wailed as he took in the scenes of bloodshed around him, sending pleas to his god above and asking why. Why had this fate befallen them?

As he turned, he saw Morgana slowly walking towards him, a serene smile on her face. "Fair maiden," he wept. "Save yourself! You must leave this place at once!"

As she stepped into the light, his features changed, contorting into horror as he recognized her. "You," he breathed, aghast, shrinking back. "You did this." She said nothing, paying him as much mind as one might pay to an ant as she nonchalantly strolled onwards towards the square.

This angered the man who raised his pitchfork and charged towards her. “Foul witch!” he spat. Without looking at him, she casually raised her left arm, pointing her first two fingers and lifting him effortlessly into the air. He began to scream and struggle, his resolve quickly crumbling. “Please! Mercy!”

She balled her hand into a fist and the man let out a strangled screech as his body condensed into a fleshy ball, with a sickening squelch. Just as easily, she opened her fist and burst his body into a cloud of blood and viscera. Before the blood even had time to hit the ground, she raised her other hand and began to weave it into great flowing ribbons which she spun and fanned elegantly in the air around her as she danced her way towards the square.

As she drew closer, she could see that the last of the surviving townspeople had gathered together around the witching pole, which still stood tall above them.

*They haven’t even taken it down.*

The demons had surrounded them on all sides, slithering and chittering as they fed on the fear in the air, while their distended bodies quaked with anticipation of yet more flesh. The men and boys of the village held their meager weapons aloft, shaking with terror while a priest recited terrified prayers, trying his best to calm them.

“Our father, who art in heaven, hallowed b–b–be thy name. Deliver us from evil—”

“Deliver you from evil?” Morgana mocked, interrupting his flimsy prayer. “Would that I could deliver you from yourselves, for the very evil you decry resides within you.”

“Silence, witch!” the priest shouted back. “The Lord will protect the faithful. He will send for us. . .” His last sentence was spoken with less conviction.

Morgana threw back her head in laughter, and the demons laughed along with her. It was a haunting, unnatural sound.

"Your *lord* sent me, priest," she said finally. "And I am the instrument of His will." As her words landed, she could see the impact they had on the priest. He knew in that moment that she was right. In his eyes, she saw his faith extinguish. Only then, when all hope had been crushed, did she signal her demons to feed. The townsfolk screamed in unison as they were torn limb from limb and slowly devoured, while Morgana wove their blood into artful ribbons in the sky above them.

Weeks came and went, and her elation slowly gave way to a hollow inertia. She had exacted her revenge. Now what? She grew restless and bored from atop her throne in The Blackwood, and her soldiers too grew unruly. Her demons hungered for blood once more.

Leading the Order was not quite how she had imagined; there was no roadmap to world domination. Part of her wished Miraneth was still here, to guide her at the very least.

*No. She just as easily would have killed me.*

Though they would not say it to her face, she could feel the seeds of dissent spreading amongst her army with each passing day of inaction. Soon ,she would have to strike again, a decisive action to remind her forces just who it was that was leading them, and why. She had promised them conquests, and conquests she would provide.

Under her guidance, construction of The Thirteenth Gate had at last been completed, and in that she took solace. What chance did humanity have in the face of Hell, itself?

The structure towered over the encampment like a great arcane arch. Her human soldiers feared it, while the demons revered it. They uttered blasphemous prayers to the structure and regularly brought it bloody offerings in the form of mutilated body parts of their unfortunate victims. Soon, The Blackstone was covered in a sticky coating of blood, and it seemed to weep constantly throughout the day, staining the ground around it a deep crimson.

Quietly, the structure instilled a sense of dread within her as well. Perhaps it was the matter of her birth, some innate glimmer of humanity which lingered within her hardened heart. It seemed to call to her. At night, she was haunted by horrific dreams and visions from the other side. It was always the same.

The portal would wink into life and blanket the world in darkness and bloodshed. She would awake in a sweat, but then lie back, and take comfort in the visions. This world was sick, full of hatred. At least the darkness was pure, it did not pretend to be anything more than itself. Evil.

Despite it all, she kept finding herself thinking of Mathias. She had hoped to see him there in Bluffton, though why, she could not say. Perhaps she wanted some sort of validation. Acknowledgement of how far she had come. Or maybe she just wanted to see him.

Such thoughts were ridiculous, she decided, unbefitting of a queen. So, she pushed them to the back of her mind. That was until, one day, when one of her scouts came to her.

A man had found his way into the woods and they had taken him. Though she could not say why, when it was reported to her, she requested that his life be spared, so that she may gaze upon him herself. This angered the demons, who's bloodlust by now could barely be contained. Still, they obeyed, begrudgingly fulfilling their oath.

The sun was high in the sky as she sat atop the Blackstone pinnacle, awaiting her audience with the hostage. He was brought before her, bound, sweating, and terrified.

One of her sharpest demons, An-Narash, who took the form of a three-eyed centaur with a crocodilian snout full of sharpened teeth, hissed at her in the ancient tongue.

"Why is it that we spare this one? We are hungry."

Morgana smiled. "I want him for myself."

An-Narash laughed, a deep, rumbling sound. "Then his fate shall be worse than death."

The demons and soldiers quickly dispersed, leaving the two of them alone. The man looked up to where she sat but the sun was behind her, obscuring her visage into little more than a silhouette in the midday sun. She, however, knew just who it was who sat before her. His features had been weathered by time and age, growing broader and more pronounced, and now his once youthful face was marked by stubble. But there could be no mistaking it. It was Mathias. His tunic was stained in blood, which gave Morgana cause for immediate concern. In an instant, she phase shifted behind him, appearing from a cloud of swirling blue energy to unbind his hands.

"I seek an audience with the lady of the wood," he panted.

"And it is she you have found," she whispered into his ear as she broke him free from his shackles. At once, she felt his body grow tense.

"Why would you free me?" he asked in disbelief.

"Because, many years ago, you once did the same for me."

"Morgana," he whispered in awe, as his eyes lit up.

"Shh," she cooed, running her fingers gently through his hair as she cast a gentle enchantment. "Sleep now."

Ω

By the time he awoke, the soft blanket of night had already fallen. Morgana had lit candles and lanterns in the cave, taking great efforts to beautify and soften her normally cold and uninviting home. She had also taken efforts to beautify herself, donning her finest and most seldom worn black gown. Its sequins glittered gloriously in the firelight, shimmering like starlight as she moved.

Despite it all, she was nervous. It was a feeling she had not felt since she was a girl, a giddiness which ebbed and flowed inside of her like the rising and falling of the tides, it made her feel young again. Innocent, almost, as if none of it had ever happened.

He awoke with a start, perspiration dripping from his brow as he sprang from his cot, reaching instinctively for the weapon at his hip, which was no longer there. He looked down at his hip and seemed perplexed. While he slept, she had healed his wounds, bathed him, and changed his clothes. Now he wore flowing white tunic and leather tights. It was a joy to use her powers once again for healing, as they were originally intended.

In his confusion, his eyes darted around the cavern, anxious for any signs of danger. That was until he affixed his gaze on Morgana, who sat at the dining table, their plates of food and goblets of wine already set. Her eyes met his own through the gloom, and through them she spoke of a deep longing years in the making.

"Will you join me?" she asked earnestly.

"Of course," Mathias said finally, his features softening. As he made his way over to the stone table, she savored the very image of him. His features had grown rugged and manly, but underneath it all she could still make out the fresh-faced youth she had fallen in love with. He carried himself with distinction and walked with the pride of a man unencumbered by the shackles of his own misdeeds. His very gait was alluring, and she yearned for his touch.

In his own eyes, she thought she could detect glimmers of the same desire. He looked at her first and foremost not as some frightful despot, but as a woman, as a human. It was a feeling she had not felt in some time. Her insides seemed to sparkle, and chills ran up and down her spine.

The very space in the air between them seemed to crackle with potential and this sheer magnetism could not be denied, even after all these years. As their eyes connected, time seemed to grind to a halt. He spoke first.

"I always knew that you lived," he said. "Somehow, I just knew. I could feel it. Night after night I prayed for you, hoping only that you were safe, that you were happy. And look at you now. You're, you're. . ." He trailed off.

"I'm?" she asked back, probing him.

"Beautiful," he sighed, stumbling over his words.

Morgana blushed then, her pale cheeks turning rosy. "Was I not always?" she teased.

"Of course!" he hastily clarified. "I only meant—"

"Relax," she broke in. "I'm only joking. And you have grown awfully handsome, might I add."

Now it was his turn to blush, and he awkwardly diverted his gaze to the meal in front of him, hearty soup with brown bread, and a skin of her finest wine.

"Dig in," she bade him. "It isn't getting any warmer."

Taking his cue, Mathias dived headfirst into his meal, devouring the soup in big gulps and the bread in even greater chunks. Each mouthful, he would wash down with a healthy swig of wine. Clearly, he was starving. Judging by the state they had found him in, this was likely his first meal in days. To that end, she did not judge his lack of decorum. In fact, she found it strangely endearing.

"How is Errol?" she asked, timing her question in between his immense mouthfuls.

Mathias features grew somber as he gulped down the contents of his food before answering. "Errol is gone," he said finally. "He passed away two winters ago."

Morgana felt her heart sink. "I'm sorry," she said softly.

"It's alright," he replied. "He passed peacefully in his sleep, though he never was quite the same after that day. After what they did to you." His words brought back a flood of harsh memories. "I'm sorry." He realized her discomfort.

"It's fine," she said. "That was a lifetime ago." There was a brief pause, then she spoke again. "Why have you come here today?" she asked pointedly. He seemed for a moment taken aback by her directness.

"Was it not enough simply to see you?"

"Not enough to risk your life, no. I saw the injuries you sustained. No sane person would risk their life for that."

Mathias sighed. "Perhaps, then, I am not sane."

Morgana could not tell if he was joking. After a brief pause his expression grew more serious. "I had to know," he said quietly.

"Had to know what?" Morgana asked.

"Bluffton. By chance I passed through, on my way north. That was when I found it. Scenes of horror. The town razed. Bodies torn apart and mutilated. Neither man woman nor child were spared. There were signs of a struggle, and of magic. So, I had to know. Was it you?"

Morgana sighed. So quickly it had come to this. "Yes."

Mathias hung his head, whether from rage or sorrow she could not say. For a while he remained so, and with each passing moment her heart beat faster. Finally, he raised his head with tears in his eyes. "How could you?" he asked, his voice breaking.

His forlorn gaze struck parts of her heart she thought she had lost long ago. Suddenly, she too was indignant, emotional. Her vision became clouded.

"How could I?" she protested. "How could they? You saw what they did to me. What they did to my mother. You said it yourself. None of them were innocent. Their fates were sealed that day. Things have changed now, Mathias. I have mastered my abilities, and my power only grows with each passing moment. No longer must I hide in the shadows, at the mercy of men. Now, it is they who must hide from me. This world shall know me, and it shall lament, for the hour of judgement is at hand."

Mathias simply stared at her from across the table, his brow furrowed with concern as his hands clenched. After a long pause she spoke again.

"What is it?" she mocked. "Do you hate me?"

"No," Mathias said softly, "I love you." In that moment her guard dropped, and the air escaped from her lungs. She was struck by the powerful remembrance of the day she had escaped Bluffton.

*He said he could never fear me.* In that moment, she was that same girl once again.

"Do you think me a monster?" she asked, tears welling in her eyes.

"You are not a monster, Morgana," he said softly. "This world has not been kind to you. It is not for me to deign what is right and what is wrong. I am simply a man. What I can say is that it's never too late to change your course. You are not the things that have happened to you, nor are you the things you have done. You are more. So much more."

In that moment, she broke into choked labored sobs as years of emotional repression and resistance came flowing out of her. On some level, she could not believe what was happening. Where was all this emotion coming from? It was as if it had laid in wait all this time, simmering just below the surface. Perhaps it made some sense after all; her heart opened only to him.

He rose from his place and strode over to where she sat, rivers of grief pouring out of her like a thaw in the springtime. He reached out his hand and she took it in her own. Slowly, he helped her to her feet and wordlessly wrapped her in his warm embrace.

So long she had waited for this. His touch. His scent. In his arms she felt safe. Not the safety guaranteed by her power and authority, a different sort of safety, the safety of home. Within that home, her tears kept flowing. She cried for the girl she once was, she cried for the world. All the while Mathias held her, saying nothing, as he gently stroked her hair.

After she felt she could cry no more, she looked up at him. He met her gaze, and then her lips. At first, their kiss was soft and slow, as their bodies opened to one another. Both of them wordlessly savored each precious moment of that bliss. Then it grew more intense, as they both succumbed to the endless reservoirs of passion that they had slowly built within themselves over the years, passion that had nowhere to go, wowhere but here, now.

Their bodies responded to one another effortlessly. It was as natural as breathing. After an eternity Mathias pulled away and looked upon her with nothing but love and kindness in his gentle eyes. "Won't you stay?" she asked him shakily. "We could rule together."

"We both know that I cannot," he replied softly. "Where you have gone, I cannot follow. For better or worse, my place is out here, amongst those people you so despise."

Morgana sighed, catching her breath in between sniffles. She knew that he was right, there was no place for him here. His presence alone would prompt too many questions and she could not appear weak, not in front of them. Her army.

"You will need my help to make it out of here alive," she said finally, regaining her composure.

Under the cover of darkness, she brought him to the edge of the Blackwood. They took shortcuts and back routes through the winding labyrinth that only she knew. They walked mostly in silence, the weight of both of their heavy hearts taking up all the space in the air between them.

On his own, death would be all but certain. She knew all too well the horrors which lurked in the shadows, horrors which were now bound to her will. At the precipice of the wood, as it opened unto the same corn fields she had once fled through, and then led an army through, she could see the faint light of dawn rising in the distance.

As Mathias surveyed the wide world in front of him, he let out an audible sigh of relief and she could not blame him, she once felt the same, suffocated by the darkness of that place. By now, however, she was comforted by it.

Mathias stared listlessly at the scene which stretched out before him. His eyes were searching for something, anything, for even a trace of the joy he once felt. For a while they were silent, as the wind of the world gently whipped at their backs.

"Where will you go?" she finally asked.

"Anywhere," Mathias replied. "Nowhere."

"Will I see you again?" she asked tentatively.

Mathias turned to her, looking in her eyes for the first time since the cave. At once she was disarmed all over again. "No," He said.

The word cut into her heart like glass, and she did her best to stem the tears which welled in her eyes. With that, he wordlessly set off, and with him he took the remains of her heart.

Sometime after Mathias's departure she heard whispers of a force coming her way. An army sent south from Kingsrest, led by a coalition of sorcerers and knights. The thought disquieted her. Such an alliance had not been brokered in three generations.

It mattered not. Within The Blackwood, she was secure, deep inside her fortress of thorns. Day by day, the ranks of her forces grew. What hope could the humans have? Even so, she thought it wise to send a message to this army. A warning. The wise amongst them would flee. Only the foolhardy zealots would stay their course, and they would face certain death.

She waited for a full moon, and in the dead of night she assembled her most powerful sorcerers atop the Blackstone pinnacle, where she had once fought Miraneth. Summoning all of her power, and the power of her arcane acolytes, she performed a ritual an order of magnitude greater than any she had ever attempted.

Drawing on their power, and the dark power of The Thirteenth Gate below them, she became the clouds, the air, and homed in on the advancing army. She found them through their stink, the stench of man, self–important and arrogant. Their encampment appeared before her like a great tumor on the landscape, spreading and corrupting all in its wake.

Below her they writhed, tiny and helpless as grubs. As she rained blood upon them, she supped on their sweet fear as it rose in great columns of towards her. She could actually see the fear radiating off of them, bright and vibrant, succulent.

As she delivered her rapturous message and delighted in the chaos it instilled, her attention focussed on one person in particular. He was a bright faced youth, perhaps around her own age, who was emitting an energetic signature which was completely distinct from the rest, he shone like a beacon amongst them. He could not have been fully human.

As she poured more of her awareness into him, she found that his energy was on par with her own. At once she knew intuitively who it was. Adam, her counterpart, or at least his present incarnation.

The prophecy Miraneth had told her rang loudly in her mind. *"When fated lovers join again, this world shall come to meet its end."*

In that moment, something clicked. At last, it all made sense. The gate required both of their energies in order to activate, and fate was bringing him right to her. The irony was almost perfect. Their rush to stop her would be the very catalyst for their undoing. Unlike her, however, she found that he was weak, an innocent almost. She could sense that he had barely begun to unlock his power, let alone master it. His mind was unguarded, and from that unguarded mind she discerned their next port of call. An abbey.

*So be it. If they march against me, they will have no ports left to call to.*

# CHAPTER 19

# Chaos

## *1033 A.D.*

The wind whipped gently at their tunics as the army stood on the precipice of The Blackwood.

Curiously, it was as if the wind was blowing towards the forest, calling them in, beckoning them to their doom. The sun was early in the sky and still rising, but its warmth today gave them no comfort.

They stood in silence, all three-thousand five hundred of them, give or take. Some had fled that fateful night, when blood had rained from the skies. More still had deserted in the following days. The only sounds across the barren, windswept field were the mild clinking of armour and blades as soldiers and mages alike readied themselves for the task ahead.

At the head of the phalanx stood Ulthian, atop his towering white elk and Lord Willock, atop his armoured stallion. The Blackwood fanned out in front of them light some primeval blight upon the landscape, stretching its unholy tendrils far and wide, poisoning the very land upon which it sat. Neither crops nor plants could grow there. The only fruit this land could yield now were corpses. One only had to follow the trail to reach its source, that great reservoir of decay. Enoch knew not the origin of this place. He only knew the curse it now carried, an evil which crept into his bones and called to him in the night.

He had been having visions, ever since the abbey. Visions of a garden, lush and vibrant, of a life, his life. And a woman, naked and exalted in all her glory. In the dreams, he too was naked, but he felt no shame. Instead, he felt a profound sense of peace.

It felt so familiar, and yet so distant. They were like daydreams, only much more vivid. Now, here, on the precipice of damnation, the visions intensified. He blinked and at once the woods had come to life, the dead pale bark turning a healthy brown as the leaves bloomed and swayed in the wind. The sky was golden and warm. Then he blinked again, and it was gone.

He had not shared these visions with Balus or Davroz. For some reason, he thought it better to keep them to himself. He put it down to grief. The loss of Adrax and the abbey was still fresh in his mind, and sleep had eluded him for days. Besides, he reasoned, now is not the time for such things. He was on the cusp of the first and most important battle of his life. Perhaps, the most important battle in history.

This was their last chance, one final opportunity to rid the world of evil for good. He thought he would feel anxious, frightened even, but he found instead that he did not. There was a strange sense of inevitability about it all, as if he had played it all out a hundred times before and would play it out a hundred times again. He was always bound to reach this place.

His emotional wounds were further cauterized by the dull

throb of loss. A scar across his heart. He would avenge his master's death, if nothing else. The thick trunks of the dead trees were packed so tightly that they acted like a great wooden palisade, highly enchanted and all but impenetrable from the outside. It would be hard for even one man to step through, let alone an army of men and horses. To counter this, the magicians were concocting an enchantment of their own, a ritual of unbinding.

"Mages!" Ulthian suddenly shouted, his voice carrying far across the desolate fields. "Step forward!" In that moment, the silent ranks of five-hundred hooded magicians of all shapes, sizes, and races stepped forward and began to silently spread out along the perimeter of the wood.

When they were positioned in points equidistant from one another along the tree line, they bowed their heads in unison and brought their hands together in a prayer motion with a resounding clap. After a few silent moments Ulthian shouted another instruction.

"Cast!"

The mages raised their heads and began a synchronized incantation with their eyes firmly fixed upon the wood. The resonance of their voices soon reached an almost deafening fever pitch as it reverberated throughout the cursed hollows. Soon, the trees began to buckle and creak involuntarily, letting out groans of protest as they were forcibly bound to the collective will of the mages. Then they began to move.

Their gnarled roots retreated from one another and they shuffled apart, creating openings wide enough to permit the passage of the men. It was a fleeting window, however, as the mages could not fight against the overpowering enchantment of the woods for long.

Once all of the men were inside, the magicians would

follow at the rear, and the woods would seal again behind them. This was no simple spell. They were crossing the boundary between dimensions. Wasting no time, the stalwart Lord Willock gave a battle cry from the saddle of his stallion, raising his sword arm high.

"Knights of the Realm!" he shouted. "Advance, for king and country!" The men gave a rapturous shout of agreement and slowly began their march into the gaping jaws of darkness. Their boots and hooves thundered underfoot and sent shivers through the earth like the very drums of war itself. To charge ahead would be folly. If they were to survive it would be together as one, carefully advancing towards the gate, wherever it lay.

Enoch, flanked on either side by Davroz and Balus, marched in with the rest of the knights. Rain, his steed, was restless, irritable as they drew closer to the mouth of the wood. He could feel the fear emanating from her and did his best to calm her nerves, whispering his reassurances.

Both Balus and Davroz were on their guard, weapons drawn, carefully surveying the trees around them for any signs of movement, a trap. As they passed over the threshold between dimensions into the forest, the air grew cold, and the light grew dim.

Suddenly, Enoch could see his breath before him in great clouds. The canopy above them swallowed almost all of the sun, so despite the early hour, it looked closer to twilight. On either side of him, the ranks of thousands of armored nights spread out like a great glistening blanket, and that gave him hope. As the army drew to a halt, at the behest of Lord Willock, he cast a glance behind him in time to watch the mages scurry through the openings they had made in the wood, led by Ulthian.

One mage who had dallied was too late. The great trunks,

no longer bound by their enchantment, snapped shut like giant teeth, crushing him and splattering their pale bark with his blood.

Their fate was sealed, and the outside world seemed distant and vague.

There could be no turning back now. Only forwards.

The men marched for what felt like hours and Enoch quickly lost track of time atop of Rain. With each careful step they took further into the wood, he could feel his life force draining bit by bit, as if his very soul was being sapped from him.

There were no discernible landmarks, only a vast expanse of pale, leafless trees which stretched far into the gloom. The place felt more like a cave than a forest. The sounds were muffled, and the air was cold, and it reeked of death. The smell reminded him of the catacombs underneath the abbey, those great crypts where the dead now slept.

"Why do they not attack us?" Balus asked indignantly from his left.

"They wait," Davroz replied from his right. "They wish to tire us out first. Only then will they strike. When we are weakened," he said, as he slowly took in his surroundings.

"Hmph. It seems like we are not making any progress at all," Balus grumbled.

"I fear you are right. We're likely no closer to the gate than when we started," Davroz replied. "This place has a will of its own. When it wants us to reach the gate is when we shall reach it."

"Then why do we have mages?" Balus asked indignantly.

"Can they not divine the gate's location? Bend the woods to their will the same way they did to enter?"

"You underestimate the magic of this place," Davroz said. "The enchantments here were not laid by men or elves, but by the gods themselves. Mortal magic holds no sway in this place. The land and the trees will not respond to it. You saw yourself how hard it was to even enter. We need to be patient. Patient and aware." Davroz continued scanning the trees around him for any signs of movement.

"Patience is one thing," Balus began. "But the light is fading by the minute. Before long it will be completely dark, and we will be helpless."

At the head of the column rode Ulthian and Lord Willock, followed closely by Lyse, the human mage-master and all of them were showing obvious signs of fatigue.

Lord Willock, in particular, seemed frenzied, almost to the point of hysteria. He was hyper vigilant, and a violent tremor had set into his body, as if he were freezing cold. Though it wasn't the cold that ailed him, it was fear. Harsh and vibrant, he practically radiated it. The more disciplined minds of Lyse and Ulthian were guarded, less beholden to their emotions. From his place in the saddle a few paces behind them, Enoch could overhear slivers of their conversation.

"We should stop now and make camp," Ulthian said wearily. "The day grows darker. Night is almost upon us."

"Just a little further," Lord Willock replied, his eyes darting frantically from tree to tree. "We're close! I can feel it." He practically shouted. Ulthian's eyes narrowed, and Enoch detected his thoughtforms, clear as day, disdainful.

HUMANS. SO FEEBLE MINDED.

His words, however, did not match his thoughts. He sighed,

collecting himself before he gave a response. "Be that as it may, we still have to make camp. The men and horses are exhausted. My mages are all but collapsing. There can be no harm in stopping for the night. In fact, we stand a better chance of survival by forming a defensive position."

Lyse chimed in from behind them. "He's right, Willock. We need to stop and rest. It will be easier to repel an attack if we are stationary."

Lord Willock let out a manic laugh, which caught some of the men's attention and caused Lyse and Ulthian to exchange a look of mutual concern. He was beginning to crack.

"Stop? Here? Are you insane? There isn't a chance in hell that I would stop in this god forsaken place. No, no, no. Besides. We have them now. That little witch is almost in our grasp. Her judgement shall match the harshness of her transgressions, and we will return as heroes." He spoke fanatically, as if trying to convince himself of the story.

This was a delicate situation. On the one hand, Lord Willock had clearly begun to lose his mind. The darkness of this place had ultimately proved too much for his fragile ego. On the other hand, Ulthian and Lyse had to maintain the chain, or at least the illusion, of command. They were responsible for the mages, but the knights answered to Lord Willock. Any signs of weakness of madness in him would be magnified tenfold in his men. Such was the nature of command. A precarious thing, Enoch reflected.

The thoughtforms emanating from Lord Willock were frayed and scattered. His mind was a soup of incoherent babble, spitting out random phrases and concepts which had no contextual bearing, and trying to form connections between them.

*So, this is what madness sounds like,* Enoch thought.

Just as Ulthian was trying to think of what to say next,

Lord Willock suddenly shouted. "There!" He pointed towards a distant tree, now little more than a shadow in the fading light. "There she is! The witch! I'll have her head!"

Enoch strained his eyes to see what he was pointing at, but he couldn't see anyone. Only the endless expanse of dead trees. "Do you see anything?" he whispered to Davroz.

"Nothing," Davroz replied.

"He's gone mad," Balus muttered wearily. His shouts had caused a stir in the ranks of the men, as confusion and panic set in amongst them.

"Lord Willock," Ulthian began, desperately trying to control the situation.

In an instant, the lord drew his sword from its scabbard and shouted. "Knights of the Realm! With me!"

He set off galloping into the darkness, chasing down his illusory phantom and quickly disappeared. Very soon, even the muffled sound of his horse's hooves was swallowed by the darkness, and the forest was silent once again.

Some of his men began to charge after him but Lyse and Ulthian quickly gave counter orders and stayed the charge, likely saving their lives. Though they did not follow him, their morale was understandably shaken. They had just watched their leader gallop off to his own death.

A cruel, inhuman laughter rang out from the woods all around them, and the men instinctively huddled in fear. It was so loud that Enoch could feel it resonating in his chest, an awful feeling, like a great anvil weighing down on his soul.

When the laughter stopped, they heard but one word. "Fools." After the laughter had passed the men began to descend into a full-blown panic, their ranks wavering until Ulthian took command, amplifying his harmonic voice through magic.

"*Enough!*" he boomed, silencing them. "We make camp here for the night. Start fires and set about making battlements. Let them not catch us unawares."

a

That night was unlike any night Enoch had ever known. The darkness descended upon them swiftly, like a thick blanket of oppression. It suffocated every breath and swallowed all signs of hope.

The pale bark of the trees was tough and brittle and the men broke many of their axes before it finally began to give. When the bark did crack, rancid black sap gushed forth from the wounds like blood, and the trees themselves emitted an ungodly whine, as if squealing in protest.

"Talking trees," Balus said to Davroz. "Have you ever seen such a thing?"

Davroz said nothing. His mind was distant as he stared listlessly into the gloom. When the men had finally collected enough wood for the cookfires, the flames were weak and pinkish, emitting an acrid smoke which hung in the air and sent the men into coughing fits. The mages had to continually cast spells to keep the fires lit, a task which soon began to drain them immensely.

When the small fires were lit, there were no songs, there was no laughter, only silence, save for the sound of cutlery on plates; they simply did not have the energy. Worse, the night had brought a fierce chill along with it.

Enoch found that no matter how many extra furs he put on, he could not stay the shiver which had set into his bones. Most of the men were the same, cold, drained, and miserable.

The horses grew restless and irritable. They had already lost a handful, succumbing to madness before whinnying away into the darkness. Shortly, they would hear a final scream in the distance, followed by a tearing of flesh. Then, nothing. It was by those sounds that they knew they were not alone.

The hordes were out there, waiting, biding their time until the final feast. Knowing that made it all the worse. That the enemy was watching them. Waiting for them to weaken, like flies caught in a web.

Davroz, Enoch, and Balus took their seats by the cookfire of Ulthian and Lyse, both haggard and desperately scanning the forest for any sign of Lord Willock.

"That fool," Ulthian fumed. "Losing his mind like an untrained dog, off chasing squirrels. Now who will lead his men?" he asked rhetorically.

"I will," Lyse said suddenly. "And you will lead the mages."

Ulthian laughed mockingly. "You? And what would you know of cavalry?"

"A great deal more than you, highborn," she shot back.

Ulthian began to rise to anger but Davroz was quick to defuse the situation.

"Enough," he said firmly. "You are the leaders of this council. We cannot let the woods turn us against each other." That seemed to bring them to their senses for the time being, but they were still shooting daggers at one another until Balus spoke up

"Gah! To hell with this cold," he grumbled.

"We may already be there," Davroz replied softly. "They say the ninth circle of Hell is the coldest, a hollow frost which does not abate." He stared into the distance.

Lyse scoffed. "Would that there was a Hell, Inferni. That

is nought but a bedtime story whipped up by those One Truth bigots. There is only the physical world, and the spirit world. The spirit world does not deal in abstractions like good and evil, right and wrong. These are earthly ideas. Nothing more," she said, matter-of-factly.

"Have you ever seen a Fellgate, girl?" Ulthian asked resentfully. "I mean, truly seen one. Up close."

"Well, no, but I have read. . ." she trailed off.

"Then you know nothing of Hell," Ulthian replied.

Enoch was struck by an awful barrage of thoughtforms which inundated his consciousness. They were harsh, piercing, and all encompassing, as if his mind were being torn apart and violated over and over again. They rang in his ears like a godforsaken cacophony of torment, a tempest of howls, shrieks and wails followed by an undercurrent of low-pitched chanting and tongues he could not recognize. They were blackish-red in color and jagged, completely inhuman. He cried out and doubled over in actual pain from the sheer weight of them.

Ulthian acted quickly, dispelling the intruders from the boy's mind with his left hand before bringing him to his feet. The first thing Enoch saw when he opened his eyes was Ulthian's own piercing violet eyes staring back at him.

"They're here," Enoch gasped.

Ulthian nodded. "I sense it, too. From which direction do they come?" he asked tensely.

Enoch winced as he felt the demonic thought forms gnawing at him again. "All around us!" Davroz, Balus, and Lyse raised the alarm and the army quickly sprang into action.

Ulthian still stared into Enoch's eyes. "I am casting a ward upon you," he said. "It will make it harder for them to penetrate your mental defences. It will not last for long, but it should be enough time for you to steel yourself to the onslaught. Remember, they are weaker than you, though they may not seem it. As creatures of darkness, they fear the light. It is you they fear, Enoch." He wordlessly let go of Enoch and sprang himself into action, rallying the mages and knights around him.

"Soldiers! Mages!" he bellowed, casting his harmonic voice around them like thunder. "Form a defensive phalanx! We are beset on all sides. Mages! Take position behind the front lines and make ready for defensive and offensive casting. Activate the rune shields. Now is the time."

Very quickly, the troops had assembled. The knights, atop their horses, formed a defensive square around the mages, leaving the mages just enough space to have a clear line of sight between their ranks. Enoch was quietly impressed. Despite everything they had been through, and their exhaustion, the thousands of knights and mages were quick to organise and stood resolutely at attention. This was due in no small part to Ulthian's commanding presence on the battlefield, Enoch supposed.

Once set in their places, the phalanx bristled with metallic anticipation as they waited for their enemies to arrive. The woods were deafeningly silent. Then they heard it. War drums. From all directions. Their cursed vibrations shook the very ground on which the army stood. Then they heard the war cry.

A deafening amalgamation of shrieks and howls from all around them which seemed to stem from the very trees themselves. The sound was so awful it brought many of the men to their knees.

Even worse was the psychic aftershock that reverberated in Enoch's mind. Pure terror. Pure rage. And utterly inhuman. He remembered Ulthian's words and fortified his mental defences. Now was not the time for weakness.

"Mages!" Ulthian suddenly cried, radiating white light from the staff atop his elk. "Luminus!" In an instant the mages shouted in agreement and sent hundreds of floating orbs of blinding white light surging to hang in the air in the woods all around them. It lit up the darkness of the woods far brighter than any daylight, and the land itself seemed to shriek in protest, it was then that they were able to properly survey their demonic adversaries for the first time.

They were surrounded on all sides by seething masses of flesh, blasphemous combinations of Earthly creatures overflowing with rancid appendages, hooks, whips, and claws.

There were so many of them that it looked more like a sea of gnashing teeth and claws than an organised army. Among them, Enoch could make out dark sorcerers in hoods, some of whom rode atop the demons. To his disbelief, he also saw human foot soldiers, replete in black armour.

What human would forsake their own race like that?

"Dear gods," Balus breathed from the saddle beside him. They were outnumbered at least five-to-one, and the ranks of darkness spread far in every direction, as if they were springing forth from the cursed ground itself.

Davroz had taken one of the opposite sides of the square, while Lyse had taken another, and Ulthian the final side. He took some comfort in that, there would be at least one powerful sorcerer leading each face of the formation.

*Except on my side. It's only us.*

Even so, as craned his neck to catch sight of Ulthian's face he detected a hint of horror. That hint was quickly replaced by determination as he once again assumed command.

"*Hold fast!*"

In an instant, the first ranks of demons descended upon

them from all sides, covering ground impossibly fast as they haggardly swept in to feast. Just as the knights were bracing to counter charge, when the snarling hell beasts were within a few strides of him, Enoch watched in disbelief as they encountered some type of invisible wall, which upon activation incinerated them all in a burst of white hot sparks, turning them to little more than clouds of ash.

*The rune shields,* Enoch thought. *So, that's what they were, a trap.*

As the dust settled, the demons screeched in dismay and hesitated before sending a second wave, while the knights and mages bellowed in defiance. Their celebration was short lived, however, for as soon as they rallied, the demons sprang forth with yet another wave, even bigger than the last.

This time, the dark sorcerers wasted no time in firing off elemental blasts of their own, and within seconds the air was coursing with deadly spells of all kinds as the mages returned fire, whizzing past Enoch's ears at blistering speeds.

Lyse barely had a chance to shout her command before the horde was upon them. "Lancers!" she screamed, straining to be heard about the roar of the magical firefight. "Charge!"

The first rank of knights on all sides of the defensive square charged headfirst into the advancing mobs of demons. Enoch watched in horror as many of the horses and riders were swallowed whole by gaping mouths much larger them and chewed before their blood and organs were sprayed back out of twisted blowholes and which rained down all around them in a red mist; this gave the demons sickening moans of pleasure.

Hundreds of men and horses died in the first few seconds. Others who were not so lucky were bitten in half, or torn limb from limb by multi–armed beasts as they screamed for mercy. At once, any illusions he had about chivalry or honor disappeared.

He was struck by the truth of battle, and that was chaos. He barely had time to collect himself before a towering insect-like creature, with great barbed arms dripping with blood, began to stagger towards him and Balus. Its harsh flesh was coarse and mottled like that of a toad and blood soaked, its body causing it to glisten horrifically. Its head ended in a pointed snout covered in eyes and a chittering maw of needles for a mouth.

As it ran towards them, Enoch could sense from its singular thoughtforms that it was focussed on him. Still, there was little he could do, and he found himself paralysed by fear as he watched it stalk ever closer, smashing armored knights aside as it did so as if they were little more than insects themselves.

When it was upon them and raised one of its great claws to crush him and Balus, a flaming disk cut through the air above them at lightning speed, instantly decapitating the hulking beast and dropping it to its knees. He spun his head and made eye contact with Davroz across the square.

"Focus!" Davroz screamed, before jumping back into the fray. He then heard Lyse yell out orders for the second rank of lancers to charge. To his left, he saw Ulthian let out an eldritch blast of chain lightning from his staff which decimated over a hundred demons and sorcerers in one fell swoop.

All around him, his comrades were fighting and dying for his sake and he had to do something. As soon as the thought crossed his mind, another demon stalked towards him. This one looked like a giant salamander covered in eyes. As it thundered towards him it hissed, revealing a mouth full of rotting teeth, filed into poisonous pointed barbs.

This was it. No one was there to save him. All around him, the scenes of the battle unfolded as if time had slowed. Soldiers fell screaming to their deaths, into the waiting jaws of the foulest machinations of Hell, while spells whizzed through the air, incinerating or vaporizing anything they touched. The Blackwood was awash with the sound of pain, screams of agony.

The music of battle.

As the demon closed in on him, he cast his mind into its own, as if outstretching his hand in desperation to shield himself. He was not just inside the demon's mind, he became the demon itself. In that final desperate moment, he assumed control of the creature's mind and it froze in its tracks.

The hulking salamander towered over him like two packhorses stood on top of one another. For a while, the two stood transfixed, the boy, and the beast, locked in a mental stalemate as the battle raged around him.

The inside of the demon's mind was even more awful than he could have expected: a cold, bloody place, ruled by animal instinct and a deep-seated hunger. Inhospitable as that place was, there could be no mistaking it. In there, he was in control. The creature was bound to his will.

As the shock of his newfound power wore off, he sprang to action. He willed the great demon to turn around, and charge back into the ranks of the order. There was no delay between his own thoughts and that of the demon's actions, as if he was operating it, like a demon marionette, an extension of his own body.

Channelling his spirit through this new vessel, he launched into the ranks of sorcerers and demons, their eyes awash with terror and confusion as they were attacked by one of their own. The salamander flayed and thrashed wildly, sending great plumes of black blood and viscera high into the air around it as it went.

The demons were quick to react, retreating momentarily from their mortal foes to subdue the massive beast. This, however, was futile. As they gnashed and tore at their hellish brother, Enoch cast his awareness even wider, infecting their minds and passing himself between them one after another.

Soon, he could feel himself within the mind of every last sorcerer and demon. Then, and only then, did he force them on one another, and the ranks of the order crumbled all around them in an orgy of bloodshed and confusion.

The allied forces of men staggered back, horrified, and equally confused by the chaos unfolding around them. Ever astute, Davroz was the first to notice young Enoch as he stood quivering, his body reeling from each impact as his eyes rolled back into his head.

He was feeling them; each blow, each bite, each spell, each body. All of it. Only when the last demon had fallen, surrounding the men in a moat of silent black blood did Enoch finally drop to his knees, gasping as his life force flickered and his soul traversed the place between life and death.

Ulthian was the first to his side, moving with swiftness only an elf could muster. As Enoch's consciousness faded, his last sight was Ulthian's piercing violet eyes boring into him as he whispered incantations.

When Enoch awoke, a dull light had returned to the sky and filtered down through the branches of the trees above him. They passed over his head like great veins, black against the dawn sky. He was in the saddle, though not his own, and was wrapped safely in a set of great trunk-like arms. He did not need his powers to know who's they were.

"Balus," he whispered. "What happened?"

Balus was silent for a while, composing his thoughts before he responded. "You saved us," he said solemnly. "You saved us, and then you fainted." He trailed off, emotion creeping into his voice. "I thought you were dead. But then that elf, he did something."

Enoch craned his neck to see Ulthian upon his elk at the head of the column, leading the men with that same unshakable air of pride. He was haggard though. His tunic was stained with blood and earth. In fact, all of them were shaken, and understandably so. As he looked around at what remained of the men, Enoch could at last appreciate the full magnitude of the battle. More than half of their rank had fallen, their bodies quickly swallowed by the earth which had opened up in great maws and the gnarled roots of the trees which sunk into their flesh like sharpened teeth. Those that remained were badly scarred, some still leaking blood from their wounds as they barely held their place in their saddles. The mages afoot were exhausted.

"Where are we going?" Enoch asked Balus.

"Forward," Balus said. "To that." He pointed to the horizon.

Enoch followed the line of sight from his finger, and sure enough found a pale cliff face looming towards them in the distance, glowing strangely with the light of dawn.

"It appeared at first light, like a mirage," Balus said. "So, we march towards it. Though I cannot say why, it is as if we are called there. All of us can feel it."

Davroz pulled alongside them, his demeanour remarkably chipper. Enoch could see he had Rain in tow, and let out a sigh of relief. "May I request an audience with the hero of The Blackwood?" Davroz asked, smiling.

Enoch laughed. "You may."

"We owe you our lives, young master. You honor us all."

Enoch blushed, not quite knowing how to respond. "Thank you for seeing to her," he said, nodding to Rain.

"She would not leave your side," Davroz replied.

"And where are we going now, Davroz?" Enoch asked earnestly.

"To face the music," he replied. "An audience with God."

Up ahead of them, the path widened and grew into a clearing. As they drew closer, Enoch could see what looked like an enormous archway of composed gnarled black stone that loomed overhead ominously.

Curiously he found that this structure was emanating a kind of thoughtform of its own. It whispered and bickered in strange tongues as it heralded their arrival. He could feel its presence within his own mind; it recognized him, called to him.

There could be no mistaking it, the The Thirteenth Gate, the very same thing they had been sent there to destroy.

A great tumult of dread welled inside of him. Though they had heard tales of it, to see it in the flesh was something far worse. The energy it emitted was foul, all wrong. There was a strange tension in the air, like that which came before a storm.

As they reached the edge of the clearing, they were faced with what remained of The Order of Sanguine, a daunting assemblage of demons, men at arms, and sorcerers, standing before them, dwarfing their own exhausted ranks one or two times over. They were fresh and unencumbered by the scars of battle. As if the demons that had assailed them the night before were only an advance guard.

He could feel the morale of the men plummeting around him as they surveyed their forsaken adversaries. This would not be an easy fight. At the head of the army, directly in front of the towering gate, stood a woman in a glorious black cloak that whipped in the morning wind, with long flowing raven hair which moved just the same. The contrast only highlighted the paleness of her flawless skin. She was the most beautiful woman Enoch had ever seen. Her beauty was eclipsed only by her cruelty. He did not need to ask, for his soul spoke her name, as hers spoke his.

"Morgana."

She smiled triumphantly as the haggard forces of men arrived, acutely aware of the advantage she possessed. To her left stood a towering warrior in tempered clay plate armor. The warrior watched them silently from beneath his helm, his eyes occasionally catching in the light. Her champion, Enoch assumed.

For a while, there was silence while the two armies faced off. The wind whipped the dust around them, and Enoch noticed a dark cavern which sunk into the earth like a great mouth, near to the site of the Gate.

Without antecedent, she began to address them. When she spoke, her eyes spoke to him, and only him, but her voice boomed across the clearing as it was amplified by her magic.

"Watchers!" she shouted commandingly. "Do you know the ground on which you stand?" There was silence from their side as she continued her tirade. "Atop this cliff," she pointed toward the pale stone cliff which loomed over them, "there was once a tree. And it was from this tree that the fruit of knowledge was picked. It was at this very site that the original sin occurred, and the first act of free will by a human was made. I am that human, though now I inhabit a new body. My counterpart shared in the fruit, and he joins us today. At last, we have come full circle. The snake eats itself. Where else to build the ultimate doorway? The final bridge between worlds."

"Where is Miraneth?" Ulthian shouted back contemptuously. "Where is my sister?"

"Dead," Morgana replied with a smug smile. "By my hand."

A look of shock passed over Ulthian's face, his façade of coolness momentarily broken. He began to send Enoch rapid thoughtforms.

IF THAT IS TRUE, THEN SHE IS NOW MORE POWERFUL THAN WE CAN COMPREHEND. WE HAVE TO TREAD LIGHTLY HERE, OR WE WILL SURELY PERISH.

"You think you know what you are doing, but you do not," Ulthian shouted back. "My sister was insane and harbored an innate hatred for all living things, even among her own kind. She was outcast for her madness. Whatever will you have inherited from her need not be your own. Make no mistake, Miraneth wanted nothing more than the total destruction of the mortal plane. It is a fool's gambit, one that could only be conceived by her twisted mind."

"Silence!" Morgana shouted. "I will not be lectured by you, nor any other. What could you possibly know of the great game? If I am to end the world, so be it. This world is sick. You think I am unleashing Hell, but have you ever stopped to look at the world around you? We are already in Hell.

"Now, I have a proposition. Enough blood has been shed on both sides. We need not fight to the last man. Both Enoch, and I, could lay waste to each other's forces in moments. And then we would have to kill each other. I propose, then, that we face one another in single combat. Now. Try though you might, your powers will not work on me, Enoch, nor will mine on you. Such is the nature of our bond. Instead, we must settle this in the old way. With tooth and nail." She withdrew a gilded steel saber from its scabbard. The blade shone darkly in the sun, and it gave off a reddish hue.

"That steel has been tempered with blood," Balus breathed from behind him.

In comparison, Enoch's own faithful blade seemed measly.

"You will have to go through us first," Davroz said calmy, striding forth on Star. "Not a hair shall fall from his head."

"Ah yes," Morgana smiled. "The flame elemental. I was expecting you. I have someone here I think you'd very much like to meet."

From her side, the armored warrior removed his helm, revealing a middle-aged man with long blonde hair and piercing blue eyes, who's skin was badly disfigured by burn scars.

"Davroz," he said warmly, his facial movement restricted by his scars. "We meet again."

"*You!*" Davroz shouted, bristling as his eyes glazed over with rage. Enoch had never seen him lose his composure, not once. As the white hot thoughtforms poured unbidden from Davroz's mind, Enoch saw images of his family, his burned house, and the searing pain within his heart.

At once he knew this man in the armor was Fenris, the man who had killed Davroz's family. The man he had hunted across the ocean, only to meet him here, at the very last.

*But of course,* Enoch reflected. *It could never have been any other way.*

Davroz took to one knee, joining his ring finger to his thumb on both of his hands while he circled them slowly in the air, whispering incantations. Finally, he snapped them back together in the air in front of him, releasing a torrent of cinders from his fingertips.

Blazing orange sigils and runes began to spread all over his body, snaking their way up from his heart center until they reached his head and he at last opened his eyes, which now burned with ancient magic. As he took to his feet, he issued only one phrase as he pointed towards his adversary.

"Today, you die."

"Davroz," Ulthian began, "wait."

In an instant, Davroz disappeared, leaving only a trail of smoke, or so Enoch thought, until he heard the sounds of an explosive impact across the clearing. To his astonishment, he saw Davroz in combat with Fenris, ducking and weaving with all his might, raining down fiery fury upon his towering foe.

He had set upon him in an instant, moving faster than the eye could see. In that time, he had conjured a staff, wreathed in flame, with three spokes protruding from each end. As he spun it faster, the prongs became as wheels, each spin of the staff landing scores of searing impacts on Fenris's clay armor, sending cracks throughout.

Fenris was quick to counter, materializing an enormous clay warhammer in his hands, bringing it crashing down to the Earth. Enoch felt his heart jump into his throat for a moment, only to be immediately met with relief as he saw Davroz spring back with lightning quickness, backflipping into the air as he evaded the blow.

He sent his staff skyward, in a great arc. It took on a will of its own, bearing back down upon Fenris with renewed fury. The staff snaked all around his armor, evading his clumsy clutches as it hammered him with flaming blows. The ground, however, had been turned to quicksand by Fenris's blow.

Still airborne, Davroz clasped his hands together and muttered another incantation before a great set of flaming wings protruded from his back, keeping him afloat. Cursing him, Fenris drew up great pillars of hardened earth from the ground and sent them flying towards him like giant projectiles, all the while the enchanted staff harassed his armour from behind.

Enoch noticed that his armor would quickly repair itself after each blow, as if it was regenerating. Davroz countered the projectiles by conjuring a blistering wall of flame, which turned them all to dust. Fenris was an earth elemental, that much was clear. For a while, their battle raged in a stalemate as both wizards became more and more exhausted.

For all the progress Davroz made with his spells and his enchanted staff, Fenris would counter them as his thick earthen plate armour regenerated around him. Sensing his magic waning, Davroz made a decision. Enoch was inside his mind, reading the thoughtforms which emanated from him.

I'M SORRY, ENOCH, he thought, sensing Enoch's presence. BUT NOW IT IS MY TIME. I MUST PLAY MY PART. He began to glow hotter and brighter, blistering as he soared higher into the sky on wings of fire until he disappeared into the glare of the overhead sun.

On the ground below, Fenris strained frantically to catch sight of his adversary.

PROMISE ME. PROMISE ME YOU'LL STOP HER. WHATEVER IT TAKES.

"I promise," Enoch whispered aloud, as tears rolled down his cheeks.

Balus and Ulthian gave him a curious look as they too squinted into the blazing sun trying to keep track of him. A resounding screech echoed across the clearing, like that of an enormous bird.

Davroz swooped down, only he was no longer Davroz at all. He had transformed into an enormous flaming phoenix, hurtling down towards the earth at lightning speed, almost too quick for the naked eye to follow. All that remained of Davroz, the man, were his eyes, steely and determined, as they hurtled towards their foe.

Fenris barely had time to react as the smouldering phoenix plunged towards him. Enoch watched his eyes widen in horror the moment before Davroz collided with him, instantly vaporising them both in a storm of dust and fire, which sent a deafening shockwave in all directions, knocking both armies off of their feet.

The ground itself shuddered, threatening to crack open, and when the dust settled, only a smouldering crater remained.

His last thoughts were of his family.

Enoch went to cry out, but the sound would not come. His ears still rang from the impact and his heart had yet to process the shock.

Across the clearing, he watched Morgana stagger to her feet as she was helped by two of her familiars. She wasted no time on recovery.

Within moments, she was sprinting towards him, saber in hand. Despite himself, he found his own body responding the same way. Against the protests of Ulthian, Balus, Lyse, and the others, his legs willed him inexorably forward and he found himself reaching for his own scabbard. It was as if he was bound.

His body and mind responded to hers. Behind her, the empty space in the middle of The Thirteenth Gate began to flicker and spark with red light. It was awakening.

As they met in the clearing, Enoch had just enough time to retrieve his short sword from his scabbard before she was upon him, flying through the air with downward momentum to deliver a blow that very nearly knocked him off of his feet. The impact of their blades colliding sent its own shockwave rippling through the air around them. This was a battle thousands of years in the making.

She was a formidable and fierce fighter, unrelenting as she delivered blow after vicious blow. It was all he could do to simply parry her hits. She moved like a black blur, like ink through water. At once, she was all around him, her tenacious eyes speaking nothing but hatred.

Already, he could tell that he was far outmatched. As he tried to enter her mind, he found that he could not. His powers were seemingly blocked in her presence. At once, his years of swordplay with Balus came rushing into his mind. He could hear Balus's voice in his mind: *Parry, thrust, duck, move your body!* Enoch almost landed a glancing blow on her side, but she took that opportunity to sidestep and slash at the ligament behind his left knee. She was deadly accurate.

He quickly faltered and almost fell. As the first drops of his blood touched the earth, the gate rumbled into life and tore open a howling red rift in the fabric of reality as the screaming abyss of Hell itself beckoned them.

The demons began to sing in reverence whilst the men, both of The Order and The Watchers, began to instinctually howl as their souls lamented what had been unleashed. Morgana was momentarily entranced by the gate opening, the fruition of her and her masters work at last within her grasp.

Enoch took advantage of this lapse in concentration and thrust his sword into her leg, sending her howling and bringing her back to the present moment. It was only then that the true wrath was awoken within her.

Her eyes darkened as she rained down, blow after blow, until he was laid low on his back. Her eyes filled with terrible zeal as she raised her saber high to deliver the killing blow.

Just as she brought down her sword, a flash of purple energy appeared in the air between them, and from it Candilia phased into reality, wincing as she caught the downward impact of the blow with her spell staff.

Enoch could not believe his eyes.

Within moments, Candilia was all around them, phase shifting in and out of reality at rapid speeds as she rained down blows and magical projectiles on Morgana. Enoch did not need his powers to know what was happening here: she was buying him time. He quickly staggered to his feet, ignoring the protests of his severed tendons as he steadied himself.

As Candilia's aerial onslaught continued, they edged closer to the edge of the portal, the threshold between worlds.

"*Enough!*" Morgana finally shouted, her voice booming across the clearing. She raised one hand, waiting for Candilia to phase back into reality and then caught her in her psychic grip.

Candilia was helpless, unable to struggle, unable to move; Morgana was inside her luminous body, within every cell. In one deft movement, she raised her arm in an arc and brought it crashing down, slamming Candilia's dainty frame into the dust. Her wings crumpled and her body twitched as she lost consciousness.

Enoch screamed in anger and hurtled towards her as she stood at the edge of the portal. Smug satisfaction was replaced by shock as Morgana spun around just in time for Enoch to launch into her with his full bodyweight, knocking them both into the howling vortex.

As they disappeared into that realm of madness, the black rock of The Thirteenth Gate buckled and swayed as if digesting their energy. The very fabric of reality began to bend and unravel around it as the Gate swayed and spiralled. Time slowed, second by second, inch by inch, until it came to a halt.

Then, there was silence and stillness in the clearing. An

eternity in one infinite moment. The expressions of horror were masks, frozen onto the faces of The Watchers. The jaws of the confused demons lay open and agape.

Then, the gate began to absorb. First, time. Then, sound. Finally, light. The gate absorbed, until there was nothing left.

ᒧᒥ

No matter, no form, only darkness, and within that darkness, awareness, an omnipresent life force that permeated all things, finally stripped bare of all its many layers and distractions.

Divested of everything it had ever conjured, the awareness was reminded again reminded of a simple truth.

It was alone.

## CHAPTER 20

# THE END & THE BEGINNING

### *2033 A.D.*

Confusion. That was Adam's immediate response.

One minute, he was atop the lookout, staring down at the city below him. He felt the sun on his skin, the power in his veins. Then, he began to glow, to shimmer. The bracelet, he remembered.

Instantly, he was someplace else. The shock of the teleportation had rocked his body and clouded his mind. As his senses returned, he became aware that he was in some type of cavern. It was cold and harsh artificial light bore down on him from above.

To his despair, he recognized at once where he was, as if his spirit could intuitively detect it.

*No. Anywhere but here.*

The timing was cruel, the very moment he tasted true freedom. He felt his heart sink as he resigned himself to his fate, to the crushing energy of this insipid place. He felt foolish.

*Did you really think it would be so easy?*

As he opened his eyes, he knew already who's face would greet him. There, standing before him with that same smug detachment, was Myra Cole, the director of the facility.

"We have need of you, Adam," she said, without emotion. As he looked around, he realised he was standing on a high podium, one which led directly to center of that huge structure she had shown him before he left.

Now, it was complete, standing high and mighty in its terrible glory. Still, it made him deeply uneasy, though he could not say why. Gently, she walked him towards the edge of the podium, until he was inches from the center of the structure.

"You know what to do," she whispered to him, before stepping back.

Though exactly why, he could not say, he did indeed know what was required of him in that moment. He was to open a rift, a portal to the dark place. His left arm began to raise itself, as if moving on its own. When it was aligned with the middle of the ring, he closed his eyes and began to concentrate, picturing a portal in his mind's eye.

From below him, he heard a piercing shout, a woman's voice, who he had never heard before. She knew his name.

"Adam! Don't!" she screamed. In that moment, his trance was broken. He opened his eyes, casting his gaze down to the left of the podium where the shout had come from. As he looked upon her, the air left his lungs, and he was struck by the most powerful déjà vu of his life. She was beautiful, her brown skin matched the color of her eyes and her curly dark hair framed her gentle face in the most stunning of ways.

Though he could not say why, or how, he knew at once that he had known her before, and flashes of distant and forgotten memories flickered through his unbidden mind. In her, he saw himself and he knew at once the magnitude of their connection.

But just who was she? Why here, and why now? At once, she looked sympathetic and terrified. She could feel it, too. Whatever it was, he knew right away that he could not open that portal, no matter what. To his horror, as he returned his gaze to the structure, he saw that he had cast the tiniest red blip before she stopped him. It was no larger than a coin, and it hung curiously in the air in front of him, glowing brightly and crackling.

What he could not understand was why it had not disappeared. Without him feeding it power it should have gone away. As he reached out to touch it, the glowing point began to expand as the structure powered up.

He heard the tearing sound as the fabric of reality, which separated his dimension from the dark realm, was ripped away. Soon, the entire gigantic structure was awash with howling red energy as it erupted into a maelstrom. To his horror, he realized at last what the structure truly was.

A man-made portal, and it was self-propagating.

He staggered back, desperately clutching his ears in an effort to drown out the wails of torment and sorrow which emanated from that forsaken place.

Once the portal had reached its full size, for a moment, a smaller portal appeared at its center and he saw a strange scene unfolding. It was some type of battle in a clearing, though everyone was dressed strangely, as if it was taking place in ancient times.

It was morning, that much he could tell, and all around them were the same blackened trees that surrounded the facility. Standing in front of the portal, with her back facing it, was a woman. She was slender and strong, and her raven black hair flowed down over the similarly black garments which hugged tightly to her frame.

Her skin was pale, heightening the contrast even more. She obstructed much of his view, though he could see that across the clearing from her were armored soldiers. They looked battle scarred and exhausted. The woman in black raised her arms high and brought what looked like a fairy slamming into the earth from out of the sky.

A young man sprinted towards her, in her blind spot, kicking up a trail of dust as he went. His leg was badly slashed and hemorrhaging spurts of blood onto the soil behind him, but he did not seem to notice, his body ignoring the pain. He had anger in his eyes, a seething determination. She did not see him coming, she was too caught up in her spell. At the last moment she caught sight of him, but it was too late.

He tackled her through the portal. Adam recoiled instinctively, expecting them both to come crashing out into him. Instead, they disappeared in a flash, as if melting into the very framework of the portal itself. The scene disappeared, and once again was replaced by the red rimmed void of the elder portal, the doorway to the dark place.

The screaming stopped, and the gigantic portal fell silent. He turned around just in time, to his astonishment, to catch the director transforming into some type of tall, glowing banshee.

She still looked somewhat like herself, though now her features had elongated, and her white hair flowed around her like glowing, living silk. Her clothes had disappeared, exposing only glowing, vibrant, pale flesh. She was beautiful, in a strange and terrifying way. At once he knew instinctively that this was her true form.

She floated up towards the portal and began to address them from above. When she spoke, it was as if he was listening to a choir of voices, all singing in harmony. Not gone, however, was her smugness; if anything, it was only amplified.

“And now, I have become death. The destroyer of worlds!” she said triumphantly. Her voice echoed through the vast complex as she beamed with joy. “Don’t look so surprised, Adam,” she teased, reading the expression on Adam’s face. “You never really believed I was human, surely.

"Ah yes, you wanted to believe. You humans. Even the best amongst you are so. . . weak minded. Unable to face the truth, to grapple with the harshness of reality.” She laughed.

“Even Zane!” she went on. “You knew exactly what you did to him, and yet you were unable to face it.” At the mere mention of his name, the fragmented memories came flooding back to him like harsh, painful shards.

At once, he was vindicated. Zane did exist, she acknowledged him, but with that vindication came the shackles of a deep, mortifying guilt.

He did it. He killed Zane. There could be no denying it. The realisation was crystal clear.

“You lied to me,” Adam finally said, through tears, his anger rising.

“I had need of you,” she said. “I merely presented to you a version of events that you would accept. I could not have you refusing to comply. Not at this final, most pressing hour. I suppose I should thank you, Adam. I have waited a thousand years for this day, and hundreds more upon that.

"None of this would have been possible without your continued compliance every step of the way. Without your fear. Such a good little lamb you were, following each and every order, right up until the very last.

"We had a few hiccups here and there, but ultimately that

business with Zane proved to be your grand catalyst, as I foresaw it would be. Ask yourself this, why else then would I have allowed it? I have been watching you from the start, Adam. I have been within your mind, within your soul. I, more than any other, know the truth of what you are. A coward."

Her words cut him like daggers. She was right. He knew it. His father knew it. Everyone knew it.

"Don't listen to her!" the mystery woman shouted from below, breaking the spell. "Her words are poison."

"Silence, mortal," Miraneth commanded, raising one arm and effortlessly sending the woman hurtling into the concrete wall with a burst of psychic energy. She collided with a sickening thump and collapsed in a heap on the floor.

Miraneth smiled exultantly. "Fool." Her eyes began to glow and great tendrils of white-hot energy coursed through her body, amplifying her voice even louder. "Do you not know what this means? I, Miraneth Enarel Moonshade, first of my name, and last of my house, have at last completed the great work.

"The Thirteenth Gate now stands before you, and all other gates across the earth open along with it. Not since the war in heaven has a living being accomplished such a feat. I have transcended mortality and now stand on the threshold of godhood. I have become more powerful than you could ever comprehend. The age of magic has returned, and the era of man is over."

Adam could do little more than shrink back, edging himself away from the horror that stood before him.

She continued: "At last, I take my rightful seat amongst the gods. At last, I—" She trailed off mid-sentence. Adam heard it, too, an ominous low frequency rumbling coming from deep in the inky bowels of the portal. After a brief pause, she continued her monologue with renewed fervour.

"At last! A crossover. The first of many. Dark one, child of the night, rejoice as you step into the light, for this world is yours!"

With no warning, and without sound, an enormous gray hand with black pointed fingernails emerged from the darkness and clasped itself tightly around Miraneth as if she were a small cricket.

Adam watched as Miraneth's expression shifted from joy to confusion, as she squirmed in its iron grip. "Let me loose, dark one," she said shakily. He could see that the hand was attached to an arm, which disappeared into the darkness. Its skin was strangely flawless and supple, unlike the demons he had previously summoned. In truth, it looked like the hand on a young woman, if only gigantic and gray, like that of a cadaver.

Slowly, it tightened its grip and Miraneth's confusion turned to terror as she began to scream, an awful sound, which would come to haunt Adam's dreams. It was like glass being broken in a pipe organ.

"*No!*" she wailed with her last breaths, desperately struggling to break free and trying every piece of magic she could as she hurriedly half muttered incantations. In her eyes, he could see nothing but utter shock and despair. For all her prescience, she had not foreseen this. He should have been glad, but he just felt sorry for her. All that power meant nothing. She was helpless.

Bit by bit, the hand tightened its grip until her scream turned to a guttural growl as her lungs filled with blood. Her face began to bulge, and bright blue blood poured from all of her orifices; she was being crushed to death. Her eyes soon burst out of her head, leaving gaping holes whil she continued to howl in pain.

Then, and only then, did the hand finally slam shut upon her with all of its power, balling itself into a fist and sending a fine mist of blue blood and organs flying in all directions. What remained of Miraneth leaked between the uncompromising fingers of this gargantuan being, dripping onto the polished concrete below.

Just as wordlessly as the first, another hand appeared. This one appeared on the upper edge of the other side of the portal and its gray fingers snaked out like huge tarantula legs to gain purchase, which it used to hoist itself through, into their world.

Adam's gaze turned upon its face for the first time. It was a woman, or at least it appeared as such. Giant and fearsome though she was, there was no mistaking it. Her lips and hair were black and luscious, as black as the portal from whence she came. Her features were flawless, breathtaking even, but that was entirely secondary to the utter terror Adam felt by even looking upon her. This being's energy was different. Ancient. Every fiber of his spirit was telling him only one thing. Run.

She brought her bloody fist below her nose, craning her neck further and inhaling deeply, basking in the scent. Only then did she open her eyes. Adam saw that they too were black, though the iris's glowed bright red. She slowly opened her hand and carefully inspected the sticky blue resin of bones, organs and fluids which coated her palm. She opened her mouth wide, exposing animalistic teeth, and extended a long black salivating forked tongue with which she lavishly licked her palm clean.

She took extra care for her fingers, pushing them slowly between her lips, one by one, and savoring each and every drop of blood as she shuddered with ecstasy.

She finally cast her gaze upon Adam, and her lips pursed into a slight smile, before she licked them clean as well. He was transfixed. Utterly terrified, but far too frightened to move.

"Adam!" a voice shouted from below him. "We have to go. Now!" It was the mystery woman from before. She had recovered from her impact on the wall and was now beckoning him down from the podium. "Hurry!" she shouted, casting an equally horrified look at whatever it was that was crawling out of that portal.

Adam scrambled down the long ladder at the end of the podium and sprinted across the cement floor towards the woman, just in time to catch sight of the enormous creature as she pulled her upper body out of the portal, exposing huge, jet black, leathery wings.

She groaned as she stretched, and her wings fanned out shaking the very foundations of the entire complex. When Adam reached the mystery woman, he was struck once again by an intense sense of familiarity as he looked into her eyes. "Who are you?"

"I'm Evie," she said. The mention of her name was like a bomb going off in his mind, as something clicked. At once, he was struck by lifetimes upon lifetimes of memories which fell upon him like a raging torrent. In any case, there was no time to unpack that now.

"How do we get out of here?" Adam asked her breathlessly.

Eve looked at him in horror. "I was hoping you could tell me that."

All around them, the structure was collapsing. Adam hazarded a glance at the portal and to his horror saw that the being had already planted one foot on the ground. By now, her gaze was fixed upon them and her smile was widening.

When all hope seemed lost, a small golden portal opened on the solid cement of the wall behind them, revealing the misty woods from whence they came. Adam was perplexed, until he remembered that he had seen a portal once like that before.

Lucifer.

"Let's go!" Evie said, jumping through the portal. Realizing what was happening, the giant being howled in anger and lunged towards the portal with terrifying speed. Adam and Evie collapsed on the cool earth on the other side, and the last sight before the portal winked shut was an enormous eye, staring at them furiously across the threshold.

For what seemed like hours, Adam and Evie ran through The Blackwood. Hopelessly lost though they were, they had to put as much distance between themselves and the facility as possible. Little was said between them as they made their escape. They would run until the point of exhaustion before taking short breaks only to press on again. Occasionally, the ground below them churned and tremored.

In the distance, far behind them, they heard heavy and unmistakable rumbling, like colossal footsteps. Worse still, a red glow had begun to build up behind them from the direction of the facility. It did not bear thinking about. The trees began to creak and moan as dark energy snaked its way through the air: the woods were coming to life.

Adam was following Evie's lead, and he was quite comfortable doing so, though he was reminded all too well of the first time he had tried to flee the facility with Zane. Quietly, he could feel her desperation growing. He could sense it within her.

"It's hopeless," he wheezed finally, as they pulled up for yet another stop. "These woods go on forever. Not only that, but they're constantly shifting. We might have barely moved at all."

"And do you have any better ideas?" Evie asked in exasperation.

"No," Adam conceded meekly.

"Then we push on," Evie said, resolutely.

"Until what?"

"Until our legs give out! And then more. We have to get as far away from here as we can, and right now this is the best option we have. So, if it's alright with you I'd like you to quit your moaning and get it together. We have a job to do."

A twig snapped in a nearby thicket and both of them jumped to attention, ready to face whatever horror was about to beset them. Adam shook with anticipation, barely able to contain his rising terror.

A dark shape at the bottom of the thicket caught his eye. It cautiously poked it's head out of the gloom and what little light there was reflected in its large eyes. It was a black cat. Upon seeing Evie, its eyes noticeably widened, and its ears pricked up as it rushed towards her, purring incessantly and nuzzling her.

"Hermes!" she shouted, dropping to her knees to cuddle him as tears rolled down her cheeks. "I thought you were dead."

At once, the cat cast a suspicious gaze at Adam.

"That's him," Evie said, wiping the snot from her nose. Hermes gazed deeply into his eyes. He was like no cat Adam had ever seen. Such a brilliant coat, and with eyes that seemed to pierce into the very depths of his soul. "And the others?" She asked.

Hermes looked towards the thicket, which bustled with activity once again. Out crawled a tentative elderly woman with kind eyes and beautiful bristling silver hair. Her skin was as warm and brown as Evie's, only with a few more wrinkles, the marks of a long life. She all but collapsed herself at the sight of Evie, who quickly caught her in her arms as she again broke down sobbing.

"Grammie! Oh god, you're alive!" She was closely followed by a dark-skinned priestess, wreathed in gold, and a towering creature that looked like a hybrid between a man and a goat.

Adam staggered back from it instinctively, losing his footing and crashing awkwardly to the ground.

"What's the matter, boy?" the creature grumbled sullenly. "Never seen a satyr before?"

Quickly, the priestess' gaze was fixed upon him, as she all but bypassed Evie to look straight to him. Crouching next to him, her eyes grew large and her mouth practically gaped. "Then you are he," she breathed. "The other child of the prophecy. And you yet live."

The satyr cast her a sideways glance, scoffing. "This runt? He can't be."

"It's true," Evie cut in, casting her gaze up from the old woman's arms where Hermes now purred. "He opened the gate."

"As he once closed it, a thousand years ago," the priestess replied. "The cycle has come full circle. The snake eats itself. . ."

The satyr sighed. "Speak plainly, Athena."

Athena shot him an intense look. "The prophecy has been fulfilled, but the roles have now reversed. On this date, a thousand years ago, the gates were sealed. Now, they have been opened, but the roles have reversed. The sealer becomes the opener, the hunter, the hunted. That they would both survive is unforeseen. Unprecedented. Not only that, but they've come together. Now the rest is—"

"Up to them," the old woman said, finishing her sentence.

At once, all eyes turned and were fixed upon Adam.

Under the guidance of Athena, the group navigated their way out of The Blackwood, back to the physical realm. As Athena explained, The Blackwood was bound to certain rules, a place that could not be navigated by maps, but by intention, by willpower.

As they crossed back into the physical, there was a collective sigh of relief, as if they could finally breathe. The air in that place was stagnant and foul, like a tomb, marred by the eons of death and decay it had endured.

They were led them back to a humble white van, which sat on the forest's edge, at a scenic overlook. Pan's van, Adam would come to understand. He was not sure what he expected. A chariot? A golden carriage? He did not quite know, but certainly not a 1980's panel van. It seemed at odds with their personas.

"We like to keep a, low profile," Athena said, reading his expression as he looked at the van. This drew a laugh from Evie's grandmother as she hopped in the back. In time, Adam was the only one outside, and Evie extended her hand, beckoning him in.

There it was again. Her soft skin. Her gentle smile. And those eyes. He lost himself in them and time slowed. Those eyes told stories of ages past. Entire lifetimes together. When her eyes met his own the rest of the world fell away. It was just them.

Was this love?

*Don't be ridiculous.*

"You can trust me," Evie said softly, sensing his hesitation. Instinctively, he knew she was right. What choice did he have? Above them, the blood red sky thundered as eldritch energy crackled through it, like constant lightning which did not abate, glowing tendrils of arcane power which forked their way through the upper atmosphere.

He had never seen a sky like that. The concepts of night and day seemed meaningless now as the entire world was blanketed in a bloody twilight. As they sped back towards the city, they discussed what transpired at the Gate.

"She was huge," Evie said in hushed tones as the others listened in. "I could feel her energy, and it was. . . ancient. Unlike anything I have ever felt."

"A greater demon," Athena reflected grimly. "Possibly even one of the queens of Hell. You were right to flee. Even your powers would have been no match. But how? How did you escape that place?"

"There was a portal." Adam said, speaking up for the first time. "Lucifer." He knew just how much gravity that name carried. Athena mumbled something indiscernible as she rubbed her temples.

"That he would intervene directly is both perplexing and troubling," she said. "He must still have a significant stake in this. Though why, I cannot say. The prophecy has been fulfilled. The Thirteenth Gate is completed, and all the other Gates have opened along with it. Chaos and magic have returned to the physical world."

"The time that was promised," Pan said from the front seat.

"The time that was promised," Flora and Athena replied in unison.

Evie and Adam exchanged looks then. Just what kind of car was he riding in right now? Please don't let this be a cult, he thought. That was the last thing he needed.

"Whatever it may be, I suspect it has something to do with whatever it was that came through that gate. He was protecting you," Athena said.

"But protecting us from who?" Evie broke in.

"Not from whom, child, but from what," Athena corrected.

"That much, I cannot say. Only that it is an ancient power. Possibly on par with his own. There are few beings in creation which possess such power. In our case, it's better the devil you know than the devil you don't."

When they reached the city, they found it in abject chaos. The glowing red sky was aflutter with the flapping wings of demons as they swooped and dove, plucking up screaming humans from the sidewalks as they fled, tearing them limb from limb in great aerial orgies of bloodlust which painted the city streets red.

More than once, Pan had to jerk the wheel suddenly to avoid the flaming vehicles and desecrated bodies which littered the roads.

Hermes surveyed the scene from Athena's lap in the passenger seat, his hair standing on end. Adam watched on in horror as the city, the only home he had ever known, burned before his very eyes.

It was as if they had stepped into a nightmare. The cries of terror and pain all around them became deafening as they swirled in his ears. Above them, the sky roiled and rumbled like some great churning cauldron of malice.

It was Hell on Earth. The flood. Beneath it all, he felt a snaking sense of guilt, which seared his insides like a hot poker.

YOU. THIS IS YOUR DOING. It sounded like Miraneth. Try though he did to shut the thoughts out, they just kept coming. When he closed his eyes, he could see her face leering at him, mocking him.

ADAM.

"Adam!" He opened his eyes and returned to the present moment to find Evie clutching his hand with a look of concern in her eyes.

The small freckles on her face danced like constellations as she spoke. "We need you with us Adam, here and now," she said softly. Meeting her gaze was like staring into a mirror. Though for once, this reflection he admired.

"Where are we going?" Flora shouted anxiously.

"The library," Athena said confidently. "We need to make contact with the other chapters, if we are to stand any chance of a coordinated response. Besides, there are artifacts within the sanctum that are too precious to be allowed to fall into the wrong hands."

"The sanctum?" Evie asked. "We'd be sitting ducks in there."

"The sanctum was built to withstand this very event, child. It is sealed by ancient magic. Right now, it is the safest place we could be," Athena said.

"And then?" Evie retorted. "We'd be sealed inside!"

"There are numerous tunnels beneath, some of which lead far beyond the city limits," Pan said.

"And what about the people?" Evie asked indignantly. "Do we just leave them to die?"

"You're of no use to them if you're dead, child," Athena shot back. "Our priority right now is to protect you and Adam. Your survival is paramount to the survival of the entire human race."

Evie slunk back in her seat sullenly, her conscience at odds with this seemingly basic truth.

"And you, Adam," Athena said, turning around from the passenger seat to face him. "We will need your help in this fight. Your strength. Can we rely on you?"

"I can't," Adam said, breaking his gaze away. "I don't want to hurt anyone else. I've already caused enough pain," Emotion crept into his voice.

"Your power was misdirected. You were used, Adam. You must acknowledge that. No one blames you for what happened. You were deceived by one of the darkest and most cunning minds to have ever walked this Earth."

"Hmph. Miraneth," Pan spat, muttering her name as if it were a curse.

Adam looked around the van, at the gentle faces which waited for his next words. Already, he felt closer to them than he had ever felt to his own family. His eyes welled over with tears as he choked back sobs. He felt undeserving of such care, of any care, after everything he had done. Perhaps one day he would feel worthy of their graces. For now, all he could do was give them his word. "I'll try."

As they reached the steps of the library, they found it swarming with demons and creatures of darkness. They screamed and chittered, calling sounds of alarm to one another in their demonic tongue as they caught sight of the van.

Blood ran down the ancient steps like the Mayan pyramids of old as the distended and deformed figures cast aside the bodies they were feasting upon to face their would be attackers. One thing was certain, they had a battle ahead of them.

Adam could feel his heart leaping into his throat as he shook with anticipation. This was it.

Pan hurriedly parked the van and, on the count of three, The Watchers sprang forth, leaping into the action. Pan and Athena led the way, their weapons materializing from thin air as direct manifestations of their intent, hardened and condensed magical energy, bound to their will.

Athena lead with a huge glowing golden spear, which she quicky put to use, impaling the first line of attackers as she advanced up the stairs, whilst Pan unsheathed two glowing green scimitars as he quickly dived into the fray, forming graceful pirouettes through the forsaken masses, leaving a trail of bouncing, decapitated heads as he went.

Most surprising of all to Adam was Hermes. Armed with a small but deadly sharp dagger, the cat moved faster than the eye could see, almost appearing to teleport as he jumped from one festering, tentacle ridden entity to the other, effortlessly lacerating their most critical points as they howled in frustration.

At the top of the stairs, there was a thundering from within the library, and within seconds a towering beast of a demon burst through the library doors, breaking them off the hinges and sending bricks and mortar flying everywhere.

Its body was like that of an enormous, hairless gorilla, and it had the bloody, fleshless skull of a ram for a head. Within the gaping eyeholes of the skull, two blazing fires burned. It had four huge arms, each carrying a bloodstained sword.

When it saw them, it stood tall on all ten feet of its haunches and roared, a deep rumbling penetrating sound. In panic, Adam quickly set about making a portal to be of use, but he hesitated.

*What good would bringing in more demons do? It's useless. I can only summon more darkness.*

In that instant, he felt the reassuring touch of Evie's hand on his left shoulder. He felt her energy spread throughout his body like warm gold, filling him up with light.

"Breathe," she said. He complied and breathed deeply.

He felt her energy swirling throughout every part of him, it concentrated to the point between his eyes before he felt an electric pulse of pure beaming light shoot directly down from the heavens through the crown of his head and deep into the earth below him.

He was overcome with more love in that moment than the entirety of all twenty-two years of his life combined. That spark, that source, whatever it was, took all of his doubts, his sorrow, his grief and his pain, and scattered it like ashes in the wind. When he opened his eyes, he saw the world with abject clarity, a clarity he had never known before.

"Now, try again," Evie whispered.

Adam directed the energy, raising first his left, and then his right hand, drawing it back like a bow. In an instant, a large glowing blue portal appeared, as easily as opening a window.

Straight away, a blindingly bright glowing white being, which Adam knew at once to be an angel, flew out of the portal with effortless grace, unsheathing a bow as she rose higher before raining down a volley of hundreds of rays of light.

Each demon that was touched burst into flames before disappearing into a cloud of ash, without even the time to scream. The ram headed demon turned its head, but not soon enough as it was quickly split in two by one of the beams before burning up and disintegrating.

In mere moments, Adam had cleared the entire entryway of the library of all demons. Its job done, the angel arced gracefully back down towards the portal, but not before pausing in front of Adam and giving a small bow. It disappeared back into its realm and the portal winked shut.

The Watchers looked down in awe from the steps above, their mouths agape. Adam could scarcely believe it himself. Evie simply smiled and wrapped Adam in a warm embrace.

"I knew you could do it," she whispered. "All you needed was a little nudge."

# The Last Judgment

For a time, there was only silence, mere awareness in an endless void.

Then, there was light.

It started from a single point, then expanded infinitely in all directions. The light was not blinding, nor was it warm, like that of the sun. It enveloped everything around it like a great sea of milk.

There was no time, there was no pain, only the gentle embrace of eternity.

Eventually, matter began to coalesce into shapes. Figures.

Enoch and Morgana materialised. They sat side by side, naked, and laid bare. Their minds were interlinked. Words seemed pointless and crude, there were no secrets here; they were one.

*So, this is death.* For a time, they simply gazed into each other's eyes. All their bitterness and all of their many sorrows seemed so distant now. It was only them.

A great golden star tetrahedron spun rapidly into existence in front of them, a merkabah, its radiance stark against the endless expanse of light.

When it stopped spinning, it collapsed with a flurry of sparks into its two-dimensional form; the hexagram. Only then did its occupant appear, sitting peacefully cross legged in the lotus position.

Lucifer.

He appeared before them as an angel, androgynous, embodying both masculine and feminine features. A closer look revealed that he was a hybridisation of their own forms. He was perfect, a bewitching countenance which transcended mere beauty.

Huge leathery wings fanned out behind him, still scarred and scorched from his fall from heaven. Atop his head, floating above his shining curls, was a radiant golden halo, an ouroboros, the snake which eats itself. It shone like the sun as it slowly rotated.

So turns the wheel of life.

Morgana sat to his left side, Enoch to his right. Gently, he opened his eyes, spheres of molten gold which creased with joy as he spoke to them. His mouth did not move. Instead, his voice seemed to come from all directions as he spoke. That voice alone carried with it harmonies that no mortal choir could ever hope to muster.

*"Dearest sister, dearest brother,"* he whispered gently. *"So hard have you fought. Such trials have you faced. You have each played your part with immaculate grace. Now you exist, without time, without space. The end of the bargain. The goal of the chase. Now, I may offer your hearts greatest wish. You need only utter, I promise you this."*

Enoch and Morgana exchanged glances, their souls reeling at the magnitude of his proposition. Anything they wanted. The possibilities were endless.

*"Enoch,"* Lucifer said finally. *"What is it that you desire most?"*

Enoch searched himself for a while. He reflected on his earthly life, and the true motivations behind all of his actions. In truth, it was curiosity. He reflected, too, on the ones he loved.

Adrax, Balus, Davroz, Candilia.

More than anything, he reflected on the great mystery of life, and the unnumerable questions he still pondered. Finally, the word left his mouth, and he knew then that it was true. His heart's greatest desire.

"Knowledge."

Lucifer smiled warmly. *"Very well."* Then, he addressed Morgana. *"And what is it you desire most, Morgana?"*

As he asked the question, she again turned inward, facing the driving forces in her own life, and she found herself reliving one painful memory after another. Throughout it all, there was one key theme.

The cruelty of man.

Over and over, she had been subject to it, molded by it, before finally coming to wield it herself. Ultimately, her reckoning had been cut short, stolen from her by the cruellest hand of all: Fate. She felt cheated.

The world would know suffering, as she had known it. And it would be by her hand. As the word left her lips, she too knew that it was true. Her only wish, her sole motivation.

"Revenge."

Lucifer smiled even wider then, though there was pain in his eyes, the pain of one who had once shared in that same wish and knew just what it meant. "*Very well. By the powers vested in me, I grant thy wish to thee. As it is. As it was. And so it shall be.*"

He raised his right arm upwards, with his index and middle fingers extended. At the same time, he lowered his left arm in the same fashion, pointing downwards. When they were in position, a great thunderclap of energy surged through the fallen angel, hurling the souls of Enoch and Morgana with blistering speed in opposing directions.

Morgana awoke gasping in the darkness on a cold, wet surface. This darkness was different to that of the void. It was foul, rancid, and dripping with fear. She could feel the ground squirming beneath her, heaving.

Wet tendrils began to ensnare her body, binding her. She jumped up with a start and quickly cast a spell of lumination, a bright white light emanating from her fingertips and hanging in the stagnant air, illuminating the world around her.

To her horror, she saw that the very ground itself was a mass of bloody, writhing flesh, and organs. The wetness was blood, oceans of it. This place heaved with sickness and suffering, stretching on as far as the eye could see.

There were faces, too, amongst the gore, contorted and howling with mournful sorrow or snapping at her feet as she stepped over them. She realized with grim absolution where she was.

Hell.

There could be no doubt about it. Fear began to overtake her, to paralyse her. Worse still, she knew that she had done this to herself. It was her own will which had brought her here, the sunken place.

Soon, she heard howls and screeches in the distance drawing closer. She knew what was coming; demons, the foul machinations of this place. They were drawn to her fear like moths to a flame. She knew that they would not bow to her here. She was in their realm now. Within moments she was set upon.

The first of them that approached her looked like an obscene spider, a towering abomination of pale limbs and appendages which skittered rapidly towards her, its mouth gaping like a salivating maw, barely able to contain its own bloodlust as it lunged at her.

She sprang gracefully into the air, casting an enchantment of lessening so that she floated above it. She narrowly escaped its snapping jaws and quickly focussed her attention on it, casting her awareness into its body and raising it up into the air.

It squealed furiously in the grip of her magic as she coursed her energy through its body, tearing it limb from limb with her powers, before effortlessly bursting it into a fine mist of blood and gore. The blood soaked her naked body and she winced in revulsion, but there was no time for revulsion. More of them were coming.

She cast lights in as many directions as she could and only then did the full magnitude of horror overtake her. Stretching far into the distance, over valleys and mountains of corpses stacked high, endless uncountable hordes of demons were descending on her from all directions.

She steadied herself, for there was nothing else that she could do. She would face them. Curiously, she noticed that her powers seemed amplified in this place. She had more energy than ever. It only makes sense, Hell is made from flesh and blood. This was her domain.

She raised up her arms, summoning her power, and gigantic arms bubbled up from the ground below her, made up of the very flesh and blood of Hell itself. She hardened and sharpened the bones within them into great towering scythes and swung and tore at the advancing hordes of howling demons as they set upon her, drenching her with yet more blood.

They would not touch her, they could not, her power was far beyond their own. They were but mere servants, and she was their master. She would see that they remembered that.

Strong though she was, the hordes kept coming. They were endless, and she was but one, a single light in the darkness. Her fight against them was valiant, but ultimately, it was folly. Holding them back was like holding back the tides of the ocean.

She did not know how long she fought them. Days? Weeks? Months? It made no difference, this place was without time. Eventually, she found her immense power waning as she reached the point of exhaustion. She could not hold them off forever.

Just as she began to falter and buckle, and the demons surged to overwhelm her, she heard a low rumbling in the distance, like the footsteps of a giant.

She watched the demons pause, turning in the direction of the sound before scattering in all directions. They were afraid. Whatever was coming was far beyond their power.

As the thundering approached, Morgana also grew frightened, but she steadied herself. Whatever it was, she would face it without fear, as she always did.

In the distance, she saw two glowing red eyes. Soon, out of the gloom, an enormous figure appeared before her, its features outlined by her floating enchantments.

It was that of a towering woman, gigantic and voluptuous, perfect in all of her dimensions. Her skin was grey, and her long black hair shone in the light. Behind her, huge black wings extended, and atop her head was a floating halo, the blackest of all, so black that it seemed to absorb the light. She knew at once that she was in the presence of a god-like being.

The being hunched over and extended her massive hand, replete with black claws, opening her palm, as if beckoning Morgana to stand on it.

Morgana did not know why, but she accepted this invitation. Quickly, she dispelled her enchantment to float gently down into the being's outstretched hand. The skin felt cold beneath her feet. As the stood in the center of the outstretched hand, it drew her up through the air, gently cradling her like one might hold an insect.

She was brought eye to eye with the being. The whites of her eyes were black, but her irises glowed a deep red. Her face was beautiful, flawless, like every other aspect of her being. Morgana felt a deep sense of intuitive awe and reverence.

"Hello, little one," the being whispered, her voice deep and rumbling. "Vessel of Eve. Long have I watched you. So tenacious you are, in the face of such peril. And yet you refuse to submit. You remind me of myself, so long ago."

"Who are you?" Morgana asked.

"I am Lilith," she said. "The first, and the last. She who did not bend. She who refused to bow to the will of man. She who was scorned."

"What is it that you want with me?" Morgana asked.

"I want what you want, young one," Lilith whispered. "Judgement. Vengeance. I seek what is owed to me. To us." Her voice lowered. "But I require a vessel. Long have I waited, but no suitable candidate has arisen. Until now. Until you. All I ask is that you give yourself to me. Body, and soul. Together, we shall visit upon the Earth a judgement the likes of which has never been seen."

Morgana pondered this proposition. It would mean sacrificing a measure of her sovereignty, that much was clear, but the power Lilith offered was immense. There was no denying the energy she felt: this was the power of a god.

In that moment, it all made complete sense. Her entire existence, every decision she had ever made, in life and in death, had led her to this exact moment. It was so clear.

"What say you, Morgana?" Lilith asked.

"I accept," Morgana said, resolutely.

Lilith smiled widely then, her luscious black lips parting to reveal a mouth of monstrous teeth. Morgana watched a third glowing red eye appear in Lilith's forehead, and as Lilith raised her palm towards the eye, its pupil expanded rapidly.

Morgana reached out and touched it and found it to be almost like liquid, a flowing membrane somewhere between fire and water. She gently pushed her hand in, and then her arm, before stepping in, and disappearing entirely.

The eye winked shut and closed behind her. Above them, an enormous red portal thundered into existence, bathing Lilith in bright artificial light. She raised her gaze towards it, and with one powerful beat of her wings, soared skyward towards the opening.

The hour of judgement was at hand.

# ACKNOWLEDGMENTS

Writing this book has been one of the most rewarding and challenging experiences of my life. I started writing in 2018, after returning from the Peruvian Amazon with the beginnings of an idea. In 2019, during my first very hard year of University in Cairns, I didn't write at all. I moved to Copenhagen on a scholarship in 2020, and found the inspiration to write again, completing the first draft of the text after my return to Australia in late 2021.

Though help was limited along the way, there are some people whom I'd like to thank.

Firstly, to my sister, Lauren Norman, who was the first person to read my first draft of the text, and offered sound advice and fair, measured criticisms. An avid reader and writer herself, her analysis and support proved invaluable. Thank you, Lauren.

Secondly, to my dear friend, Sami Draper, the second person to read the first draft of the text. Thank you for your constant support, friendship, and genuine interest in this story.

Having someone who was as fired up about this as I was, and with whom I could delve into the nuances of the world with was priceless, and reminded me that this was indeed a story worth telling. Thank you, Sami.

Lastly, I'd like thank my editor, Jason McCord. Jason has been nothing but professional throughout the entire publication and editing process, and his drive and enthusiasm to see this through to completion has brought us here today. Thank you for taking a chance on me, Jason, and for believing in this story.

# ABOUT THE AUTHOR

**Daniel Norman** was born in Malaysia, and grew up between Zimbabwe, Australia, and Tanzania, which instilled him with a deep love and admiration for the human spirit. He found a deep love of the arts from a young age, and he maintains that art, in all its forms, when utilized correctly, has the power to uplift and awaken humanity.

He can mostly be found by the beach, on an archipelago somewhere, or wandering the streets of a nameless town.